Ledger Of The Damned

A Judgement of the Wicked Dark Romance

Yvonne Hamilton

GOLDEN LIGHT PUBLISHING HOUSE

ISBN: 978-1-970692-02-0

First Edition
Printed in the United States of America

Cover art: Get Covers
Interior design: Yvonne Hamilton

Published by Golden Light Publishing House

For those who have walked through fire and learned to whisper to the
smoke.
For the ones who burn quietly, who see beneath the veil, who hear the
hum between heartbeats.
May you remember what the light erased—
and become what the shadows always knew you were.

Content Warning: Ledger of the Damned

Ledger of the Damned contains mature, intense, and psychologically dark content.

Please read with care.

This book includes, references, or thematically explores:

Violence & Death

Graphic and non-graphic depictions of murder

The killer's point of view, including internal motivations and ritual elements

Blood, wounds, and death imagery

Themes of justice, vengeance, and moral ambiguity around killing

Psychological & Emotional Triggers

Dissociation, missing time, intrusive thoughts

Gaslighting, manipulation, and emotional coercion

Trauma responses

Identity fragmentation and the loss/return of memory

Scenes depicting panic, disorientation, and intense mental strain

Sexual Content & Power Dynamics

Sensual scenes involving supernatural influence

Seduction tied to hunger, magic, or compulsion

Non-physical power imbalance (supernatural allure, siren/succubus abilities)

Note: No non-consensual sexual acts occur in this book, but some scenes involve magical influence tied to desire and temptation.

Ritual, Occult, & Supernatural Themes

Ritual magic

Cult-like societies and esoteric ceremonies

Mythic or religious symbolism involving judgment, sin, and balance

Transformation scenes (physical and metaphysical)

Abuse & Systemic Harm (Referenced)

Mentions of human trafficking, exploitation of vulnerable women, and institutional cover-ups

Corruption in legal, medical, and philanthropic systems

Foster care trauma (implied and referenced)

Other Themes

Alcohol consumption

Blood-related supernatural hunger

Moral grayness in both protagonists and antagonists

Dark romance elements threaded through a psychological thriller framework

If you need to pause, breathe, or step away while reading, please do.

Your wellbeing matters more than finishing a chapter.

This story walks willingly into the shadows—

but you never have to follow it alone.

Playlist

Dream Girl Evil — Florence + The Machine

WILDFLOWER — Billie Eilish

Eternity — Alex Warren

Technicolour Beat — Oh Wonder

Human — Of Monsters and Men

Strangers — Kenya Grace

Yellow Flicker Beat — Lorde

Just Keep Watching — Tate McRae

The Reaper — Jonah Kagen

Beggin for Thread — BANKS

The Line — Twenty One Pilots (Arcane)

Supercut — Lorde

Which Witch — Florence + The Machine

Empire Now — Hozier

Take Me to Church — Hozier

affection — BETWEEN FRIENDS

The Roads — Jonah Kagen

Ace of Hearts — Zella Day

Fantastic — King Princess (Arcane)

Lose It — Oh Wonder

Humankind — David Kushner

Taste — Sabrina Carpenter

Mr. Brightside — The Killers

Talking Body — Tove Lo

make you mine — Madison Beer

Devil's Backbone — The Civil Wars

Solo — Myles Smith

ilomilo — Billie Eilish

Frozen Pines — Lord Huron

Team — Lorde

Contents

Chapter 1
Celeste

The bell over the door gives a soft, familiar chime as I step into The Witch's Brew. The smell of espresso and baked bread wraps around me, a small reprieve from the storm outside. I've caught the sweet spot between rushes. Thankfully, only a few people wait in line ahead of me, their voices low, the room calm in that brief pause before the world picks up again.

I let my gaze drift over the usual early-morning crowd until it catches on the stand by the counter, the day's paper propped in plain sight.

I step forward and lift the paper, the ink still smelling faintly of rain.

Prominent Businessman Found Dead in Seaport Home

By Rachel Alden | The Salem Gazette | August 28

BOSTON —

Eduardo Lexington, 52, a well-known Boston businessman and philanthropist, was found dead late Thursday evening in his Seaport District home. According to police, the body was discovered by his wife, Margaret Lexington, who had just returned from a business trip.

Authorities have not yet released an official statement regarding the cause of death. Detectives on the scene confirmed there were no immediate signs of forced entry or theft.

*Mr. Eduardo Lexington, founder and CEO of **Lexford Holdings**, built his empire on real estate and regional manufacturing, owning several textile and processing factories across Massachusetts and the North Shore. Over the past two decades, his company expanded into urban redevelopment, frequently partnering with city officials on "revitalization" projects that critics claimed displaced working-class families. Publicly, Lexington was praised for his philanthropy and contributions to youth and housing initiatives throughout the Boston area. Associates described him as disciplined, intense, and unyieldingly focused on his work—a man who measured his success in numbers and neighborhoods, not names.*

Neighbors told police the Lexington home was quiet that evening, with no disturbances or visitors reported. The case remains under investigation.

A normal person might frown. Concern would crease their brow. They'd reach for the paper, already bracing for the name printed across the front page.

But what rises in me isn't concern. It's curiosity—sharp, alive, bubbling at my fingertips.

Gently, almost reverently, I set the paper back on the stand. There's no fear. No concern. Only a quiet hum beneath my skin, a faint thrill I don't bother to name.

A smile finds its way to the corners of my mouth.

Justice.

"Morning, Celeste. Your usual?" June asks, her smile as bright as the café lights. Her curly brown hair's pulled into a messy bun, blue apron cinched at her waist with a bar towel tucked into the side. She's been the one constant in my mornings since I moved to Salem from Seattle.

"Yes, please," I say, matching her smile. I don't even have to wait. By the time I pay, my large dirty chai and chocolate croissant are already waiting on the counter.

I thank her, slip the pastry into my bag, and take my drink. At the door, I pause for that first sip. The warmth slides down my throat—cinnamon, spice, comfort wrapped in heat. It hits like a habit I never had. I've never smoked, but I imagine this is what that first drag feels like—the quiet rush, the moment before the world crowds back in.

Stepping outside, I'm greeted by dark clouds and the steady fall of rain. Tugging my hood forward, I duck into the storm and make my way toward the station a few blocks over. This is my routine—coffee shop, train station, Boston. It's reliable. Unlike my work.

Just as I step onto the train, the rain intensifies, pelting the windows in steady percussion. The city slides past in a wash of gray—brick buildings, cobblestone streets, shopfronts half-swallowed by fog. Salem fades quick, replaced by stretches of marshland and skeletal trees bowing under the weight of the storm.

The horizon blurs where the ocean meets the sky, all of it the same bruised color. Power lines flicker by, vanishing into mist. Water pools along the tracks, reflecting the occasional flash of headlights from a distant road.

Inside, the carriage hums—the overhead lights buzzing softly, the scent of wet wool and stale coffee hanging in the air. I watch the world smear itself across the glass, the reflection of my face ghosting over every passing shape.

My thoughts drift back to the headline. I remember the case. A week in courtroom A, cataloging every lie that rolled off his tongue, every smirk that followed. His attorney twisted the facts until guilt wasn't even on the table anymore. On paper, it looked airtight—inspection reports, safety logs, testimony lined up like dominoes.

A safety violation that turned into tragedy. The company ignored repeated maintenance requests, refusing to upgrade the machinery to meet current standards. Workers filed complaints—dozens of them—but no one listened. Then, on an overnight shift, the compressor on lane two caught fire. Three people died before help could reach them. Several more were pulled out burned and broken.

And somehow, between the accident and the trial, the entire factory went up in flames. No suspects. No answers. Just another crime reduced to ash before anyone could be held accountable. Now it seems karma has paid a visit to correct what the justice system failed to do.

The train reaches Boston, carrying me toward the next set of cases I'll record like a modern scribe. The rain has followed from Salem—trailing behind like a quiet reminder of what the day expects.

The Boston courthouse looms like it was built to outlast guilt itself—stone and glass stitched together with ego. Its steps are slick with rain, a dark sheen catching flashes of headlights from the street below. Inside, the air smells of polish and paper, bureaucracy layered over decay. Voices echo in the marble atrium, rising and falling in practiced tones of authority.

Security wands beep. Shoes scuff. The rhythm of procedure never changes. Even the light here feels filtered, cautious—thin stripes spilling through tall windows to illuminate faces that would rather stay in shadow.

Everything about the building demands reverence, but underneath the polish is exhaustion. The kind that seeps into walls, into the grain of the benches, into anyone who's stayed too long trying to believe justice is anything more than performance.

The routine is soothing. Step to the metal detector. Remove my shoes, coat, and bag. Place them on the conveyor, step through, wait for the nod. Gather everything again and move on. The predictability helps—there's comfort in repetition when the rest of the world refuses to make sense.

My office sits on the second floor. Most weeks I split time between Judge Josephine Abrams and Judge Alister Gathers. Their dockets rotate between me, Gertrude Bethers, and Abigail Lockley—always courtroom 2A or 2B.

This week it's Gathers. A medical malpractice suit in 2B. All procedure and politics, dusted with ego.

The hallway hums with the sound of early arrivals—heels clicking against polished floors, muffled greetings, the low buzz of fluorescent lights. The air smells faintly of disinfectant and rain-soaked coats, the kind of sterile calm that pretends nothing bad ever happens here. Light filters in through tall windows, pale and cold, glinting off plaques that promise justice in serifed gold.

I gather my things—stenography machine, case notes, terminology list, digital backup. The weight of it all is familiar, grounding. Aside from Bailiff Jefferson, I'm the first to reach the courtroom. The ritual is a tether, steady and sure.

If I can't give the victims the justice they deserve, I can at least make sure every word survives. Every sound. Every silence. It's a small way to help, a promise I can keep when the system forgets how to.

The quiet doesn't last. Within minutes, the room begins to fill—the shuffle of papers, the muted thud of briefcases hitting desks, the clipped rhythm of heels against tile. The attorneys file in, their conversations low but charged, already rehearsing arguments they'll pretend are sponta-neous.

Judge Gathers steps in from chambers, tugging at the cuffs of his robe, the faint exhaustion of the day clinging to him. He's a man who still be-lieves order can be wrung from chaos if you say it with enough conviction. The bailiff calls for everyone to rise, and the room obeys.

I take my place at the front, fingers poised above the keys. The air is thick with perfume, coffee, and nerves. For a brief, impossible moment, it almost feels sacred—like truth might actually find its way into the record today.

Then the first witness is sworn in, and the illusion breaks.

The rhythm settles in fast. The hum of fluorescent lights, the soft thud of folders being opened, the clipped phrases traded like currency. My fingers move on instinct, chasing words before they vanish into air. Every keystroke is a pulse, a heartbeat keeping time with the voices around me.

Courtroom 2B feels smaller once the day starts—like the walls lean in to listen. The air thickens with caffeine, perfume, and quiet desperation. The attorneys move through their opening statements with rehearsed precision, their voices calm, their questions surgical. It's all routine, but the subtext hums—tension wearing a polite face.

Three days blur together in the rhythm of procedure.

Day one: the plaintiff, Clara Mendel, takes the stand. Thirty-four. Pale. Too composed for someone speaking about the loss of her own body's future. The diagnosis came fast, she says—a hormone irregularity flagged by her doctor as "critical." Within days she was pushed into a fertility preservation plan, told her reproductive system was on the verge of failure. Her voice shakes only once, when she says the word *barren.*

Day two: medical experts dissect her chart. Numbers. Test results. Lab codes. The kind of data meant to sound objective but always feels like translation. One specialist testifies the original readings were inconclusive at best. Another implies her treatment was chosen for profit, not preservation. The name of the cryo facility keeps surfacing—*NovaGen Fertility Labs.* Each mention lands heavy, like a stone dropped in still water.

Day three: the defense fights back. Calm. Polished. They call it a coincidence, a referral, standard practice. The same few phrases loop through the air like a metronome of denial. "No evidence of kickbacks." "No documented agreement." "Nothing improper."

Through it all, I type. My hands ache, but I don't stop. Every word matters—especially the ones spoken too smoothly. There's something deliberate in the defense's cadence, a rhythm too even to be honest.

By the end of the third day, the testimony blurs into the soft whir of ceiling vents and the mechanical click of my keys. The words feel heavy, like they know what they're worth.

Outside, the rain hasn't stopped.

By the fourth morning, the defense has found its rhythm. They bring in their own experts—polished, confident, armed with jargon and rehearsed sympathy. Charts and case studies fill the projection screen, glossy exhibits meant to look like truth.

They talk about *unknown variables, lifestyle factors, environmental influence.* They make the human body sound like a rumor.

One doctor—a specialist with a résumé too long for humility—leans forward as he testifies. He suggests that *Clara's* condition might stem from "extended stress, inconsistent routines, or hormonal instability brought on by lifestyle choices." His tone softens just enough to make the implication sound like concern.

Another witness takes it further. Mentions a "social phase" in her twenties, a "fast-paced job," late nights, travel, exhaustion—all unverified, all irrelevant. They use her life as misdirection, a distraction wrapped in clinical phrasing.

Each word lands dull and heavy through the microphone. Each one feels like a verdict waiting to happen.

When the closing statements come, even the air feels tired. The defense leans on protocol. The plaintiff's attorney fights for empathy, but the energy in the room has already turned. No one's listening anymore—just waiting.

Judge Gathers delivers the ruling two days later. His tone is measured, his phrasing careful. The verdict: partial compensation. Legal fees covered. Storage fees for the frozen eggs waived. No damages. No fault. No real justice.

The plaintiff nods as if she expected it. The defense shakes hands, papers rustling like applause. The local reporter marks the final entry.

When the gavel falls, the room exhales, but nothing feels settled. Just another file closed, another name filed away.

I pack my notes and power down my machine, the silence between clicks louder than anything said in the last four days. Outside, the sky's still gray, the city still wet.

Justice didn't die here. It just forgets to show up. The verdict echoes long after the gavel falls. The sound follows me down the hallway, bouncing off marble and glass, softening until it's nothing but a low ache behind my ribs.

Outside, the air smells of wet stone and exhaust. I pull my hood up and step into the rain. It's lighter now, almost gentle, but it still finds its way through the seams. The city hums the same as it always does—indifferent, efficient, alive.

I should feel angry. Outraged, even. But what settles in is heavier than anger. It's the quiet kind of injustice, the one that doesn't scream. The one that just keeps happening.

By the time I reach the station, I've already filed it away in my head. Another case, another name, another loss dressed up as procedure. I tell myself it's balance—the scales tip both ways. But the truth is, the losses outweigh the wins. They always do.

The train pulls in, brakes hissing like a sigh. I step aboard, the warmth of the cabin clashing against the cold that's settled in my bones. Through the window, the city slides by in streaks of gray and gold, and I can't shake the thought that somewhere between verdict and silence, justice got tired of waiting.

Chapter 2
Elias

Late August used to be my favorite time of year. The rain, the cold, the city winding down. It used to mean something steady. Now it's just a reminder—a sound that drags me back to the Jensen case and everything I got wrong. Some mistakes don't wash away, no matter how hard the storm tries.

The call came just after three a.m. I'd be annoyed if I actually slept anymore. Most nights I just lie there, running through the details in my head, retracing every bad call so I don't make them again.

Dispatch said Seaport District. By the time I reach Seaport, the rain's turned mean—thin needles against the windshield, streetlights bleeding into streaks of gold and red. The harbor smells like salt and diesel, the kind of cold that cuts straight through fabric.

Two cruisers block the street, blue and red lights strobing against wet pavement. Yellow tape flutters in the wind, snapping like it's trying to break free. I park a few feet back and step out, the air thick with that mix of curiosity and dread that always hangs around fresh death.

Neighbors cluster under umbrellas, drawn to tragedy like it's theater. They whisper in tight circles, trading speculation for warmth. On the periphery, reporters hover—microphones tucked under raincoats, waiting for someone careless enough to talk. A few flashbulbs pop as I duck under the tape.

A uniformed officer nods in my direction. "Detective Shaw?"

"Yeah."

He jerks his chin toward the house. "You're late to the party."

"Wasn't invited," I say, stepping past him. The porch light flickers overhead, and somewhere behind me, a reporter calls out my name. The flash of cameras follows, but I don't look back. I've got enough ghosts in front of me already.

The Lexington house looks exactly like the kind of place bad things aren't supposed to happen. Three stories of glass and steel overlooking the harbor, lights from the skyline bleeding across the wet façade.

Inside, the air's too warm, heavy with the smell of coffee, perfume, and something sharper—like ozone after lightning. The kind of stillness that doesn't belong to grief yet, just shock.

A uniform I don't recognize meets me in the entryway. "Detective Shaw?"

I nod, taking in the polished floors, the art-lined walls, the harsh geometry of money. "What've we got?"

"Male, early fifties. Eduardo Lexington. Found by his wife around one-thirty. She's in the kitchen."

We move through the house, the air shifting with every step—carpet muffling footsteps, voices echoing off glass and marble. The low hum of forensics work carries through the hall: quiet instructions, the soft pop of flashbulbs, the mechanical sigh of the camera reset.

In the kitchen, Mrs. Lexington sits at the table wrapped in a gray blanket that's already slipping from her shoulders. A patrol officer leans beside her, notebook open, his tone gentle but practiced. She doesn't respond. Her hands are locked around a mug gone cold, knuckles white, eyes fixed on nothing. Her nails are perfect—pale polish, clean lines—except for a faint streak of blood along one cuticle, a single imperfection she hasn't noticed yet.

Upstairs, a flash flickers through the glass railing—crime scene techs marking evidence, someone murmuring measurements under their breath.

"Scene's contained?" I ask.

The officer nods. "Yeah. No forced entry. Wife says she got in around one-fifteen, found him upstairs. No one else present."

"Neighbors?"

He gestures toward the window. "They saw the lights when she called it in. Press showed up before the second cruiser."

Of course they did.

I glance back at the kitchen table. Mrs. Lexington hasn't moved. Just stares into the dark mouth of her coffee like it might have answers.

Upstairs, the air feels heavier—like the house itself knows what's waiting. The bedroom door hangs half open, yellow tape tugging in the draft from the vent above.

Inside, the scene is quiet. Too quiet. Expensive furniture, minimalist layout, not a thing out of place except for the body on the floor beside the bed. The smell hits first—ozone, faint smoke, and something metallic that clings to the back of my throat.

Freddy Haven crouches beside the victim, flashlight steady in one hand, penlight in the other. "You finally decided to show," he says, voice flat, not unkind.

"I like to make an entrance," I reply, stepping closer. "What do we have?"

"Male, fifties. Burn marks along the right side—arm, neck, shoulder. Not thermal burns from a house fire. More like direct contact with something hot or electrical."

He gestures to the body. The skin's blistered in narrow lines, uneven, angry red against the gray tone of death. It looks fast, deliberate.

"No sign of arson," Freddy continues. "No soot. Power's off in the room, so whatever caused it wasn't from here."

I scan the space—the bedding's barely disturbed, no overturned furniture, no clear sign of struggle. Just an expensive room and a body that doesn't belong in it.

"Other injuries?" I ask.

"Minor bruising along the ribs and forearms. Could be defensive, could be from the fall. We'll know more once I get him on the table." Freddy straightens, pulling his gloves off with a snap. "I'll have tox screens later today. If there's anything foreign in his system—alcohol, sedatives, maybe accelerants—it'll show up."

I nod, eyes drifting back to the burns. They tell part of the story, but not the part that makes sense yet.

Freddy exhales, glancing toward the window. "Hell of a way to start a morning."

"Yeah," I murmur, more to myself than him. "A real wake-up call."

"Thanks, Freddy," I say, stepping back as he signals for his team to bag the body. "Keep me posted when tox comes in."

"You'll be the first to know," he replies, already scribbling into his log-book.

I take one last look around the room. Everything about it feels inten-tional—the expensive order, the curated emptiness. No signs of struggle, no forced entry. Just a dead man in a perfect room. The kind of scene that looks too neat for truth.

The rain taps at the windows, steady and hollow. I make a note of the time and head downstairs.

The air near the kitchen changes—dense, charged, the kind of stillness that presses against your ribs when something has already gone wrong. It smells faintly of stale coffee and damp wool, like the room's been hold-ing its breath too long. The officer who'd been taking Mrs. Lexington's statement stands near the counter now, flipping through his notebook. He looks up when I approach.

"Detective."

"What've we got?" I nod toward the woman at the table. She hasn't moved. Same blanket. Same untouched mug.

He glances at his notes. "Wife says she flew in from Chicago late last night. Cab dropped her here around one-fifteen. Found him upstairs about twenty minutes later. No sign of forced entry. No noise. Nothing out of place—just the light under the bedroom door."

"She touch anything?"

"Just him," the officer says. "Checked for a pulse. Said his skin was cold."

I jot that down. "What's your read?"

He hesitates, eyes darting toward the floor. "Doesn't feel like she's lying. But she's... hollow. Like she's already somewhere else. Keeps asking when she can go."

"Tell her soon," I say, closing my notebook. "Once the coroner clears out."

He nods and returns to his post. I linger a moment longer, watching Mrs. Lexington. Her hands have stopped trembling, but her stare hasn't shifted—fixed on that mug, the coffee now black and still.

The air seems to thrum faintly around her, a kind of static that doesn't belong in kitchens or grief. Upstairs it was suffocating; down here, it just waits. Like the house itself knows something it isn't saying.

It's always the quiet ones who unsettle me most—the ones who seem like they've already heard the verdict.

By the time I make it back to the precinct, the rain's tapering off, leaving the streets slick and silver. Reporters wait near the steps, their umbrellas huddled like crows.

"Detective Shaw! Any updates on Lexington's death?"

"No comment," I say, pushing through them. They call after me anyway, voices overlapping until the heavy glass doors close and the noise dies in the lobby.

Upstairs, the bullpen hums low—phones ringing, keyboards clacking, the steady murmur of half-finished conversations. I hang my coat, pour coffee that tastes like burnt regret, and pull Lexington's case file from the evidence box.

The paper smells faintly of smoke and dust. Old court transcripts. Witness lists. Depositions. His name sits bold at the top of every page, like he owned the damn trial too.

I skim through the summary:

Eduardo Lexington — Lexington Industrial Solutions.

Charges: Negligence resulting in workplace fatalities.

Outcome: Case dismissed for insufficient evidence.

Three dead, several injured. A factory fire that never should've happened. The factory itself gone before the appeal even started.

I flip to the list of employees who testified—names scrawled in different handwriting, some half-faded from photocopying. Line workers, maintenance techs, a shift manager. I start jotting them down on a legal pad, one by one.

Every case like this leaves residue—people overlooked, grudges left to fester. The ones who sat in court and watched him walk free.

My pen stalls halfway down the page. The rain outside drums against the window, steady and dull.

If someone wanted justice, they had motive.

If someone wanted revenge, they had opportunity.

Either way, Lexington made enemies the way most people breathe—without thinking about it.

I close the folder and lean back in my chair, eyes on the ceiling tiles. The building hums around me, fluorescent and tired. Boston was supposed to be a clean slate, but some ghosts don't bother checking city limits.

The next afternoon, Freddy Haven shows up at my desk with a manila envelope tucked under one arm and a half-finished coffee in the other. Rain's still tracing the windows, the kind that makes the lights look jaundiced.

He drops the file in front of me. "Tox came back."

I raise an eyebrow. "Tell me he was drunk."

Freddy huffs. "Not even close. Diazepam—small dose. Enough to take the edge off, not enough to knock him out."

"Prescription?"

"Could be. Could also be slipped. Hard to tell without a bottle to match the count." He flips open a photo. "Whatever it was, it slowed him down. Reflexes shot to hell."

I study the burn photos. Linear marks, deep and uneven. "Electrical?"

"Yeah. Portable source. I'm thinking a livestock prod or modified cattle rod. Industrial voltage but handheld. Someone knew what they were doing." Freddy's voice dips. "Pattern's too clean for improvisation."

"So he's sedated, then shocked?"

"Looks that way. Heart gave out somewhere between the second and third hit. Instant arrest."

I sit back, rubbing the bridge of my nose. "Jesus."

Freddy nods, slipping the photos back into the envelope. "Whoever did this didn't just want him dead, Elias. They wanted him awake enough to understand why."

He leaves the folder on my desk. The weight of it feels heavier than paper should. Outside, thunder rumbles somewhere over the harbor.

The file's still open on my desk when the captain knocks once and walks in without waiting for an answer.

"Shaw."

"Captain."

She doesn't bother with pleasantries. Captain Mara Kellan is built from steel and caffeine, every line of her uniform crisp enough to cut glass. She's one of the few people in this department who earned her title the hard way, and she wears that history like armor.

She stops in front of my desk, eyes flicking to the crime scene photos. "You get anything from Haven?"

I tap the folder. "Sedative in his system. Diazepam. Just enough to slow him down. Cause of death looks electrical—something portable, like a livestock prod."

Her jaw tightens. "Jesus."

"Yeah," I say. "Not exactly your average break-in gone bad."

She crosses her arms, gaze fixed on the photos. "You see any connection to the others yet?"

That drags me up short. "You mean the unsolveds?"

Kellan nods once. "Guy like this dies, everyone wants a headline. Half a dozen nobodies turn up dead in the same year, no one cares. But Lexington? That's politics. That's pressure. Vance wants it wrapped before the cameras roll."

"I don't see a match yet," I say, even though my gut twists. "No calling card, no message. Could just be timing."

"Could be," she says, but her tone makes it clear she doesn't buy it. "Pull the files on the others. I want a comparative report by tomorrow morning."

"Yes, ma'am."

She studies me for a beat longer, the kind of look that sees more than I want it to. "Try not to make this another Jensen, Shaw."

Her words land harder than they should.

Before I can respond, she's gone—heels clicking down the hall, leaving the smell of rain and command in her wake.

I stare at the folder again. Lexington's burned flesh, the faint sedation, the careful precision of it all.

If there's a connection, it's not written anywhere I can see yet. But the city's keeping count.

Chapter 3
Killer

They'll call it murder. They always do.

But murder is chaos. This—what I do—is order.

Eduardo Lexington's face fills the morning newsfeed before I've even finished washing the residue from my hands. The anchors call him a *factory magnate,* a *beloved employer,* a *self-made man who gave back to the community.* They never say the rest. They never mention the workers who collapsed on the line because he cut corners on ventilation. The underpaid staff breathing in chemicals he refused to regulate. The child who suffocated in a shipment crate because overtime meant survival.

Justice looked the other way. So I didn't.

They'll call him the first, but he isn't. He's just the first they noticed.

The others were quieter. The halfway house manager who sold the girls' medication for cash. The social worker who forged signatures to close her backlog. The nurse who traded patient files to a trafficker for a mortgage payment.

Names buried under statistics. Deaths written off as accidents, suicides, misfortune. But every one of them chipped at the same rot—the system that hides wolves under charity's skin.

I keep them all.

The ledger remembers every one. A name for every sin the courts refused to name. A truth written in ink that doesn't wash away.

Outside, the city is still half-asleep. The air smells like wet iron and burnt paper—the remnants of industry. I walk the side streets where the reporters gather, their cameras already pointed at Lexington's mansion, their voices soft with false pity. They'll talk about him as if he built something worth mourning. As if the blood wasn't already there before I ever touched him.

Lexington wasn't an accident. He was a pattern—predictable, practiced, protected. He was the first they saw, not the first who fell.

The others before him—smaller, quieter sins corrected while the world looked the other way. Each one another page turned, another weight lifted. Each one making the next easier to bear. I didn't kill them out of anger. I corrected them.

Anger is messy. It burns too fast to be useful. What I feel is slower—methodical. A steady hum that settles under the skin like gravity, pulling me toward everything the world keeps trying to ignore.

They'll say it's senseless, a killer with a cause. They always do. But this has always been here, waiting. The scales were never blind—only bound by people too afraid to cut the ropes.

Because someone has to remember what justice is supposed to feel like.

The call started as a whisper—an irritation behind thought, like a song half-heard through walls. I ignored it, the way people ignore guilt or hunger, pretending that discipline is the same as peace. But peace was never meant for me.

The first time I felt it clearly was in the courtroom. I was just another face on the back bench, one more body watching the slow, polite death of consequence. The defendant smirked when the verdict came down—*not guilty*. I remember the mother's sound when she cried; it wasn't human. It was the noise grief makes when it realizes there's no one left to hear it.

That's when the hum started.

It lived in my chest at first, steady as a heartbeat but out of sync with my own. The world sharpened—the scrape of pens, the tick of the clock, the judge's gavel like thunder. I remember gripping the edge of the bench, knuckles white, while that other pulse beat beneath my skin. *Do something,* it said. *Balance it.*

But I didn't. Not then.

Weeks passed. I told myself it would fade. That it was stress, rage, empathy turned sour. But it followed me—through the streets, the subways, every headline about another case dismissed for lack of evidence. It waited behind every lie that ended with a handshake.

Until one night, I couldn't stand the noise anymore.

The world went quiet when I picked up the blade.

Not gone—just...aligned.

The hum in my veins turned clear, harmonious, right. The air around me seemed to breathe in time with my pulse. And when it was done—when the blood stilled and the silence returned—it wasn't horror I felt. It was relief. Like a fever breaking.

That's when I understood: this was never a burden. It was a summons.

I used to tell myself it was mercy.

That lie lasted one kill.

The rush wasn't joy. It was clarity—the noise of everything else burning away until only purpose remained. Adrenaline, yes. Relief, too. The kind that settles low in the bones once the shaking stops. I can still feel the weight of it if I sit still long enough.

Paul Granger. The first name I sought out.

The first injustice I corrected.

A small-time dealer the city barely bothered to notice. His arrest record read like a punch line—petty charges, probation, warnings. Nothing that ever stuck. But what he did behind closed doors never made the papers: the girlfriends who vanished, the neighbors who turned up the TV, the woman who limped to work for weeks and said nothing.

I saw the pattern. Everyone else called it bad luck.

She tried. God, she really did. Sat in that courtroom trembling but unbroken, speaking truths that made the walls shrink. And still—still—they smiled politely and let him walk. "Insufficient evidence." Those words sounded clinical, harmless. They meant she was gone. They meant he'd done it again.

So I waited. Waited until outrage faded and the city forgot her name. Waited until his arrogance returned, until he laughed too loudly at bars and told people justice had a soft spot for charm.

The night I found him, there was no anger left—just focus. A calm so absolute it felt holy. I watched him breathe until it annoyed me, until I couldn't stand how easy it still was for him to exist. When it ended, it was clean. Quiet. No spectacle, no bloodbath. Just balance. The silence afterward felt like the world had exhaled with me.

Afterwards, they called it an accident. A robbery gone wrong. A tragedy. The paper ran three sentences. His friends shook their heads and blamed the city. But I knew better.

That was the first correction. The first whisper in the dark that sounded like truth.

Since then, I've learned patience. I've learned precision. I've learned how to hear the hum of imbalance—the faint vibration in my bones that tells me where to look next.

Because the ledger never sleeps. It remembers every dismissal, every broken oath, every name the courts erase.

I don't hunt.
I balance.

And the world, if it's honest, is grateful for the things it can't confess.

The city sleeps, and somewhere across it, a detective sharpens his questions like knives he's not sure how to use. Elias Shaw. I've watched him longer than he realizes. He moves like a man haunted by his own pulse—sleepless, restless, chasing ghosts no one else can see. The kind of man who mistakes exhaustion for purpose.

He doesn't know what he's stepping into. Not yet. He still believes truth and justice are different things, when really they're just opposite sides of the same door. He keeps pounding on one, begging it to open, never realizing he's already holding the key to the other.

He lies awake at night, trying to make sense of the patterns, the coincidences, the bodies. He tells himself he's searching for the truth, but that's not it. Truth is a mirror—it only reflects what's already there. What he's really chasing is balance. The same balance I am.

He just hasn't learned what it costs.

One day, when the system fails him again—and it will—he'll stop knocking. He'll step through. And when he does, he'll understand that we were never enemies.

He'll understand that justice was never blind. It was only waiting for someone willing to see.

Chapter 4
Celeste

The ballroom is a cathedral of excess—gold leaf and glass, candle-light caught in every mirrored surface. Waiters move like clockwork through the glittering crowd, silver trays balanced with precision. Strings hum softly from a corner stage, the kind of music meant to disappear behind conversation.

I shouldn't stand out here, but the dress makes that impossible. Deep red—liquid and deliberate—the kind of color that doesn't ask permission to be seen. Satin that catches every hint of light, fitted through the waist, the fabric pooling around my heels like spilled wine. I'd picked it because it looked professional enough for the job, but honest enough to remind me I'm still human.

The scent of wealth lingers thick in the air—perfume layered over champagne, over fresh-cut flowers that cost more than rent. The kind of luxury that hums with its own gravity, pulling everyone closer to its shine. I find my corner near the stage, the spot reserved for documentation and press.

I uncase my equipment: the compact recorder, extra batteries, my back-up drive. Routine movements. Muscle memory. The red light blinks once, ready to capture every speech, every applause break, every empty promise dressed as philanthropy.

From my angle, I can see everything—the donors leaning in too close, the polished smiles that never quite reach their eyes, the host rehearsing her gratitude in the reflection of a champagne flute. The ballroom gleams with crystal and candlelight, gold pressed into every corner like the night's wearing someone else's jewelry.

I don't belong here. Not really. The years I spent clawing my way to stability don't vanish just because I learned how to speak their language. I remember the nights of scraping tips into an envelope to cover rent, the secondhand suits that never quite fit, the exhaustion that comes from pretending you're not one bad week away from losing it all.

Now I'm surrounded by people who've never worried about late fees or bus schedules—people whose lives come with the kind of certainty I've only ever borrowed. I worked for this life, every inch of it, but sometimes it still feels like standing on borrowed marble, waiting for someone to notice the cracks underneath.

Still, I stand where I'm supposed to, adjusting the focus on the recorder, pretending I fit in among the silk and glass. That's the trick, isn't it? Looking like you belong long enough that people stop questioning why you're there.

Then, in the mirrored curve of the champagne tower, I catch a reflection—a figure moving toward me through the blur of sequins and light. Even before he speaks, I know who it is.

Silas Mercer Kade.

He doesn't belong here—not really—but somehow he always does. The crowd parts around him without meaning to, drawn by the kind of confidence that used to fill courtrooms. He's dressed in a charcoal suit that fits like a secret, no tie, shirt unbuttoned just enough to look careless in a calculated way. The same smirk plays on his mouth, the one that could be mistaken for charm if you didn't know him.

I shouldn't be surprised to see him here, but I am. After everything—the hearings, the headlines, the quiet disgrace of a man once untouchable—I expected him to be licking his wounds somewhere private, not gliding through a gala like he never left the center of the room. He should look diminished by the scandal. Instead, he looks refined by it, sharpened. Like losing everything gave him permission to stop pretending.

He moves like he's in on a joke no one else has heard yet, every glance deliberate, every pause designed to make the air bend toward him. People still gravitate to him, even when they shouldn't. Especially when they shouldn't. That's always been his talent—making ruin look like power.

And when his eyes find mine across the glass and candlelight, that same talent hits me square in the chest.

"Celeste," he says, voice low enough that I feel it more than hear it. "Didn't expect to find you buried in another speech."

I don't look up from the lens. "Someone has to document the fiction before it's rewritten."

He chuckles—a sound that doesn't quite reach his eyes. "Still poetic. Still sharp." He glances toward the stage. "Quite the performance tonight. You'd think salvation came with a guest list."

I finally meet his gaze, steady, unflinching. "You working the room or haunting it?"

"Maybe both," he says, a ghost of amusement flickering in the candlelight. "You know I have a soft spot for redemption stories."

His tone is smooth, practiced, but there's something else behind it—something quieter, heavier. He shifts his weight, hands in his pockets, as if he's been standing too long in a place that doesn't fit him anymore.

The host's voice rises from the stage, drawing the room's attention. Applause swells, bright and hollow. I hit record. Out of the corner of my eye, Silas watches me instead of the stage.

And for a second, the air between us feels charged—like a verdict waiting to fall.

The lights dim slightly as the first speaker takes the stage, a polished man with a practiced smile and a lapel pin that gleams like moral authority. His voice rises—smooth, rehearsed, just the right mix of humble and self-congratulatory. Applause punctuates each line, obedient and rhythmic.

I lift the recorder, letting the red light blink steady. The cadence of his words becomes a metronome—another courtroom, another plea for redemption wrapped in philanthropy.

They talk about *hope*. About *second chances*. About how every child deserves a home.

My throat tightens. Hope is a strange word to me. Too clean for what it feels like.

I remember the way the walls in Saint Brigid's smelled of bleach and crayons, the sound of the door clicking shut after every failed visit. The way we'd line up on Sundays, all dressed in our best, pretending not to care if someone came. Always smiling just enough for the volunteers' cameras. Always waiting. Always pretending the waiting didn't hurt.

They said families were "in review." They said "patience." They said "these things take time." But time just stretched until the only constant was leaving—caseworkers, placements, promises.

The room bursts into another round of applause. I blink back to now, the sound loud enough to drown the ghosts. Onstage, the host accepts a bouquet of lilies and gardenias, white and perfect under the lights. The image will make tomorrow's papers—*a symbol of generosity*, they'll call it.

From my corner, I keep the recorder steady. The applause fades, and another voice begins—a woman this time, her tone softer, dripping with sincerity. But I already know how this story sounds.

I was the child they're talking about.
The one they saved in speeches but forgot in practice.

And somewhere behind the hum of champagne and polite laughter, I swear I can hear the faintest echo of rain against glass—like the past, tapping to be let in.

The final speech fades into polite applause—measured claps, champagne laughter, the kind of cheer that feels more like punctuation than praise. I stop the recorder, watch the red light blink out, and begin packing up. The cables coil neatly, my fingers moving on instinct, each motion practiced enough to look effortless.

I'm halfway through sliding the recorder into its case when a familiar voice cuts through the murmur of the crowd.

"You're not really calling it a night already, are you?"

Silas again. Of course.

He's close—too close—with that same infuriating calm he carries everywhere. No tie, collar undone, sleeves rolled once at the wrist. Casual in a room where everyone else looks staged. His jacket smells faintly of rain and smoke, like he's been outside recently, watching from somewhere I couldn't see.

"My work's done," I say, snapping the case shut. "No reason to stay."

"Work's always done for you," he says, his tone lighter than it should be. "That's the problem. You never stay long enough to remember you're allowed to live, too."

I glance at him. "What are you getting at?"

He gestures toward the dance floor. "One song. You've earned that much."

"I don't dance."

He smiles—small, knowing. "You used to."

The music shifts, softer now. Couples move like color in candlelight, sequins glinting like distant stars. For a moment, the air feels less like a ballroom and more like a dream—bright, too warm, too alive.

And just like that, I remember. The last time we danced.

Different room, different night—five years ago, maybe more. A charity dinner then, too. The air had smelled like roses and ambition. He'd caught me off guard, offering his hand with the same effortless confidence that always managed to feel like a challenge. I'd said yes before I had time to think better of it.

The song had been slower, darker. I remember the weight of his palm against the small of my back, the measured press of his thumb through silk. He didn't speak much, just moved with me, steady and certain, like he already knew where I'd step next. When the song ended, I couldn't tell if I'd been led or if I'd followed willingly.

Now, standing here, that memory breathes between us like a ghost neither of us invited. The years haven't softened it—they've only made it heavier. His gaze finds mine through the shifting light, unspoken words flickering there.

"Still not a dancer?" he asks quietly, the faintest trace of amusement in his voice.

"Still not someone you can read that easily," I lie.

His smile deepens, the kind that doesn't need proof to know it's already won. "We'll see about that."

And for the briefest moment, I forget the reason I'm here, the reason he shouldn't be. All I can think about is the echo of that night—the music, the warmth of his hand, and how, even then, I knew he was a danger I would one day stop pretending to resist.

"Come on," he says, extending his hand. "Just one."

I should say no. I should pack my things and disappear back into the rain. But his hand is there, patient, waiting, and I'm suddenly too tired to pretend I don't want the moment.

I take it.

His fingers close around mine—steady, grounding.

"Fine," I murmur. "One song."

He grins, not smug, not even surprised—just quiet, like he'd been waiting for me to remember something I'd forgotten.

As he draws me toward the floor, the lights tilt golden and soft. The crowd fades into motion. My red dress catches the glow, his hand finds the small of my back, and for a fleeting second, I forget about trials, transcripts, and the ghosts that follow me home.

For a fleeting second, it almost feels like living.

The music shifts—slow, deliberate, meant for people pretending not to watch each other. Silas leads me into the tide of movement, his hand resting lightly at the small of my back. Even through the satin, his touch feels grounded, too warm for comfort.

He moves like someone who's used to control, every step measured but unforced. I hate that I notice. The faint scent of cedar and rain still clings to him; it cuts through the perfume-heavy air. Up close, I see the gray threaded through the dark of his hair, the faint bruise-colored shadows under his eyes that no amount of charm could disguise.

"You've gotten better at disappearing," he says, voice low enough that only I can hear.

I keep my gaze fixed over his shoulder. "Maybe you've gotten worse at looking."

He laughs under his breath, the sound dark and genuine. "You still use sarcasm like a shield."

"And you still think you can see through it."

"Sometimes I can." He turns me with effortless precision, my skirt whispering against his leg. "You still type every verdict like you can rewrite the ending?"

"I just record what's said," I answer, too quick.

He studies me then, head tilted slightly. "You never did believe that."

The words slide between us, heavier than the music. The chandelier light scatters across his face, catching on the faint scar at his temple—one I never asked about, one he never offered to explain.

"Why are you here, Silas?" I ask quietly.

"Same reason as you," he says, spinning me out, then drawing me back in. "To see how the story ends."

"Except you don't write it anymore," I say.

He smiles, but it doesn't reach his eyes. "Maybe not on paper."

For a moment, our steps falter, just slightly—his hand tightens at my waist, steadying me. The heat of it sinks in before I can pull away.

"You always did overthink," he murmurs. "Can't you just enjoy one song?"

"I'm trying," I say, even though we both know it's a lie.

His thumb traces the edge of my spine, subtle, almost accidental. My pulse betrays me anyway.

"Still trying to outrun ghosts?" he asks softly.

I meet his gaze then—sharp, searching, too familiar. "Aren't you?"

The corner of his mouth lifts. "Every damn day."

The song ends before I realize I've been holding my breath. Applause breaks around us, polite and fleeting. He steps back, releases my hand slowly, eyes never leaving mine.

"See?" he says. "Didn't kill you."

"No," I answer, voice quieter than I intend. "Not yet."

He grins at that, something half-sincere flickering behind it. Then he nods toward my equipment case on the table. "Go on, Celeste. Back to work. Wouldn't want anyone to think you were enjoying yourself."

And just like that, he's gone—swallowed by laughter, gold light, and people who never notice the storm still gathering outside.

I grab my bag and head for the exit before the noise can swallow me again. The ballroom fades into echo and perfume, the last fragments of music clinging to my dress as I push through the revolving door.

Outside, the rain has thickened—steady, cold, relentless. It slicks the streets into a mirror, turning every passing headlight into a smear of light. My old sedan waits at the curb, wedged between glossy black cars that cost more than my annual salary. Its paint has dulled to a tired gray, a patch of rust spreading under the driver's door.

I run my hand along the roof before I open it, the metal cold and familiar. Ten years ago, I'd scraped and saved for this car—late shifts, second jobs, living off diner coffee and borrowed hours. It was the first thing I'd ever bought for myself. My one promise that I could keep moving forward, even if the road ahead was cracked.

It coughs to life on the third turn of the key, the dashboard lights flickering like a heartbeat. The heater wheezes, spitting out air that smells faintly of dust and rain.

The music fades behind me as I pull onto the street. City lights smear across the wet pavement, reflections stretching and breaking against the windshield as I drive. The wipers keep their tired rhythm, steady enough to loosen the thoughts I've been trying to hold together.

Boston slides away in ribbons of red and gold, dissolving into the dark. Silas lingers there. He always does.

He has a way of stepping into a moment like he belongs in it, like gravity tilts just a little to make room for him. It's always been that way. When I first moved here—barely out of school, still learning how to keep my head down in rooms full of people who talked louder than they listened—he was the first one who seemed to notice I existed.

Back then, he wasn't the man in the headlines. Just a name whispered in courthouse corridors, the attorney who could charm a confession out of stone. He'd stop by the training rooms sometimes, ask about my shorthand speed, correct my phrasing like he was doing me a favor. I told myself it was mentorship. Maybe it was. Maybe it wasn't.

He's always had that confidence that borders on arrogance, softened by that disarming half-smile he wields like a scalpel. He sees through people. Through masks. Through me.

It's not the flirting that unsettles me—it's the way he listens when I don't realize I'm speaking, the way his silences press closer than words.

Every time I tell myself I'm imagining it—that the pull between us is nothing more than nostalgia, muscle memory from old trials, the echo of how he used to command a room. But deep down, I know better. He looks at me like he's already read the ending of a story I haven't started yet.

The farther I drive, the quieter the world becomes. Salem waits beyond the blur of headlights—salt-stained and patient, familiar in a way that feels almost alive.

By the time I reach the coast, the storm has caught up. The air tastes of brine and memory. I cut the engine and sit there, listening to the rain drum against the roof.

It's strange how easy it is to find my way back to the past, no matter how far I try to go.

Maybe I was never outrunning it—just tracing the same circle, waiting for it to catch me.

Chapter 5
Elias

The city smells different after rain—iron and stone, like something old trying to breathe again.

By the time I reach Beacon Hill, the streets are slick with fog, gas lamps glowing faint against the dark. Townhouses rise shoulder to shoulder, red brick shining like polished bone. The kind of neighborhood where wealth isn't shown—it's assumed.

Another early call. Another body. Second in a month.

Uniforms are already keeping the press at bay, their flashbulbs lighting up the mist across the street. I flash my badge, nod at the perimeter officer, and step through the gate. The iron fence is slick, cold against my palm.

Inside, the house feels too still. No chaos, no sign of intrusion—just quiet. Expensive quiet. The kind that absorbs sound.

Freddy Haven is waiting upstairs, crouched near the bed with his usual coffee in one hand, pen in the other. The lines around his eyes deepen when he looks up. "Morning, Shaw. Hope you like perfume."

The smell hits before I answer—sweet, cloying, heavy enough to stick in the back of my throat. A bouquet of lilies and gardenias sits on the table by the window, still damp from the rain.

The victim's sprawled half across the bed, evening gown wrinkled, jewelry still on. No forced entry. No struggle.

"What do we have?" I ask, stepping closer.

"Female, late forties," Freddy says, voice flat. "Preliminary says no trauma. No punctures, no bruising, no defensive wounds. But look at this—" He nods toward her face. "Swelling around the lips. Throat blotchy. Classic anaphylaxis, if I had to bet. I'll know more when tox comes back."

"Something she ate?"

"Maybe. Or drank. Or touched. Could've been in the air for all we know. Reactions like that can hit fast."

I glance at the flowers again. "Who sent them?"

Freddy shrugs. "Housekeeper found her this morning. Said the door was unlocked, lights still on. She was supposed to fly to New York for a board meeting today. Guess she missed her flight."

I scan the bedroom. It's pristine—too pristine. The kind of order money buys. Makeup brushes laid out in perfect lines, jewelry still on the dresser. No sign of panic, no struggle. Just stillness.

Freddy gestures toward the table by the window. "Said she got the flowers and the perfume last night at the gala. Brought them home herself."

The bouquet sits there, lush and deliberate—white lilies and gardenias bound tight with cream ribbon, the water pooling under the vase from where it had been dropped and reset. Next to it, a small velvet box holds a crystal perfume bottle—clear, elegant, label embossed in gold script: *Lueur d'Aube.*

I step closer, crouching to inspect. "Housekeeper touch anything?"

Freddy shakes his head. "She called nine-one-one, waited on the stoop until patrol arrived. Everything's as she left it."

The scent is thick, cloying—floral turned sour under the heat. I put on gloves, careful as I lift the edge of the bouquet's damp tissue paper. Something catches my eye: a sliver of paper wedged between the folds.

"Bag that," I tell the evidence tech. "Carefully."

She peels the wrapping back layer by layer, revealing a handful of neatly folded documents pressed flat between the stems. Moisture has blurred the ink, but the numbers are still visible—account transfers, donations that loop back into shell foundations, signatures that don't match.

Freddy leans in. "Well, I'll be damned. Looks like the flowers came with a side of confession."

"Or accusation," I murmur.

He straightens, rubbing his jaw. "So whoever sent this knew she'd open it. That she'd see what was inside."

"And that she'd never live long enough to tell anyone," I finish.

The evidence tech seals the papers, labeling each sheet as she works. I glance back at the perfume bottle. A faint residue glints along the rim—almost invisible, but not to trained eyes.

"Bag the bottle, too," I say. "Check the sprayer for residue. And I want the bouquet tested for any allergenic compounds."

Freddy scribbles in his notebook, frowning. "You thinking poison?"

"Maybe. Or exposure. Something slow enough not to look like murder."

He exhales through his nose. "No wonder the house is so damn quiet."

I nod toward the card still tucked into the bouquet's ribbon. "Get a shot of that before we bag it."

The photographer clicks once. The card's words gleam faintly in the flash:

For your tireless compassion. The city blooms because of you.

Outside, rain taps against the window, soft and steady, as if the storm itself is listening.

"Call me when tox comes in," I say.

Freddy's voice follows me as I head for the stairs—dry, steady, the kind of calm that only comes from years of seeing too much. "You'll be the first to know, Shaw. Always are."

The front door shuts behind me, sealing in the perfume, the silence, and the ghosts.

Beacon Hill exhales—a long, tired breath.

Another quiet death in a city built on noise.

The office hums with the kind of silence that builds pressure behind the eyes. My notes sprawl across the desk—photos, typed reports, scrawled observations that read more like confessions than leads. The Beacon Hill file sits dead center. I've gone through it four times, and it still refuses to make sense.

The phone buzzes.

"Shaw."

"Detective, it's Lina in Forensics." Her voice is sharp, efficient. "I've got results on your flowers and the perfume. You'll want to come down."

"I'm on my way."

The forensics lab is colder than usual—sterile air, low hum of machines, the faint sting of alcohol wipes. Lina's at her workstation, gloves on, eyes alert despite the hour.

"Tell me something good," I say.

She huffs out a humorless laugh. "Define good."

Evidence bags line the counter—flowers, tissue, perfume bottle, card. She gestures to the bouquet first. "Petal swabs tested positive for sesame protein—heavy concentration on two species: gardenia and stephanotis. Whoever handled these flowers deliberately coated them in a sesame-based oil. Enough to trigger anaphylaxis from a single touch or inhalation."

I jot it down. "Cross-contamination?"

"No chance," she says. "It's intentional. Uniform coverage, not random."

She moves to the next tray. "This tissue paper came from the bouquet wrap. Between the layers, we found folded financial ledgers—account transfers, falsified donor receipts. The ink bled from moisture, but you can still make out the names. And under UV—"

She flips a switch. The overhead lights fade, and the page glows faintly, dotted with yellow specks.

"Printer microdots," she says. "Each pattern is unique to a specific printer. This one traces back to a laser model registered to the foundation's office. Someone inside printed these."

"So the killer didn't just want her dead," I murmur. "They wanted her exposed."

Lina nods toward the velvet box. "It gets better. The perfume bottle—custom blend, labeled *Lueur d'Aube.* Expensive, no public record of distribution. I ran chemical analysis on residue from the sprayer and the cap threads." She slides over a chart, peaks spiking like heartbeats. "Trace sesame oil compound mixed with the fragrance base. Whoever designed this blend used sesame as a carrier note."

"She sprayed it?"

"Housekeeper said the bottle was open when she found her. One spritz on the inside of the wrist."

I look down at the report. "That's all it took."

"Contact absorption," Lina says. "Skin exposure followed by inhalation. Two routes, one reaction. Death within minutes."

The hum of the machines fills the pause.

Lina folds her arms, leaning back against the counter. "Whoever did this knew her history. Probably her medical file too. This was designed—personal."

"Have you noticed any connection to the other cases?" I ask. "The drownings, the supposed accidents?"

She frowns, scanning her notes. "Nothing chemical. But the presentation? Same precision. No mess. No hesitation. It's... ritualistic."

Ritualistic. The word fits too well.

I nod. "Send me the lab summary and the dot-map. I'll follow up with Financial Crimes on the ledgers."

She slides a folder toward me. "Already printed and signed. You're welcome."

"Thanks, Lina," I say.

"Anytime, Detective. Though you could bring coffee next time."

"Noted."

I push through the door, back into the hallway. The hum of the lab fades behind me, replaced by the slow drip of rain against the windows.

Each drop feels like a clock tick, counting down to the next name waiting to be crossed off some invisible list.

By the time I make it back from Financial Crimes, the caffeine's burned off and the city's soaked clean again — or pretending to be. My office smells like wet paper and bad coffee. The kind of mix that tells you you've been at this too long.

The ledgers sit open on my desk, rows of numbers that twist if I stare too long. Donations looping through ghost accounts, corporate shells, charitable fronts that never actually funded a damn thing. Financial Crimes pulled the metadata from the files — creation dates, edit trails. All of them trace back almost a year. All under the same authorization tag.

Eduardo Lexington's foundation.

And the late Marlene Corbett — tonight's body.

I flip through the case summaries the analyst handed me. Every financial irregularity ties to a sealed civil case. Fraud, embezzlement, mishandled funds, and a quiet out-of-court settlement that never hit the press.

The last page catches my eye:

Corbett v. State of Massachusetts — 14-376A.

Filed fifteen months ago. Dismissed nine months later.

Defense counsel: Silas Kade.

I sit back. The name punches through the fog like a blade.

Kade. I've heard it before — murmured in precinct halls, cursed in legal circles. A courtroom prodigy who fell hard. Disbarred six months ago for evidence tampering on a homicide case. He's not supposed to be anywhere near an active defense now.

But he was.

I pull the file closer. The victim list, the testimony. Kade represented Corbett's foundation during the investigation into the missing funds. His closing statement reads like gospel — righteous, measured, full of that polished poison men like him make sound like truth.

The case vanished after that.
And now she's dead.

I flip another page. Her deposition transcript. The first line under oath:

"Mr. Kade assured me no one would ever find out."

The hum in the room shifts — a low, electric pulse, like the rain syncing with my heartbeat.

I pull out my pen, scrawl his name at the top of the board in red ink.
Silas Mercer Kade.

Six months disbarred.
Tied to a dead philanthropist.
And if I dig far enough, I bet I find more bodies hidden under his brand of justice.

I pull the folders closer, flipping them open one by one. Different faces, same phrasing on every report—*no sign of forced entry, minimal struggle, cause of death inconclusive.*

Wexler's file is thinner than the rest. A quiet death, barely a whisper in the *Globe*: *Local financier found dead near the Charles River embankment.* The kind of blurb people skim over between coffee sips. No one asked how a man who couldn't swim drowned in three inches of runoff.

But the dates line up too neatly— Wexler in July, Lexington in August, Corbett at the start of September. One a month. And each tied, directly or not, to the same firm.

His name surfaces in Lexington's redevelopment contracts and again in Corbett's charity trust, buried under *Second Light Holdings.* The signatures form a paper trail no one else thought to follow—money laundering disguised as philanthropy, client funds siphoned into ghost accounts.

Neglect and greed—that was Wexler's sin. The kind that hides behind polished smiles and quarterly reports. He drowned in the same complacency he sold to everyone else.

I scribble the word *water* beside his name, linking it to the others: *fire* for Lexington's burned records, *air* for Corbett's suffocation, *earth* for what they buried beneath their foundations.

Different methods. Same equation. Someone's rewriting justice by the elements.

The coffee pot sputters behind me, the sound too human in the quiet. I stare at the board until the faces blur, until I can almost see the pattern pulsing underneath.

And for the first time since this started, it doesn't feel like investigation—it feels like translation.

The phone buzzes again.

"Shaw," I answer.

Vance's voice. "Press is all over this. Tell me we've got a lead."

I glance at Kade's name bleeding across the whiteboard. "We've got something better," I say. "A pattern."

The precinct hums low, that late-hour fatigue where even the coffee pot sounds exhausted. I've been staring at the board for an hour, the names bleeding together—Lexington, Corbett, Wexler—all tethered by the same invisible thread.

Financial Crimes sent over a supplemental packet before closing: staff logs, courtroom rosters, and administrative lists connected to each trial Silas Kade ever touched in the last two years. I sort through them, cross-referencing names like I'm building a ghost map.

Some overlap. Court personnel. Transcriptionists. Clerks.

Then one name shows up twice.

Celeste Evelyn Duvall.

Court Reporter. Boston Superior Court.

Her signature's on the transcripts from both Corbett's and Wexler's trials. Precise, neat—almost too clean.

I rub at the corner of my eye, fatigue setting in. Maybe it's coincidence. Maybe she's just another cog in the system—someone who happened to be there when justice fell asleep at the wheel. But coincidences have been getting harder to believe in lately.

The rain picks up outside, tapping harder against the glass.

I jot her name onto my notepad, underline it once.

Celeste Duvall — interview. If there's a thread running through all this, maybe she's the one holding it.

I shut the file, slide my chair back, and grab my coat. The city's still bleeding silver through the windows, restless even at midnight.

Time to start asking questions.

Chapter 6
Killer

I watch her. Track her steps until I know her schedule better than my own. To anyone else, it might look erratic—appointments shuffled, meetings moved, no pattern worth finding. But there's always a rhythm if you listen long enough. Everyone has their tells. Their habits. The little rituals that give them away.

To the public, she's a saint in heels. A philanthropist with perfect hair and a curated conscience. She funds literacy programs, shelters, charity dinners. Cameras love her; the city calls her hope.

But I've seen the rot that hides beneath all that polished grace. The way her smile falters when no one's watching. The sharpness in her eyes when the spotlight fades. They call her generous. I call her what she is—another name waiting to be corrected.

Tonight, the city gathers at the Fairmont Copley Plaza—a palace of marble and mirrors where old money and ambition still waltz in step. The gala is hers to host, the season's crown jewel. On paper, it's a fundraiser for children's programs—adoption, foster care, second chances wrapped in silver linen.

Inside, crystal chandeliers catch the light like judgment. Waiters move in seamless choreography, champagne flutes balanced with grace that borders on reverence. Every laugh sounds rehearsed. Every smile costs something.

Old wealth, new wealth, and those desperate to join their ranks all orbit one another, trading handshakes and half-truths. The glitz conceals the rot. Behind every polished compliment is a transaction; every donation comes with a receipt for silence.

They call it charity. I call it accounting.

And at the center of it all stands the host—radiant, untouchable, adored. The crowd sees a savior. I see the next correction.

I don't need to fight or force my way in. I'm already part of the crowd—expected, comfortable, polished the same as the rest of them. So I mingle. I eat. I wear the practiced smile and time the perfect laugh. All the while I watch her.

I'll let her have this night—a gala she'll remember. Let the cameras catch her glow, let the donors pat themselves on the back. Let her feel untouchable one last time. Then she'll meet her end.

Twofold, like I said. I give light; I make shadow.

The bouquet is deliberate. Not showy—too loud would ruin the il-lusion—so I pick blooms that read as innocence and ceremony: cream calla lilies, their trumpet mouths smooth as porcelain; a few pale gardenias for the waxy, close scent of motherhood; sprigs of stephanotis threaded through like confessions, tiny white stars that mean "good luck" in wedding bouquets. I tuck in a handful of baby's breath to make the arrangement look airy, charitable, like something the city would buy into without thinking. Each stem is stripped of excess leaves, the bouquet wrapped in pale ribbon and tied with a single knot so the hand that accepts it will feel the practiced weight of gratitude.

The flowers look like a benediction. They photograph well.

The second gift is quieter: a slender bottle, bespoke—bergamot top notes, a heart of jasmine softened by a warm amber base. It reads like sophistication, the kind of scent the hostess will breathe in and carry like a private award. The bottle is velvet-wrapped, a flourish that makes people lean in and cameras gobble it up.

There's a small thing no one notices: the faint grit along the underside of a few petals. It gleams like dust when it catches light. Tiny, unspectacular. Plausible as pollen. Invisible in the applause.

The ballroom hums with borrowed light. Gold drips from every surface, applause echoing off glass and good intentions. I stand near the edge of the crowd—close enough to feel the heat of the stage lights, far enough to be no one at all.

It's all already in motion. Every step timed, every gesture rehearsed. The bouquet waits offstage, roses bound in silk ribbon. The perfume bottle rests beside it—cut crystal, imported, expensive enough to look thoughtful. Gratitude made tangible.

Marlene Eliza Corbett takes the podium like she's auditioning for sainthood. She speaks of redemption, of healing, of *hope*. The crowd drinks it up, eager to believe money can cleanse what it touches. They don't see the fractures beneath her grace. But I do.

When she finishes, the handoff is seamless. The bouquet first—light enough to cradle. Then the perfume, offered as a final gift. She smiles, the flashbulbs catching her at just the right angle. She doesn't notice the faint shimmer beneath the bottle's glass. No one ever does.

Later, she'll set them on her table, dim the lights, maybe uncork the perfume to test its scent. She'll breathe it in, slow and indulgent. That's when the correction begins. Not violent. Not messy. Just inevitable.

I don't need to watch her fall. I'll feel it—the way the city exhales when balance returns.

By morning the bouquet will sit like a pale accusation. A smear of grit on a petal. The bottle uncapped. And just like that, the scales tip back into balance—if only for a breath.

I never set out to be the hand that steadied them. It wasn't fate, and it sure as hell wasn't divine purpose. It was smaller than that. Quieter. A collection of moments that started to mean something when no one else was looking—faces in crowds, the way people flinch, the way the world learns to look away when cruelty wears a familiar smile.

For a long time, I thought that was just life.

"Just the way it is."

That's what they all say, right before they stop seeing it at all.

I sit at the table with only a lamp and the low sigh of the heater for company. The rest of the world is a muted block of windows and distant traffic; here, under this light, everything sharpens. I lay the photos out like a deck of faces—some glossy press shots, some grainy surveillance stills, a few Polaroids taken when a life felt ordinary enough to be forgotten. Beside them, the notebook lives open, its edges smudged from my hands. Names, dates, small notes: why they were missed, how the system folded for them, what the court called their endings.

Paul Granger — domestic violence, multiple complaints. Witnesses too scared, testimony thin. Case dismissed after "insufficient corroboration."

Trevor Densmore — assault on a minor; mistrial; disappeared before appeal.

Harold Wexler — linked to development contracts; accident reported; odd burn patterns in clinical notes.

Eduardo Lexington — factories, safety violations, complaints buried under corporate counsel. Big name, bigger cover. The one that made the city look up.

I let a finger trace the ink beside each name. The ledger doesn't care about headlines. It cares about balance—about the moments where law and money braided together and left someone broken in the middle. That's my measuring stick: not celebrity, not cruelty alone, but the way institutions softened consequences until the harm was archived as an anomaly. The ledger remembers what they erase.

There are rules I don't write down, but they live in me all the same—old as instinct, older than language. I was never taught them. I just *knew*.

No spectacle.

No suffering for its own sake.

No correction that leaves ripples wider than the wound itself.

Every act must close the circle.

Precision. Control. Silence.

I don't need to carve these truths anywhere. They hum in my blood, the way certain people are born knowing when to look up just before lightning strikes. It isn't morality that drives me—it's something older. Something that remembers balance long after the world forgot what it meant.

The edges have to blur until no one can tell where fate ends and I begin.

I make lists. The first column is need—who the ledger is calling for. The second is access—how close they let themselves be to their own pleasures without armor. The third is cover—who will be blamed, what story the city will accept, whether the press will dig or move on. Names fall into columns like talent. Some sit in the margins for months: connections, corporate umbrellas, quiet confidants who wash the stains into other hands.

Tonight, I add three more names to the center fold. They're not famous. That's the point. They are the ones who enabled the famous—administrators who bent rules for profit, counsel who drafted indemnities with one eye closed, clinic directors who stamped reports "follow-up" until there was nothing left to follow. They have clean records by design. Their children will inherit what they built. Their grief will be discreet. The ledger hums a little louder when I place their names down.

I read witness statements with the same calm I used to read technical manuals—looking for the margin note, the slip, the line that says someone else touched the truth and then turned away. I mark each spot where a promise was made and broken: "insufficient evidence," "no sign of forced entry," "ruled accidental." Those are the soft places that invite correction.

They show where the world is hollow.

There is ritual in the choosing.

Not ceremony. Not spectacle.

Just the quiet, deliberate order of things: watch, wait, confirm, close.

I watch how a man sleeps when he thinks no one sees. How he drinks, how his voice bends when he lies. How the world unbuttons around him until there's a seam to pull.

I wait for the right night—one that offers silence and the mercy of clean exits.

I confirm the story the city will keep.

And then I close the ledger for a while and step into the space where ink becomes blood.

The candle gutters low, wax drowning in itself. I stand, stretch, and gather the photographs. Each one slides back into its envelope like evidence of a truth no one else can bear. The notebook folds shut with a soft snap.

In the hush between the radiator and the street, I speak their names. Not for power—just precision. Speaking them makes the choices real.

Paul Granger.

Trevor Densmore.

Marion Wexler.

Eduardo Lexington.

Four names. Four corrections. The most notable among the ones I've made so far.

Outside, the city exhales—unaware it's been spared something worse. Inside, the ledger waits. Not *mine*, not yet, but the one I've been reaching for. The true record. The one that hums beneath my skin like recognition every time I set a wrong thing right.

Somewhere, it exists—inked in blood and intent, its pages older than law, older than the gods that failed it.

Until I find it, I keep the rhythm. I keep the order.

I go to the window, looking down at the city lights pricking through the dark like tiny, watchful eyes. Patterns forming. Scales shifting, if only by degrees.

I listen for the hum beneath it all.

It answers me.

The ledger remembers.

Chapter 7
Celeste

The first thing I feel is pain—a slow, dull throb behind my eyes that spreads like spilled ink. My body aches, every muscle stiff, like I've been carrying someone else's weight in my sleep.

The clock on the nightstand blinks 10:47 AM. Saturday.

For a moment, I just stare at it, trying to remember when I went to bed. The last clear image I can pull is sitting on the couch, tea cooling beside me, pen still in hand. After that—nothing. Just fragments: the sound of water, the taste of salt, the feel of wind tangling in my hair. My clothes are still damp at the hem like I've been outside, but the door's deadbolt is untouched.

I stay in bed for a while, caught somewhere between sleep and the shape of morning. Rain whispers against the window, steady and thin, the refrigerator's hum threading through the silence like a pulse. Time slips in slow circles—minutes maybe, maybe more—until the chill finally pushes through the sheets.

I pull a blanket around my shoulders and make my way to the kitchen. The motion feels rehearsed, muscle memory on autopilot. The first dark drops of coffee fall into the pot, bitter and grounding, but they don't chase away the fog clinging behind my eyes.

When I finally lift the mug, my hand trembles. There's something metallic beneath the scent of coffee—something that doesn't belong.

I tell myself I'm imagining it.

Then a knock breaks the quiet. Soft. Polite. Out of place.

I set the mug down and glance through the peephole. A delivery driver stands in the hallway, rain dripping from his jacket, a large bouquet balanced in his arms with a small gift bag resting on top.

"Delivery for Celeste Duvall?" he asks when I open the door.

Hearing my name feels strange this early. "Yeah," I say, and take the flowers from him.

He nods, already turning away as the door closes behind me. The hallway light flickers once, then steadies.

The bouquet is striking—long-stemmed lilies, pale roses, and sprigs of baby's breath, all wrapped in crisp white tissue paper. Elegant. Familiar. The same arrangement from the gala. The scent rises faintly, warm and expensive, like it's been waiting here for me.

I set the bouquet on the counter and find a small envelope tucked between the stems. The handwriting is neat, deliberate.

> *Dinner tonight? I'll pick you up at seven—unless you decide to cancel.*
> *— Silas*

Inside the gift bag sits a perfume bottle—cut crystal, vintage, the liquid inside catching the gray morning light like trapped fire. I twist the cap. The scent is deep, smoky, laced with something rich I can't quite name.

The migraine sharpens behind my eyes. I press a hand to my temple and stare at the note until the words blur.

He always finds a way to slip through the cracks.

He did it the first time I met him—when I was twenty, fresh out of training, still learning the rhythm of the courtroom and how to keep my nerves from showing in my hands. Silas Kade had been the rising star of the bar back then, the kind of attorney who didn't just win cases—he *orchestrated* them. I was the stenographer tucked in the corner, transcribing every carefully chosen word. He'd glance my way sometimes between statements, like he was studying punctuation instead of people.

When I moved to Boston, he was already there, somehow waiting—introducing me to the city like it was his to share. He told me which neighborhoods were safe, which cafés stayed open late, which judges hated being interrupted. Always helpful. Always just distant enough to make me wonder what he wanted in return.

Back then, I thought he was untouchable—elegant, calculating, immune to the kind of chaos that swallowed everyone else. Then came the scandal, the disbarment, the fall. But even that didn't break him. It just made him quieter. Sharper. Like the edge of something tempered by fire.

Now, standing here again, nearly ten years later, I can feel it—the difference. The air around him carries a charge it didn't before, heavier, magnetic, like something unseen has started to pull the world slightly off its axis. Maybe it's time. Maybe it's me. Maybe we've both changed in ways we don't have names for.

All I know is this feels different. His presence isn't just familiar anymore—it's *inevitable.*

He always finds a way to slip through the cracks.

But this time, it feels like he's stepping through something larger.

And somehow, I'm already waiting on the other side.

A knock comes again before I've even cleared the first delivery from the counter. Sharper this time. I freeze, mug halfway to my lips, a drop of coffee sliding over the rim and onto my wrist.

Another delivery.

The driver waiting in the hall is new—older, polite, holding a long garment bag and two stacked boxes. "Ms. Duvall?" he asks.

"Yeah," I say, already knowing.

He nods once and hands everything over. No clipboard. No signature. Just that faint look people wear when they know they're carrying something expensive.

The apartment feels too still when I close the door. I set the packages on the couch and just look at them, that old ache starting low behind my ribs. When I finally unzip the garment bag, red spills out—dark, deliberate, the kind of shade that dares you to touch it.

The dress is silk. Smooth, cool, and heavy enough to matter. Off-the-shoulder neckline, fitted bodice, a skirt that moves like it remembers how to breathe. It's elegant, but it's intimate in a way that feels almost personal—like it was tailored from memory.

The first box holds accessories: black heels with a wine-colored sole, a matching clutch, gold earrings shaped like teardrops, and a thin bracelet that glints like fire when it catches the light.

The second box is smaller. Lighter. When I open it, soft tissue paper parts to reveal something folded and red—lingerie. Silk and lace. Minimal. Precise. The kind of thing no one should guess and yet somehow he got it exactly right.

A card rests on top, written in Silas's unmistakable hand—clean, measured, intentional.

> *For tonight. Dinner at seven.*
> *— Silas*

The paper smells faintly of his cologne: amber, smoke, and something darker beneath it. The scent finds its way under my skin before I can stop it.

Silas Kade never sends gifts without purpose. He doesn't flirt—he strategizes. Every gesture, every word, is a calculation designed to make you forget where the line was drawn until you've already crossed it.

The flowers from earlier still sit on the counter, their perfume thickening in the air. The lingerie rests in my hands, light as a secret I shouldn't be keeping.

This isn't a gift. It's a test.

And still, my fingers smooth the silk as if it might tell me what he's really after. He always makes control feel like choice.

The apartment feels smaller now, crowded with flowers, fabric, and meaning. It's absurd. It's calculated. And yet, it's beautiful. I tell myself it's just dinner—a meal, a conversation, nothing more. Maybe a thank-you for helping at the gala. He isn't expecting anything. I'm not, either.

I carry the garment bag and the opened boxes into the bedroom, balancing them against my hip like something fragile. The lids sit askew, tissue paper spilling over the edges in pale waves. Silk, lace, jewelry—each piece chosen too precisely to be coincidence. Even the faint trace of his cologne clings to the wrapping, subtle and deliberate.

I set them down gently on the chair, trying not to think about how easily he's learned me. The dress. The lingerie. The accessories that match so perfectly they feel like prophecy. It's unsettling—being known this well by someone I've spent years pretending to keep at arm's length. I turn to take a shower before the thought can linger.

The water takes a moment to warm, sputtering through old pipes before settling into a steady stream. Steam gathers quickly, fogging the mirror and softening the edges of everything. I stand beneath the spray, letting it beat against the tension in my neck and shoulders until the ache begins to ease.

The scent of my shampoo mixes with the faint trace of lilies still clinging to my hands from the bouquet. It's too sweet, almost cloying, but it reminds me of the night before—the shimmer of glass, the quiet hum of strings, the sound of Silas's voice close to my ear. I rinse slower than I should, the heat chasing away the chill that's settled deep in my bones.

When I step out, the air feels heavier, the kind that sticks to skin. I towel off and move back toward the garment bag, condensation cooling along my arms. I tell myself again that it's only dinner, just an evening. Nothing more.

Still damp from the shower, I find myself unzipping the garment bag, letting the silk slide through my fingers. The color is deliberate—rich and deep, somewhere between blood and wine. It catches the light when I move, soft and liquid, the kind of fabric meant to be seen. My reflection in the fogged window shifts with every motion, red spilling across the pale morning like a secret trying to escape.

In the bedroom, I open the smaller box. Inside, folded neatly between layers of tissue paper, lies the lingerie. Red lace. Thin straps. A suggestion of transparency. My pulse stutters. I shouldn't even touch it, but I do. The silk is impossibly smooth beneath my fingers, cool at first and then warm as it learns my skin.

I was raised to see beauty as something dangerous—to hide it, silence it, pray it away. Purity meant safety, control meant virtue. Desire was something whispered about only when it ruined someone. Yet standing here now, I can't stop thinking that maybe it was never desire that was dangerous, only the shame attached to it.

I unfold the pieces slowly and slip them on, the lace settling against my skin with a sigh. It feels indecent, too intimate, as if it knows me better than I know myself. Every movement draws my awareness inward—the whisper of silk, the press of breath against fabric, the pulse thrumming low beneath it all. I should feel ashamed. Instead, I feel awake.

I stand there for a moment, just breathing, the quiet drip of water still echoing from the shower. Heat clings to my skin, mixing with the faint trace of perfume that lingers in the air. The lace feels like memory—soft, dangerous, impossible to ignore. I smooth the straps into place and meet my own eyes in the mirror. The reflection staring back feels half mine, half something older, something that's been waiting to be seen.

I move back to the bedroom, letting my hands stay busy—powder, brush, the slow rhythm of drying my hair, the soft click of jewelry clasps. Each motion steadies me, gives me something to hold onto. But my mind doesn't quiet. It drifts where it always does when his name surfaces.

Silas has asked me to dinner before. Years of near-misses and polite refusals. He always made it sound effortless, almost careless, like the invitation didn't matter—but it did. It always did.

The first time was after a long case we both worked—when he still wore arrogance like armor and charm like a weapon disguised as warmth. I said no, and he smiled like he'd expected that answer all along. Like it was part of a longer game.

The second time, months later, he showed up with chai and that same half-smile—the one that turns every question into a promise. I said no again, and again he didn't seem disappointed. Just... patient. As if he already knew that someday, I'd stop saying it.

Now, when he asks, there's something different in the way he looks at me. A quiet certainty. A secret I'm not being told but somehow already part of.

And the worst part is, I think I want to know what it is.

As I pin up my hair, I can almost hear his voice, smooth and deliberate, the kind that threads through a room until you forget it's there. It's the tone he uses in court—control disguised as curiosity. It shouldn't affect me anymore. I tell myself it doesn't. Still, my pulse betrays me.

The dress waits where I left it, red spilling over the chair like something alive. I step into it carefully, pulling the zipper up my spine. The silk slides over the lace, cool meeting warmth, restraint meeting invitation. It fits perfectly. Of course it does. He never guesses.

I turn toward the mirror. The woman staring back doesn't look like someone who's spent her life saying no. She looks like someone who's finally considering the cost of restraint.

I slip on the bracelet last, the clasp snapping shut around my wrist with a soft click. Outside, a car horn echoes faintly down the street. Seven o'clock is closer than I thought.

I look once more at my reflection—the painted lips, the calm eyes, the faint tremor in my chest—and whisper, "It's just dinner."

But even as I say it, I know he'll hear something else entirely.

Chapter 8
Celeste

The knock comes exactly at seven. Not a second early. Not a second late.

I take a breath before opening the door, one last attempt to steady the flutter in my chest that refuses to listen to reason. The hallway light spills in as I turn the handle.

Silas stands there like he's been painted into place—perfectly composed, perfectly aware of it. His dark hair is swept back, silver threading through it just enough to look intentional. The charcoal suit fits him too well to be off the rack, the shirt open at the collar in that careful way that suggests he didn't try at all. He's holding a box wrapped in simple brown paper and tied with black twine, his expression caught somewhere between casual and calculated.

"Evening," he says, voice low and smooth, like the sound of a match being struck. "You look—" He pauses just long enough to make me feel it. "Exactly how I imagined."

My pulse betrays me. "You shouldn't have."

"I should," he says easily, lifting the box slightly. "Peace offering."

"What is it?"

"Coffee and chai. A few rare blends." The corner of his mouth curves. "I noticed last night at the gala that you still ran on caffeine and willpower. Thought you might need a better version of both."

I fold my arms, half to hide the tremor in my hands. "That's thoughtful. And unnecessary."

"Most things worth doing are." His smile is the kind that could pass for kindness if you didn't know better. "Besides, you've had a rough docket lately. Medical malpractice, fraud, the Lexington trial. Heavy cases. You deserve something pleasant."

I blink, the weight of his words settling. "You remember the cases I cover?"

"I make a point to remember the people who record the truth," he says. "Even when no one else does."

It's a line. I know it is. But the way he says it—quiet, measured—makes it feel less like flattery and more like something he believes.

The box is still between us. I should refuse it. I should tell him it's too much, too personal. Instead, I find myself reaching for it. His fingers brush mine as I take it, warm and steady.

"Thank you," I manage.

"Don't thank me yet," he says, stepping back just enough to let his gaze travel, deliberate but not crude. "Save that for after dinner."

He offers his arm like a gentleman from another century, his eyes catching the faint light from the hallway. They look almost silver when he smiles.

For a moment, I just stand there, one hand clutching the gift, the other hovering between refusal and surrender. His confidence hums in the air—quiet, assured, practiced. It would be easier if he were arrogant. Easier if he didn't know exactly how much space to take up, or how to leave just enough silence for me to fill.

I step back, just enough to break the tension, and set the gift on the small table by the door. The tissue-wrapped flowers from this morning sit beside it, their scent heavy and familiar. The sight of them grounds me, or maybe warns me.

When I turn back, he's still there, the faintest smile ghosting across his lips, like he already knew what I'd do.

"Shall we?" he asks.

Outside, the rain has calmed to a mist, the kind that clings instead of falls. His car waits at the curb—a sleek black sedan that gleams under the streetlight. The windows are tinted, the interior visible only when he opens the door.

The seats are blood red, soft leather that looks too expensive to touch. Even the air inside smells like him: cedar, smoke, something sharp beneath it. He circles around to the driver's side as I slide in, the door closing with a satisfying thud that feels more like a seal than a sound.

Everything about the car feels deliberate, curated, like him. The low purr of the engine, the faint jazz murmuring from hidden speakers, the heat set to exactly the right temperature.

As he pulls into traffic, the city lights streak across the windshield in ribbons of gold and white. For a while, neither of us speaks. The quiet isn't awkward—it's studied, like he's giving me time to settle into the rhythm he's already decided on.

Finally, he glances over, one hand loose on the wheel, the other resting against the console. "You almost didn't open the door," he says, not as a question, but as a knowing.

"I almost didn't," I admit.

"And yet, here you are."

His tone is light, but there's something underneath it—something testing, searching.

I turn my gaze to the window. "It's just dinner."

He laughs softly, low and genuine. "Of course it is."

But when I glance back, the smile he gives me says otherwise.

The drive is quiet, the city falling away behind us until only the hum of the tires and the low rhythm of the radio fill the space between us. I can feel him watching me in small glances, not intrusive—just observant. Measured.

The air outside is cool, unnaturally so after days of rain. The clouds have finally given up their hold on the sky, leaving it stripped bare and endless. The moon hangs full and pale above the road, a coin of light surrounded by a scattering of stars. The kind of night that almost feels like forgiveness.

Every so often, the headlights catch the wet sheen of the asphalt, and for a second the world blurs—moonlight and motion and that strange pulse beneath my ribs that I can't quite name. It's not nerves. It's something deeper, a tug that feels familiar and foreign all at once.

When he finally speaks, his voice cuts through the quiet like a slow exhale. "You're thinking too hard."

"Occupational hazard," I say, keeping my eyes on the dark stretch of coastline ahead.

He smiles, just enough to show it in the corner of his mouth. "You analyze everything, don't you?"

"Someone has to."

"And yet," he says, glancing over at me again, "you came anyway."

I don't answer. I'm not sure I could explain it even if I tried. There's something about him that draws me in—the way he speaks, the way he seems to already know what I'll say before I do. It isn't the usual kind of attraction. It's slower. Heavier. Like gravity finding a new center.

We leave the highway, turning down a narrow coastal road that winds along the cliffs. Waves crash far below, the sound carrying even through the closed windows. The lights ahead resolve into a building perched at the edge of the world—glass walls glowing golden against the dark sea.

The sign reads *Astra Mare*. I've heard of it. A reservation months out. The kind of place that doesn't just serve dinner; it orchestrates it.

When he parks, the engine quiets to a soft purr, leaving only the wind and the waves. He steps out first, coming around to open my door before I can reach for the handle. The chill hits me instantly, cool and briny, carrying the scent of the ocean and something metallic beneath it.

For a moment, I just stand there, looking up. The stars feel impossibly close, scattered across the sky like a secret someone finally decided to share.

"Beautiful, isn't it?" he says softly.

"It doesn't feel real."

He studies me for a beat, the wind catching his hair, the moonlight cutting across his jaw. "That's the trick," he says. "The best illusions never do."

I don't know if he means the view or himself. Maybe both.

Inside, the warmth hits immediately—soft lighting, linen-draped tables, the hush of money and good wine. The hostess greets him by name and leads us toward a corner table overlooking the ocean. The glass windows reflect the moonlight, blurring the line between sea and sky.

As we sit, I feel that pull again, quiet but insistent. Like something deep in me remembers him from somewhere that doesn't exist on paper.

He smiles across the table. "You look like you're still deciding whether this is a mistake."

"Maybe I am."

"Then I'll do my best to convince you otherwise."

The way he says it—soft, certain—makes me wonder if I even want to be convinced.

The waiter returns, menu in hand, but Silas waves it off with that same quiet confidence that's always made people pause mid-motion.

"She'll have the pan-seared halibut," he says, tone even, practiced. "With the saffron risotto. And the Pinot Gris to pair."

He glances at me—polite, but knowing. "Unless you'd prefer something else?"

I arch a brow, meeting his gaze squarely. "Actually, I'd prefer the ribeye. Rare."

The faintest flicker of surprise crosses his face—gone as soon as it appears. "Of course," he says easily, signaling to the waiter. "Make that two ribeyes.

Both rare. Cabernet"

The moment lingers as the waiter leaves, tension threading between us like smoke. I take a sip of water, just to steady my hands.

"I may have come to dinner, Silas," I say finally, keeping my tone measured, "but that doesn't mean it's anything more than dinner."

He leans back, the ghost of a smile playing at his lips. "Then I'll do my best not to make it more."

"Do you ever?" I ask.

He tilts his head, studying me in that way he does—like he's cataloging the truth beneath my words. "Only when someone deserves it."

I should look away. I don't. Something about the way he says it—quiet, unhurried—makes it hard to breathe for reasons that have nothing to do with the candlelight or the wine.

He studies me across the table, the flicker of candlelight caught in his eyes.The waiter returns with the wine, pours two perfect glasses, and disappears again. The first sip rolls over my tongue—light, bright, familiar. He was right about the pairing. Of course he was.

"So," Silas says, fingers tracing the stem of his glass, "how does it feel to hold the truth for a living?"

I glance up, caught off guard. "You mean transcribing court proceedings?"

"I mean hearing everything people won't admit once they leave the room."

I let out a quiet laugh. "It's just a job."

He tilts his head slightly, voice soft but sure. "That's not true."

The words linger—steady, deliberate, unsettling. I reach for my glass again just to have something to do with my hands.

The food arrives then, breaking the spell. Steam rises in delicate ribbons from the plates, filling the space between us with warmth and scent. My steak glistens dark and red, the juices pooling like wine. His is the same, of course. He always matches without asking.

"Well?" he asks as I take the first bite.

I hate that I have to swallow before I can speak. "It's good."

His smile curves slow, almost private. "I wouldn't have expected you to settle for less."

He cuts into his own steak with the kind of precision that feels intentional—every motion smooth, quiet, practiced. The silence that follows hums low and charged, like the pause before lightning strikes.

And though neither of us says a word, I can feel him watching. Not openly. Not boldly.

Just enough to make me wonder if I've already stepped into something I won't be able to come back from.

"You know," he says finally, "I didn't think you'd agree to dinner."

"I didn't either," I admit.

"What changed your mind?"

I toy with my wineglass, tracing the rim with a fingertip. "Curiosity."

He nods, slow, approving. "A dangerous habit."

"I could say the same about persistence."

"Ah," he says, eyes narrowing in amusement. "Then maybe we're both in trouble."

The smile he gives me is quiet but deliberate, and I feel it like a slow burn beneath my skin. I should look away, but I don't.

Outside the glass wall, the ocean stretches out in silver and shadow, the waves catching the moonlight as they break against the cliffs. I can almost feel the pull of the tide in my chest, the same rhythm that hums beneath the table between us.

It's just dinner, I tell myself again. Just conversation.

But when his hand brushes mine as he reaches for his glass, the thought collapses completely. The touch is barely there—an accident, a nothing—but it unravels something I didn't know was wound so tight. My breath catches, shallow and sharp, and suddenly the air between us feels too small, too aware.

I should move. Say something. Anything. Instead, I sit perfectly still, watching the way the light skims across the line of his wrist, the faint movement of his throat when he swallows. Every inch of him feels deliberate, measured—the kind of danger that doesn't announce itself, only waits to be invited in.

Desire hums low, steady as a pulse. It's not sudden. It's the quiet kind that's been waiting, building in the spaces between words and glances, disguised as familiarity. I tell myself it's only proximity, the wine, the conversation—but the lie dissolves before it can even form.

When he looks up, our eyes meet, and the world narrows to that single point of contact. The noise of the restaurant fades. The candle burns lower. And for one dangerous heartbeat, I forget who I'm supposed to be—what lines I've promised myself not to cross.

I pull my hand back first.

He lets me.

But the ghost of his touch lingers long after, threading through the quiet as the night deepens around us.

And somewhere between restraint and ruin, I realize—

I don't want to stop thinking about him anymore.

Chapter 9
Killer

The anchors' voices spill from the television in smooth, measured tones. *Prominent philanthropist found dead in her Beacon Hill home.* They make it sound like poetry, grief rehearsed and performed for the evening broadcast.

The blue light from the screen washes over the room, catching on the edges of books. Rain threads against the window, sharp and uneven. The apartment smells of damp paper and something faintly metallic—ordinary, grounding, safe.

They speak of her charity work, her "immeasurable generosity." No one mentions the embezzled funds, the foster programs that collapsed, the children who vanished when the lights went out. Marlene Eliza Corbett. The name tastes wrong even now. I remember her in court—steady voice, immaculate suit, crocodile tears. The city forgave her before the ink on her defense was dry.

Now they call it tragedy.
I call it balance.

The report cuts to footage of her house—ambulance lights washing the pavement red. *Authorities suspect an allergic reaction.* Convenient, how mercy always comes wrapped in euphemism.

The hum starts low beneath my skin, the one that means equilibrium has been restored. It isn't joy. Joy burns too fast. This is quieter—peace disguised as fatigue. For a moment, the world feels right again.

The black notebook lies open on the table, pages rippled with ink. I trace a fingertip along the edge, half-expecting it to pulse. Each name steadies me, each line through a name quiets the static behind my eyes. It's not a list. It's a heartbeat.

And yet—something's missing. The notebook feels lighter than it should. I can't remember when I started keeping it, but I dream of the *real* one—the way the air around it shifts, how the ink shimmers faintly red as if alive. The original. The world's memory bound in flesh and gold. Sometimes I dream of the pages whispering in a language I almost understand. When I wake, I reach for this one instead.

It's never the same. But it keeps the silence at bay.

The TV fades into static. I watch the rain crawl down the glass, my reflection breaking apart in the ripples. For a second, it looks like two faces instead of one—mine, and something older staring back. The one that remembers what I've forgotten.

I turn back to the notebook and write the name that's been circling me for days.

Elias Caleb Shaw.

The ink bleeds darker, heavier, like it knows it belongs here.

I've read his file—the Jensen case, the fallout, the guilt he still wears like armor. A detective who chases truth the way others chase absolution. He believes justice can be earned. I used to believe that too. Before I learned justice doesn't live in courtrooms—it lives in what's left when the lies are stripped away.

Maybe that's why I can't stop thinking about him.

He's circling closer. Each question, each connection—it's all gravity. And when he finds me, I wonder if he'll see what I really am. If he'll understand that I'm not the monster. I'm the balance the world keeps trying to deny.

The hum under my skin deepens—almost melodic now. I close the notebook and rest my palm against the cover.

"Balance," I whisper. The word tastes like prayer and confession both, dipped in ink and blood.

Outside, thunder rolls across the city, low and steady. A train horn echoes through the rain, the line that runs through Boston. I imagine him on it—Elias Shaw, eyes hollowed by another sleepless night, still believing truth is something he can chase down and catch.

He doesn't know yet that justice isn't a pursuit. It's what's left after.

The flame gutters out. The city light takes its place, pale and cold against the window. My reflection fades, but the melody stays. Stronger now. Restless.

He's getting closer. I can feel it.

Soon, he'll start asking questions. And when he does, I'll give him answers—just not the ones he's ready to hear.

The apartment goes still again, only the rain whispering against the glass. I should get up, turn off the lights, do something ordinary to remind myself I'm still here. But my body feels distant—like I've already moved and left it behind.

The hum in my veins won't fade. It builds, low and constant, until it drowns out thought itself. The room blurs at the edges, the television's glow flattening to white.

I blink, and it's gone.

When I come back to myself, the screen is black, the clock on the wall reads 3:17 a.m., and my pen is on the floor. There's ink on my fingers, dark and wet, though the notebook is closed—its pages dry.

For a moment, I just stare at the stain on my hand, the color too red under the lamplight.

Then I close the book, slide it back into the drawer, and tell myself I was only tired.

Outside, the train passes again, its distant horn long and low—like something calling me back to a place I've already been.

Chapter 10
Elias

Monday mornings in Boston always feel like unfinished business. The kind of gray that promises rain but doesn't deliver—just hangs there, heavy, waiting. The air's cool enough that my breath ghosts when I step out of the car, and the courthouse looms ahead like it's judging me for showing up again.

I run through my notes in my head as I climb the stone steps—Wexler, Lexington, Corbett. Three dead in as many months. Different backgrounds, different neighborhoods, but the same precision in every scene. No forced entry. No struggle. Each one found alone.

The pattern's there. I can feel it under my skin like a pulse, but every time I reach for it, it shifts.

Inside, the courthouse hums with its usual brand of bureaucracy. Voices echo off marble, heels click like metronomes, and the smell of burnt coffee lingers somewhere near the clerk's desk. Same old temple to justice—polished, indifferent, pretending to care.

I nod to the security guard at the metal detector, empty my pockets, flash my badge. The detector beeps anyway. It always does.

"Morning, Detective Shaw," the guard says, already bored.

"Morning," I mutter, grabbing my keys off the tray.

On the second floor, the courtroom doors are closed. The plaque reads *Courtroom 2A – Judge Alister Gathers.* I've been through these doors a hundred times, but it still feels different walking in now. Maybe it's the weight of the last few months. Maybe it's the fact that I'm back where I swore I wouldn't be—inside another case that smells like something more than coincidence.

I pause just long enough to catch my reflection in the glass panel of the door. Same tired eyes, same permanent shadow of a five o'clock beard. I look like someone who hasn't slept in days. Which, to be fair, I haven't.

Pushing the door open, I find the room half full—lawyers shuffling papers, a bailiff setting up, the quiet strain of people who live on deadlines.

And there, at the front, already seated, is the court reporter.

Celeste Duvall.

I've read her name on enough transcripts to recognize it before I ever met her. Her work always stood out—precise, balanced, every word struck like a heartbeat. That kind of discipline doesn't come from training. It comes from instinct. From someone who listens to the world a little too carefully.

In person, that precision looks different. Her posture is perfect, deliberate, but there's a tension in it—like she's holding herself together by will alone. Long black hair with a red undertone catches the weak morning light, and her skin has that kind of warmth that makes everything around her seem colder by comparison.

She doesn't look up when I walk in, but somehow I know she knows I'm here.
It's in the way her fingers pause—just long enough to remind me I'm not as invisible as I should be.

I take a seat in the back, flipping open my notebook. I'm supposed to be here for the Lexington follow-up—cross-checking timelines, making sure the legal department isn't sitting on something useful. But part of me's here for something else.

The same instinct that's been scratching at me since this all started. The feeling that the truth's sitting in plain sight, just waiting for me to look in the right direction.

Maybe today's the day I finally do.

The docket's light today—mercifully so. Judge Gathers runs his courtroom with efficiency, the kind that borders on impatience. Every case moves like clockwork: methodical, predictable, soulless.

First up is a petty theft charge—corner store clerk caught pocketing unclaimed lottery tickets. He looks young, maybe mid-twenties, too nervous to meet anyone's eyes. His public defender does most of the talking, pleading circumstance and desperation. Gathers listens, unmoved, before handing down probation and a fine that probably costs more than the tickets ever would've paid out.

Next, an eviction appeal. A mother of two standing too straight for how small her voice is. The landlord's attorney reads the lease terms like scripture, and I can already see where it's heading. Gathers doesn't draw it out. He rules by the book. He always does.

Then there's a workplace injury claim—janitor versus contractor. Nothing sensational, just one more reminder that bureaucracy bleeds slower than truth.

Each case passes like a breath held too long. Names, dates, consequences—all of it washing over the room in the steady rhythm of order pretending to be justice.

Through it all, Celeste types.

Her fingers move in a precise, almost metronomic rhythm, each keystroke deliberate but effortless. It's not just transcription—it's translation. The chaos of human failure turned into something clean, permanent, undeniable.

Every so often, she pauses, adjusts a key, glances up to confirm a quote. Her eyes are calm but alert, tracking everything without revealing a thing. It's the kind of focus I envy—the kind that shuts the world out completely.

I should be watching the witnesses, the attorneys, the judge. Instead, I'm watching her. The way her posture stays perfect even after hours of stillness. The way her expression never cracks, not even when the defense attorney fumbles through his objections like a kid learning his alphabet.

There's something steady about her—something that doesn't match the rest of this room full of restless people waiting to get through their day. She's stillness, and I can't decide if it's born from control or exhaustion. Maybe both.

I catch myself leaning forward a little, trying to read her face when one of the lawyers raises his voice. Nothing. Not even a flicker. Whatever she feels, it never reaches the surface.

The judge adjourns early. The clerk begins to pack up, papers shuffling like leaves in a breeze. Celeste doesn't rush. She finishes her notes, double-checks her file, then begins disconnecting the cables from her stenograph with the same precision she uses to type.

As people start to filter out, I stay seated. There's no reason to, not officially. But something about her composure draws me in—the way she seems untouched by the chaos around her. Or maybe it's the opposite: maybe she's holding it all inside, too contained to let it spill.

Either way, I can't shake the feeling I've seen that kind of restraint before. In the mirror. After Jensen.

By the time I stand, the room's nearly empty. She slips her laptop and machine into a black case, shoulders her bag, and heads for the door. I hesitate just long enough to make it seem unintentional before following her out into the hallway.

She's halfway down the corridor when I catch up, my boots echoing against the marble floor. "Ms. Duvall?"

She stops, turning with that same poised calm she wears on the stand—composed, unreadable.

"Detective Shaw," she says, polite but careful.

"Didn't expect you to remember my name."

"You were sitting in the back," she replies. "Most people in the back are either press or police. You don't look like press."

"Fair point." I offer a half smile. "I was hoping to ask you a few questions—off the record."

Her brow lifts slightly. "About the hearing?"

"Not exactly. I'm reviewing some older cases—cross-checking transcripts and expert testimony. When I asked around about who to consult, your name came up more than once."

She tilts her head, considering that. "And you believed them?"

"Figured I'd find out myself."

Her lips twitch, the ghost of a smile. "You could go through the clerk's office."

"I could," I say, "but I was hoping for something less official. Maybe coffee? There's a spot around the corner from here—"

She shakes her head before I finish. "Not in Boston."

That catches me off guard. "No?"

"I live in Salem," she says, adjusting the strap of her bag. "If you really want to talk shop, The Witch's Brew. It's quieter. Tomorrow morning."

"Bit of a commute."

"You can handle it," she says, tone dry but not unkind. "Nine o'clock."

There's no invitation in her voice—just certainty. The kind that makes it sound like she already knows I'll show up.

"I'll be there," I say.

"Good." She nods once, efficient, and turns down the hall. Her heels strike the tile in an even rhythm that shouldn't sound as steady as it does.

I tell myself I'm just watching her leave—habit, awareness, the usual cop reflex. But there's something about the way she moves that makes it harder to look away. Purposeful. Controlled. Every motion measured, like she's always one thought ahead of whoever's watching.

Her hair catches the light when she passes beneath the skylight, a muted red that doesn't quite belong in this building full of gray walls and fluorescent hum. Even the way she carries her bag—neat, careful, deliberate—feels like its own language.

She disappears through the double doors, and the echo of her steps lingers longer than it should. While, I stand there a few seconds too long, staring at the space she left behind.

Coffee, I tell myself, is just an interview.
But the way my pulse stirs says otherwise.

The drive to Salem takes just under an hour, though it feels longer in the morning gray.
The sky's still heavy, clouds hanging low enough to scrape the tops of the old brick buildings along the highway. It isn't raining yet, but it's close—the kind of air that feels like it's waiting for permission to break.

My sedan groans its way through the miles, every rattle and hum a reminder that I'm overdue for an oil change I haven't had the time—or patience—to deal with. The check-engine light flickers occasionally, like it's just checking to see if I still care. I do. Barely. The car's paid off, which makes it worth every sputter.

The closer I get to Salem, the quieter the city becomes. Boston's noise fades behind me, replaced by the low hum of the coast. The streets here are narrow, uneven, built for horse carts instead of traffic. Old buildings lean against each other, their paint faded but proud. It's the kind of place that feels like it remembers everything you've done.

The Witch's Brew sits at the corner of a sloping street, wedged between a bookstore and a record shop that looks like it's survived the last three decades out of sheer stubbornness. The sign in the window glows faintly against the morning gloom—OPEN—a beacon for the kind of people who don't sleep right.

I find a spot along the curb, kill the engine, and sit for a second, letting the quiet settle. My thoughts drift back to yesterday—to her.

Celeste Duvall.

In court, she was all restraint and precision. Not cold, just... contained. The kind of stillness that comes from knowing more than you're willing to say. I've seen witnesses try to fake that kind of composure before. Hers was real.

I step out into the chill, pulling my coat tighter as the wind cuts through the damp air. The scent of the sea rides on it—salt, metal, a faint sweetness beneath it all. The streets are half-awake, locals moving slow, coffee cups in hand, the morning pressing down like a weight.

When I push open the café door, the bell gives a soft, familiar chime. The warmth hits immediately—coffee, cinnamon, old wood.

She's already there.

Back corner booth by the window, same as yesterday's courtroom posture—upright, steady, a sense of order in the chaos. But the light in here does her no favors in staying invisible. Her hair looks warmer in the amber glow, her skin soft against the gray morning pressing against the glass.

She's not typing, not focused on anything but her cup and the rain that hasn't started yet. For a moment, I just stand there, watching the quiet play across her features.

She looks different outside the courthouse. Less guarded. Almost human.

When she glances up and catches me looking, there's the smallest flicker of something unreadable—surprise, maybe, or recognition she won't name. Then the mask slides back into place, smooth and polite.

"Detective," she says, voice even but softer than yesterday. "You found it."

"Wasn't hard," I say, stepping closer. "This place stands out."

She gestures to the seat across from her. "That's part of the charm."

I slide into the booth, the smell of spice and espresso settling between us. The rain hasn't started yet, but it will soon. I can feel it.

Maybe it's not the weather tightening the air this time.

Chapter 11
Elias

The place smells like cinnamon and rain.

If I believed in omens, that'd mean something.

Celeste sits across from me, hands folded around her cup like she's trying to memorize the warmth. She doesn't fidget, doesn't fill the silence. It's the kind of calm that makes people talk too much just to fill the gap. I've seen it a hundred times in interrogation rooms, but this feels different—less strategy, more instinct.

"Appreciate you meeting me," I say, wrapping my fingers around the mug the barista dropped off a few minutes ago. The coffee's strong, bitter enough to wake the dead. "I know this isn't exactly part of your job description."

"It's fine," she says. "I like this place. It's quiet."

I nod, glancing out the window. The sky hangs low and gray, the kind of overcast that makes time blur. "You always commute from here?"

"Every day," she says. "The courthouse is less than an hour, if the train runs on time."

"And if it doesn't?"

Her mouth curves slightly. "Then I remind myself patience is a virtue."

There's humor there, buried under the words. Subtle. Sharp. It surprises me.

I pull the notebook from my coat pocket and flip it open. "I've been reviewing some older cases—Lexington, Wexler, a few before that. You transcribed at least two of them."

Her eyes narrow just slightly. "You've been busy."

"Trying to make sense of a pattern," I say. "One that doesn't fit the usual statistics."

"Pattern?"

"Each victim was cleared of something in court before they died. Different crimes, different times, but similar endings. No struggle, no sign of forced entry, all of them found alone."

She's quiet for a beat, staring into her cup. When she looks up again, her expression is unreadable. "You think someone's targeting them for revenge."

"I think someone's making sure justice catches up."

Her fingers tighten around the porcelain. "And you think that's a bad thing?"

"I think murder usually complicates the definition of justice," I say.

Her gaze flicks to mine. There's something there—amusement, maybe.

Or challenge. "Usually," she echoes.

The air between us shifts. For a second, I forget we're sitting in a café surrounded by normal people doing normal things. It feels like the rest of the world's gone quiet just to listen.

I take another sip of coffee, watching her. "You knew Lexington, right? You worked his trial."

She nods. "I remember him. Most people in that courtroom do."

"Ever get a sense something was off?"

"Off?"

"The way he acted. The way anyone acted."

She considers this, tracing the rim of her cup. "Courtrooms are built on performance, Detective. Everyone's acting. Some of them are just better at it."

I can't argue with that.

Outside, a gust of wind hits the window, rattling the glass. The storm's close.

She glances toward it, then back at me. "You came all this way to ask me about old cases."

"I'm thorough."

Her mouth tilts. "No. You're looking for something. You just don't know what it is yet."

She lifts her cup, takes another slow sip, eyes never leaving mine—steady, unreadable. "So you really drove all the way from Boston to talk transcripts?"

I raise a brow. "You think I'd make the trip for small talk?"

"I think you're the kind of man who doesn't know how to stop working," she says. "Even when you tell yourself it's a vacation." Her gaze flicks toward the folder on the table. "Homicide, right? That's what you do?"

I hesitate, just long enough for her to notice. "Used to be," I say finally. "Now it's... complicated."

"That sounds like a story."

"Most of them are."

She studies me over the rim of her cup, like she's cataloging every detail. "You're not like the others who come through the courthouse," she says. "They look at people like me and forget we exist the second the gavel hits. You—" she pauses, searching for the word, "—you look like someone who carries what he finds."

The way she says it makes something tighten in my chest. "Occupational hazard," I say.

"Or maybe," she murmurs, setting her cup down, "you were built for it."

"I've done worse for less," I say.

Her mouth curves faintly. "You don't strike me as someone who does anything for less."

"That supposed to be a compliment?"

"Observation." She sets her cup down carefully, the faintest clink against porcelain. "You look like someone who doesn't stop until he finds what he's looking for. Even when he's not sure what that is."

"Maybe I'm just stubborn."

"Maybe," she says softly, tilting her head. "But stubborn people usually chase ghosts."

That pulls a half-laugh from me. "You sound like my captain."

"Smart woman," she says.

"She's not wrong."

Her smile lingers, brief but real. For a moment, the air between us feels less like interrogation and more like something alive—something pulling at the edges of reason.

"You ever get tired of it?" she asks.

"Of what?"

"Carrying what other people can't face."

The question hits harder than I expect. "You learn to live with it."

She studies me for a moment longer, the light from the window catching in her eyes—gold flecks, sharp even in the gray morning. "That's not the same as letting it go."

I don't answer.

The rain still hasn't started, but the sky's gone darker, the wind pressing harder against the glass. The café feels smaller now—like the air's closing in just enough to make it personal. I glance down at my notes, trying to find something solid again.

"So, about the Lexington case—"

"Detective." Her voice cuts through the space between us, soft but certain. "Some things don't want to be solved. They just want to be understood."

It shouldn't sound like a warning, but it does.

Her words hang there, quiet and steady, threading through the hum of the espresso machine and the low murmur of conversation around us. I meet her eyes, and for a moment, I forget why I came. There's something in her gaze—something knowing. Not judgment, not fear. Just... recognition. Like she's already seen the thing I'm still chasing.

If we'd met somewhere else—somewhere that wasn't soaked in death and evidence and unanswered questions—maybe I'd have asked her name without a badge between us. Maybe I'd have watched the way she stirs her chai just to hear her talk about something that isn't measured in blood and motive.

But that isn't how this works. Not for me. Not for her.

"I don't want to understand it," I say finally. "I want to stop it."

Her lips curve, but it's not quite a smile. "Maybe those are the same thing."

The words land heavier than they should. I can feel them under my skin, pulsing in rhythm with the storm building outside.

For a second, the thought crosses my mind—how dangerous it is to want someone who speaks like that. Someone who feels like a mirror I never meant to look into.

The first drop of rain hits the window, and I realize I haven't written a single note since she sat down.

Before I can ask what she means, she's already sliding out of the booth, smoothing her coat like she's brushing off the weight of the moment.

"Thanks for the chai," she says, and that faint smile is back—polished, polite, but with an edge that doesn't quite fade. "Be careful with your patterns, Detective. Sometimes they start to look back."

The words land softer than a warning, sharper than a joke.

She gathers her bag, smooths her sleeve like she's sealing the moment shut. "My recommendation?" Her eyes flick to mine, steady and deliberate. "Look at the big picture."

Something in her tone makes the air between us shift—like a current pulling in two directions at once. For a second, I forget how to breathe.

I watch her walk toward the door, that same quiet precision in every step. Outside, the rain blurs her reflection against the glass, turning her into light and shadow and motion. By the time I stand, she's already gone.

And I can't shake the feeling she wasn't just giving advice.

She was issuing a challenge.

Coffee, I tell myself, is just an interview.
But the way my pulse stirs says otherwise.

I leave a few bills on the table and step outside. The air hits colder than I expect, heavy with the kind of damp that seeps into your bones. The wind carries salt from the harbor and something faintly metallic beneath it. Overhead, the clouds hang low and swollen, ready to break but still holding back, the entire sky balanced on the edge of a storm.

By the time I reach my car, my hands are numb. I slide behind the wheel, start the engine, and let the heater cough itself awake. The café's reflection glows faintly in the rearview mirror—warm light spilling onto the street, rain-speckled glass blurring the inside. Through it, I catch the faint outline of Celeste moving past the window, graceful, composed, unknowable. She doesn't look back, and I tell myself that's a good thing.

The drive to Boston stretches longer than it should. The highway is half-empty, and the silence that comes with it leaves too much room to think. Her voice lingers, precise and even, replaying in my head like an echo I can't shake. *Be careful with your patterns, Detective. Sometimes they start to look back.* She said it with the kind of certainty that doesn't come from curiosity. It felt like warning. Or confession.

Rain starts halfway down the interstate, soft at first, then harder, blurring the lanes into streaks of motion. My wipers drag across the windshield, uneven and tired, a slow rhythm that keeps time with the names running through my head—Lexington. Wexler. Corbett. Three different people. Three similar endings. Each acquitted. Each alone. Each death too clean to be coincidence.

The pattern is there. I can feel it. But every time I try to pin it down, it slips away. No prints. No witnesses. No motive that holds. Just the same precise silence after every scene, as if whoever's doing this understands what evidence to leave behind—and what to take.

I try to shake off the thought, focus on the road. The city lights start to bleed through the fog ahead, faint halos of gold and white. But my mind keeps circling back to Celeste—her calm, her unflinching eyes when I said the names, the way she seemed to already know where my questions were heading. Most people crack under the weight of implication. She didn't even blink.

I tell myself it's professionalism. Years in courtrooms make people immune to tragedy. But part of me—the part that still trusts instinct over logic—can't let it go. There was something measured in her response, like she was taking my pulse with every word I said.

The rain thickens as I cross into Boston, the world narrowing to the hiss of tires and the hum of the engine. My car rattles like it's begging for the oil change I keep putting off, but I don't have the time, or maybe the will, to deal with it. The heater barely keeps up. The smell of wet asphalt seeps through the vents, and thunder rolls somewhere behind the skyline, low and patient.

When I pull into the precinct lot, I kill the engine and sit for a minute, listening to the rain drum against the roof. The streetlights cast long streaks across the hood, orange reflected in water, and for a second, the world feels suspended—everything holding its breath before the next move.

I should go inside, file my notes, pretend this morning was routine. But I stay where I am, staring at the building through the blur of rain, thinking about the way she said my name—soft, deliberate, like she was memorizing it for later.

The storm hasn't eased. It just changes its rhythm—less violent now, more deliberate. Each drop sounds like a thought I can't quite finish. The wipers drag across the windshield, smearing city light into ribbons of gold and gray.

I should get out of the car, but I don't. Not yet. The longer I sit here, the quieter everything feels—and that's dangerous. Quiet makes room for memory, and memory has never done me any favors.

Somewhere behind the rain, a siren wails, distant and directionless. Boston keeps breathing, even when it shouldn't. And I can't shake the feeling that whatever's been haunting this city just changed direction—subtle, but certain—turning its gaze toward me.

The Jensen case still plays on repeat whenever I let my guard down. A year later, I can still hear the hum of the interrogation room lights—the faint flicker that made the shadows crawl. I can still smell the stale coffee, the sour edge of adrenaline that clung to the walls. And I can still see his eyes—darting, calculating—just before I pushed too hard.

One bad call. One assumption I couldn't prove. And everything collapsed with it.

A woman died because I chased the wrong lead. The real suspect walked free for three months before another department caught him. Three months of silence I couldn't fill. Three months of headlines calling me reckless, arrogant, unfit. I used to argue with them in my head, replaying every decision, every step. But eventually, I stopped. They weren't wrong.

Before Jensen, I was the one they called when things got impossible. The one who could see the pattern everyone else missed. Seven years on the force, four in homicide, two commendations for investigative merit—and all it took was one mistake to burn it down.

Sometimes I think that was the day I stopped believing in the system altogether. We call it justice, but half the time it's theater—scripts, cues, people pretending truth and law are the same thing. They aren't. They never were. The courtroom's just a stage, and I was stupid enough to think I could change the script.

Now I sit through trials and tell myself I'm just collecting evidence, just doing my job. But underneath it, there's always that same question gnawing at the back of my mind:

What if the system can't be fixed?

What if it isn't broken at all—just built this way?

I rub at my temple, trying to force the thought down. The heater hums, too loud in the quiet, and the windows start to fog. I drag a sleeve across the glass, clearing just enough to see the reflection of the building. The precinct stares back at me like a monument to my own bad choices—order carved from chaos, all the cracks hidden under polish.

The system saves the right people when it's convenient. The rest get lost in paperwork.

I think about Lexington again. About the others. People who should've faced consequence and instead walked out into sunlight like nothing touched them. And now they're all dead.

Someone out there decided the system wasn't enough. Someone decided to balance it by hand.

I should be angry. Instead, I feel something closer to understanding.

Maybe that's what scares me most.

The rain begins to slow, a softer rhythm now, the kind that makes the city sound like it's breathing again. I finally pull the keys from the ignition and step out into the damp air. It smells like iron and electricity. The storm's moved on, but the weight of it still lingers.

As I head for the precinct doors, I can't shake the thought that maybe whoever's doing this isn't entirely wrong—just further gone.

And maybe that's a line I've already started to blur myself.

Chapter 12
Celeste

The streets of Salem are half-asleep when I leave *The Witch's Brew*. The air smells like rain that hasn't started yet—salt, iron, and the faint sweetness of wet leaves clinging to the edges of fall. Clouds press low over the harbor, bruised and swollen, waiting for permission to break.

My heels click against uneven brick as I head down Essex, the rhythm sharp against the hush of early morning. This town absorbs sound when it wants to—so much history packed into so little space that it feels like the walls have learned to listen.

I tell myself the walk will help clear my head. It doesn't. Elias Shaw has a way of asking questions that stay lodged under the skin long after he's gone. His voice still hums in the back of my mind—low, steady, the kind of calm that hides its fractures too well. He watches people the way I listen to them: closely, deliberately, like he's cataloging every heartbeat.

He shouldn't be interesting. Men like him never are—too focused on rules and ruin. But there's something about the way he carries silence, like he's afraid of what might spill out if he lets it go. It makes me want to listen longer than I should.

He was polite, careful, almost charming in a way that felt unintentional. But underneath it, I could feel the weight he carries—the kind that doesn't come from the badge but from guilt. His questions were about cases and evidence, but what he really wanted was something harder to name. Proof that the system still means something. Proof that he still does.

I didn't have the heart to tell him it never did.

A train horn sounds somewhere beyond the harbor, low and distant. I stop without meaning to, the sound threading through the fog like something familiar. The morning air feels too still, the kind of stillness that hums just before thunder.

When I start walking again, my steps are slower. Every light in every window feels like an eye watching. The scent of saltwater thickens as I cut down the narrow lane toward my building, the sea's breath mingling with the oncoming storm.

By the time I reach the front steps, the first drops of rain have started—soft, deliberate, more promise than downpour. My key sticks in the lock, as it always does, and the door gives with a tired click.

Inside, the quiet waits for me. The apartment is dim and still, the air heavy with the ghost of cinnamon and chai from this morning's routine. I set my bag on the table, hang my coat, and glance toward the window. My reflection stares back through the fogged glass, haloed in gray light. For a second, I almost don't recognize her—the woman in the reflection. There's something older in her eyes. Something patient.

I blink, and she's gone.

The kettle hums to life behind me. I move through the motions—water, cup, tea—trying to let the noise fill the space. But underneath it, the hum beneath my skin hasn't quieted. It's faint, like a heartbeat half out of sync with my own, waiting for something I can't name.

Elias Shaw.

Persistent. Controlled. Dangerous in his curiosity.

He doesn't know what he's walking into yet.

The rain outside thickens, threading down the glass in silver veins. I watch the city blur behind it, and for a moment, it feels like everything is holding its breath.

The sound of footsteps in the hallway pulls me from the window. A soft knock follows—two taps, then silence.

I wait a beat before opening the door. No one's there. Just a small parcel on the floor, the kind wrapped carefully enough to feel personal. The label bears my name in neat handwriting, inked with the kind of precision that says habit, not haste.

For a moment, I consider leaving it there. Ignoring it. Pretending curiosity doesn't win as easily as it always does. But the hum under my skin—the one that started when I left the café—hasn't faded. It feels almost like anticipation.

I bring it inside, set it on the kitchen table, and pull at the string. The paper gives way easily, folding back to reveal a slim black box tied with a ribbon the color of dark wine. Inside, nestled in tissue, is a notebook—leather-bound, the kind that smells faintly of ink and memory. Beneath it, a set of fountain pens rests in a velvet-lined case, their brass trim catching the low light. They're beautiful, deliberate, the kind of tools meant for someone who takes words seriously.

There's a note folded between the pages of the notebook. The paper's thick, edges pressed clean.

> You mentioned once that you love a good pen—and that you journal when you need to make sense of things.
> Consider this an encouragement to keep writing.
> Lunch this time? Something less formal.
> —S.

The handwriting is as elegant as the rest of it—calm, composed, the ink flowing without hesitation.

I read it twice before setting it down, the words hovering somewhere between intimacy and restraint.

The gift itself shouldn't mean anything. It's thoughtful, harmless even. But the weight of the notebook in my hands feels like more than paper and leather. It feels intentional. The kind of gesture that listens, that remembers details people usually miss.

Silas Kade.

I should have expected this. He's always known how to blur the line between generosity and control. A conversation becomes a confession; a thank-you becomes a test. He doesn't push. He just... waits.

I trace the edge of the notebook with my fingertips. The leather's soft, smooth, warm where it shouldn't be. The pens glint faintly, their barrels engraved with some foreign script I don't recognize. Expensive. Too much for a casual gesture.

Outside, the rain deepens, streaking the glass with silver trails. I tell myself I won't respond—not tonight. Not until I decide what this is.

But later, when the apartment's gone still and the storm's found its rhythm, I find myself sitting at the table with the notebook open in front of me. The first page is blank, waiting.

My hand hovers over it for a moment before I start to write. I uncap one of the pens, the ink a deep, storm-dark blue that spreads across the page like thought made visible. The leather spine creaks softly as the book settles open. For a long moment, I just sit there, listening to the rain and the faint scratch of metal against paper.

October 27th

Journal Entry

I told myself it was just dinner. A courtesy. A simple thank-you for helping at the gala. But Silas has never been simple. Everything about him feels calculated, and yet it never feels forced. Every word seems chosen, but never rehearsed.

He'd already arranged the table when we arrived, the view facing the ocean like he knew I'd want to watch the waves. The conversation moved easily—too easily. Work, travel, court gossip, old cases that brushed too close to memory. He listens differently than most people. It's not just hearing; it's study. Like he's trying to memorize the rhythm of my thoughts.

And still... he didn't cross the line.

Even when the air between us shifted, when my pulse betrayed me and I could feel the warmth of his gaze slide down my neck like a touch, he didn't push. He never has. That's what makes it dangerous.

He sent me home with a smile that wasn't quite a smile. Walked me to my door. Said goodnight like the word still meant something. And then—

God, I can still feel it.

He took my hand first, tracing his thumb across my fingers before lifting them to his lips. His mouth was warm, deliberate, reverent in a way that felt centuries old. Then, just before he stepped back, he turned my wrist slightly and pressed another kiss to the inside—slow, lingering. It wasn't possessive. It wasn't a promise. It was permission to *remember*.

And I do.

I can still feel the ghost of it when I breathe.

He's dangerous in a way that doesn't announce itself. Not the kind of danger that threatens, but the kind that invites. Like standing at the edge of the ocean in the dark—knowing the tide will take you if you stay too long, but staying anyway just to feel it move around you.

I should know better.

I should lock the door, put this notebook away, and pretend I don't care. But the truth is, I do. Not just about him, but about what I feel when I'm near him. Something buried and electric, something that hums under my skin like recognition.

I close my eyes, and it's still there—the heat where his lips touched, the pulse that answered.

Maybe that's the real danger. Not him. Me.

—C

I set the pen down, the ink still glistening on the page. The words feel too intimate, too close to something I shouldn't have said out loud—even to myself. I blow gently to dry the last line, then close the notebook with a soft snap.

The phone rings, slicing through the quiet.

My heart jumps. Silas.

Without thinking, I grab it and answer, a small smile already forming.

"Thank you for the gift," I say, warm and unguarded.

A pause—then a voice I wasn't expecting.

"Gift?"

The bottom drops out of my stomach. It's not Silas.

It's Elias Shaw.

I freeze, closing my eyes for a beat. "Detective—sorry, I thought you were someone else."

"That much I gathered," he says, his tone roughened with a hint of humor. "Did I catch you at a bad time?"

"No," I lie, forcing a steadier breath. "Just finishing up some writing."

"Of course you were," he says, and somehow it sounds less like a guess and more like he's been paying attention. There's a faint shuffle of papers on his end, the muted buzz of the precinct in the background. "Actually, I wanted to ask if you'd come by the office tomorrow. I'm going through a few more of the old case files—ones that overlap with your transcripts.

Thought it might help to get your perspective."

"Sure," I say, still trying to quiet the rush in my pulse. "What time?"

"Come by around noon," he replies. Then, after a pause that lingers just a touch too long, "I'll order lunch. What do you like?"

The question catches me off guard. It's simple, but there's something about the way he asks it—careful, like he's testing how much ground he's allowed to stand on.

"Depends," I say. "I'm easy to please. As long as it's hot and not instant noodles, I'll eat it."

He huffs a quiet laugh. "Noted. I'll surprise you then."

"Detective—"

"Elias," he corrects gently. "If we're going to work together, you should probably use my name."

My grip on the phone tightens. "Alright. Elias."

"Tomorrow, then."

The line clicks, leaving me in the stillness of my apartment, the faint sound of rain brushing against the window.

I lower the phone, staring at the closed notebook on the table. The words inside feel suddenly heavier, as if they've been heard somehow.

Two men. Two invitations. Two kinds of gravity.

And somehow, I've already started orbiting both.

That night, I dream of touch.

It starts innocently—fingers brushing mine as I reach for a glass, the press of a palm against my back as I step through a doorway. The air smells faintly of chai and something darker—cedar, smoke, the sharp bite of rain on stone. Two shadows move through the room with me, close enough that I can feel the warmth of their breath but never close enough to see their faces.

Silas's voice comes first, low and deliberate, the kind that slides beneath your skin and stays there. *You keep pretending you don't want to be seen.* His fingers trace the edge of my wrist, right where the pulse beats hardest.

Then another touch—rougher, steadier. Elias. He doesn't speak, but when his hand finds the side of my throat, I feel the unspoken question in it. The choice. The pull.

The dream folds over itself—Silas behind me, Elias in front. The air crackles with tension, desire and warning braided together until I can't tell which one belongs to whom. My heart stutters, my breath catching between them. The world hums, low and alive, as if waiting for me to choose.

But I don't. I can't.

When I finally reach out, the space between them collapses—and everything burns white.

I wake gasping, tangled in sheets that feel too warm, skin damp as if I've run a mile. The clock reads 3:17 a.m. The rain has stopped, but thunder murmurs far off, rolling over the city like a held breath.

For a long time, I just lie there, staring at the ceiling, my pulse refusing to slow. I can still feel the ghost of hands on my skin—one that steadies, one that tempts. Both pull me toward something I'm not sure I'll survive.

Chapter 13
Killer

Two nights before Halloween, the air carries that sharp sweetness of rot and rain. Salem hums beneath it—streets thick with tourists, cheap masks, and laughter that curdles at the edges. Everyone's pretending to be someone else. It's the perfect night for monsters to look ordinary.

The house sits beneath a canopy of skeletal trees. Its windows glow faintly, not with warmth, but with that hollow, yellow light that pretends to be alive. Every October, he opens the doors for charity—ghosts for the children, smiles for the cameras, redemption by donation. They call it *heartwarming.* I call it camouflage. Monsters love philanthropy; it keeps their hands looking clean.

The house breathes as I step inside—warm, damp air steeped in fog-machine residue and burnt sugar. The scent clings to the back of my throat, sweet and chemical. Props litter the hallway: severed foam limbs, tangled webs, rubber bats dangling from the ceiling. Everything is arranged to frighten without consequence. Fear for entertainment. Fear that doesn't bite back.

He thinks the spectacle keeps eyes off the truth—that the same hands that handed out candy also signed prescriptions that silenced complaints. That every shriek echoing off these walls can drown out the real kind that came before.

My fingers trail along the wallpaper, the once-rich pattern faded into something brittle and gray. I can almost hear the applause he used to receive for his generosity, the soft, careful words of those who owed him favors. They'll mourn him when they find him, of course. They always mourn the illusion, never the rot.

Downstairs, the music changes—a distorted carnival tune looping endlessly through the speakers. It makes the walls pulse. Somewhere beneath it, the fog machine hisses again, the sound too close to breathing.

The perfect misdirection.

And tonight, I'll make sure the fear they feel is real.

Dr. Malcolm Harren's Victorian creaks beneath the weight of October. The house breathes fog and heat from within, every window pulsing faint gold. Laughter filters up from below—neighbors, volunteers, teenagers paid in pizza to help set up the annual haunted house.

He's in the attic when I find him.

Bent over a crate of props, sleeves rolled to his elbows, sweat darkening the collar of his shirt. His movements are brisk, confident. He doesn't know yet that confidence is a luxury only the living get to keep.

"Almost done?" I ask softly.

He doesn't look up at first, just waves a hand behind him. "Almost. Still need to fix the wiring on this light." His voice carries that genial tone he used on patients—warm, careful, rehearsed.

The fog machine hums below us. A faint red light pulses up through the cracks in the floorboards. The attic smells of dust, rubber, and machine smoke. Somewhere downstairs, a girl laughs too loud. He smiles at the sound.

"Charity's looking good this year," I say.

That gets his attention. He straightens, turning toward me, pride softening his expression. "You think so? We're hoping to raise double what we did last year. Every dollar counts when you're saving lives."

His words hang in the air like perfume—sweet and stale. I take a step closer, until I can see the sheen of sweat on his temple, the pulse working in his throat. "You save lives?" I ask.

He chuckles. "Do my best."

"That's interesting," I say. "Because some of them didn't make it, did they?"

The smile falters. Just slightly. "What?"

"Those women from the clinic. The interns who filed complaints. The patients whose charts were altered. You remember their names?"

His eyes narrow. "Who are you?"

I touch his shoulder lightly—just a gesture, grounding. The same way he used to when calming a frightened patient. "Someone who remembers."

The syringe slides in before the question forms. His body goes rigid, the breath catching in his throat. His hand twitches, fingers flexing once, twice.

His eyes are wide now, reflecting the attic's dim light.

He can't move, but he can hear. That's the point. Paralysis keeps people honest.

"You always said you wanted to save lives," I whisper, leaning close enough for him to feel the warmth of the words. "Consider this a correction."

His breathing is fast now, shallow. I guide him backward toward the chair beneath the slanted window. His body obeys, unwillingly graceful, the way all bodies are when the nerves give up. The moonlight catches in his glasses.

The first cut is clean, surgical. A line just below the wrist—deliberate, practiced. Blood wells slow and steady, like ink rising in a fountain pen. His stethoscope coils tight around his hands, its tubing darkening as the red creeps upward.

I move the stack of patient files beside him—his true legacy. The folders are brittle, edges yellowed. Some marked *Closed*, others *Pending Review*. A few I found shredded in his office trash last month. I lay the *Hippocratic Oath* across his lap. The parchment curls at the edges as the blood seeps through.

He watches me, his eyes glossy, wet. If he could speak, he'd offer another excuse. They always do—mistakes, stress, clerical errors. But the body never lies. It trembles, then stills.

"You swore to do no harm," I murmur, "but you made harm an art."

I descend the stairs, slipping into the sound of laughter and creaking floorboards. Outside, the street is alive—costumes and cider, strings of orange lights swaying in the wind. I buy a cup of hot cocoa from a vendor.

The warmth bites at my palms.

From here, the Victorian looks harmless again—its porch lights glowing soft amber, the faint sound of canned screams drifting from the open doorway. A group of costumed families walks past, chatting about how *realistic* the decorations are this year. Someone laughs, says, "Guess the doc finally went all out."

They keep moving. No one looks twice.

The cocoa tastes sweet, cloying. I sip slowly, watching the line thin as the night deepens. Then a group of teenagers breaks off from the main crowd—too loud, too bold, the kind who dare each other to be brave. They push through the front door, flashlights cutting across the dark interior.

I wait.

At first, it sounds like laughter—sharp, breathless, the kind that carries down the street and folds into the night's noise. Then the pitch changes. Higher. Raw. The sound of something breaking open.

The scream rips through the air, slicing through the chatter of tourists and the hum of street music. It's not the fun kind—the rehearsed kind. This one curdles, catches, claws its way up until the entire block goes still.

The front door bursts open.

The teenagers tumble out in a flailing tangle of limbs and terror. One of them—the smallest, in a vampire cape—stumbles down the steps and lands hard on his knees, palms skidding through the puddled rain. Another clings to the railing, breath hitching between sobs.

"It's real—it's real—it's *real!*" the tallest one gasps, voice cracking as he backs into the street. His friends talk over him, the words tumbling, half-choked, too fast to make sense.

"Blood—"

"—he's not moving—"

"—I slipped—God, I slipped in it—"

They're shaking. One of them lifts an arm to wipe his face, and I see it—a crimson smear across his sleeve, the imprint of a hand dragged in panic. The blood is darker now, drying, clotted.

Someone in the crowd laughs nervously, still half-convinced it's part of the show. Then another scream comes from inside the house—this one deeper, adult. Realization hits like thunder.

The laughter dies.

Phones come up. Voices rise. A woman shouts to call the police. A siren starts somewhere down the block, that lonely, hungry sound winding closer.

I finish the last sip of my cocoa. The cup's gone cold.

The hum beneath my skin softens, satisfied, steady. Around me, the world stumbles into chaos, flashing lights reflected in puddles like red veins pulsing through the street.

Balance restored.

Just in time for Halloween.

I walk with the crowd, the rhythm of their footsteps folding around me until I'm just another body moving through the night. Salem is alive in a way that borders on feverish—candles flickering in shop windows, laughter bubbling too loud, tourists clutching paper maps like talismans. Masks grin from every corner, their hollow eyes catching flashes of streetlight.

The air smells of woodsmoke, caramel, and something metallic beneath it all—faint, but there. The scent of truth bleeding through the costume.

Children dart past with pumpkin buckets clutched in their fists, their parents trailing behind, pretending this is all harmless fun. It always fascinates me—how easily people flirt with fear when they think they're safe. They crave it in small doses. A ghost story. A jump scare. A brush with darkness that ends in laughter. But the real thing terrifies them. The real thing demands something back.

I move past a busker playing violin near the fountain. The music cuts through the chatter like silk over glass. For a moment, I let myself stop, watch the bow glide, the notes trembling in the cool air. The song's familiar—I can't name it, but it hums against something buried deep inside me.

I think about the faces I've seen—the guilty ones smiling for cameras, shaking hands, pretending their charity could wash out the blood on their ledgers. I think about the ones the system forgot, their pain filed away like misplaced paperwork. And then I think about the names I've written. The balance I've kept.

The hum starts again beneath my skin, faint but steady, as if the city itself breathes in rhythm with me. Salem has always had a pulse that doesn't belong to the living. It remembers. It listens.

Across the street, a couple argues softly, their words dissolving into the crowd. A man in a pirate costume drops his drink and curses. Somewhere, church bells toll, too slow for the hour.

Everything feels suspended—like the whole city is holding its breath, waiting for something unseen to finish.

I pass a storefront window, catch my reflection in the glass between the candlelight and shadows. For a moment, I don't recognize the face looking back—familiar but distant, like a memory I can't quite place. My reflection blurs with the faint shimmer of the rain starting again, and I wonder, just for an instant, if the water remembers too.

The wind shifts. A siren wails faintly in the distance.

I turn toward the harbor, the sound of the waves pulling against the rocks, steady and certain. There's always another name. Another balance waiting to be restored.

The night exhales, and I keep walking.

Chapter 14
Elias

Dispatch says Salem PD's asking for a consult—possible connection to the other deaths. I'm halfway through my first cup of bad coffee, running on four hours of sleep and the regret of rescheduling lunch with Celeste. I told her it couldn't be helped, that another case came in. She'd sounded like she was smiling—professional, polite—but there was a hesitation in her voice before she said goodbye. Something small. Something I can't stop hearing now. Now I'm wondering if that was disappointment or relief.

The drive north is gray and endless, the kind of morning where the sky looks too heavy for the hour. Clouds hang low over the highway, a dull bruise bleeding light through the horizon. My sedan rattles in protest every few miles, the engine coughing like it's got opinions. I should've gotten the oil changed two weeks ago, but like everything else lately, it keeps slipping down the list.

By the time I reach Salem, the streets are already crowded. Patrol cars clog the block, lights throwing blue and red veins across the damp pavement. The Victorian sits at the end of Lafayette, cordoned off with police tape that flutters in the wind like torn ribbon.

Tourists are still gathered behind the line, phones raised, eyes wide. The Halloween decorations on nearby porches suddenly look obscene—fake blood, rubber skulls, a mannequin hanging from a tree limb by a rope of fairy lights. Someone's trying to sell cider two doors down. The world doesn't stop for corpses.

I duck under the tape, flash my badge at a uniform near the steps. "Detective Shaw, Boston PD."

He nods, relief flickering across his face. "They said you'd be coming. It's bad, sir."

"Show me."

Inside, the air smells like metal and sugar—copper and carnival. Fog still drifts from a machine near the entryway, mixing with the iron sting of blood. The floorboards creak underfoot, tacky in spots where the red's already dried. I follow the sound of murmured voices up the narrow stairs.

The attic is too bright. Forensics has set up lights that turn everything pale and unreal. The smell hits first. Then the color.

Dr. Malcolm Harren sits upright in a chair near the window, hands bound with what looks like a stethoscope, head tilted toward the moonlight. A printed oath lies across his lap, soaked through. The blood on the floor has dried in patterns that don't make sense yet.

"Jesus," I mutter.

Freddy glances up from beside the body, his gloves streaked red. "Hell of a show, huh?" he says, voice dry. "Our victim liked drama. Looks like someone finally gave him a taste of his own medicine."

"Cause?"

"Wrist lacerations, both sides. Precise. Arteries nicked just enough to bleed him slow," Freddy says, crouched beside the body. "There's something else off, though—no sign of struggle. No defensive wounds, no overturned furniture. It's like he just...sat here and let it happen."

"Shock?" I ask.

He shakes his head. "Maybe. Or something chemical. I'll know more once tox comes back, but I'd bet he wasn't fighting when the cuts were made."

Freddy stands, pulling off one glove with a soft snap. "Whatever it was, he was awake for it."

I glance at the body again. The chair. The oath. The stacks of files like witnesses.

"He watched himself die," Freddy adds quietly.

I stand there for a long moment, taking it in. The precision of it. The stillness. The way every piece seems placed, not dropped. The oath on his lap, the careful angle of his head, the files stacked like an audience that already knows the ending. Whoever did this didn't rush. They curated it.

It isn't a murder scene. It's a verdict.

I crouch beside one of the stacks, careful not to disturb the blood that's crept across the floor. Each folder's labeled in his handwriting—patient names, dates, conditions. Some go back over a decade. I open the top one: a malpractice complaint that vanished from the records years ago. The woman's name hits me like static. I remember reading the case summary, the quiet settlement, the way it just disappeared after.

There's something methodical about the pattern—like the killer is pulling names straight out of a ledger no one else can see.

Freddy mutters something behind me about timing the blood loss, but his words fade into static. My focus narrows to the arrangement: the symmetry of the wounds, the ritual precision. It's not rage. Rage doesn't sit someone upright and fold their hands. Rage doesn't quote oaths in blood.

"Whoever did this knew him," I say quietly.

Freddy glances over. "That's your read?"

"Yeah. Or at least knew what he was."

He nods, not arguing. "You think this ties to the Beacon Hill case?"

I straighten, my knees cracking in protest. "Same balance, same message. Public virtue, private rot."

Freddy wipes a line of sweat from his temple. "You sound like you're starting to see a sermon in it."

"Maybe I am."

Outside, thunder rolls again—closer now, low enough to rattle the windowpane. I can smell rain coming through the cracks in the wood. The air feels charged, waiting.

"Send me copies of everything," I tell him. "Files, photos, tox as soon as it's in. I'll compare it to the others tonight."

Freddy gives me a look. "You really think we've got a pattern?"

"I don't think," I say. "I know."

He exhales, a slow, skeptical sound. "Guess you're the one chasing ghosts now."

"Not ghosts," I mutter, stepping toward the stairs. "Something worse. Something patient."

I pause at the doorway, glancing back one last time at the doctor's still form—how the fading moonlight catches the glasses, how the blood has dried into neat arcs. It feels less like chaos and more like calculation.

Outside, the sirens fade. The crowd noise turns to murmurs. The first drops of rain start to fall against the windows, quiet, deliberate, like fingers on glass. I can feel it again—that hum under the surface. The rhythm that's been following me through every scene like an echo I can't shake.

I don't know what it means yet.
But I know it's getting closer.

"Detective," one of the uniforms calls from the stairwell. "Reporters are already outside. They're asking if it's connected to the Beacon Hill case."

"Tell them nothing." My voice comes out sharper than I mean it to. "Not until I'm sure."

Outside, thunder rolls low over the harbor. I glance through the attic window—rain threatening but not yet falling. Somewhere in that stillness, I can almost feel it again: that hum under the surface, the rhythm I can't quite name.

A dull pressure blooms between my shoulder blades—small at first, then sharper, like something trying to push its way out. I roll my shoulders, trying to shake it off, but it lingers, pulsing in time with the distant thunder.

It feels like the city's holding its breath.

And for the first time, I wonder what—or who—it's waiting for.

By the time I step back outside, the sky has faded to that thin gray that lives between night and morning. The horizon looks bruised, the kind of color that never quite decides on dawn. The air tastes like copper and wet leaves, sharp enough to wake the dead.

Uniforms are corralling the last of the onlookers behind the tape. Tourists who should've been asleep by now huddle together under umbrellas, their voices low and eager—already trading versions of the story before the body's even cold. Coffee steams in paper cups, breath ghosts in the chill.

Somewhere nearby, a camera shutter clicks. Flash. Silence. Flash.

It's too early for the city to care, too late for me to sleep.

"Haunted house murder," one kid says to a reporter's camera, eyes wide. "There was so much blood—it looked fake until it didn't."

I pull my collar up and keep walking. The sound of the word *murder* feels too small for what's happening. This isn't chaos. It's orchestration.

At the edge of the tape, the press waits like vultures. I spot a few familiar faces from the Beacon Hill coverage. They've learned nothing since then—same microphones, same rehearsed questions about monsters, patterns, justice.

"Detective Shaw!" someone calls. "Can you confirm if this victim's connected to the other deaths?"

I don't break stride. "No comment."

Flashes pop behind me, white light cutting through the fog. I get into the car, shut the door, and for a second just sit there with my hands on the wheel. My reflection stares back from the windshield—tired eyes, three-day stubble, the faint tremor of adrenaline that still hasn't worn off.

I could drive straight back to Boston, file the report, wait for the lab results like protocol says. But I already know I won't.

The pattern's tightening.

Wexler—accountant, fraud charges buried.

Lexington—developer, safety violations ignored for profit.

Corbett—philanthropist, charity darling turned embezzler.

And now Harren—doctor, malpractice wiped clean.

Four names. Four pillars of respectability. All fallen clean, quiet, and precise.

I rub a hand over my face. It's too deliberate to be coincidence, too clean to be rage. Whoever's behind it isn't killing for pleasure—they're correcting something. I've seen messy revenge before, the kind that spirals. This isn't that. This is surgical. Purposeful. Like someone's keeping score and evening it one name at a time.

The rain starts as a mist against the windshield, then deepens to a steady tap. I stare at the ripples crawling down the glass, the city lights fracturing through them. It looks like the world's trying to wash itself clean.

My phone buzzes on the passenger seat. A text from the captain:

Press wants a statement by noon.

Keep it tight.

No theories.

I lock the screen. I've been told to stay quiet before. Didn't work out so well last time.

My thoughts drift to Celeste. The way she spoke about the transcripts—how carefully she catalogued every detail without ever passing judgment. I remember her voice on the phone when I canceled our meeting. Calm, but not cold. Like someone who's learned to make disappointment sound polite.

She'd understand patterns like this. She's seen every side of the system—heard every lie dressed in legal phrasing. Maybe too many.

I start the engine. The wipers drag across the glass with a tired squeal.

If anyone can help me trace the line between these victims, it's her.

Thunder rolls over the harbor as I pull away from the curb, the sound low and deliberate, echoing off the empty streets. By the time I get home, it's past nine. The rain has tapered off to a drizzle, enough to make the streetlights look like they're bleeding. I shrug out of my coat, toss it over the chair, and drop the case folders across the kitchen table.

The apartment's quiet except for the hum of the refrigerator and the steady tick of the clock above the sink. I like the noise. It sounds like something keeping time when I can't.

Four folders. Four names.

Wexler. Harren. Lexington. Corbett.

Four neat endings to cases that never really closed.

And every one of them has Silas Kade hiding somewhere in the fine print.

I already knew it—had a gut feeling the day Lexington's name hit the news. A sense that Kade's shadow stretched longer than his disbarment. But seeing it laid out on paper, black and white, makes it real.

Wexler's file sits open in front of me. Kade's signature curls at the bottom of every motion, every objection. His last big case before the Bar cut him loose. I flip to the next page—photographs, transcripts, testimony—and feel the familiar bitterness rise. The same charm, the same manipulation, the same smirk that sold a jury on innocence they shouldn't have believed.

Then the Beacon Hill gala. The photos glare up at me from the glossy printouts—crystal glasses, red gowns, and polished smiles.

There he is again. Kade. A name on the guest list, his face in the background of a news photo. Standing just behind the victim, hand raised mid-toast.

He didn't just defend the guilty. He celebrated with them.

I close my eyes, rub at the bridge of my nose. Maybe I'm seeing ghosts. Maybe I'm desperate to make sense of a string of bad coincidences. But it's the same hum I felt in Hartford before the Jensen case fell apart—the sound of something that doesn't add up, whispering until you can't ignore it.

Silas Mercer Kade.

Every time I think the trail's gone cold, his name surfaces again like oil on water.

I jot a few notes in the margin of the Beacon Hill file—dates, cross-references, circles and arrows that only I'll understand. My handwriting's getting sloppier, the lines darker, heavier.

He's at the center of this. He has to be. Either he's orchestrating it, or someone's making sure every stain he touched gets wiped clean the hard way.

Outside, thunder rolls over the harbor, a long, tired groan that rattles the glass. I look toward the courthouse dome, faint and gold through the clouds.

"Still playing savior, Kade?" I mutter under my breath. "Or did you finally find someone better at it than you?"

The rain picks up again, light against the window, steady as a heartbeat. I gather the files into one stack, clip them together, and lean back in my chair. The case isn't just close anymore—it's circling.

Chapter 15
Celeste

By Thursday, the week feels longer than it should. The courthouse hums with routine—same halls, same stale coffee, same shuffle of papers passed between hands pretending to hold justice. Outside, the sky threatens rain again but never follows through, leaving everything gray and waiting.

Sleep hasn't been kind. Every night since the gala, my dreams have been strange—too vivid, too heavy with sound and color.

Sometimes it's just the flicker of candlelight behind my eyes, shadows moving where they shouldn't. Other times, it's a house I don't recognize but somehow know: narrow stairs, creaking wood, walls that breathe. The air smells of copper and fog machine smoke, and somewhere above, something drips.

Last night was worse.

I dreamed I was standing in an attic. My hands were clean, but the floor was not. There were papers scattered around me—medical charts, signatures, names that blurred when I tried to read them. A shape slumped against the wall, and though I told myself not to look, I always do. I wake just before I see his face. Always before.

Even in daylight, the edges of it stay with me. A faint ache in my chest, a phantom weight in my hands. My reflection in the courthouse restroom mirror looked off this morning—hair damp though I'd showered the night before, wrists marked faintly like I'd worn something too tight.

I keep telling myself it's nothing. Just exhaustion. Just the job wearing me thin.

But the dreams have been getting worse—same screams, same flashes of light behind my eyelids. They've followed me for years, shadows stitched into my sleep. Lately, though, they're louder. Closer.

Sometimes, when I blink too slow, I can almost hear it again—a scream echoing through the back of my mind, faint but familiar, like a memory I was never supposed to keep.

Silas shows up that morning with a paper cup in one hand and that knowing smile that always lands somewhere between charming and dangerous.

"Dirty chai, extra spice," he says, setting it beside my files before I can protest.

"You're going to make me dependent," I tell him, though I still take the cup.

He leans against the doorframe, the picture of easy confidence. "There are worse vices."

I roll my eyes, but my pulse betrays me. There's something about him that unsettles the air—too calm, too observant, like he's always two thoughts ahead of me. We've fallen into a rhythm without meaning to: chai in the mornings, small talk that lasts too long, the kind of glances that carry more than they say.

It isn't supposed to mean anything. I remind myself of that every time he smiles.

He calls around noon. "Tell me you've eaten," he says.

"I was about to."

"Good," he replies, and somehow that's an invitation.

Lunch is at a restaurant tucked into the top floor of a downtown high-rise, glass walls framing the city below. From this height, Boston looks almost peaceful—streets reduced to veins of motion, the harbor a sheet of dull silver under the gray sky. The clouds hang low, pressing against the skyline, but the light still manages to find the water, glinting off it like scattered coins.

He holds the door open for me, his hand brushing lightly against my back as we step inside. It's nothing, but it sparks all the same.

The host leads us to a corner table by the window. Linen napkins, polished silverware, a single candle that doesn't need to be lit this early. It's the kind of place built for being seen.

"You've been busy," he says as we sit. "Your docket this week looked brutal."

I shrug. "Medical malpractice, eviction appeals, insurance fraud. Nothing glamorous."

"Still," he says, "I noticed the way you type when the witnesses talk. Like you're listening for something beneath the words."

I glance at him. "You notice too much."

"Occupational hazard."

The waiter arrives before I can even reach for the menu. Silas doesn't hesitate. "The salmon with lemon risotto," he says, nodding toward me, "and the ribeye for myself. Bottle of the house red."

It's smooth, unhurried—like this is a script he's already performed and perfected.

"You always do that?" I ask once the waiter's gone.

"What—order for people?"

"Assume you'll be right."

His mouth tilts, that easy half-smile I've never figured out how to read. "Only when I am."

I lean back in my chair, crossing one leg over the other. "Then let's see if you are this time."

He laughs quietly, low and genuine, and something in the sound pulls the edge out of the room. Maybe that's his gift—making defiance feel like an invitation.

For a while, it feels... easy. We talk about nothing—music, coffee, the absurdity of courthouse politics. He's funny when he wants to be, sharper when he doesn't. But beneath it all, there's something else—a pull I can't name.

When the plates are cleared, Silas leans forward, his voice low enough to blur with the hum of the room.

"You should let me take you somewhere different next time. Doesn't have to be dinner. Just... someplace you don't have to think so hard."

I huff out a quiet laugh. "You say that like I know how to stop."

"Maybe that's what you need," he says, almost to himself.

The waiter slips by, clearing glasses, and the silence that follows feels heavier than before. Light glances off the rim of his wine glass, staining the white tablecloth the color of blood and dusk.

He studies me for a beat, then sets it down. "You've heard about the doctor, I assume?"

I nod. "It's hard not to. Everyone at the courthouse has been whispering about it since Monday. You can practically feel the gossip crawling through the halls."

"Salem's favorite pastime," he says wryly. "The more gruesome the better."

"They're saying it happened during his haunted house," I add. "Kids found him in the attic. Can you imagine? You go out for a night of fake blood and come home with a story the police can't explain."

His mouth twists into something thoughtful, not quite a smile. "There's always more to stories like that. A man like Harren—he didn't end up on anyone's list by accident."

I tilt my head. "You sound certain."

"I've met his kind," he says, fingers tracing the stem of his glass. "Men who hide behind philanthropy. The more they perform virtue, the darker the secrets they bury."

His tone isn't casual. It's quiet and deliberate, carrying an undercurrent that makes me shiver before I can stop it. "You talk like you knew him."

"I didn't," he says, meeting my gaze again. "But I know patterns. And if someone like Harren finally met their end, I doubt it was random."

The words hang there, heavier than they should. I look down at my napkin, suddenly aware of how tight my fingers have curled around it.

"Do you really think one person could be behind all of these?" I ask, trying to sound curious, not uneasy. "Lexington. Wexler. Corbett. Now Harren."

Silas leans back, studying me. "If there is, they're not impulsive. They're organized, meticulous. They understand how to stay invisible." His voice softens, almost intrigued. "And if that's true... they're probably closer than anyone realizes."

A flicker runs down my spine, gone before I can name it. For a moment, I forget to breathe.

"Don't look so haunted," he says gently. "You spend all day surrounded by death. It's not healthy to take it home with you."

"Easier said than done."

"I could help with that," he offers lightly. "Dinner this weekend? Something with less murder in the conversation."

I laugh under my breath and shake my head. "You don't give up, do you?"

"Not when I want something," he says again, and there's a gleam in his eye that's half-challenge, half-promise.

"Fine," I say after a beat, my voice softer than I intend. "Saturday."

His smile widens, slow and deliberate. "Perfect. Something more casual this time. No suits, no candlelight. Let me surprise you."

"That sounds dangerous."

He tilts his head. "Only if you don't trust me."

The words hang between us, teasing and sharp. I tell myself not to read into it, but I can feel the warmth creeping up my neck. He knows exactly what he's doing—how to keep the tone just light enough to make me wonder if it's a game or something more.

By the time the check arrives, it already feels like we've stepped into a rhythm I can't quite name. It started with chai and stolen minutes in courthouse corridors. A joke here, a knowing look there. Now it's lunches that last too long and gifts that make my pulse stutter. Somewhere along the way, the boundaries shifted. I just can't remember when I stopped noticing.

Outside, the afternoon light has turned pale and thin, the city washed in that soft gray that always seems to linger over Boston this time of year. The streets blur past—brick, glass, and streaks of wet pavement reflecting the skyline like a half-forgotten memory.

Silas drives with one hand on the wheel, the other resting easy against the gearshift. His ring catches the light—gold, understated—the kind of detail you'd only notice if you were already looking too long.

We don't talk much. The silence between us isn't awkward; it's deliberate. Comfortable, even. Every so often, I catch him glancing my way, a small, knowing smile tugging at the corner of his mouth—like he's in on a secret I haven't decided to share yet.

When we pull up outside the courthouse, he kills the engine but doesn't move to open his door right away. The world outside the windshield feels suspended—clouds low, light diffused, the faint hum of traffic a reminder that the city keeps moving even when I'm not sure I am.

Then Silas turns to me, voice low and sure. "Come on," he says, unbuckling his seat belt. "I'll walk you in."

I start to protest—it's unnecessary, too formal—but he's already out of the car, circling around to open my door like it's second nature. By the time I step out, he's offering his arm with that same easy confidence that makes it hard to refuse.

And so I don't.

It's quiet enough that his voice sounds too intimate when he leans closer.

"Saturday," he reminds me, his tone low. "Don't be late."

"I won't," I say, and hate how it sounds like a promise.

He smiles—small, satisfied—and tucks a strand of hair behind my ear before stepping back. "Good."

Someone clears their throat nearby. The sound slices clean through the moment.

I turn, startled. Elias Shaw stands halfway down the corridor, coffee in one hand, file in the other—expression unreadable. That detective stillness again, the kind that sees everything and says nothing.

"Detective," I manage, straightening. "Didn't expect to see you here."

He glances at his watch, then back at me. "Could say the same. Thought most people were still on lunch."

"Working through it," I reply.

His eyes flick briefly to Silas, then back to me. "Didn't realize you two knew each other."

Silas's smile is smooth, unbothered. "Boston's a small city when you work in law."

Elias hums, a sound that lands somewhere between doubt and warning. "Right."

The silence stretches, taut as wire. I reach for professionalism like armor. "If you'll excuse me, I have transcripts to finalize."

Elias nods, but his gaze lingers. "Of course. Don't let me keep you."

Silas steps aside, gesturing for me to pass. His hand brushes mine—deliberate, fleeting—and something sharp sparks beneath my skin. I don't look back until I'm halfway down the hall.

When I do, they're still there—two men cut from the same shadow in very different ways. One restraint. One control disguised as charm. And me, caught in the space between them, wondering which will break first. Then I keep walking.

Silas moves through the world like it bends for him—controlled, deliberate, the kind of man who already knows the ending and waits for everyone else to catch up. Even his words seem to hum with something beneath them, a quiet current that pulls when he speaks, like gravity disguised as charm. There's safety in his certainty, even when it feels like standing too close to an open flame.

Elias is the opposite—steady but frayed at the edges, a man who still carries the weight of something he can't forgive himself for. His gaze doesn't pierce like Silas's; it searches, careful and human, as if he's still trying to prove the world can be fixed.

Silas draws me like a tide I don't remember stepping into. Elias lingers like memory.

And somehow, I keep finding myself caught between current and shore, wondering which will pull me under first.

Chapter 16
Elias

When I look back, Kade's already watching me. That faint smile still plays at the corner of his mouth—patient, knowing, like he's testing how close he can stand to the edge.

"You seem to turn up everywhere these days," I say.

"Coincidence," he replies easily, straightening his cuff. "Or maybe Boston's just smaller than it looks when you're not behind a badge."

I take a slow sip of coffee, eyes on him. "Small towns breed familiarity. You start recognizing the same faces—especially when they keep turning up around crime scenes."

His smile doesn't falter, but something in it sharpens. "And here I thought you only questioned the guilty."

"Just the ones who like to walk with them," I say.

He tilts his head, considering. "Maybe that's the difference between us, Detective. You think proximity makes you complicit." His gaze flicks toward the courthouse doors, then back to me. "I think it just makes you human."

The words could mean anything—or everything. His voice carries that quiet pull again, the kind that hums just beneath reason, dangerous in how natural it sounds.

He steps past me, close enough that the air shifts. "Careful what you look for," he adds softly. "Some truths don't like being found."

Then he's gone, footsteps fading into marble silence.

I stand there longer than I should, the echo of his tone still vibrating under my skin. The rain seeps through the air vents, faint and metallic. My coffee's gone cold, but the heat in my chest isn't.

Instinct tells me this wasn't a warning. It was an invitation.

The drive back to the precinct feels longer than usual. Boston's after work traffic hums against the quiet—buses sighing at curbs, wet tires hissing over pavement still damp from an earlier drizzle. The streetlights blur into long ribbons of white in the windshield, and my thoughts move just as fast, just as directionless.

Silas Kade. Disbarred defense attorney. Reputation polished smooth by charm and power, cracked open by scandal. And somehow, he's resurfaced—grinning in the middle of my investigation, walking beside Celeste Duvall like the world forgot what he did.

By the time I pull into the garage, the sky's turned the color of old steel. Inside, the bullpen's mostly empty. The few night officers left nod as I pass, their voices blending with the low murmur of the vending machine and the endless hum of fluorescents overhead. I drop into my chair and stare at the evidence board. The photos, the headlines, the names.

Lexington. Wexler. Corbett. Harren.

And now Kade—threading through all of it like a shadow that refuses to disappear.

My gut says he's connected, but nothing on paper backs it up. Not yet.

I take a sip of coffee gone bitter and cold, then open my notepad. If Kade's protecting something—or someone—I'll need an angle that doesn't make him retreat. Celeste might be that angle. She's close enough to see what I can't. Maybe she's seen him slip, heard something he didn't mean to share.

The thought sits wrong, but I don't stop it. I'm not using her, I tell myself. I'm investigating.

Still, the memory of her expression—surprised, uncertain, caught between two men who both know too much—sticks with me longer than I'd like. I push the image aside and pick up the phone.

"Records," I say when the line clicks. "Put in an appointment for Court Reporter Celeste Duvall. Friday morning, eleven o'clock. Tell her it's about documentation from the Wexler case."

"Got it, Detective."

When I hang up, I sit there for a long minute, staring at the city lights bleeding through the blinds. I should go home. Instead, I pull another file from the stack, flip it open, and let the paper whisper its secrets.

If Kade's playing some long game, I need to find the pattern before he moves again. And if Celeste's caught in the middle—willingly or not—I need to know which side she's standing on.

The clock ticks past midnight before I finally shut the folder. The office is silent except for the rain starting up again against the windows, a low rhythm that sounds too much like warning.

I lean back in my chair, rubbing at the ache between my shoulders. The files blur if I stare too long—names, dates, faces bleeding into one another until they're just patterns on paper.

I tell myself I'll close my eyes for five minutes. Just five.

When I do, the rain changes sound—no longer on glass, but water dripping in a tunnel. My desk light flickers, and the shadows stretch, thin and long, reaching toward me. Somewhere ahead, a woman hums softly—a song without words, rising and falling like breath. My feet move before my thoughts catch up, the floor slick underfoot. Every step echoes.

The hum turns to whispering. I can't make out the words, but they crawl under my skin like recognition. Something warm presses against my shoulder blades from the inside out, a pulse that doesn't belong to my heartbeat.

Then I see her. Or think I do. A figure at the far end of the hall, hair dripping, eyes too bright, too knowing. When she opens her mouth, the sound is both thunder and water—a voice that feels older than language itself.

"Wake up, Elias. It's time."

I jerk upright. Papers scatter to the floor. The lamp buzzes steady again, the only sound the rain on the window and my own pulse hammering in my ears.

The clock reads 3:42 a.m. I don't remember falling asleep.

Friday morning comes too fast. The sky over Boston hangs low and colorless, the kind of gray that looks permanent. I'm already at my desk by seven, half-running on caffeine, half on unease. The precinct hums with tired movement—phones ringing, printers sighing, officers exchanging clipped words about arrests and reports.

I tell myself this meeting is routine, just a follow-up for record-keeping. It isn't.

By eleven sharp, Celeste Duvall steps into the bullpen. She's precise as ever—pressed blouse, hair pinned back, a folder tucked neatly under her arm. The faint scent of chai drifts with her as she approaches.

"Detective Shaw," she greets evenly.

"Ms. Duvall." I stand, gesturing toward the chair across from me. "Appreciate you coming in."

"I was told this was about the Wexler case."

"That's right," I say, flipping open a folder already marked with colored tabs. "I've been cross-referencing transcripts. Trying to find a rhythm—see if any patterns carry over between defendants, counsel, or testimony."

She raises an eyebrow. "You think there's a connection?"

"I think the same names keep turning up. You've seen enough courtrooms to know that isn't always coincidence."

Celeste nods once, thoughtful, though her expression doesn't give much away. "Which cases?"

"Lexington, Wexler, Corbett and Harren," I reply. "And a few others I'm still digging into. All had a similar defense style—controlled pacing, heavy emphasis on procedural flaws. That sound familiar?"

Her lips press together, eyes narrowing slightly. "It sounds like Silas Kade and his old firm."

"That's what I thought."

Her gaze flicks toward me, sharp for the briefest second. "This isn't about transcripts, then. It's about him."

I lean back. "It's about what connects them. I'm just trying to understand the full picture."

Before she can answer, there's a soft knock at the doorframe. One of the officers from downstairs steps in, balancing a small takeout bag.

"Your lunch order, Detective."

I glance at my watch. Eleven on the dot. "Perfect timing. Thanks." I motion toward the empty spot on the desk. "Set it down."

Celeste tilts her head slightly. "You planned this?"

"I thought better results came with better food," I say, passing her one of the two takeout boxes. "Turkey club and dirty chai latte, if I remember right from the courthouse café."

Her eyes narrow again, half suspicion, half amusement. "You don't forget much, do you?"

"Occupational hazard."

She hesitates, then accepts it, setting the folder aside. For a few minutes, we eat in silence. The city murmurs faintly through the windows, sirens somewhere far off. The normal sounds of people pretending everything's fine.

Finally, I speak again. "You transcribed Kade's cases. You've heard how he works. What's your read on him?"

Celeste wipes her hands with a napkin, considering. "He's a man who likes control. He listens more than he speaks. Uses silence as a weapon. He has presence, but it's... unnerving. Like standing near a current you can't see but know could pull you under if you step too close."

I nod slowly. "And you?"

"Meaning?"

"You've spoken with him recently?"

Her cup pauses midair. "I don't see how that's relevant."

"It might be."

She exhales through her nose—soft, sharp. "You saw us yesterday. Let's not pretend this is subtle."

"I'm not pretending anything."

"Yes, you are," she snaps quietly. Then her tone softens, like she's forcing herself to find center again. "You think I'm a lead. I'm not. I'm just the one who writes everything down."

"Maybe," I say. "But sometimes the one writing it down is the only person who notices what everyone else misses."

She studies me across the desk. For a long moment, neither of us moves. The air between us hums—uneasy, alive.

Then she sighs. "Fine. You want my help? Tell me what you're really looking for."

"Patterns," I say simply. "Something that ties them together."

"And if there isn't one?"

"There is." I lean in, lowering my voice. "Silas Kade. His name keeps coming up—different cases, different victims, always near the center. I think he knows more than he's saying."

Her expression flickers, the faintest break in composure. "And you want me to spy on him?"

"I want you to pay attention," I correct. "If something feels off—something he says, someone he meets, anything that doesn't fit—you call me."

She lets out a breath that's almost a laugh, but there's no humor in it. "You're asking me to risk my job for a hunch."

"I'm asking you to help me stop whatever's happening before someone else ends up dead." I pause, meeting her eyes. "You wouldn't just be a witness, Celeste. You'd be my informant. Off record. Protected."

"Protected?" she repeats, quiet but sharp. "From who?"

I don't answer right away, because the truth sounds paranoid when you say it out loud. "Just... trust me on this."

Her gaze narrows. "You sound like a man who's already lost too much to trust anyone else."

That one lands. Harder than it should.

I look away first, staring down at the notepad between us. "If I'm wrong, you'll never hear from me again," I say finally. "But if I'm right—if there's something moving under all this—you'll be glad I came to you now."

For a long moment, neither of us breathes. Then she reaches for her cup, fingers steady even though I can see the pulse in her wrist.

"You really think you can protect me from someone like Silas Kade?" she asks softly.

"I don't know," I admit. "But I'm going to try."

Her lips part like she's about to say something—maybe to refuse, maybe to ask why it sounds like a promise—but instead she just nods once, slow and deliberate.

"Fine," she says. "I'll keep my eyes open."

And when she says it, I can't tell if she's agreeing to help me—or warning me that it's already too late.

Before I can respond, she pushes her empty lunch box aside and gathers her folder. "I'll have copies of the transcripts from those cases delivered by tomorrow morning. If I notice anything unusual, I'll let you know."

"Appreciate it," I say, standing as she does.

She lingers by the door just long enough to glance back. "You might be a good detective, Shaw," she says quietly, "but you're a terrible liar."

Then she's gone, her heels fading down the hall, leaving the smell of chai and something sharper in her wake. I stand there for a while, the lunch untouched beside me, and think about the way she said it—not like an accusation, but like a warning.

I watch the door long after it shuts, the words still hanging there like smoke. *Terrible liar.* She isn't wrong. I've built a career on reading tells, on dissecting every twitch and hesitation in a suspect's face, but when it comes to my own? I've never been good at hiding the things that matter. Not from people like her.

The bullpen hums around me—phones, keyboards, the sound of other people moving forward while I circle the same ghosts. The file on my desk is a mess of names and faces: Lexington. Wexler. Corbett. Harren. Four bodies, one pattern I can feel but can't name.

And every line I draw leads back to Silas Kade.

His name splinters under my skin—familiar, wrong, impossible to shake. He's too close to everything: the cases, the galas, the paper trails that look too clean to be real. The timing's perfect. Too perfect.

Then there's Celeste. Always in orbit. Always exactly where she shouldn't be.

She's not just a court reporter—she listens like someone trained to remember what others try to forget. When she caught me watching her, there was something in her eyes I can't explain—fear, maybe. Or recognition.

I glance at the takeout box on the desk, the half-drunk coffee cooling beside it. I told myself lunch was about information. It wasn't.

She got under my skin faster than I expected—something about the way she held her ground, how she could look at me like she already knew what I'd ask next.

I lean back in the chair, staring at the whiteboard.

Silas. Celeste. The victims.

The pattern's there—I can almost see it forming behind the noise.

I should keep my distance.

But distance stopped working the moment I saw the way she looked at him.

I flip open the notebook I keep for personal notes. Not the official log, but the one that matters. My handwriting wavers slightly, the ink heavier than usual.

Patterns — similar timing, public virtue, private rot. All connected through the same defense network. Kade's name recurring. *Duvall* as transcriber on most of them.

I underline her name once. Then again.

Outside, thunder rolls over the harbor—low, deliberate, the kind that sounds like a warning. I tell myself it's just the weather, but part of me doesn't buy it.

I push back from the desk, rubbing at the ache between my shoulders. The bullpen's gone quiet, most of the lights dimmed, only the hum of the vending machine filling the dark. I could go home. Pretend I know where the line is.

Instead, I find myself thinking about the drive to Salem.

It wouldn't take long. An hour, maybe less at this time of night.

I could park down the street, watch which lights in her building come on,

see who she's meeting when she thinks no one's looking.

It's a bad idea. I know that even as I picture it—her silhouette behind a

rain-streaked window, the flicker of motion I can't quite name. But some

part of me—the same part that doesn't sleep anymore—wants to see the

truth for myself.

She said it like a warning. *Some things don't want to be solved. They just

want to be understood.*

Maybe she's right.

But understanding has never been enough for me.

I glance back at her name underlined twice on the page.

Tomorrow, I'll start pulling harder on the thread.

And if it leads to her door, then maybe that's where I need to be.

Because something tells me when it finally snaps, it's going to take all of

us down with it.

Chapter 17
Celeste

I leave the precinct with my jaw tight and my pulse still tripping from irritation. The air outside is crisp, cool enough to bite, and the gray sky hangs low over the city like it's waiting to rain again. I shove my hands into my coat pockets, replaying every second of that conversation.

Elias Shaw.

He doesn't ask questions—he *digs*. Peels them open like he's trying to see what color the nerves are underneath. I held my own, mostly. But something in his eyes told me he didn't buy everything I said. And that line about me lying—God, it still rings in my ears.

By the time I hit the sidewalk, the crowd has thinned, just the shuffle of a few commuters and the distant hiss of a passing train. My phone buzzes in my pocket.

Silas.

I hesitate. Then answer. "Hey."

His voice comes smooth through the receiver, warm like smoke. "Rough day?"

I exhale, slow. "You could say that."

"Then let's fix it." There's a smile in his tone; I can hear it. "Come away with me this weekend. Nothing formal—just the lake house. You could use quiet, and I could use company that doesn't talk about indictments."

I stop walking, caught somewhere between laughter and disbelief. "A weekend?"

"Casual," he assures. "Hiking, fishing, bonfires. Maybe I'll teach you poker if you're brave enough."

"I don't fish," I say, but it comes out softer than I mean it to.

"Then you can read by the fire while I embarrass myself trying."

He knows exactly how to make it sound easy, harmless. Just a weekend. Just us. But the idea of quiet with him feels anything *but* harmless.

"Silas..." I start, then stop.

"You've been running too long, Celeste." His voice dips, gentler now. "Let something catch you for once."

My throat tightens. I tell myself it's ridiculous, that I should say no. But what slips out instead is, "When?"

"Tomorrow. I'll pick you up early."

"Okay," I whisper, surprising myself. "Tomorrow."

When the call ends, I keep the phone pressed to my ear for a moment longer, as if the echo of his voice might tell me why I agreed. The street around me hums with life—cars passing, lights flickering on—but everything feels slightly off-balance, like I've just stepped onto a path I can't quite see the end of.

The lake. The quiet. The promise of calm.

Maybe that's what I need.

Or maybe it's exactly what I should've avoided.

The next morning, the air smells like rain even though the sky's still clear—clean, metallic, expectant. I pack light: jeans, sweaters, a worn paperback I'll probably never open, and the small leather bag that's followed me through every move I've ever made. It's scuffed at the corners, the strap fraying, but I've never been able to throw it out. It holds things the way I hold secrets—tight, careful, pretending the weight doesn't matter.

I fold the last sweater, double-check that I packed my charger (and something that passes for courage), then zip the bag closed. It looks casual, harmless. Nothing inside it says I don't trust myself to go.

Before leaving, I catch my reflection in the mirror by the door. My face looks the same—hair neat, lips soft, eyes steady—but something beneath the surface hums like a warning. A shift I can't name. Maybe it's anticipation. Maybe it's guilt. I tell myself it's just a weekend. Fresh air. Quiet. No courtrooms.

When Silas's car pulls up—sleek, black, and predatory—I take a deep breath and grab my bag. The sound of the zipper scraping against my palm feels too loud in the morning stillness.

He steps out before I can reach the curb, dressed in dark jeans and a wool coat that somehow still looks expensive. The sunlight catches in his black hair, gleaming faintly like ink.

"Morning," he says, opening the passenger door for me.

"Morning." My voice sounds steadier than I feel.

As I slide into the seat, I set my bag at my feet, keeping one hand on the strap out of habit. The scent of him—cedar and smoke with something sharper beneath—fills the car before the door shuts.

The city recedes in layers: first the brick and traffic, then the glass, followed by the gray ribbon of highway. Silas's driving mirrors his every action—precise, patient, confident that the world yields to his presence. For a time, only the soft jazz from the radio and the steady beat of tires on asphalt fill the air.

"You've been restless," he says eventually, eyes on the road. "I noticed it even at the gala."

I look out the window. "Maybe I'm just tired of watching the same things happen to different people."

He hums, faint approval in the sound. "Or maybe you're tired of watching others decide what justice means."

That makes me glance back at him. "And you think you know?"

His mouth curves just slightly. "I think justice isn't decided—it's balanced."

The silence that follows feels heavier than it should. I stare out at the blur of trees and coastline, my fingers tracing the edge of my worn leather strap.

By the time the lake comes into view, the sky's dipped to gold, the water catching fire where the light hits. The cabin waits at the edge of the forest—quiet, elegant, the kind of isolation that feels chosen.

Silas kills the engine, his voice smooth and calm when he says, "Welcome to stillness."

But the way his reflection lingers in the window beside mine, dark and certain, makes me wonder if he means peace—or surrender. The cabin is a contradiction—much like him.

From the outside, it looks rustic and unassuming. Weathered cedar siding, black-trimmed windows, and a wide porch draped in creeping ivy. The lake stretches behind it, still as glass under the fading light. But once Silas unlocks the door and gestures for me to enter, I realize appearances are just another layer he controls perfectly.

Inside, the space is *too* refined to belong to a simple lakeside retreat. Polished wood floors catch the amber light filtering through wide windows. A stone fireplace anchors the main room, unlit but ready, the scent of cedar and old smoke lingering in the air. To the left, a professional-grade kitchen gleams beneath brass fixtures—sleek black counters, copper pans hung in symmetrical rows, knives lined with surgical precision. It's the kind of kitchen meant for someone who doesn't just cook, but *curates*.

"You cook?" I ask, setting my bag near the door.

"When it suits me," he says, his tone mild. "There's something therapeutic about control measured in teaspoons."

I glance around. "I can't picture you with an apron."

He smiles faintly. "I prefer not to get messy."

Past the main room, an open archway leads to a personal library. The sight makes me stop. Shelves reach from floor to ceiling, crowded with books in every size and color. The air smells of parchment and dust, warm and faintly metallic—like old secrets. A reading chair sits by the window, worn just enough to prove it's used. A few antique pens rest on the desk beside an open notebook filled with looping script.

"This is... impressive," I say quietly. "You must spend a lot of time here."

"Not as much as I'd like," he replies. "But it helps to have a place that remembers silence."

The phrase lingers with me as I drift toward the back of the cabin. Glass doors open onto a wide deck that stretches out over the lake itself. The boards are smooth underfoot, sanded to a soft gleam. The view steals the rest of my breath. Water ripples in the wind, catching what's left of the light like liquid gold.

The world feels too still. Too perfect.

Silas steps up beside me, close enough that the warmth of him brushes through the cool air. Our reflections overlap in the glass—two outlines that blur together before he looks past me toward the dark horizon.

"I thought you could use a weekend that isn't dictated by deadlines or transcripts," he says. His voice is low, the kind that carries without needing to rise. "Just quiet."

"Quiet," I echo. The word feels heavier than it should, like it means something he isn't saying.

He turns his head slightly, enough that I can feel the weight of his gaze trace the side of my face before it moves to my mouth, then back to my eyes. "You don't trust quiet, do you?"

"Not when it's this deliberate."

The corner of his mouth curves. "Then maybe it's time you learned to."

The space between us hums—too close, too charged. I can smell the faint spice of his cologne, the smoke from the fire catching in his hair. Behind us, the hearth crackles softly, and the faint heat against my back makes the cool air between us feel sharper, more intimate.

I tell myself to step away, but I don't. His arm brushes mine, barely a touch, and something in me answers—a pulse, a memory, a hunger I can't quite name.

The lake murmurs against the pilings below. Stars surface in the bruised twilight, patient, watching, as if they already know how this story ends.

For a moment, I let myself breathe. Just air, silence, and him—close enough that the warmth of him seeps through the thin space between us without ever crossing it. The kind of nearness that feels intentional. Dangerous.

The glass catches our reflections again, doubled in the fading light. Two shapes—one standing still, one moving just slightly closer. But when I blink, there's only me, and the ghost of something that shouldn't feel as intimate as it does.

"I'll start dinner," Silas says quietly, his voice brushing against the moment like a hand smoothing over flame. He turns toward the kitchen, the sound of his footsteps soft against the wood.

As soon as he's gone, the stillness presses in. The reflection in the window lingers half a second too long before dissolving into the dark outside. I turn away from it and drift toward the only space that feels like it might explain the weight in the air.

The library feels older than the cabin itself—walls of polished oak lined with shelves that reach nearly to the beams. The scent of cedar smoke and old paper wraps around me, grounding and electric all at once. The quiet here isn't absence—it's intention. Like the room is waiting to be entered, or remembered.

I drift between the shelves, fingertips grazing the spines until one catches the dim firelight. The leather is deep brown, worn smooth from use, the gold lettering pressed faintly into its cover:

The Ballad of Ash and the Thirteen Gates
by Valora Morgraven.

The title feels familiar in a way I can't quite place—like a name half-heard in a dream. When I open it, the scent of parchment and dust rises like a held breath. The pages are thin, soft-edged with age, the text alternating between poetry and prose—a song disguised as scripture. The first lines hum against my fingertips:

When heaven split, the sky did burn,□
And ash fell thick as rain...

The words stir something under my skin—faint, electric, unsettlingly familiar.

By the time I return to the main room, Silas is already in the kitchen. The smell of seared salmon and caramelized butter fills the space, rich and grounding. He moves with unhurried precision—sleeves rolled, wrist flicking neatly as he turns the pan. Every motion feels intentional, as though even dinner is part of some quiet ritual.

"Find something good?" he asks over his shoulder.

I hold up the book. "*The Ballad of Ash and the Thirteen Gates.* Can't say I've heard of it before."

He glances back, the faintest smile tugging at the corner of his mouth. "It's old. A myth cycle, mostly forgotten. People used to think it predicted the fall of thirteen kingdoms—or the rise of one."

"That's dramatic," I say, though my thumb is already tracing the edge of a stanza.

"History usually is." His tone softens, almost reverent. "That one's been bound and rebound more times than most books survive. You could say it's... persistent."

I glance down at the cover, the worn leather glowing faintly in the firelight. "Persistent sounds dangerous."

"It is," Silas replies. Then, with a quick shift of tone, "Your tea's ready. Chai, extra spice."

I take the cup from him, the warmth seeping through my palms. "You always notice things."

He shrugs, returning to the stove. "I listen. It's a dying art."

The fire murmurs softly behind me. I settle into the chair by the hearth, opening the book again. The verses weave through flame-born crowns and ash-stained gates, betrayal and prophecy—the language heavy with ruin and beauty. The rhythm of Silas's movements in the kitchen seems to match the cadence of the lines, as if the words and his motions belong to the same quiet pulse.

Outside, Hollowmere lies still beneath the moon, its surface silver and unbroken. For a moment, the reflection of the cabin ripples faintly—then steadies again, as though the world itself is holding its breath.

For the first time in a long while, the silence feels alive—like something ancient breathing just beneath the surface of the world.

Chapter 18
Celeste

The scent of butter and rosemary lingers in the air long after the pan leaves the stove. Silas sets two plates on the table—a meal that looks effortless but isn't. Seared salmon, roasted vegetables, wild rice threaded with herbs. Simple, elegant. Like him.

He pours the wine without asking, the motion deliberate, almost ceremonial. The bottle catches the firelight—dark red glinting like blood behind glass. "You read when you're thinking," he says, settling across from me.

"I didn't realize I was that transparent."

"You're not," he replies, a faint smile ghosting across his mouth. "Most people wouldn't notice. But I've had time." His gaze lingers—too long to be casual, too calm to be impulsive. "Ten years, give or take."

The words land heavier than the air between us. "You've been paying attention that long?"

"Let's call it... consistency." He lifts his glass, studying the wine like it might answer for him. "You don't read for escape. You read to remember. To touch something the rest of the world pretends isn't there."

I trace the rim of my glass, trying not to flinch under the weight of being seen. "You talk like a man who's been studying me."

"Observation," he corrects softly. "It's part of the job."

"And what job is that now?"

He leans back, and the fire shifts across his face—gold catching on the sharp line of his jaw, the rest lost to shadow. "The same as it's always been," he says. "Understanding what people bury in themselves. The things that hum under the skin when they think no one's listening."

His voice dips, lower now. "Tell me, Celeste—what do you make of things unseen? The ones that linger just below the surface. The ones you feel before you believe."

The room seems to tighten around us. My pulse catches, and for a heartbeat, I swear the wine trembles in my glass.

"I think," I say quietly, "some things don't need to be believed to be real."

His smile deepens—not satisfaction, not surprise, but something more dangerous. "Then maybe you've always known what most people spend their lives trying to forget."

The air hums between us, charged in that quiet, invisible way that feels more like current than conversation. I look down at my plate, pretending to focus on the food, but every movement feels too deliberate, every breath too loud.

"And what is it you think I'm hiding?" I ask, forcing the words out lightly.

He doesn't answer right away. He lifts his glass instead, studies the wine as if it might reveal something only he can read. The silence stretches, intimate and unhurried. When he finally speaks, his voice is low—measured, careful, dangerous.

"Maybe the better question," he says, "is what you've had to bury to survive."

The knife stills in my hand. My chest tightens. For a second, I can't tell if he's talking about the past I've tried to outrun, or something deeper—something I don't have a name for yet.

I manage a quiet laugh, thin and brittle. "That's a little heavy for dinner talk."

"Maybe." His eyes find mine again, steady, searching. "But you strike me as someone who's never had the luxury of small talk."

The flicker of firelight catches in his eyes, green gone molten, and suddenly I can't remember what I was about to say. There's a gravity to him, something that pulls—not just attention, but confession.

For a heartbeat, I swear the air itself leans closer. The fire crackles, the lake outside whispering against the shore. Then, almost mercifully, he changes direction. "How's the chai?"

"Perfect," I admit, and it is. Spiced and sweet, grounded.

"I figured you could use something familiar," he says, eyes holding mine just a second too long. "You've had a long few weeks."

He's not wrong. Between the cases, the endless transcriptions, and the weight of the courthouse air, exhaustion has woven itself into my bones.

But here, in this strange place with him, the world feels suspended—like time has been folded into something softer.

"Thank you," I say finally.

"For the chai?"

"For dinner. For... all of it."

He tilts his head, studying me with that same unreadable curiosity. "You're welcome, Celeste."

The way he says my name—low, deliberate—wraps around me like a secret I'm not sure I want to keep.

I take another sip of wine, trying to focus on the warmth in my throat instead of the flicker of heat that rises somewhere deeper.

Outside, the lake gleams under the full moon, calm and endless. Inside, Silas raises his glass in quiet toast. "To balance," he says.

I hesitate before clinking mine against his. "To what?"

He smiles faintly. "To finding what was lost."

The words hang in the air longer than they should, stirring something I can't quite name.

The wine burns a quiet path down my throat, low and steady. I tell myself it's the alcohol making my pulse quicken, not the way Silas watches me. Not the way he says my name. The silence between us stretches—not awkward, not empty. Just charged.

He cuts another piece of salmon, gestures toward my plate. "You're barely eating."

"I'm not used to food that looks like it belongs in a magazine."

He smirks. "You'd prefer diner coffee and cold croissants?"

"Maybe." I tilt my head, pretending to think. "Less pressure to look impressed."

His laugh is soft, unguarded. The sound slides under my skin before I can stop it. "You always have an answer ready, don't you?"

"Occupational hazard," I say. "When you spend your days transcribing other people's words, you learn to find your own before they're used against you."

"That sounds lonely."

"It's practical."

He studies me for a long moment. "And which are you tonight—practical or curious?"

The question lands somewhere between a challenge and an invitation. I can't quite tell which. My hand tightens around the stem of my glass.

"I'm off duty," I manage.

"Good." His smile doesn't fade. "Then you can stop trying to read me."

"I'm not—"

"You are," he interrupts, calm and certain. "And I'm not complaining. But it's not a fair game, is it? You listen for a living. You catch what most people miss."

There's truth in that, though I wish there wasn't. I glance at the book beside me, its cover catching the light like it's waiting to be opened. "Maybe I just like puzzles."

He leans forward, forearms resting on the table, the movement slow enough to make it feel deliberate. "Then tell me—what am I?"

My pulse skips. "Persistent."

"Accurate," he counters, the ghost of a grin tugging at his mouth.

"Controlled."

He hums, low and amused. "And that's a flaw?"

"It's a warning."

That earns a full smile—quiet, sharp, the kind that feels like a hand pressed to the small of your back, urging you closer. "You always this good at deflection?"

"Only when someone's trying to study me," I say, lifting my glass. "Or undress me with philosophy."

His laughter is soft, rich, genuine. "You think that's what I'm doing?"

"I think you like to see how far you can push before someone calls your bluff."

He tilts his head. "And you? Are you calling it?"

"Not yet," I say, too easily. The words slip out before I can catch them.

The pause that follows is alive—thick with implication. His gaze lingers, not hungry, but intent, like he's tracing a thought he hasn't decided whether to say out loud.

"You shouldn't look at people that way," I murmur, breaking the silence.

"What way?"

"Like you already know what they'll do."

He studies me a moment longer, the air between us charged and humming. "Maybe I just have faith in patterns," he says finally.

"Or maybe," I say, matching his tone, "you make them."

His lips curve, slow and deliberate. "You make me sound dangerous."

"Maybe I like dangerous," I say, setting my glass down, my pulse betraying me. "In theory."

The fire pops, a spark jumping in the quiet. His voice drops, low and rough-edged. "Careful, Celeste. Theories have a way of becoming practice."

"Are you? Dangerous?"

His silence answers for him.

The air feels heavier now—thick, electric, like the moment before a storm breaks. Every shift of movement, every breath between words hums with something I don't have the language for. I've spent years mastering control, keeping emotion in neat, tidy lines, but sitting here under his gaze, the foundation trembles.

I've never been the kind of woman who invites chaos. I've never been the kind who lets it feel this much like gravity.

"Celeste," he says softly. Just my name. But it lands like a touch.

I force a quiet breath, pretending to focus on the way the candlelight flickers against the glass. "You're very sure of yourself."

"Only when it comes to knowing what I want."

"And what is that?"

His eyes catch the firelight—gray-green, unreadable. "Dinner. For now."

The words are too simple for the way they sound. My pulse stumbles; he doesn't move closer, doesn't reach for me, but somehow the space between us feels smaller, charged. It's restraint disguised as ease, patience that borders on predatory.

I glance toward the window, pretending to look past him. The lake outside is dark and still, the moon caught like a coin on its surface. My reflection flickers faintly in the glass—eyes too bright, lips parted, shoulders not quite as steady as they should be. I look like someone I don't quite recognize. Someone who isn't afraid of wanting.

When I turn back, Silas is still watching, his expression calm, unreadable, but there's something deliberate in his stillness—like he's letting the moment unfold just to see what I'll do with it.

"You should eat," he says finally, the faintest edge of amusement ghosting his tone. "It's going to be a long night."

I pick up my fork, pretending not to hear the promise in it.

The silence that follows is softer now, dense with unspoken things. I focus on the food, on the warmth of the wine, on anything that might anchor me. But beneath it all, that pulse remains—steady, insistent, alive.

When I finally push my chair back, I tell myself I just need air. A walk. Distance.

But as I cross the threshold into the library, I can still feel his gaze trailing after me—measured, patient, and entirely too knowing.

The night folds in soft around us. I remember the warmth of the fire, the rhythm of our voices dipping and rising, laughter catching between sips of wine. I remember eating—slow, measured bites, the salmon dissolving like smoke on my tongue. I remember the book still open beside me, the pages whispering lines I no longer recall.

At some point, Silas stands. The motion is unhurried, his expression unreadable in the shifting light. "You should rest," he says. "It's late."

He shows me to the guest room, one door past the library. The air smells faintly of cedar and linen. There's a small lamp on the nightstand, its glow amber and soft, a stack of books beneath it. He lingers just long enough to brush a kiss against my forehead—light, deliberate.

"Goodnight, Celeste."

I remember nodding. I remember the weight of the moment, the strange wish that he'd stayed. Then the memory cuts—clean, abrupt—like someone's spliced the reel of my life and left the rest blank.

When I wake, it's still dark. The window's open, curtains shivering with the wind. My hair clings damp to my neck, the sheets heavy with cold. For a moment, I can't move. The scent hits first—salt and water and something metallic just beneath it.

I sit up slowly. My nightshirt is damp, the hem cold against my skin. I touch my hair—it's wet, tangled, as though I've just stepped out of the lake.

A shiver crawls up my spine. The last thing I remember is standing in this room, the lamp still on, Silas's voice soft in the doorway. Everything between then and now is... gone.

I push the blanket back, my bare feet finding the hardwood. The room creaks in protest. The lamp flickers once, steadying as I cross to the window. Outside, Hollowmere lies still under the moon, perfect and silver—untouched. But the faint imprint of footprints darkens the deck boards below.

Mine.

I know it before I even look down.

My hands tremble as I pull the window shut. The latch clicks louder than it should. I lean against the sill, trying to piece the night together. Dinner. The book. The fire. His voice. The way the air felt charged, like the world was holding its breath.

And then nothing.

I check the clock on the nightstand. 3:12 a.m. The sound of the ticking fills the space between thoughts, steady and dissonant.

Maybe I sleepwalked. Maybe the exhaustion, the wine, the months of long cases and sleepless nights finally caught up. That's the logical answer. The only one that fits.

Still, when I catch my reflection in the window—pale face, damp hair, eyes too dark in the half-light—it feels like I'm looking at someone else entirely. Someone who knows where she's been.

I close the curtains. The clock ticks on. And somewhere outside, beneath the hush of the trees, I think I hear the faint lap of water against the dock—soft, rhythmic, like something breathing just below the surface.

Chapter 19
Elias

It's past midnight when the pattern finally fractures open.

The precinct's been empty for hours—just the hum of fluorescents, the stale bite of coffee, and the rain tapping the windows like it's trying to get in. I should've gone home hours ago, but "home" doesn't mean much when the case won't let go. The board keeps staring back at me, all red string and unanswered questions, each connection tightening instead of coming loose.

I'd driven to Salem earlier, hoping distance might make sense of it all. Sat outside her building for hours, engine off, watching the glow from other people's windows fade one by one. Celeste's apartment stayed dark. No movement. No silhouette. Nothing but the steady blink of the streetlight reflected in the glass.

I told myself I was there to clear my head—to see if the pattern really touched her or if I'd just started seeing ghosts in the data. But the longer I waited, the thinner that excuse became. I could feel the temptation crawl under my skin—the urge to move, to check the door, to look inside.

By the time I admitted she wasn't home, the rain had turned the street into a mirror. I sat there longer than I should've, watching the building blur in the downpour, the wipers moving slow enough to make it feel like time itself was dragging.

In the end, I drove back to Boston before I did something I couldn't take back.

Now, sitting here, the precinct feels hollow. My reflection stares back from the window, tired and sharper than I remember. The evidence board looms over my desk, the names bleeding together—Lexington, Wexler, Corbett, Harren—all orbiting the same invisible center. All wealthy. All untouchable. All dead.

Celeste Duvall.
Silas Kade.
Patterns, connections, gravity.

And I can't tell anymore if I'm chasing the killer or being pulled into the same current that made them.

But something about it feels too... clean. Too curated. Like I'm only seeing the surface of a larger design.

It starts with a hunch and ends with a stack of coffee-stained folders taller than my good sense.

I pull up case records from Boston, then branch out—Cambridge, Salem, Lynn, Revere—anywhere the paperwork might still smell of neglect. Most of it's routine: bar fights, DUIs, domestic disturbances that died in bureaucracy. But the more I dig, the more something sour seeps through the cracks.

I call in favors from the other precincts. "Just a few old files," I tell them, keeping my tone easy. Nobody asks why a Boston detective wants sealed records from Essex County. They never do when you sound like you already know what you're looking for.

The pattern doesn't surface all at once. It builds.

A small-time landlord in Salem accused of assault—case dismissed when the victim recanted.

A probation officer in Cambridge charged with falsifying statements—mistrial.

A state employee in Revere tied to missing evidence from a trafficking case—charges dropped after "procedural errors."

Different towns. Different defense attorneys. But each file ends the same way: nothing sticks.

Most of these never even made the papers. The kind of offenders the system forgets on purpose—men who hurt people who couldn't afford to matter.

I spread the folders across the table, tracing the timelines with my finger. Ten years back, the incidents scatter like debris. Then, five years ago, the rhythm changes. Faster. Cleaner. Almost deliberate.

A nurse found dead in her car outside Marblehead.

A corrections officer from Plymouth "fell" from his balcony.

A retired judge with a history of harassment died of carbon-monoxide poisoning in his own garage.

No witnesses. No suspects. No noise.

Each one a quiet subtraction.

The chair creaks when I lean back. My coffee's gone cold, rain tapping the windows of the precinct like a metronome.

It's not random. It's a pattern stitched across counties—someone working the gaps between jurisdictions so no one notices the overlap.

A ledger of names that should've carried sentences but didn't.

A list of sins the law ignored.

And somewhere out there, someone's balancing it.

For a long minute, I just stare at the files—at the faces staring back through time and paper. The air hums against my ribs, heavier than it should be. I tell myself it's just the caffeine, or adrenaline, or too many hours under the same flickering light. But it isn't.

It's something sharper. Something like recognition.

And maybe that's what scares me most.

I scoop the files into my arms before I can second-guess it. The hallway feels longer than it should—empty desks, the low buzz of fluorescent light, the smell of burnt coffee and rain-soaked wool. My pulse keeps time with my footsteps, quick and uneven.

Rivera's still here—of course she is. Her light bleeds through the blinds, music low enough to hide under. She looks up when I push the door open, one brow lifting.

"Jesus, Shaw. You look like you wrestled a ghost."

"Maybe I did." I drop the stack of folders on her desk. Paper fans out like a broken deck of cards. "I need you to look at these."

She exhales through her nose, leaning back in her chair. "Tell me this isn't another one of your late-night theories."

"Just look."

Rivera starts flipping through the reports. I watch her expression shift—confusion first, then focus, then something closer to unease.

"These are all dismissed cases," she says.

"Yeah. And all tied to the same circles—defense firms, private investigators, corrections officers. Different towns, same endings." I tap the top file. "They all walked free."

Her brow furrows. "And you think whoever's been killing the high-profile ones—Corbett, Lexington, Harren—connects back to this mess?"

"I think it's all part of the same ecosystem," I say. "These early ones weren't random. They were testing the water—correcting the kind the system forgot to punish."

Rivera shuts one file, eyes narrowing. "That's a hell of a leap, Shaw."

"It's not a leap if the ground's already cracking."

She studies me, the quiet between us thick enough to hum. "Alright. What are you asking me to do?"

"I need you to widen the net. Pull every unresolved homicide across Boston, Salem, Cambridge—hell, all the North Shore. Cross-reference them with dismissed or sealed cases from the last ten years. Pay attention to overlapping legal representation."

Rivera lets out a low whistle. "That's gonna light up the whole damn map."

"Good," I say. "Then we'll finally see what's been hiding between the lines."

She shakes her head, muttering something about my sleep schedule. "You realize this could blow up careers, right?"

"Yeah," I murmur, eyes drifting to the rain-smeared window. "Maybe that's the point."

For a moment, neither of us speaks. The hum of the lights fills the space, steady and merciless. Outside, snow has started again—soft, relentless, burying the city in quiet absolution.

Rivera finally nods, resigned. "Alright, Shaw. I'll run it. But if this spirals, you're buying coffee for a month."

"Deal."

I'm halfway to the door when she calls after me. "Hey, Elias."

I pause, hand on the frame.

"If you're right about this," she says quietly, "then whoever's doing it—they're not just cleaning house." Her voice drops. "They're building one."

I don't answer. Just glance through the glass at the board—red lines webbed like veins, a map of correction drawn in blood and ink.

"Yeah," I say finally. "I know."

I don't go home right away. I tell myself I'm clearing my head, but the truth is I'm circling the noise. The streets bleed reflection—headlights smearing across puddles, neon trembling in the snowmelt. Boston never really sleeps; it just hums under its breath. I drift through it like a ghost, the engine idling low, the city flickering past in wet glass and memory. The files ride shotgun, edges curling from heat and rain, whispering against each other every time I take a turn.

I pass the Common, the old courthouse, the brick shoulders of Beacon Hill. Every block holds some echo of the job—sirens that once carried my name, cases I never fully closed. The air tastes like salt and exhaust. Somewhere near the harbor, I stop noticing the road and just follow the pulse in my chest until I'm home.

The building's quiet when I pull in. Back Bay looks drowned in silver—streetlights soft through the snow, the Charles blurred to mercury. I take the stairs instead of the elevator; the hum of machinery feels too loud tonight. My key sticks in the lock before it gives. Inside, the apartment greets me with the faint smell of rain-soaked paper and the low whine of the radiator. It isn't much—two rooms, one view—but it's enough to hold the silence.

I drop the keys in the bowl, hang my coat, and stand by the window. The city stretches beneath me, lights flickering like they're breathing. A siren starts somewhere near Fenway, fades before it reaches me. I tell myself to stop thinking, to let the night go, but something in me won't unclench. The rhythm hasn't left my ribs; it never does.

I pour a drink, the motion automatic. The bourbon catches the light, amber over my fingers. When I bring it to my mouth, the glass trembles—not from nerves, just the same old tremor that comes when the world shifts and doesn't tell me why. I've felt it my whole life, that sliver of warning in the air before everything goes wrong. The fire on Temple Street. My mother's accident. The prisoner who smiled a second too long before he shot himself in holding.

The scent hits first—ozone, faint and metallic, like lightning behind the walls. Then the lights flicker. Once. Twice. Long enough to draw the breath out of me. I set the glass down carefully, waiting for the hum to settle. It doesn't.

I move through the apartment, hand brushing the doorframe, the counter, the back of the chair. Everything hums—low, alive, vibrating at a frequency I can't name. I stop in front of the window again. Snow drifts sideways through the wind. My reflection looks wrong—split by the glass, one half moving slower than the other.

It passes as suddenly as it came. The air stills. The lights steady. The smell fades. But the feeling lingers—the quiet recognition of something near and watching.

And in that moment, I think of her. Celeste Duvall.
The way the room shifts when she walks in, like the air recalibrates around her. The same current that moves through me before disaster, but softer. Calmer. Like she carries the opposite frequency—something that steadies what the rest of the world keeps unraveling.

Every time I'm near her, that hum quiets.
Not gone. Just... tuned.

I finish the drink, though it tastes different now, sharper somehow. Below, the city moves on, unaware. Somewhere out there, someone's correcting the world's mistakes, and for a moment, I can almost hear the echo of their work in the static.

When I finally turn away, the glass leaves a ring on the sill—thin, perfect, balanced.

Chapter 20
Celeste

The sky hangs low over Salem, the kind of heavy gray that promises snow but refuses to give in. The air is sharp and metallic, like a held breath that never quite exhales. Inside, my apartment feels dim despite the lamp on the desk. The light flickers, catching on the edges of my journal, the steam curling from a half-finished cup of chai gone lukewarm hours ago.

I stare at the open page, the words already blurring together.

November 26th.

Back from the lake.
Still tired. Still dreaming. Still wanting.

My handwriting falters at that word again—*wanting*. It feels like a confession every time I write it.

Once, I could keep that part of myself locked away, neat and silent. Desire used to be something I could catalogue and shelve—an impulse pressed flat between pages. Now it moves through me like current. No permission. No control.

I close my eyes and the film plays again: water against my skin, breath that isn't mine, fingers at my throat tracing where pulse meets bone. His hand. *Silas's.*

At least, I think it was.

The dreams bleed too easily into memory now.

I remember him after dinner, the scent of chai and smoke clinging to the space between us. He spoke about *The Ink-Bound Society*—a circle of minds devoted to truth and consequence, he said. "A place for those who see what the law refuses to name."

He said it like an invitation. And maybe that's what it was.

I shouldn't have leaned closer, but I did. There was something in the way he watched me—like he was reading a secret written under my skin. I wanted to know what he saw.

I wanted *him* to find it.

And yet, there's another pull. Quieter, steadier. Elias.

He doesn't see me the way Silas does. With Elias, it's not seduction—it's gravity. He moves like someone who believes in order, in the kind of truth you can measure, and still... something in him trembles when our eyes meet. He has layers he isn't even aware of—an ache he hides behind discipline. I keep wondering what he'd become if that restraint ever broke.

Sometimes I think I'm seeing both of them through the same dream—two reflections in the same pool. One made of firelight, the other of static and storm.

But then the blank spaces come.

Whole hours vanish like pages torn out. I'll look up from a transcript and it's dark outside. My tea is cold. My body feels used but not exhausted, as if I've been *somewhere*, doing something that memory refuses to translate.

When I sleep, it's worse.

Dreaming doesn't feel like rest anymore. It feels like travel—like I'm stepping through a mirror into a life that remembers me better than I remember myself. There, the lake hums like it's alive. There, I am not afraid.

I should tell someone. Silas would listen, but he'd twist it into prophecy. Elias would analyze it until it lost its meaning.

And if either of them looked at me too closely, they'd see what's shifting beneath the surface—what's been waiting to wake.

No. Better to stay silent. Better to write it down, let the ink take the weight.

At least the page doesn't ask who I am when the lights go out.

The pen trembles against the page as I write *I'm fine* three times, each word pressed harder than the last until the ink feathers through the paper like a wound that won't close. Outside, snow drifts past the window—thin, uncertain flakes that vanish as soon as they touch the glass. The world feels muted, wrapped in a hush so complete I can hear my own heartbeat and the faint whisper of the radiator breathing through the walls.

I think about Silas's voice, the calm certainty of it when he said, *You don't have to be afraid of what you feel.* He doesn't understand. I'm not afraid of what I feel; I'm afraid of what happens when I stop trying *not* to. With him, it's too easy to lose the edges of myself, to forget which parts belong to wanting and which to warning.

Then Elias's face flickers in my mind—the steadiness of his eyes, the quiet way he watches me as if waiting for something I can't name. There's discipline in him, a deliberate control that feels both safe and dangerous. I wonder what he'd say if he knew how deep the cracks go, if he'd still look at me like I was something worth saving. The thought hurts more than I want to admit, a kind of ache that feels older than the both of us.

My pulse won't steady. It stumbles instead, too strong one moment and too faint the next, like it's trying to find rhythm between two different hearts. When I glance back at the page, the last line isn't one I remember writing. *The lake remembers.* The ink glistens wetly, the words darker than the rest, as if something just beneath the surface wanted to be heard.

A chill works its way through me that has nothing to do with the weather. I snap the journal shut and push it away, the sound too loud in the quiet room. Outside, the snow thickens, soft and relentless, erasing the streetlight glow one flake at a time. The city feels smaller, folded in on itself, as if the whole world is holding its breath. I'm still staring at the closed journal when my phone vibrates against the desk, sudden and sharp, the sound cutting through the silence like a heartbeat that isn't mine.

Silas.

For a second, I consider not answering. I'm too raw, too unsettled. But

I swipe to accept anyway, pressing the phone to my ear.

"Celeste," he says, my name a slow exhale. "I was hoping you hadn't gone into hibernation yet."

His voice does that thing it always does—finds the small crack in my armor and slides through before I can stop it. "Not yet," I say, forcing lightness. "Give it another week of overcast skies and snow."

He chuckles softly, low enough to feel rather than hear. "Then I'll have to intervene before you disappear completely. How do you feel about spending Thanksgiving in the city?"

I blink. "Boston?"

"Mm. My place. I'm hosting something small—some friends, a few from the society..." He pauses, then adds, "You'd like it. Nothing formal. Good food, good wine, terrible board games."

"I wouldn't want to intrude."

"Celeste." His tone gentles, coaxing. "If I didn't want you there, I wouldn't ask. Besides, I made too much pie last year. You'd be doing me a favor."

The corner of my mouth lifts despite myself. "That's a hard sell."

"I'm persuasive."

"I've noticed."

He laughs again, soft but edged with something that tugs at my pulse. "Then take pity on me. Say yes. I'll even make your chai the way you like it—extra spice, extra patience."

I hesitate, watching the snow drift down in faint spirals. Thanksgiving. A crowded table, laughter, warmth. It's been years since I've had that—years since anyone asked.

"Okay," I say quietly. "I'll come."

"Good." His voice lowers, the warmth turning intimate. "I'll pick you up at noon. Dress comfortably, but... maybe keep that red dress in mind. It suits you."

The line hums for a beat longer, and I think he's about to say something else. But then it's just silence and the soft click of the call ending.

I set the phone down and stare at my reflection in the dark window. Snow streaks across the glass in thin white veins, tracing my outline like the world is trying to redraw me.

It's just dinner, I tell myself.

But the words sound like a lie.

***

Boston feels sharper than Salem tonight—alive with light and movement, the air holding the first edge of winter. Silas's car glides through the narrow streets, headlights sweeping over brownstones strung with the last traces of autumn. The closer we get to the waterfront, the quieter it becomes—money buys silence in this part of the city.

When we stop, the townhouse looks like something pulled from another century: tall, narrow, its brick façade washed gold by the streetlamps. Candlelight glows behind mullioned windows, warm and deliberate.

He steps out first and circles around to open my door, offering a hand. "You're safe now," he says lightly, as if the city itself might've been waiting to test me.

Inside, the scent hits first: cinnamon, smoke, roasted herbs—warmth layered over something faintly metallic, like old paper and ink. It's the smell of history, not just a home.

He takes my coat, fingers brushing mine, the touch fleeting but electric. "I'm glad you came," he murmurs. "Holidays can be cruel company without warmth to balance them."

The entryway opens into a world that feels curated and lived-in all at once. Tall shelves brimming with leather-bound books rise to the ceiling; a grand staircase curls upward beside a wall lined with portraits whose painted eyes seem too alive.

The fireplace in the next room spills golden light over a long dining table. A handful of guests have already gathered—men and women dressed with that subtle kind of wealth that never needs to announce itself. Their laughter is soft, practiced, as if they've shared too many secrets over too many years.

"This is Celeste," Silas says, his hand resting at the small of my back. "A friend."

The word hangs between us. Polite. Untrue.

I murmur a few greetings, though I can feel their attention shift and linger—studying me, appraising, measuring what I might know. The weight of their gazes prickles at the base of my neck.

Dinner begins in a low hum of conversation. Crystal glints beneath candlelight; silverware moves in quiet choreography. I try to focus on the food, but the rhythm of it all—the murmured voices, the clink of glass—feels ritualistic. Intentional.

At the center of the table, a woman with silver-streaked hair lifts her glass. "To remembrance," she says, the words soft but absolute.

The others echo in perfect harmony. "To remembrance."

I hesitate, then raise my glass because not doing so feels like a breach I can't afford. The word tastes strange, familiar, like a prayer I don't remember learning.

Across the table, Silas is watching me. His eyes catch the firelight—gray-green deepened to storm. For an instant, it's like he's seeing through the moment, past the dinner, past the years. Then the others laugh, and the air eases again.

Later, when the plates are cleared and the guests drift toward the adjoining library, Silas leans close, voice pitched for me alone. "You look like you've been here before."

"Maybe in a dream," I say, only half joking.

"Dreams remember more than we do," he murmurs. "And sometimes, they tell us what's coming."

The way he says it sends a shiver down my spine—half fear, half something else.

Most of the guests leave before midnight, coats and laughter trailing into the cold. I linger near the fire, the last sip of wine warming my throat, while Silas sees them out. When the door closes behind the final goodbye, the townhouse exhales—its grandeur shrinking into quiet.

He returns with his sleeves rolled up, the top buttons of his shirt undone, carrying a stack of plates to the kitchen. "You don't have to stay and help," he says, glancing back at me.

"I know," I answer, setting my glass aside and following anyway. "But you cooked."

"True," he concedes, mouth curving faintly. "And I don't argue with a woman offering to restore balance."

The kitchen feels different than the rest of the house—less museum, more heart. Copper pans hang above a butcher-block island, and herbs dry in bunches from the beams. The smell of rosemary and lemon lingers in the air. I roll up my sleeves and start rinsing plates, aware of him beside me, close enough that the space between us hums.

He dries a glass, the sound of the cloth against crystal barely audible. "You were quiet tonight," he says. "Did the company unsettle you?"

"Not exactly." I pause, watching the water swirl down the drain. "They were... familiar. But not in a way I can explain."

His reflection meets mine in the dark window above the sink. "You don't have to explain. Familiarity has many names."

Something in his tone makes me look away. "That toast—'to remembrance'—what was that about?"

"A tradition." He places the glass down, neatly aligned with the rest. "A reminder that forgetting is a choice, and remembering is a burden worth carrying."

"That sounds like something from a sermon."

He smiles, faint but genuine. "Or a warning."

We finish the dishes in silence. The warmth from the oven and the soft glow of the fire through the doorway make everything feel hazy, intimate. When I turn to hand him the last plate, he's closer than I expected.

"Thank you," he says quietly. "For trusting me enough to be here."

The words land deeper than they should. My pulse catches. "You make it sound like trust is a rare thing."

"It is," he replies. "But not impossible."

Something shifts between us then—something that feels both inevitable and forbidden. His gaze dips to my lips, then lifts again, restrained. He doesn't move closer, doesn't touch. The restraint itself feels like a touch.

"Come," he says at last, breaking the tension with practiced grace. "You haven't seen the library properly."

He leads me through an archway lined with carved molding into a room that smells of smoke, ink, and age. The shelves rise nearly to the ceiling, filled with volumes bound in leather and cloth, spines stamped in fading gold. A fire burns low in the hearth, its reflection dancing across the glass of a framed map above the mantel.

Books fill every corner—stacked, layered, alive. Yet one shelf catches my eye immediately: a collection behind glass, each spine marked with a sigil I recognize from the night's toast.

"What are those?" I ask.

Silas's voice lowers, almost reverent. "Records. Histories. Some truths need protection more than others."

"Protection from what?"

He meets my gaze. "From time."

Something about the answer makes the air feel too thin. I step closer to the case, the faint heat from the fire brushing against my skin. My fingers hover above the glass but don't touch. Inside, one of the volumes looks newer—its leather less worn, its seal uncracked.

Before I can ask, Silas moves beside me. "Some things aren't ready to be remembered yet."

His proximity pulls the question right out of me. The words die unspoken.

He gestures toward the hallway instead. "Your room is just down there—the second door on the left. I made sure it was warm."

"Thank you," I manage, though my throat feels tight.

At the doorway, I pause and look back. He's standing by the fire, a shadow carved in gold and smoke, watching me with that same quiet intensity that feels almost like knowing.

"Goodnight, Celeste," he says softly.

"Goodnight."

When I reach the room, the warmth hits me first—subtle, like someone turned the sheets just before I arrived. My bag sits by the window, the glass clouded with frost. I sit on the edge of the bed, heart still steadying, the echo of his voice in my mind. Trust. Remembrance. Protection.

All words that sound like promises.

Or warnings.

Chapter 21
Elias

The precinct feels hollow today. Half the desks sit empty, chairs left in half-turns like the people who use them just vanished mid-sentence. The smell of old coffee and reheated takeout lingers under the hum of the fluorescents. Somewhere outside, Boston exhales in quiet celebration—parades, football, laughter rising through the cold. Inside, the only sound is the tick of the clock and the slow scratch of my pen.

Thanksgiving. A holiday built on pretending everything's fine. That we should be grateful.

I push the thought aside and face the board again. Four victims now—Wexler, Lexington, Corbett, Harren. Each file stacked with color-coded tabs, each scene arranged like a sermon disguised as tragedy. The rhythm's undeniable now. Each month, a new body. Each death deliberate.

Each message written in method, not words.

Which means the next one is close.

I draw a slow breath, eyes following the red thread stretched between the photos. July. August. September. October.

November's square is still empty. It won't stay that way for long.

Outside, the city looks rinsed clean from last night's rain—pavement slick, trees stripped bare. Cold light cuts through the blinds, thin and gray. Freddy left early this morning, muttering something about "stuffing over corpses" and refusing to let me ruin his appetite. He's not wrong.

I should've gone to my sister's in Providence. She texted twice—said there'd be pie, that the kids keep asking about Uncle Eli. I told her I had a deadline. That's the lie I tell every year.

Corbett's photo catches the light, her smile too bright beside the glossy shots from the gala. I still see her house when I close my eyes—the pale walls, the glass cases of awards, the careful perfection of it all. And underneath, the rot.

The coffee's burnt. I drink it anyway, let it bite.

Beside her, the file marked *Harren* feels heavier. The doctor who turned his home into a theater, who thought he could play savior. His death was louder than the others—bloodier, more deliberate. Which means whoever's doing this is escalating. Or getting comfortable.

The names blur if I stare too long. I drag a hand over my jaw, flipping through my notes. The thread isn't proximity—it's legacy. They're all tied to the same machinery: courtrooms, settlements, verdicts that bent instead of broke. Every single one of them touched by justice, then let go.

I turn another page in Corbett's file and stop at a name I almost missed. Robert Vennett. Property developer. Major donor to her foundation. Frequent guest at her events.

He was there the night she died.

The chill that moves through me isn't imagination. He fits the timeline. The pattern. The escalation.

If the rhythm holds, he's next.

The thought lands heavy, settling somewhere between instinct and inevitability. And beneath it, that same faint hum—the one that's lived under my skin for as long as I can remember. It sharpens when danger's close, when truth gets near.

But it quiets when I'm around her.

Celeste.

There's something about her I can't explain. The air steadies when she's near, like the noise in me finally finds its key. Maybe it's her voice, the calm in it that doesn't match the chaos she transcribes. Or maybe it's something older—recognition wrapped in disguise.

I look back at the board, the empty square waiting for November's name. The thread between them all feels alive, humming through the air like current.

And I can't shake the sense that whatever this is—this rhythm, this reckoning—she's woven into it. The only question is how.

I flip to the map pinned behind me. Salem. Boston. Seaport. Beacon Hill. Each mark is connected by faint lines, stretching toward the harbor. The pattern almost looks intentional—like a spiral folding inward. If that's true, the next point lands somewhere south. Ashwell. Maybe Dorchester.

My phone buzzes. A message from Freddy.

"Don't forget to eat something. And if you start seeing patterns in your mashed potatoes, call me before you go full Beautiful Mind with your gravy."

I almost smile. Almost.

The clock reads 4:17 PM. Outside, the light is already dying, the city dressed in that thin gold that only lasts a minute before it turns to gray. I close the folder, but my thoughts won't stop.

Someone out there is planning their next move.
And this time, I intend to get there first.

The thought settles in like static, low and insistent. I tell myself it's just the job—one more lead to clear before the weekend. But halfway across the city, the lie thins, and I can feel the truth waiting on the other side of it.

Ashwell Commons rises out of the fog like a monument to wealth pretending to be modest—glass walls, pale stone, manicured hedges trimmed too neatly for November. The kind of place that smells like money even from the curb.

Vennett's home sits at the end of a private drive, lights glowing warm through tall windows. I half expect someone else to answer the door—an assistant, a wife, a housekeeper—but it's him.

Robert Vennett. Mid-fifties, fit, silver at the temples that probably costs more than my monthly rent to maintain. The man smells faintly of cedar, scotch, and success.

"Detective Shaw," I say, flashing my badge. "Sorry to interrupt your evening. I know it's Thanksgiving."

He gives me a smooth smile that doesn't quite reach his eyes. "No trouble at all. I was just catching the second half. Family's out of town, so it's just me and the dog. You want a drink?"

"Appreciate it, but I'm on duty."

"Suit yourself." He steps aside, gesturing me in. The foyer gleams—marble tile, minimalist art, the kind of silence you can only buy. "So, what brings Boston's finest to my door on a holiday?"

"I wanted to ask a few questions about Marlene Corbett," I say, keeping my tone even. "You attended her gala last month, correct?"

He nods, walking toward the sitting room. "Of course. I was one of the sponsors. Terrible what happened to her. The city lost a good one."

The same rehearsed line I've heard a dozen times.

I take in the room while he talks: the football game muted on a widescreen, glass decanter sweating beside a half-empty tumbler, family photos turned just enough to look casual. "You two knew each other well?"

"Well enough. She was persuasive when it came to fundraising." He chuckles, takes a sip of his drink. "You don't say no to Marlene Corbett. Not if you want to keep your name off her bad side."

"You had joint ventures together, didn't you? Real estate acquisitions, redevelopment projects?"

Vennett lifts a brow. "Every business deal has a paper trail, Detective. I'm sure if you've dug that far, you already know which ones were legitimate."

"I like to hear it from the source."

His smile tightens. "Then here's your sound bite: everything I did with Marlene was aboveboard. You can check the filings. Hell, I'll even have my attorney email you the records if it helps you sleep better."

"Appreciate the offer," I say, letting a faint edge into my voice. "You also knew Lionel Harren?"

He sets the glass down, eyes narrowing just enough to notice. "We sat on the same charitable board. Why?"

"Just mapping connections. Similar circles, overlapping events."

"You think I'm next, is that it?" His laugh is too quick, too practiced. "That's why you're here? To warn me?"

"Maybe." I meet his gaze. "You've been in proximity to three victims. All of whom had... flexible interpretations of ethics. You see why I'd be concerned."

Vennett exhales through his nose, a ghost of a smirk returning. "Detective, I appreciate your vigilance, but I'm not in the habit of dying for other people's sins."

"No one ever is," I say quietly.

He studies me for a beat longer, then tilts his head. "You look tired, Shaw. You ever take a day off? Go home, have dinner, watch a game?"

"Not lately."

"Maybe that's your problem." He raises his glass in a mock toast. "You spend too long staring at the dark, you start thinking it's looking back. Take it from someone who's seen his share of headlines."

"Headlines don't kill people," I say.

"No," he agrees, "but they sure as hell bury them."

The air shifts. He turns back toward the television, dismissing me without saying it outright. I close my notebook slowly.

"Thank you for your time, Mr. Vennett."

"Anytime, Detective. Happy Thanksgiving."

I nod once and step out into the cold. The night air hits like clarity—sharp, bracing, full of the kind of silence that comes before a storm. His lights stay bright behind me, gold and steady against the gray.

I linger by the car longer than I should, watching the reflection of the house ripple in a shallow puddle by the curb.

He's too calm. Too confident.

Either he's innocent—

or he already knows he's next.

The air outside Vennett's house bites sharper now, the kind of cold that seeps through gloves and into bone. The streets are mostly empty—Boston's quiet for once, emptied out by food and football. I start the car and drive a few blocks before pulling into a dimly lit lot beside a closed florist shop. The irony doesn't escape me.

There's a diner still open across the street, its neon sign flickering between *EAT* and *AT*. I duck inside, order black coffee and whatever passes for dinner this late. The waitress gives me a look that says she's seen too many of me—tired men in rumpled coats chasing ghosts instead of holidays.

By the time I'm back in the car, the sky's gone slate-dark, and the city's hush feels heavier. I park halfway down Vennett's street, engine off, lights out. From here, I've got a clean line of sight to his house—the broad front windows, the faint movement of the television, the silhouette pacing every now and then across the second floor.

Stakeouts are ninety percent waiting, nine percent self-doubt, and one percent gut instinct you can't shake.

Right now, that instinct feels like static in my veins.

I eat in silence, the sandwich dry and forgettable, my focus locked on the golden square of light from his living room. Every now and then, a passing car throws a brief flash of color across the wet pavement, then it's gone again. The neighborhood feels too still—too composed, like the world's holding its breath.

I jot a few notes between sips of lukewarm coffee: **Pattern proximity. Behavior steady. Timeline approaching reset.**

The radio murmurs through the static, a half-hearted holiday song about gratitude and forgiveness. I turn it off.

Hours slide by. The moon drifts behind a thick bank of clouds, and the temperature dips another few degrees. Around ten-thirty, the house lights shift—second floor going dark, ground floor still glowing. Vennett's moving slower now, the way people do when they think the night's over.

I should go home. But I don't.

Instead, I roll the window down just enough to feel the cold. The air carries the faint scent of pine and salt from the harbor. There's something else under it too—something I can't quite place.

At 11:04, the motion changes. A shadow crosses one of the windows, quick, deliberate.

Then nothing.

I sit forward, pulse tightening. The light from the living room flickers once, twice—then cuts out entirely. The house is swallowed by darkness.

I wait. Count the seconds in my head. One minute. Two. Three.

Then the sound reaches me.

A short, sharp noise—like glass breaking somewhere deep inside.

"Shit."

I'm out of the car before I can think about it, badge in one hand, flashlight in the other. The wind knifes through my coat as I move up the street, quiet but fast. The house looms ahead, all glass and shadow, and for a moment it feels like walking toward a mouth that's just learned how to smile.

I reach the front door, listen. Nothing. No movement, no sound. Just the soft rattle of branches against the siding.

When I try the handle, it gives. Unlocked.

Every instinct screams wrong.

Still, I push the door open.

Chapter 22
Killer

The knife's reflection trembles in the glass, thin and bright as a breath.

He doesn't hear me at first. Most of them don't. He's talking to someone on speaker—slurred, jovial—thanking a friend for a good game, promising to call again soon. His voice fills the house like the ghost of a man who believes himself untouchable.

I stand behind the archway, watching the light of the television dance across the marble floor. Everything about him hums with comfort—the loosened collar, the bare feet, the scotch sweating on the table. A man who built his kingdom on other people's roofs and called it progress.

Robert Vennett.

Urban developer. Philanthropist. Parasite.

He calls it "revitalization." I call it eviction. Families displaced for profit. Subsidies pocketed, inspections bypassed. He built towers where homes once stood and sold the sky by the square foot.

"You took what wasn't yours," I whisper, voice almost drowned by the wind.

He doesn't turn until the lights flicker.

"Hello?"

The sound of his voice tightens something inside me—familiar, inevitable. The hum beneath my skin steadies, finding rhythm. I step forward.

He spins, half-laughing at first, mistaking me for the security he swears is always on call. Then he sees my eyes. His confusion curdles to fear.

"What—who—"

He doesn't finish. The syringe slides neatly against his neck, quick as a heartbeat. His body stiffens, mouth opening but no sound escapes. The paralysis hits fast, clean.

"I told myself I wouldn't intervene again so soon," I murmur, guiding him backward into the study. "But balance doesn't wait for convenience."

His breath rasps, shallow. His pupils dilate, wide and pleading. He tries to move—fails.

Stacks of folders line the desk—tenant reports, construction bids, environmental assessments all marked *APPROVED*. The perfect camouflage for decay. I sweep them aside. The hum in my chest grows louder, almost like a pulse echoing through the house.

"Do you know what they said about you?" I ask softly. "That you made neighborhoods better. Safer. Cleaner." I trace the blade across his wrist, just enough for the first crimson bead to bloom. "You made them empty."

He jerks, soundless, eyes wet now with tears he'll never shed in apology.

"Don't worry. It'll be slow. Awareness is part of penance."

The cut is measured, surgical. Not deep enough for mercy. The second mirrors it perfectly. Blood pools over the papers, soaking the ink until words blur and run together—deeds, permits, signatures dissolving into one red smear. The smell is thick and metallic, curling through the air like a struck coin left too long in a closed hand.

He stares at me—lips trembling, breath shallow, eyes wide with the terrible clarity of someone who finally understands what's been done in his name. The pulse at his throat slows. Each drop that slides from the edge of the desk lands softly on the hardwood, a metronome keeping time with his fading life.

I move around him with careful precision. This part always matters—the symmetry, the silence, the sense of order restored.

From the stack of documents, I draw out a single sheet—a blueprint of his latest "redevelopment." A plan that erased an entire block of homes and called it progress. I fold it once, twice, until it fits neatly in my palm. My gloves are slick with blood, leaving faint smudges across the paper as I smooth it over his chest. A map of greed covering the heart that never knew guilt.

"You built foundations from displacement," I whisper, angling his chin toward the window. "Let the city see what it cost."

The moonlight filters through the blinds, pale and unwavering. It cuts across his face in perfect lines, dividing him into light and shadow. For a moment, it looks like fire flickering under his skin.

I turn back to the desk. The files are stacked high—tenant lists, acquisition contracts, relocation forms—each one stamped and initialed by his steady hand. I sweep them into a loose circle around him, edges touching, forming a ring of confession. The last page I set before him reads *Approved for demolition.* His name loops clean and proud at the bottom.

When I step back, the scene feels whole. Balanced. The hum beneath my skin slows to a rhythm that feels almost sacred.

"You thought legacy was something you could buy," I murmur. "Now it's something you've paid for."

The knife slides back into its sheath with a soft click. I wipe the handle clean and leave it beside the ledger of documents. Then I switch off the lamp.

Darkness folds around me, but the city's glow spills faintly through the glass—thin, silvery, enough to paint the room in quiet ruin. The hum beneath my ribs doesn't fade; it deepens, a pulse steady as breath, thrumming with something that feels less like peace and more like warning. I sense him before I see him, the sweep of headlights sliding slow across the far wall, deliberate as a thought. I move to the window. Down the road, under the edge of the streetlamp, a car idles—engine low, exhaust ghosting into the cold. I can feel him even from here. **Detective Shaw.** Always closer than he should be.

"You're early," I whisper. "Too soon, Detective."

The hum sharpens, crawling beneath my skin, restless and knowing. I step away from the window, crossing the carpet in silence. By the time I reach the back stairwell, the house feels suspended between breaths—no wind, no sound, only the slow spread of blood over paper and the faint rhythm of my pulse echoing through the walls. Outside, the air is brittle, the sky wide and indifferent. Boston sleeps under its thin layer of snow, unaware that justice has shifted again. Another name crossed from the ledger that isn't mine. Another balance restored.

But the hum won't settle. It climbs, urgent, pressing against my ribs like it wants to speak. Maybe it's because he's here—the detective who doesn't know what he's chasing, the one who keeps finding me anyway. I turn toward the streetlight, toward the car still waiting at the curb. "You shouldn't have come," I murmur, almost tenderly. Then I slip into the night, the air closing behind me like water.

Snow whispers against the ground as I move through the alley. The city's usual rhythm has gone still, muted beneath the hush of cold and distance. I tell myself it's over—that the balance is kept—but the hum trembles on, low and insistent, a warning I can't yet name. Then I hear it: a faint mechanical whine from up the street, headlights dimming, engine cutting out, a door opening and closing with deliberate care. Sound travels differently in weather like this—clean, exact. Whoever it is doesn't want to be noticed.

I freeze near the treeline, breath ghosting white in the dark. The hum sharpens until it buzzes behind my teeth. He's here. I can't see him yet, but I know the rhythm of his movement—the steady, measured stride, the pause before each step. Elias Shaw doesn't stumble into places; he haunts them.

I edge back toward shadow, keeping low. The house sits behind me like a heartbeat—light leaking faintly through drawn curtains, warm and un-aware. Then the hum changes again—higher, impatient—and something shifts inside. A flicker of movement at the window. Light sputters once, twice, and dies. The night inhales.

Glass breaks—sharp, sudden—and I flinch, instinct dragging my gaze toward the sound. It came from inside, the kind of shatter that means struggle, not accident. He's closer now. I can hear the scrape of his boots on asphalt, the low growl of breath between clenched teeth. "Shit," he mutters, just loud enough to carry. The flashlight cuts through the dark, slicing across the lawn as he starts up the walk—badge out, jaw tight, that edge of recklessness he wears like a second pulse.

For one brief heartbeat, the urge to warn him flickers through me—absurd, dangerous, human. I swallow it down. He's already inside the story. All I can do now is keep it from devouring me too. The hum steadies, turning cold and clear. I step backward, one foot at a time, until the street curves and the light from the house disappears.

Behind me, the night swallows the sound of shattering glass and rushing footsteps, leaving only the echo of balance shifting again—subtle, inexorable, inevitable. I stop at the end of the street, half-hidden in shadow, the cold cutting deep enough to remind me I'm still here. The hum begins to slow, settling into something quieter, something that almost feels like grief. It's never supposed to linger, this ache after the act, but lately it does. The stillness doesn't soothe anymore; it presses in—heavy, watchful, aware. Each time the scales even out, the silence grows louder, as if the world is waiting for me to admit what I already suspect.

This was never only about justice.

It's about remembering what I was before I became this—

a name, a promise, a wound that never healed right.

Chapter 23
Elias

"**D**ispatch, this is Detective Shaw," I say into the radio, keeping my voice low. "Possible break-in at the Vennett residence. Lights out, possible movement inside. Requesting backup and forensics on standby."

Static crackles before the reply cuts through. *"Copy that, Detective. Units en route. ETA six minutes."*

Six minutes can mean a lifetime.

I move closer to the house, flashlight steady in one hand, badge glinting faintly in the other. The front yard is too quiet—no wind, no motion, not even the rustle of leaves. The kind of quiet that waits for something to happen.

The glass on the porch door catches the beam of my light. A hairline crack spiders out from the corner—fresh. I crouch, brushing my fingers along the edge. Cool. Still wet from the last trace of condensation. Whatever broke it happened minutes ago.

"Vennett?" I call softly. No answer.

I should wait for backup. But the thought of standing out here while something unfolds inside…

I can't. Not again.

I ease the door open. The hinges whisper, and the smell hits me first—copper and ozone, faint but sharp. Blood. Old wood polish. A trace of paper dust.

I step inside, careful, the beam sweeping over framed photographs, the edges of an open briefcase, a half-empty tumbler of bourbon. Everything is in place except the silence—it's too complete, the kind that only happens when a room has already decided to hold its breath.

"Boston PD," I call again, voice low but firm. "Mr. Vennett, if you're home, I need you to answer me."

Nothing.

The house feels wrong—too still, too curated. Like it's waiting for me to see what I shouldn't. I take another step, boots creaking against hardwood, the smell of iron growing thicker.

The hum of the radio on my shoulder is the only sound. *"Units are two minutes out,"* dispatch says.

"Copy," I mutter, but I barely hear myself. My pulse is already syncing to that other rhythm—the same one that's haunted me since Salem, since the rain, since the first body that made no sense.

The flashlight finds the trail next: a faint drag mark across the floorboards, thin but deliberate. It leads down the hallway toward the office door, cracked open just enough to show the edge of a desk lamp.

I tighten my grip on the light, swallow hard, and step forward. I stop at the threshold. The door is half-closed, angled just enough for the light to slide through and kiss the edge of a desk.

Everything in me says don't.

Procedure says wait for backup. Logic says six minutes is nothing. But instinct—the thing that's kept me breathing this long—leans forward anyway.

The handle is cold under my fingers. Too cold. The metal's slick, maybe from the condensation or maybe from something else. I ease it down, the latch clicking softly like a held breath giving out.

The door shifts. A narrow strip of the room opens before me.

The smell hits first—thick and metallic, riding the air in waves. It's familiar, the kind of scent that settles into your clothes and refuses to leave. Blood, and too much of it.

My flashlight finds the floor—shadows twisting under the desk, the faint shine of liquid across the hardwood, lines intersecting like a blueprint gone wrong. My stomach tightens.

The silence feels alive now. A weight pressing against my ears, daring me to move another inch.

Somewhere down the block, the first wail of sirens cuts through the night—thin, sharp, and closing fast. The sound fractures the moment, breaking the stillness into something fragile and temporary.

I take a step closer but stop just short of the doorway.

"Vennett?" My voice sounds wrong in the quiet, too human for the space it lands in.

No answer. Just the faint tick of cooling metal.

I could step inside. Just one foot. Just enough to see. But the voice that's kept me alive—the one that remembers Jensen, the one that still wakes me up at night—says don't. Not yet.

The sirens are louder now. Red and blue flash faintly through the window blinds, painting stripes across the hall.

I pull back, jaw tight, flashlight beam trembling against the edge of the doorframe. Whatever's in that room isn't going anywhere.

"Yeah," I whisper to myself, the words barely sound. "We'll do this by the book this time."

I back away just as the first cruiser turns the corner, tires spitting gravel.

The door swings a little wider behind me—only an inch—but enough for the smell to pour out stronger. Enough to tell me, without seeing, that I was right to wait.

Headlights flash through the narrow front windows, washing the hallway in white before fading to pulsing blue and red. Tires grind against the curb, car doors slam, and the silence fractures into motion—radio chatter, footsteps, the clipped tones of first responders switching gears from routine to alert.

I step out onto the porch, hand raised in a brief signal. "Single scene," I call to the nearest uniform. "Probable homicide. Don't contaminate the entryway. Blood's fresh."

The techs move fast, efficient even in the cold. Plastic boot covers, gloves, rolling cases of evidence kits. The kind of choreography that only comes from too much practice.

Freddy's van pulls up a few minutes later, his headlights flickering once as if in greeting. He steps out with his usual half-finished coffee in hand, coat collar up against the November wind, dark hair tied back loosely. "You couldn't wait until after the holiday, huh?"

I huff a dry sound that isn't quite a laugh. "Trust me, not my plan."

He joins me at the door, scanning the porch and the faint trail of blood that stops just before the entry. His eyes narrow slightly. "That smell's not hours old."

"Minutes," I say quietly. "Light flickered out when I got here. I called it in before moving further."

Freddy gives me that look—the one that sits somewhere between respect and reprimand. "You actually waited this time?"

"I'm learning."

He snorts. "Miracles do happen." Then, to his team: "Set up containment from the front hallway. Lights, angles, full coverage before we touch a damn thing."

Inside, the rhythmic click of camera shutters begins. The flash bounces off the walls in sterile bursts, painting the house in staccato glimpses. Every sound feels too loud—gloves stretching, boots squeaking, radios murmuring static.

I stay in the doorway, watching the line of tape go up, the slow bloom of light from their portable rigs.

Freddy leans closer. "You see anything before we arrived?"

"Not much. A broken pane on the porch door. Trail leads into the office."

He nods, already pulling on a second pair of gloves. "Then let's hope whatever did this left us something worth chasing."

He disappears down the hall, his flashlight beam joining the harsh glow of the portable lamps. I don't follow. Not yet.

From where I stand, I can see just enough—the slant of the office door, the glint of something metallic on the floor, the smear of red reflecting the light. The smell hits again, thicker now that the air's moving.

Another voice calls from inside: "We've got pooling—north corner, heavy saturation. Paper soaked through. Looks like files."

Freddy's voice, steady and low: "Don't touch them yet."

I rest my hand on the doorframe, thumb pressed against the grain of the wood until it hurts. The hum of the scene fills the space between my thoughts—the sound of people documenting, recording, preserving. The only kind of order we can make from chaos.

I should go in. That's my job. But for once, I let myself wait.

Outside, the night feels colder. The sirens have gone quiet. Somewhere down the street, a porch light flickers on, then off again.

I take a breath and keep my eyes on the threshold. Whatever's waiting in that room, I already know it won't be justice. Just another entry in a pattern I can't stop seeing.

"Okay," Freddy calls, his tone shifting into that steady, clinical cadence he uses when a scene starts to open up. "We've got arterial spray low, consistent with deep cuts—probably self-defense or restraint before bleed-out. No immediate sign of struggle beyond displacement on the desk. Everything else..." He trails off, crouching. "Too neat."

I step closer now, the sound of my boots softened by the plastic mats the team has already laid. The office smells like copper and dust, like the aftermath of a burned wire.

The light catches the edges of Freddy's gloves as he lifts a sheet of paper from the desk. It's soaked through, edges curling from the moisture, the ink running into illegible veins.

"Blueprints," he says, turning the page slightly. "Some kind of property layout. Blood pattern suggests it was placed intentionally—centered."

I move around the edge of the desk, careful not to cross into the marked perimeter. Vennett's body slumps in the chair, his head tilted toward the side window. His hands rest flat against the blotter, palms up, the wrists slit with precision.

Freddy adjusts his flashlight. "Both cuts mirror each other. Same depth, same angle. Surgical precision. Not a panicked attack—measured."

"Same as the others," I say quietly.

He glances at me, the briefest acknowledgment of what we both know but can't yet say out loud. "You think we're dealing with the same person?"

"I think whoever did this has a sense of ritual."

Freddy exhales through his nose. "Well, that narrows it down to anyone who's ever watched a true-crime documentary."

One of the techs lifts a blood sample into a vial. Another photographs the documents spread across the floor. They're arranged in a rough circle—permits, contracts, letters—each overlapping the other, all of them stained in the same deep red.

"Paper trail," Freddy murmurs, crouching again. "Looks like zoning permits, environmental assessments. City records."

"Same type of target," I say, half to myself. "People tied to money, construction, law. Corbett with her charities, Lexington with his factories, now Vennett with zoning and redevelopment."

"Pattern," Freddy says softly.

"Yeah," I answer. "But it's more than that. It's... symbolic."

He nods once, standing. "Maybe. Or maybe it's someone with a flair for the dramatic."

A camera flashes again, white light bouncing across the papers and catching the thin glint of something on Vennett's cuff—gold ink, faint but visible. Freddy notices it too, bending close.

"Looks like someone marked him," he says. "You ever see anything like this?"

I lean over his shoulder. The sigil is simple but deliberate, drawn in a looping, circular hand. It's too clean to be random.

"No," I say. "But whoever they are, they're getting bolder."

Freddy straightens, scribbling notes into his pad. "I'll get tox rushed. Let's see what his bloodstream has to say."

I nod but don't answer. My gaze drifts back to the blueprint—creased, blood-soaked, still perfectly centered on the desk like a signature.

The hum of voices fades behind me. All I can hear is the faint ticking of the wall clock, counting down to something I can't name.

This wasn't just a killing. It's a message.

And whoever's writing it knows I'm starting to read between the lines.

Chapter 24
Celeste

I come back to myself standing in the library. For a few long seconds, the world won't focus—the shadows blur at the edges, the air cold enough to sting when I breathe. The fire has burned to embers, faint red veins pulsing against the grate. Somewhere behind me, a clock ticks soft and patient. 3:07 a.m.

I'm still dressed. My sleeves are damp, my hair clings to my neck, and the chill in my clothes feels bone-deep, like I've been outside for hours. When I flex my fingers, dirt flakes from beneath my nails. The faint smell of wet stone and smoke clings to my skin. My hand is raised, hovering inches from the glass case of books—the same locked shelf as before, the one with the sigiled spines. The nearest volume catches what little light remains, gold embossing flickering like a heartbeat. I shouldn't be this close. I shouldn't even be awake.

"How did I get—" The question dies before I finish it.

A voice answers from the dark. "You shouldn't be here."

The sound roots me where I stand—low, measured, steady as breath. I turn slowly. Silas steps out of the shadowed doorway, the darkness clinging to him like it belongs there. His clothes are immaculate—black shirt, black slacks, not a trace of color. His hair falls loose across his forehead; his eyes catch the emberlight and hold it. Gray-green. Unreadable.

"I—" My voice catches, too loud in the stillness. "I must've been sleep-walking. I don't remember—"

"I know." His tone is calm, almost kind. "You've done it before."

My pulse falters. "What?"

He studies me with quiet precision. "You've wandered like this every night since the lake. You always end up here."

I step back, the edge of the rug bunching beneath my heel. "You're saying this isn't the first time?"

He tilts his head slightly, as if weighing how much to tell me. "You don't remember."

"I—no. I don't."

"That's all right." His voice lowers, smooth as smoke. "Memory's an unreliable witness. It keeps what serves and buries the rest." He moves closer, slow enough that I can hear the soft drag of his shoes on the floor. The firelight bends around him, dimming everything else. My breath hitches, though I can't tell if it's the cold or the pull of his voice.

"Does this room draw you?" he asks quietly.

I glance toward the case. The shimmer on the glass looks almost alive. "I don't know. Maybe."

"You do." He stops beside me, close enough that I feel the warmth of him through the chill still clinging to my clothes. "Something in you remembers."

The words slip into me like a hook, gentle but sure. "I should go back to bed," I whisper.

"Should you?" His gaze drops to my sleeves, still damp, then returns to my face. "You've been outside."

"I don't—remember."

"I know," he murmurs again. "You never do." For a heartbeat, something like regret shadows his expression. "I always manage to get you home before you wake."

The room tilts slightly. My throat tightens, and I don't know if it's fear or shame or something far more dangerous. I take a step back, needing distance, needing breath. The air hums between us, charged and quiet, as the clock ticks on—3:08, 3:09—each second too loud, too deliberate.

"What's happening to me?" I mean to whisper it only to myself, but the sound breaks open the stillness anyway.

Silas watches me for a long moment before he answers. "You're remembering what you were," he says softly. "And what you're becoming."

The silence between us thickens until even the house seems to hold its breath. Silas reaches past me, fingers brushing mine as he locks the glass case. The faint click sounds final—like the closing of a confession.

"I'll walk you back," he says.

I nod, unable to look away from him. Together we step into the hallway, the fire's glow fading behind us. When I glance back, I swear the glass catches one last flicker of light—as if another face is watching from inside.

The corridor feels too long, the air too still. A single wall sconce spills gold along the banister, painting half his face in light and leaving the rest in shadow. The house waits around us, quiet and listening. I mean to thank him, to apologize, to make the night small again—but the words never come.

He walks a half step behind me, the sound of his shoes soft against the floorboards. When I reach the guest room door, I pause with my hand on the frame. My pulse beats too loudly in the silence. "Thank you," I manage, though it comes out thinner than I expect.

He nods once but doesn't step back. His presence hums against the edge of my awareness—warm, steady, unyielding. The scent of smoke and chai clings to him, threaded through with something darker, metallic, like rain on iron.

"You shouldn't have to be afraid of yourself," he says quietly.

I meet his gaze. "Then why do I feel like I should be?"

"Because you were taught to. To fear what you can't explain. To mistake power for danger."

His words settle over me like truth and warning all at once. "And what do you see when you look at me?" I ask. "Power? Danger?"

"Both," he answers without hesitation.

The space between us closes before I realize I've moved. His hand lifts, slow enough for me to stop him if I wanted to. I don't. His fingers find a loose strand of hair and trace it back behind my ear, his touch barely there, almost reverent. The heat of it spreads down my throat like a pulse remembering itself.

"You're cold," he murmurs.

I should step back, but I don't. "You found me in the library," I whisper. "You said I've done it before. Why didn't you stop me?"

"I did." His voice roughens. "Every night since the lake. You wander until the world calls you back, and I always manage to get you home before you wake."

The words land heavy—tender, unsettling, intimate in a way that feels wrong. My breath catches. "Why?"

He studies me for a long, silent moment. "Because there's more to the world than you remember. And I'm here to bring that to the surface."

His gaze holds mine until the rest of the house fades away. There's a devotion in it that feels like worship, and for one dizzy heartbeat, I wonder if I've been mistaken all along—if he's not guarding me, but guarding whatever *this* is, whatever he thinks I am.

"Silas..." My name in his mouth would sound like prayer, I think, if he said it now.

He steps closer instead, close enough that his breath warms my cheek. "The time is coming," he says softly, "when you won't need to hide from what you are."

I don't know if he's warning me or promising something holy. His hand lifts again, and before I can decide, I reach for him. Our fingers brush, and the air between us sharpens. Then his other hand finds the back of my neck, and the distance disappears.

The kiss is barely there at first—a tremor, a question—but it deepens before I can stop it. He tastes like warmth and ruin, like smoke and salt, something ancient and consuming. When he finally breaks away, his forehead rests against mine, his breath unsteady.

"This isn't wise," he whispers.

"No," I breathe. "But it's real."

Something flickers behind his eyes—devotion, grief, maybe both. He presses one last kiss to the corner of my mouth, softer than the first, and steps back. "Sleep," he says. "You'll need it."

He turns and walks down the hall, his shadow stretching long behind him until it fades into darkness. For a long time after he's gone, I stand there with my hand on the doorframe, the taste of him still on my lips and the echo of his words still in my chest. When I finally step inside my room and close the door, my hands won't stop trembling—not from fear, but from the certainty that something vast and unseen just shifted. Something I can't take back.

His footsteps fade down the hall, but the silence he leaves hums through the walls, low and steady. It crawls across my skin, syncs with the pulse still hammering in my throat. I lean against the dresser, forcing a slow breath that won't steady. *God, what did I just do?*

The mirror catches the flicker of lamplight as I unfasten the top button of my blouse, then another. The fabric slides against my skin, his warmth lingering beneath it like an echo. My reflection looks altered—eyes too bright, lips still parted, color high in my cheeks. I barely recognize the woman looking back. "This isn't you," I whisper, though even I can hear the lie in it.

Every sermon, every warning, every whispered threat of damnation presses against my ribs like a hand. Virtue as armor. Desire as sin. The body as evidence of guilt. I spent years making myself small enough to be good, quiet enough to be safe. But tonight, that discipline cracks. What fills the space isn't shame—it's pulse, heat, hunger. Want is the only thing keeping me upright.

I peel away the rest of my clothes, restless, each layer heavier than the last. The air bites cold against my skin, but beneath it my blood burns. I stop by the window, moonlight spilling pale across the floorboards, turning the room into something sacred and strange. I tell myself it's exhaustion, adrenaline, the intimacy of being seen. I tell myself it meant nothing. The lie frays as soon as I think it.

Because every time I close my eyes, I see the way he looked at me—steady, reverent, as if he were waiting for me to remember something I've forgotten. The memory of his hand at my throat feels less like danger and more like belonging.

I pull a thin nightdress over my head, the fabric clinging to skin too aware. My fingers tremble as I braid my damp hair over one shoulder. "Control," I whisper, like penance. The word feels weightless, already obsolete. Because underneath the guilt, something older stirs—patient, certain, familiar. The same hum that thrums through my dreams. The same pulse that answers his.

I sink onto the edge of the bed, burying my face in my hands. The air tastes electric. My heart won't calm; it beats like it's trying to tell me something I've spent a lifetime denying. When I look up, the clock reads 3:48 a.m. I don't remember sitting down, don't remember how long I've been caught between shame and something dangerously close to awe.

The house is too quiet. The silence presses against my ears until I can hear every breath, every tremor in my chest. And then I feel it—the pull.

Low, magnetic, alive. It isn't thought; it's instinct. My bare feet move before I can stop them, carrying me into the hall. The air thickens as I go, like the whole house is holding its breath again.

I stop outside his door. The handle is cold beneath my fingertips. Every rule, every lesson screams *turn back,* but the warnings sound distant, hollow. I can feel his heartbeat before I touch the door, steady and human—and something else beneath it, deeper, calling to me.

I open it.

The room is dim, silvered by moonlight that slips through tall windows and drapes itself over him. He lies turned toward the light, face half in shadow, chest rising slow and even. Peaceful. Vulnerable. A man at rest—or something pretending to be.

I linger in the doorway, my breath catching. I could still leave. I could close the door, bury this moment in denial. But the hum inside me grows louder, pulsing in rhythm with the faint rise and fall of his chest.

The floor creaks as I step closer. His breathing shifts, a soft intake that's almost a sigh. "Celeste," he murmurs, voice threaded with sleep and something that sounds too much like recognition.

I freeze. "I didn't mean to—"

"Yes, you did." His tone isn't unkind. It's factual. Absolute.

He doesn't move, and somehow that stillness pulls me closer. My pulse stumbles. "I couldn't sleep."

"I know." He exhales slowly, deliberately. "Come here."

The words settle in the air like a command—or a prayer.

The command is quiet but absolute. I don't remember crossing the distance between us, only the moment his hand finds mine, steady and warm, guiding me down beside him. The world contracts to sensation—the heat of his skin, the rhythm of his breath, the pulse of something unseen binding the space between us.

When his fingers brush the side of my throat, it feels like recognition—as if he's tracing a mark I've carried all my life without knowing it was there.

"This," he whispers against my skin, "is what you're afraid of."

He's right. But fear isn't what holds me still. It's the opposite. It's how right it feels—how my body answers before my mind can intervene. The hum inside me unfurls, widening until it fills everything, until it's all I can feel.

I tilt my head and his lips find mine—slow, searching, inevitable. The air seems to shiver, the faint taste of ozone and salt threading through the heat. When he pulls back, I'm breathless, heart hammering hard enough to hurt.

"You should go," he murmurs. "Before you forget how to stop."

Neither of us moves. The silence stretches until it feels like the house itself is listening.

"I already have," I whisper.

The world seems to pause, waiting. Then his hand slides to the back of my neck and the distance disappears.

Everything dissolves—sound, shape, thought—until there's only pulse and heat and the hum thrumming through both of us. The air vibrates, real, physical, like the space is alive. When his hands slide over my shoulders, down my spine, warmth blooms outward and the hum answers in kind. The scent of smoke, rain, skin. Beneath it all, something metallic, electric. For a heartbeat I forget where I end and he begins.

He breaks the kiss first, eyes searching mine. There's no arrogance there, no triumph—only recognition. Like he's waited lifetimes for me to remember.

"This isn't new," he says.

My breath stutters. "What do you mean?"

His thumb grazes my lip. "You've been dreaming of it long before you met me."

He's wrong—and yet the words ring true. Fragments flash behind my eyes: moonlight on water, gold reflected in glass, hands clasped in a place that doesn't belong to this world. The hum deepens, thickens, spilling through my veins until I can taste it. His breath catches; I see the crack in his composure, a flicker of awe, of fear.

"Celeste..."

The sound of my name in his voice feels like invocation, like the instant before lightning strikes. He leans forward again, giving me every chance to stop him. I don't.

When our mouths meet, the world tilts. The air rushes out of the room. The hum erupts into something vast—too big for breath, too deep for language. Light blooms behind my eyes; for a heartbeat, I see it clearly: veins of gold curling through the dark, ink spilling across creation. His hand, warm and seeking, drifts down my side, over my hip, and settles, cupping the warm curve of my pussy. A soft gasp escapes me as his thumb finds my clit, circling gently, then pressing, sending a jolt of pure pleasure through me.

Then everything goes white.

When I wake, the room is cold. The sheets are smooth beneath my palms, untouched, but my dress still clings damp to my skin. The faint smell of rain lingers in the air, sharp and clean, though the windows are closed. My heart slams once—hard—like it's trying to remember something my mind has already lost.

The clock reads 5:11 a.m. The house holds its breath. I sit up slowly, every muscle sore, as if I've been running in my sleep. My hair hangs heavy and wet down my back, curling against my collarbone. There's dirt beneath my nails again—dark, fine, the kind that comes from deep soil, not city dust.

"What…" The word disintegrates.

The lamp on the nightstand flickers once before settling. My reflection stares back from the mirror—pale, wide-eyed, pupils blown too large. For an instant the glass ripples, as though something beneath the surface moves with my pulse.

I tell myself to breathe. To stand. To believe it was a dream. But when I reach for the lamp, I see them—faint streaks of mud across the floorboards, leading from the door to the bed.

And beneath it all, that sound again: the hum. Low, steady, patient.

I sit there listening, heartbeat pounding in counter-rhythm. The air feels dense, as if the night itself is leaning close to listen. My fingertips find my mouth without thought. The touch ignites a spark—warmth, pressure, the ghost of a kiss that shouldn't be there. The memory dissolves as soon as I reach for it, leaving only sensation: heat, breath, surrender.

Pleasure curls through the cracks of memory, unwanted and unstoppable. It's too vivid to dismiss, too physical to be imagined. I remember wanting—helplessly, completely. I remember the way it felt to be *found*.

The rest scatters into flashes: his voice in the dark, the weight of a hand at my throat, light blooming behind my eyes.

I draw my knees up, the nightdress clinging damp to my skin. My throat burns, scraped raw from words I don't remember saying. I should feel shame, or fear, or both. Instead, there's only ache—a hollow pulse beneath my ribs that hums with something perilously close to longing.

My gaze drifts to the door. Closed. Silent. The house beyond is still, unbroken. It would be easy to pretend none of it happened—to tell myself the dream slipped too close to waking, that my imagination mistook desire for reality.

But when I lower my hand, the faint warmth on my lips lingers. Real. Solid. Unmistakable.

And I know, even without memory, that something crossed the threshold of this night.

Something that touched me, claimed me, marked me.

Something that isn't finished.

Chapter 25
Elias

New York smells the same—steam vents, exhaust, burnt coffee. It's almost comforting in the way old wounds sometimes are. The train down from Boston gave me too much time to think. About the case. About Corbett and Harren and Vennett. About Celeste. Especially her. Every line I draw, every thread I chase, circles back to her orbit—even when the dots don't connect.

The precinct hasn't changed. Same flickering fluorescents, same dent in the file room door, same front-desk sergeant who still calls everyone kid no matter how gray they get. I sign in, flash the badge out of habit, and make my way upstairs. Raines's door is open.

He looks older, or maybe I've just stopped pretending he isn't. White shirt sleeves rolled to the elbow, tie loose, glasses low on his nose. Coffee stains mark nearly every sheet of paper within reach. When he glances up and sees me, a grin breaks through the fatigue. "If it isn't my favorite headache. Shaw. Thought you'd fallen off the map."

"Boston's close enough," I tell him, stepping inside.

"Close enough to make trouble?"

"Something like that."

He gestures to the chair opposite his desk. "Sit. Tell me what kind of mess you're neck-deep in this time."

I drop into the seat, the wood groaning beneath me. "A series of deaths. All tied, at least loosely, to the justice system. Former defendants, attorneys, witnesses. They look clean on paper, but the edges don't fit."

He whistles, low. "Sounds like your kind of storm."

"Yeah. And maybe my kind of mistake."

His expression shifts. "You thinking Jensen?"

"I'm always thinking Jensen," I admit. "That's why I'm here. I can't shake the feeling the ghosts I'm chasing started back then."

Raines leans back, steepling his fingers. "You want my advice?"

"That's why I took the train."

"Stop chasing ghosts. The Jensen case was rotten from the start. Everyone wanted a villain, and you gave them one. You were the only one still pretending the system gave a damn about truth."

The window behind him cuts the skyline into glass-edged shards—gray, endless. "You ever wonder if that's where we lost the line?" I ask. "When justice stopped being about right and wrong and started being about what sticks?"

He exhales through his nose, something between a sigh and a warning.

"You don't lose the line, Shaw. It just moves."

"Maybe it's moving in Boston too."

Raines pours coffee into a chipped mug, slides it across the desk. "You want the truth? Boston doesn't want your kind of detective. They want headlines. You dig too deep, you start pulling names that were never supposed to surface."

"Like Silas Kade?"

That earns a raised brow. "The disbarred lawyer? He's still breathing?"

"More than that. He's circling my dead."

Raines tilts his head. "Then stop calling them victims. Start asking who the real ones are."

The words hit harder than they should. "You think they deserved it."

He doesn't answer right away. Just sips his coffee and watches me over the rim. "I think sometimes justice doesn't wear a badge. And if you go hunting whoever's passing it out in Boston, you might not like what you find."

The silence that follows settles heavy between us. I stare down at the coffee gone cold in front of me. "There's someone else," I say finally.

He smirks. "There always is."

"Not like that."

"Then like what?"

I search for the shape of her in language and come up short. "She's a court reporter—Celeste Duvall. Sharp. Composed. The kind who doesn't flinch when she should. She's not on every file, but she's near enough to all of them. A hearing here, a deposition there. And lately..." I scrub a hand over my jaw. "She's been spending time with Kade."

"The same lawyer?"

"Yeah. He defended two of my vics before he got disbarred. Now he's back in play, and she's in his orbit."

Raines studies me for a long beat. "You think he's pulling her strings?"

"I don't know. Maybe she doesn't either. But every time I get close to a lead, he's already been there—like he's cleaning the trail."

"Or maybe you're following where he wants you to look."

The thought lands like weight in my chest. "You ever feel like you're being played from both sides?"

He chuckles without humor. "Kid, that's the job." Then, softer, "If she's tangled with Kade, tread careful. Men like him don't build relationships—they build leverage."

"She doesn't feel like leverage."

He eyes me over his mug. "Then she's already under your skin."

I look away. "So what do I do?"

"Same thing I told you back in Jensen. Follow the evidence, not the impulse. If she's standing too close to the fire, let her burn on her own time. You try to pull her out, you'll go up with her."

I push to my feet, the floor creaking under my weight. "You always this optimistic?"

"Only when I care whether the idiot in front of me makes it home."

I almost smile. "Good to know I still qualify."

He waves me off. "Get out of my city before you start digging up ghosts."

I pause in the doorway. "That's the problem," I say quietly. "I think the ghosts are digging back."

The train hums beneath me, steady as a pulse. Boston's still two hours out. The window reflects more darkness than landscape, the world reduced to streaks of gray light and the faint silhouettes of sleeping towns. I meant to review my notes again, but exhaustion wins. My head tips against the glass, the rhythm of the tracks pulling me under.

At first, it's Jensen.

Always Jensen.

A warehouse, rain slick on concrete, sirens pulsing in the distance. The suspect on his knees, hands up. I see the flash before the sound — my partner shouting, the world tilting sideways. The blood. The silence afterward. The press calling it a mistake. IA calling it negligence. Me calling it penance.

But the dream shifts — it always does.

The rain turns to water, deep and black. Something gleams just beneath the surface. A hand, pale and motionless, fingers brushing the glass between us.

Celeste.

She's standing in the dark water, her hair floating around her like ink. Her eyes open slowly, not afraid, not pleading — just watching. She lifts her wrist, the same wrist I saw her brush against Silas's arm, and there's blood where the pulse should be.

"Don't," I whisper, but my voice doesn't reach her. The water fills my lungs before the word finishes.

Her mouth moves — I can't hear the sound, but I know what she's saying.

You're too late again.

The surface cracks like glass.

I reach for her and wake with a jolt.

The train lurches around a curve, lights flashing through the cabin. My chest is tight, breath unsteady. A kid a few seats ahead glances back, then returns to his phone.

I rub a hand over my face, trying to ground myself. The echo of the dream won't fade — her eyes, that stillness, the same chill that clung to every scene I've walked into lately.

Outside, the first flakes of snow drift past the window, catching the faint glow of the platform lights. Boston's skyline is just beginning to cut through the haze.

I tell myself it was only a dream.

But the part of me that still believes in instinct—the part that's never wrong—knows better.

She's in danger.

And this time, I can't afford to be too late.

The city feels different when I get back. Quieter, like it's holding its breath. The snow hasn't stuck yet, but the air carries that metallic bite that warns it's coming. My car's parked a block from the station — a streak of salt and city grime dulled against the curb. The ride home's short, but every red light stretches. The dream still clings to me like cold water I can't shake off.

My apartment greets me the way it always does — dark, still, half-empty. The kind of place meant for sleeping, not living. I drop my keys in the dish by the door, hang my coat, and let the silence settle.

Then I go to the wall.

It's supposed to be a workspace, but the corkboard's turned shrine

— threads, photos, maps, copies of case files. Corbett. Harren. Vennett. Wexler. Each one framed by neat handwriting and red pins that connect places, dates, names. I stare at it until the shapes blur.

Celeste's name isn't up there. Not yet.

Still, my eyes find the space where it would fit — just under Silas Kade's.

I sit on the edge of the desk, flipping open my notebook. The pages are full of my own scrawl, half logic, half instinct. Every thread leads back to him. Kade's clients. His cases. His connections. He defended them all before their lives fell apart — or ended.

Now he's playing host, wining and dining court reporters, journalists, anyone who might know more than they should. And Celeste—she's in the middle of it, too close to see she's already in his orbit.

I thumb through the latest report, Freddy's handwriting messy as ever: *Vennett—arterial cuts, slow bleed, same signature precision. No forced entry.*

The same phrase jumps out every time. *No forced entry.* They all trusted their killer.

I drop the file, lean back, rub my eyes. "What the hell are you doing, Shaw?"

The radiator kicks on, clanging like an old ghost. Outside, the snow finally starts — soft, soundless, relentless. The city lights smear through the glass, gold bleeding into gray.

I think of her face at the precinct. The way she looked at me when she said I was a terrible liar. She wasn't wrong.

Somewhere in the city, she's probably with him right now. Smiling. Laughing. Letting her guard down. And I can't tell if I'm more afraid that she's in danger—or that she isn't.

I reach for my phone, thumb hovering over her number. Then I stop. Not yet.

If I'm wrong, I'm just another man chasing ghosts.

If I'm right…

I look back at the board, at the thin line connecting Corbett to Kade, Kade to Wexler, Wexler to Harren, and the blank space beneath. If I'm right, she's already next.

Chapter 26
Elias

The precinct smells like coffee gone cold and snow tracked in on boots. Too quiet for a Friday night, too loud for the dead stillness sitting under my ribs.

Silas Kade sits across the table—hands folded, cufflinks glinting faintly under the bad fluorescent light. He came without a fight, no lawyer, no hesitation. Voluntary, he said. A show of good faith. The kind of confidence only a man with something to hide could wear like a tailored suit.

I drop the case file between us. The folder lands with a dull slap, photos spilling free: marble floor, blood pooled like spilled ink, the half-moon of a broken glass. Vennett's eyes frozen wide, reflecting his own living room lights.

Silas doesn't look away. "You work quickly, Detective. Thanksgiving dinner one night, interrogation the next."

"You were seen outside his home Tuesday night," I say. "You want to tell me what business you had with him?"

"Old clients don't disappear just because the bar does," he replies. "He owed me an apology, not a confession."

"He got one of those." I flip a photo toward him. "In blood."

Silas studies the image, head tilted, expression unreadable. "Efficient," he murmurs. "Almost reverent. Whoever did this understood balance."

Something hot flares in my chest. "That what you call it? Balance?"

"Call it what you like. You and I both know justice doesn't always fit inside the rules we write for it."

His voice is calm, even sympathetic, which makes me want to break the table in half. "You sound like you're admiring them."

"Admiration implies distance." He smiles faintly. "I simply recognize devotion when I see it."

The words hang there—devotion, deliberate, heavy as a confession.

I lean forward, elbows on the table. "You were the last man to defend him before the corruption probe, weren't you? Same pattern as Corbett. Same as Harren. Everyone you touch ends up in the ground."

He exhales softly, almost like a sigh. "Maybe that says more about the world we live in than the company I keep."

My jaw tightens. "Or maybe it says you're the common denominator."

He studies me for a long moment, head slightly tilted, like he's watching something unseen behind my eyes. "You look tired, Detective. Haunted. How long since you've slept without seeing blood?"

"Don't turn this around."

"I'm not turning anything. I'm observing." He folds his hands neatly. "You chase monsters long enough, you start mistaking your own reflection for theirs."

The hum of the fluorescent light grows louder. My pulse keeps pace. "You know what I think?" I ask quietly. "I think someone's feeding you names. I think whoever's doing this—whoever's keeping that ledger—works through you. Or with you."

That earns the first real change in his face. Not anger—offense. "You think I'd risk her for something so base?"

Her. The pronoun lands like a gunshot.

"Celeste," I say, watching him.

The silence between us sharpens. His composure fractures, just a hairline crack, but enough.

"You leave her out of this," he says softly.

"She's already in it."

His chair shifts an inch as he straightens, every trace of ease gone. "You think she's in danger with me?"

"I think danger follows you like shadow. And I think she's too close to see it."

Something dark flickers behind his eyes. "You're wrong," he says, quiet but precise. "Celeste isn't prey in this story, Detective. She's the balance itself."

I almost laugh, but it dies in my throat. "You sound like a zealot."

"Maybe faith and truth aren't as far apart as you pretend."

I push the photo of Vennett toward him again. "Faith didn't do this."

He looks down at the picture, then back at me. "No," he says softly.

"Truth did."

The room feels smaller now. I can hear my own breath, the hum of the heater, the faint tick of a clock somewhere beyond the door.

"Tell me where you were Thursday night," I demand.

"Home. Reading."

"With Celeste?"

He meets my eyes dead-on. "Would it matter if I said yes?"

"It would make you her alibi."

"Or her executioner." His smile is slow, deliberate. "Which would you prefer?"

My hand curls into a fist before I can stop it. "You enjoy this—don't you?"

He leans in slightly, voice low enough that it feels personal. "I enjoy clarity. And right now, you have none."

That's the moment I stand. The chair legs scrape against tile, sharp and final. "We're done."

Silas rises just as smoothly. "Then I assume I'm free to leave?"

"For now."

He buttons his coat, movements unhurried, almost ceremonial. "Then I'll do that." At the door he pauses, glancing back at me. "For what it's worth, Detective—balance doesn't wait for belief. You'll see that soon enough."

When he's gone, the silence rushes in to fill the space he leaves behind. The photos on the table curl slightly under the heat of the light. I stare at the one on top—Vennett's lifeless eyes reflecting something I can't unsee.

It isn't guilt that hits me. It's recognition.

Silas leaves the room like he owns it. Calm, unhurried, unmarked. He doesn't glance back when the door closes behind him—he doesn't need to. The echo of his presence stays long after he's gone, like the air itself remembers the shape of him.

I sink back into the chair, elbows on my knees, trying to slow a pulse that won't listen. The file still lies open between us—photos, transcripts, fragments of people who thought the law would save them. I stare at Vennett's face until the image blurs. The way the wounds were laid out, precise, deliberate, symmetrical—it isn't rage. It's ritual.

Balance. That's what Silas called it.

Not revenge. Not justice. Balance.

The word crawls under my skin.

He's too polished to make mistakes, too composed for panic. A man like that doesn't walk into a precinct unless he's already written the ending. He came here to be seen, to measure me, to decide whether I'm worth the trouble.

And the way he spoke about her—Celeste—like she was part of something sacred. Like she wasn't a woman at all but a revelation. The devotion in his voice wasn't admiration; it was possession.

I rub a hand over my jaw, the scrape of stubble grounding me just enough to breathe. The whole room smells like him now—cedar, smoke, and something sharp beneath it, like ozone after a storm. It's in my lungs, my clothes, my head.

Rational thought says he's clean. No prints, no record, no proof. But every instinct I have says he's playing me.

I flip the last photo over to the blank side, can't stand the eyes anymore.

My reflection stares back from the polished surface—tired, hollow, too close to the thing I'm chasing.

"You're not untouchable," I murmur to the empty room. "You just haven't slipped yet."

The heater clicks on, the lights hum. Outside, snow falls slow and soundless against the glass. For a moment, I catch my reflection superimposed over the night—my eyes lined up with his, the killer's, both staring out into the same dark.

I turn away before I start to believe it.

But even as I gather the files, I can't shake the feeling that he left something behind—not a clue, but a promise.

He's not running. He's waiting.

And until I prove it, every drop of blood that follows is on me.

The city blurs past in streaks of amber and white, headlights bleeding across black ice and rain-slick asphalt. Snow drifts through the air in slow spirals, catching light before disappearing into shadow. Boston feels hollow tonight—muted, emptied out, the kind of quiet that only follows confession.

By the time I pull onto my street, the heat in the car's gone cold. The wipers drag across the glass in tired arcs, smearing light instead of clearing it. For a moment, I just sit there, engine ticking, watching the flakes collect on the hood. The precinct hum still echoes in my head—Silas's calm voice, his half-smile, the way he said *balance* like a prayer.

I kill the ignition and step out into the wind. The snow's heavier here, muffling everything—sirens, traffic, even the sound of my own footsteps. My building waits at the end of the block, a narrow silhouette against the dim wash of the city. Warm light seeps from one window on the second floor—mine.

By the time I climb the stairs, the parking lot's turned to slush that seeps through my shoes. My breath ghosts in the air; the railing bites cold against my palm.

Inside, the air smells faintly of dust and coffee left too long on the burner. The silence hits harder than it should. I hang my coat on the hook, set my badge on the counter, and let the weight of the night settle.

Boston sleeps under its thin layer of snow, but the case—him—is still awake in my head.

Silas Kade.

Still calm.

Still smiling.

Still guilty.

The apartment feels lived in by absence—bare walls, unopened mail stacked by the counter, case files scattered across the coffee table. I tell myself I'll clean up. Instead, I pour two fingers of whiskey into a chipped glass and carry it to the window.

Outside, the streetlights smear gold across the snow. From up here, the city looks softer—distant, almost peaceful. If I try hard enough, I can almost pretend I don't see the shadow of a Beacon Hill townhouse every time I blink.

Silas Kade.

That smirk. That calm. That flicker of movement on the landing.

He's hiding something—I can feel it. But it's not just him that lingers. It's her.

Celeste Duvall.

The way she looked at him in the courthouse hallway—steady, unreadable. Not fear, not guilt. Something else. Something like allegiance.

I toss back the rest of the drink, the burn cutting through a chill that's settled too deep to shake. The glass lands on the counter with a dull thud. I lean forward, palms braced, eyes on the open file spread before me.

Corbett. Lexington. Harren. Vennett.

Different names. Same pattern. The quiet rot under every verdict, every signed page. And now Celeste, somehow caught in the current of it all.

I drag a hand over my face. The whiskey helps, but not enough. Sleep feels like a dare I keep losing.

I stretch out on the couch instead, case notes scattered across the table, my badge glinting faintly in the low light. Outside, snow keeps falling—steady, relentless—covering the city like an unfinished confession.

In the silence, I swear I hear it again: a faint hum, low and rhythmic, like a train passing somewhere deep underground. Or maybe it's something older. Either way, it follows me into sleep.

Sleep doesn't come easy. When it does, it doesn't feel earned. It feels borrowed. Like falling into someone else's memory.

The apartment shifts around me, edges melting into shadow. The hum deepens—steady, deliberate—until it sounds like a heartbeat beneath the floorboards. Then comes the whisper.

Low. Genderless. Everywhere at once.

The Ledger must be fed.

I jolt upright—or think I do—but the room keeps moving. The air thickens. The shadows breathe.

Justice waits for no man.

The words coil through the dark, smoke curling under my skin. My chest seizes; the ache behind my ribs sharpens. I try to speak, to move, to demand who's there, but the sound dies in my throat.

A face flickers in the dark—half-formed, shifting. For a heartbeat, it's Celeste. For another, it isn't.

You're too late, Elias. You always are.

My pulse hammers against the silence. The whisper fades into static, then nothing.

When I claw my way back to waking, the room is gray with early light. My neck aches. My shirt clings damp with sweat. Case files litter the floor. The whiskey glass lies overturned.

And on the coffee table sits a note.

Not typed. Not printed. Just a single sheet of paper, the edges curled as if it's been waiting all night.

The handwriting is neat. Unfamiliar. Elegant.

You can't save her from what she is meant to become.

For a long moment, I just stare. The room feels too still, the air too heavy. My heart tries to fill the space where reason should be.

The phone rings—sharp, jarring. I flinch, scattering another pile of files before fumbling for the receiver.

"Shaw," I manage, voice raw.

Freddy's on the other end, half-awake, all nerves. "You might want to get down here," he says. "We've got the tox results back on Vennett."

I glance again at the note, its edges trembling in the draft from the window.

"Yeah," I say quietly. "I'm on my way."

I slide the paper into an evidence sleeve, grab my coat. The mirror by the door catches me in passing—bloodshot eyes, jaw tight, a reflection that looks nothing like the man who walked into that interrogation room.

Outside, the snow's still falling. The city hasn't woken yet.

But something has.

Chapter 27
Celeste

When I wake, the first thing I feel is the ache. Not the dull throb of a bad night's sleep — deeper. Older. A pulse low in my stomach that won't quiet, humming through my veins like something alive.

The sheets are twisted around my legs. The air in the room feels too warm, too still. My mouth tastes faintly of salt and smoke.

I press a hand to my chest, trying to steady my breathing. It's been happening more often lately — waking like this, every sense sharp and wrong. The space between dreams and daylight thinning until I can't tell which one I'm still in.

The clock on the nightstand says 6:47 a.m. I don't remember going to bed. I don't remember coming home.

Just fragments:

Silas's voice, low and certain.

The feel of his hand brushing mine across the table.

The way his eyes caught the light — gray-green, unreadable, like the sea just before a storm.

And then water. Always water. Cold against my skin. My hair clinging to my neck. My pulse echoing like it's underwater too.

I sit up, my body aching in places that feel newly aware of themselves. The mirror across the room catches my reflection — flushed cheeks, eyes darker than they should be. For a heartbeat, I think I see someone else looking back. Someone older. Hungrier.

The journal waits on my nightstand, where I always leave it. Open to a page I don't remember writing.

He calls to me in the dark.

The water listens.

I am not afraid.

My breath stumbles. The ink is dry, but the handwriting is mine.

I flip to a clean page and uncap the fountain pen, my hand already trembling.

December 1

I don't know what's happening to me.

The days have lost their edges. They bleed together until I can't tell when I'm dreaming and when I'm awake. Sometimes I lose whole hours—whole nights. I wake with my hair damp, my skin cold, dirt beneath my nails. The sheets smell faintly of rain and something older, something that doesn't belong to this world.

Every dream feels like a memory trying to surface. Every heartbeat feels borrowed.

My thirtieth birthday is coming—December 21. I used to imagine thirty as a kind of arrival: solid ground, steady breath, a life that made sense. But the closer it gets, the more it feels like a deadline. The date hums in my chest when I write it down, as if it's counting toward something inevitable.

I should tell someone. I should tell *him.*

But I don't know which *him* I mean anymore.

Elias watches me like he's afraid of what he might see if I break. His questions sound gentle, but they carry weight. He wants to help, I think—but part of me wonders if he's really trying to save me or understand me enough to put me in a report.

Silas never asks. He just looks, listens. When he's near, the air changes—denser, charged. He talks about truth as if it's a living thing, something that feeds on the people who chase it.

And lately... there's something else.

A voice. Not loud, not clear—just there.
It slips between sounds: in the radiator's sigh, in the hum of fluorescent lights, in the rhythm of my own pulse. Sometimes it sounds like wind moving across water. Sometimes it whispers my name.

Come home.

I don't know what it means. Or where home even is. But every time I hear it, the ache beneath my ribs deepens, like something inside me recognizes the call.

I find notes I don't remember writing. Words that don't feel like mine: *The water remembers what the body forgets.* The handwriting matches, but the voice behind it doesn't.

I think about telling Elias—the lost time, the dreams, the voice—but something in me stops every time. It feels like warning. Like saying it out loud would draw it closer.

If I tell him, he'll look at me differently. And once he does, I don't think I'll come back from it.

So I'll keep it here, pressed between paper and breath.
Maybe that's safer.
Maybe this is what I am now—half witness, half echo.

And somewhere out there, the voice keeps calling.
Soft. Certain. Patient.

Come home.

The pen slips in my hand. A drop of ink bleeds into the page, spreading outward until the words blur.

I close the journal too fast, pressing my palm against the cover until my pulse stops racing.

The room feels heavier. Denser. Like the air's waiting for me to admit something I'm not ready to say out loud.

I shove the journal into my bag, grab my coat, and force myself to breathe. Work will help. Routine always does.

But as I step out into the hallway, the faint smell of lake water clings to me — impossible, unmistakable — and the ache returns, low and insistent, like the echo of a name I've forgotten how to say.

The cold bites the second I step outside. It's been snowing for weeks now—thin layers that never melt, just stack and settle, softening the edges of the world. The air smells like pine and smoke, sharp enough to clear my head for half a heartbeat. My breath ghosts in front of me as I pull my coat tighter, boots slipping through a mix of salt and half-frozen slush.

The Witch's Brew waits at the corner, glowing against the gray like a held breath. Its windows fogged, haloed with twinkle lights that flicker against the frost. Someone's gone overboard with the decorations again—garlands sagging under their own weight, red bows crooked from the wind, a paper snowflake taped unevenly to the door. It's imperfect in a way that almost hurts. Too human. Too alive.

Warmth hits the moment I step inside. Cinnamon, espresso, and burnt sugar wrap around me like a memory. The speakers hum with something cheerful—bells and sleighs and promises that sound like they belong to another world.

"Morning, Celeste," June calls from behind the counter. Her curls have staged another rebellion, haloed wild around her face. "You look half-frozen. Dirty chai, extra spice?"

"Always."

She grins, already moving—steam hissing, metal clinking, the rhythm of someone who never questions the world outside her door. I drift to my usual spot by the window, fingertips tracing the condensation on the glass. Outside, the snow falls thicker now, blurring streetlamps into watercolor streaks.

When June sets the mug down, the smell hits first—sweet, spiced, grounding. The first sip burns, the second soothes. Cardamom, clove, a trace of smoke. It tastes like control. Like pretending everything still makes sense.

For a moment, I almost believe it. I watch Salem wrap itself in lights and lies, the world pretending at peace while garlands bow under the weight of snow.

But the hum is still there. Low. Patient. Curling somewhere at the base of my spine. It's been days since it started—weeks maybe—and I still can't tell if it's coming from inside me or something that's waiting just beyond reach.

The lights overhead flicker once. Then steady. I tell myself it's the wiring. The age of the building. Anything but what I feel.

Still, when I glance at the window, my reflection wavers—cheeks flushed, eyes too bright, something alive and unfamiliar glinting beneath the surface.

I take another sip. Let the heat settle in my chest. Pretend it's enough. Pretend I'm not changing.
Pretend I can still stop it.

I pull my journal from my bag, the leather worn soft around the edges from too much handling. **December 1st.** The date looks too clean at the top of the page, too stable for the way my hands tremble. Outside, the snow keeps falling—slow, deliberate—as if the world's trying to bury something it can't quite forget.

Steam curls from my chai, fogging the edge of the paper as I tap the pen against the margin. For a long moment, I just stare at the blank space beneath the date. What do I even write anymore?

I could write about the weather. About the Christmas lights strung down Essex Street, blinking through the gray like small, desperate promises. About how June hums off-key while she wipes down the counter, or how Salem looks almost holy under the snow. But my hand doesn't move for any of that.

Instead, I write about the ache that hasn't left since Thanksgiving. The way I wake drenched in cold sweat, the taste of saltwater on my tongue when there shouldn't be any. I write about the gaps—the missing hours that swallow whole nights—and the memories that bleed into dreams until I can't tell the difference. I write about how I blinked and somehow, it was already December.

I write his name, too.

Silas.

Then I cross it out.

My handwriting looks steadier than I feel. I tell myself I'm being paranoid—that exhaustion can twist memory into something unrecognizable. But when I close my eyes, I still see flashes: bookshelves that hum when I touch them, a mirror that ripples like water, his voice in the dark saying my name like it's a prayer—or a warning.

The pen stills.

Outside, the snow has deepened, muting the world into a soundless gray. I press my fingertips to the page, to the faint outline of the name I tried to erase, and the paper feels warm beneath my touch—as if it remembers what I'm trying to forget.

I close the journal carefully, slide it back into my bag, and wrap my hands around my chai. The spice burns sharper now, almost metallic.

December 1st, I repeat silently. The beginning of something—or the moment I stop pretending it hasn't already begun.

By the time I board the train, the cold has settled deep enough to hurt. The windows fog with every breath, the world outside reduced to gray streaks and motion. The snow hasn't stopped—it just thins into mist halfway down the coast, soft enough to cling to my coat but not enough to hide the city's sharp edges.

Boston waits ahead, restless and awake.

And somewhere between the sound of steel and storm, I swear I hear it again—

a voice I can't name, soft and certain, threading through the hum of the rails.

Come home.

By the time I reach the courthouse, my fingers are numb, and the hum of the lobby feels like static pressing at the base of my skull. People move in the same tired rhythm—security wands, the beep of scanners, the shuffle of papers clutched too tightly. The smell of burnt coffee hangs in the air, a scent so woven into this place it might as well be part of the marble.

I slip through the familiar corridors toward my office, my boots leaving faint wet prints on the tile. When I reach for the doorknob, my phone buzzes in my bag.

Elias Shaw.

I hesitate before answering.

"Detective."

"Morning," he says, voice rough from too little sleep. "Didn't catch you at a bad time, did I?"

"Not yet." I set my bag down, balancing the phone between my shoulder and ear. "Though I have a full docket today, so if this is about transcripts—"

"It's not." There's a pause, the faint scrape of movement on his end. "I just... had a few questions about a case you might've covered. Lexington.

Maybe Corbett."

The names hit harder than I expect. I press a hand to the edge of my desk, grounding myself. "Those were months ago."

"I know," he says quietly. "But something's come up. Patterns, maybe. I'd rather ask you in person."

I glance at the stack of files waiting for me, the blinking cursor on my monitor, the weight in my chest that hasn't gone away since the lake—or whatever memory my mind has twisted into one. "Is this official?"

"Not yet." Another pause. "But it's important."

I exhale slowly, watching the condensation ghost against the phone screen. "You have a strange definition of timing, Detective."

"Comes with the job," he says. "Lunch? There's a place near the station—quiet."

Something in his tone gives me pause. He sounds tired, yes, but there's more beneath it. Concern, maybe. Or suspicion. Either way, it tugs at me.

"Fine," I say. "Twelve-thirty?"

"Twelve-thirty," he repeats. "And, Celeste?"

"Yes?"

There's the faintest breath before he answers. "Thanks for picking up."

The line goes dead, leaving the steady buzz of the courthouse around me. I slip the phone back into my pocket, telling myself it's just lunch. Just work. Just another conversation with a man who looks at me like I'm part of a mystery he's half afraid to solve.

Still, when I sit down to start transcribing, my hands won't stop trembling.

Chapter 28
Elias

The diner's half-empty when I get there—one of those old corner places that hasn't changed its neon sign or furniture since the seventies. Chrome trim, cracked red vinyl booths, coffee that smells like it's been burning since dawn. The kind of place cops gravitate to without meaning to.

I slide into a booth facing the door. It's 12:20, snow starting again outside, soft flakes catching in the traffic lights. The waitress tops off my mug without asking; she doesn't need to. I've been here enough times that the staff barely glance up anymore.

The windows fog around the edges, blurring the street into shapes of gray and motion. For once, I don't mind the quiet. The last few days have been nothing but noise and static—calls, reports, leads that spiral clean until they don't. But this? This is a pause. A held breath before whatever comes next.

My thoughts drift to Celeste before I can stop them. The way she looked last week in the courthouse—composed but brittle, like a statue that's learned to breathe. She hides it well, but something's unraveling beneath that calm. I saw it in the way her hands trembled when she passed me those files, how her eyes lingered on something I couldn't see.

It's not just the cases. I know that kind of fracture when I see it. I've lived it.

The bell over the door rings. She steps inside.

She shakes off the cold, brushing snow from her coat, hair catching the weak winter light. It's darker today, with a copper undertone that burns when she moves. Her cheeks are flushed from the wind, and for a moment she looks—human. Not the composed witness from the courtroom, but the woman beneath it.

When her gaze finds me, something flickers—hesitation, maybe, or calculation. Then it's gone, replaced by the practiced neutrality she wears like armor.

"Detective."

"Celeste." I nod toward the seat across from me. "You found it."

"Hard to miss." Her voice is smooth, measured. "Not many places still have working neon."

She slides into the booth. The waitress arrives with a refill before either of us speaks. "Thanks," Celeste murmurs, wrapping her hands around the cup like she's trying to steal its warmth.

I study her over the rim of my own coffee. "Rough morning?"

She lets out a breath that almost counts as a laugh. "Define 'rough.'"

Fair enough. I let it go. "I appreciate you coming. I know you didn't have to."

"You said it was important." Her tone's polite, distant.

"It is," I say quietly. "I just haven't decided if it's something you should be worried about yet."

Her fingers still on the cup. Outside, a plow grinds past, spraying slush against the glass. For a moment, the world is all noise and white.

Then she leans back, eyes narrowing slightly. "You think I'm involved."

I don't answer right away. I've never been good at lying to her.

"I think," I say finally, "that you're closer to all of this than you realize."

Her jaw tightens. "And you think lunch is the best place to interrogate me about it?"

I shake my head. "No. Lunch is where I remind you that if something's coming—and it is—you don't have to face it alone."

Something flickers behind her eyes at that—soft, fleeting, gone before it settles. She looks away, watching snow gather on the ledge. The silence stretches thin, fragile as glass. For the first time, I'm not sure which one of us is closer to breaking it.

I turn my mug in slow circles, watching steam ghost toward the ceiling. "The victims—Lexington, Corbett, Harren, Vennett. They all ran in overlapping legal circles. Same defense networks. Same consultants."

Her brow furrows, faint but sharp. "Silas Kade."

The name lands between us like a dropped blade. I don't confirm it. I don't need to. She reads it in the quiet that follows, and the way my hands won't stop tightening around the mug.

I shift in my seat, the leather creaking beneath me. "He defended Wexler and Lexington before his license got pulled. Now he's showing up on the fringes again—galas, charity boards, donor lists. Always just outside the frame."

She takes a slow sip of her chai, eyes fixed on the table. "And you think that means he's involved in the murders?"

"I think..." I stop. The words don't come clean. "I think there's a pattern, and every time I follow it, it ends near him. But it's never enough to hold."

Her gaze lifts, steady and knowing. "You're leaving something out."

I exhale through my nose, thumb drumming against the handle of my mug. "It's not that simple."

"It never is with you, Detective." Her tone softens, but there's still a blade hidden under the calm. "You've been circling this for weeks. You wouldn't have called me if it wasn't eating at you."

She's not wrong. I lean forward, elbows on the table, the smell of cinnamon and burnt coffee thick between us. "You've been in the same rooms as him, Celeste. You've seen the way people move around him. They don't say no. They don't even think no. It's like he already knows what they'll do before they do it."

Her fingers tighten around her cup. "That's just influence. Charisma."

"Maybe." I pause, watching her reflection shimmer faintly in the fogged window. "Or maybe it's something else."

For the first time, she looks unsettled—not frightened, exactly, but aware. Her eyes narrow slightly, the gold flecks catching in the dim light. "You sound like you're talking about magic."

The word lands heavier than it should. "I sound like a man running out of explanations," I say quietly.

Outside, snow presses the daylight into gray. Inside, the hum of an old radio fills the space—a Christmas song warped just out of tune. The sound makes the air feel charged, alive.

Celeste breaks the silence first. "You're afraid of him."

I meet her eyes. "I'm afraid of what he touches."

Her jaw tightens, but her voice stays even. "You're still not telling me everything."

"No," I admit. "Because I'm not sure what's truth and what's coincidence anymore. But if I'm right about where this is heading, you might be the only one close enough to see what I can't."

Her lips part slightly. "And if you're wrong?"

"Then we both get burned."

The words hang between us, smoke and static. She doesn't look away this time.

Then she leans back, voice quiet but steady. "Then I guess we'd better find out which one it is."

Celeste traces the rim of her cup, her gaze drifting to the window where the snow falls in slow, hypnotic spirals. "What if it isn't just influence," she says, almost to herself. "What if there really is something more to it? To all of this."

I study her, unsure if she's humoring me or finally letting herself wonder. "You mean magic."

She hesitates, then exhales. "Maybe not the fairy tale kind. But something underneath it all—something that doesn't fit into our neat little categories. Energy, intent... maybe even consequence." Her eyes flick toward me, sharp and golden in the muted light. "What if belief itself makes it real?"

Her words settle in the space between us like a challenge—quiet, dangerous, and already true.

I let out a slow breath, leaning back. "You sound like one of those mystics who hang out near the harbor—reading palms between tarot sessions and storm warnings."

A small smile ghosts across her lips. "Maybe they're the only ones paying attention."

Her tone is teasing, but her hands betray her. A faint tremor as she sets her cup down too carefully, porcelain kissing the saucer with a soft clink that sounds louder than it should.

"You've seen things, haven't you?" I ask. My voice comes out quieter than I mean it to.

She goes still. The rest of the diner blurs into a distant hum—the murmur of other patrons, the hiss of the espresso machine, the scrape of forks against chipped plates. It's just her and me, the silence drawn thin as wire between us.

When she finally speaks, her voice is calm, deliberate. Too deliberate. "I've seen enough to know the world doesn't stop where we think it does."

I study her, searching for the tremor beneath the words. "That sounds like experience talking."

"Maybe," she says softly. "Or maybe it's just... recognition."

The way she says it sinks into me like a blade turned slow. Recognition. The kind that doesn't come from memory but from something older—something waking up behind her eyes.

Outside, a snowflake hits the glass and melts instantly, leaving a single streak of water that catches the light. She watches it fall, her reflection warping in the window before turning back to me.

"If you're right about Silas," she says, "then maybe what scares you isn't that he's manipulating people."

My pulse stumbles once. "Then what is it?"

"That he's right about something you've spent your whole life pretending doesn't exist."

The words land with the quiet weight of truth. For a heartbeat, all I hear is the faint hum of the lights overhead—steady, pulsing, almost rhythmic. Like the sound knows something we don't.

I open my mouth, but nothing comes out. Because somewhere beneath all the logic and law I've built my life on, I can feel it too—something moving just out of sight, old and patient, waiting for both of us to catch up.

And for the first time since this started, I'm not sure if I want to.

Chapter 29
Killer

The harbor is quiet tonight.

Wind off the Atlantic cuts through the alleys, carrying salt and exhaust and the faint scent of iron. Snow drifts sideways under the streetlights—fine, needling flakes that sting when they touch skin. The kind of cold that strips sound down to essentials: breath, footsteps, heartbeat.

I walk without haste. The city's rhythm has thinned to whispers—the rumble of a distant truck, the cry of a gull too stubborn to migrate. Every window I pass glows soft gold, small worlds behind glass. Warmth I will not enter. Warmth I do not need.

The call hums beneath all of it.

Not a sound exactly—more a vibration that threads through bone. Each step syncs to it, an old metronome keeping time with something the world has forgotten how to hear.

The harbor water is half-frozen, black beneath its crust of slush. It moves even when the air is still. That's what balance is—motion inside stillness. The living pretending to be calm.

I pass the piers, counting them without meaning to. Wooden pilings rimed with ice, ropes stiff as bone. The hunger builds with the wind, steady, patient, neither cruel nor kind. It isn't about blood. It's about correction. The scale tips. The hand steadies it.

Somewhere behind me, a church bell sounds—dull through the snow, carrying only half a note before the wind devours it. Time measured, then erased.

Across the harbor, the skyline burns faint orange against the storm. I can feel the city's pulse from here, faint but strong enough to guide me. Its wrongness hums like static under glass.

They never see it coming, the ones whose names hum in that pitch. They live inside their triumphs, believing law and wealth will keep them safe from consequence. But nothing human lasts without balance. Everything stolen must be paid for.

I stop at the end of the pier. The water licks the ice with a sound like breath drawn through teeth. The next name is already forming—a vibration in the air, a tremor in the dark between lights. It's not spoken aloud. It doesn't have to be.

I close my eyes. The wind threads cold fingers through my hair, across my mouth. The hum inside me steadies.

Soon.

When the solstice comes, the voice that calls will no longer need a vessel.

It will simply speak, and the world will listen.

I turn from the water and start back toward the city, the snow erasing my tracks as I go. The wind hardens as I turn inland. Snow drags sideways through the alleys, clinging to the brick, to my sleeves, to the edges of the world. The harbor's rhythm fades behind me, replaced by the hum of the city—tires hissing through slush, the far-off wail of an ambulance swallowed by distance.

The call quiets a little when I move.

It likes motion. It likes the promise of purpose.

By the time I reach Market Street, the snow has turned to fine sleet. The neon from the taverns smears across the wet pavement—red, blue, gold, a pulse beneath my boots. That's when I hear it.

A voice.

Then another.

Sharp. Frantic. The language of fear.

I pause at the mouth of an alley.

Two figures, half-hidden by shadow: one pressed against the wall, the other blocking the only exit. The sound of a struggle carries in short bursts—pleading, then the thud of a fist, the crack of bone against brick.

The call stirs.

It doesn't roar; it hums—low, approving, a pulse answering a pulse.

I step closer. The man doing the hitting wears a heavy coat, hood up, boots too clean for the alley he's chosen. The woman's purse dangles from his hand, torn strap slick with snow. She's small. Shaking. Whispering prayers to no one who's listening.

For a moment, I just watch.

The wind lifts my hair into my face; I don't move it away. The scene before me is simple, perfect in its imbalance.

A choice presents itself, but it isn't moral. It's mechanical. The scale tilts. The weight must return.

"Hey."

My voice sounds strange to my own ears—calm, almost gentle.

The mugger freezes, half-turned, eyes narrowing beneath the hood.

"Mind your own business," he says.

He doesn't see the shape in my hand until it's too late.

The motion is clean. Not fast—measured.

A single breath, a single shift of weight, the sound of impact muffled by the snow. He collapses to his knees, clutching the place where his strength used to live. His breath fogs white against the air.

The woman stares at me, too stunned to scream. Blood stains the snow in a slow bloom. I crouch and retrieve her bag, set it beside her trembling hands.

"You should go," I tell her.

She nods, eyes wide, voice lost.

When she runs, she leaves no sound behind her.

I stay there for a moment, watching the man struggle to breathe, the steam of his life curling into the night. The hum inside me steadies. The tension in my spine eases. It's not satisfaction—it's silence. A temporary stilling of the noise.

A bandage. Nothing more.

The call recedes, soft for now, purring under my ribs. The city resumes its rhythm around me—sirens, snow, the pulse of light reflected in puddles.

I stand, wipe my gloves clean against the brick, and step back into the wind.

The hunger will return. It always does.

But tonight, the scales are quiet.

And for a few fleeting breaths, that's enough.

I turn toward the direction of the courthouse lights, their glow faint through the storm, and walk until the footprints behind me vanish into the dark.

Chapter 30
Celeste

The radiator hums a weary rhythm beneath the silence, its heat pulsing in uneven breaths. Outside, snow drifts down in slow spirals, blurring the city until it looks half-imagined.

I haven't been sleeping right. When I do, the dreams stick to me—wet, heavy things that follow me into morning. The taste of rain in my mouth. The ache of something I can't name.

The journal waits on the table beside my cooling mug of chai. I uncap the pen before I can talk myself out of it.

December 3

The nights feel longer than they should.

I lose hours again.

It isn't emptiness—it's the opposite. Like the missing time is full, crammed with something I'm not allowed to see yet. The air feels heavy when I wake, thick with salt and static, like something's just left the room.

I dream of water that doesn't exist. Hands pulling me under. Light breaking apart until all that's left is sound.

And when I wake, my hair is damp, my skin cold, my heart racing like I ran from something I can't remember. I tell myself it's just a dream, but the sheets smell faintly of ocean water—brine and iron, like the sea found its way inside while I slept. There's sand under my nails, a bruise blooming on my thigh I can't explain.

I dream of Silas too. His voice like smoke. His hands warm against my skin, tracing lines that burn long after I open my eyes. The way he says my name—it feels like he's pulling it from somewhere ancient. Somewhere I've heard it before.

But it's Elias who lingers.

In the dream, I'm standing in the ocean. The waves are calm, but deep—dark enough to hide anything. Moonlight scatters across the surface like a broken mirror, and he's there—close enough that I can see the breath fog between us.

He looks at me like he's trying to remember who I am. Or maybe like he already knows. His hand lifts, slow, cautious, fingers brushing the side of my neck. "Celeste," he whispers, and it feels like the name belongs to both of us.

The water rises around us, curling at my waist, cold enough to sting. I should step back, but I don't. He leans in, and when his lips touch mine, the world stills. The sea hums beneath us—steady, alive—and for a heartbeat, I feel whole. Like I've been found after a lifetime of being misplaced.

Then it changes. His grip tightens. The waves climb higher, swallowing the light. His eyes shift, silver bleeding to gold, and the air tastes like static. My chest burns. I can't tell if he's saving me or drowning me.

I wake gasping, salt on my lips, the echo of his name caught between breath and prayer.

Elias asked if I believed in magic.

I told him I didn't. But I lied.

Something is changing. The edges between things feel thinner.

Streetlights flicker when I walk beneath them. Radios hum with no signal. The elevator in my building stops on the wrong floor, doors opening to hallways that don't exist. And when I close my eyes, I hear a voice—a low, melodic whisper calling my name in the same rhythm as the tide.

It doesn't sound cruel. It sounds like home.

I used to dream about home a lot when I was younger. Back when "home" was just another house on another street with another last name that didn't fit. Every new room smelled different—bleach, dust, lavender—but none of them ever felt like mine.

Maybe that's why the voice doesn't scare me. Maybe it's the only thing that never has.

My thirtieth birthday is eighteen days away—December twenty-first.

The solstice. The longest night of the year.

When I was little, I used to say I wouldn't make it to thirty. I can't remember why. Just that I believed it with a certainty no one could talk me out of. My foster mother once called it "dramatic," said I'd grow out of it. I never did.

Now it feels less like superstition and more like prophecy.

I can feel something pressing against the edges of me—like memory, or heat, or power. I don't know if I'm breaking apart or waking up. I just know the line between who I am and what's inside me is thinning.

Maybe this isn't falling apart. Maybe this is remembering.

—C

The ink ripples faintly, like the page itself takes a shallow breath. I freeze, the pen hovering midair as a low vibration hums beneath everything—under the radiator, under the soft mechanical exhale of the city itself. It's not sound exactly. It's something smaller, stranger, a pulse that doesn't need to be heard to be felt. I close the journal slowly, tracing my fingers over the date once more. The twenty-first glows faintly in the lamplight, ink still wet, bleeding toward the paper's edge like it's trying to escape the confines of the page. Outside, the snow keeps falling—soft, relentless, endless.

The cold hits me the moment I step outside. Salem looks washed in pewter this morning, every line of the old town blurred beneath the crusted ridges of last night's storm. My boots crunch over ice, the sound small and sharp against the hush that's settled over everything. The iron lampposts still wear their Thanksgiving wreaths, ribbons stiff with frost, half-forgotten gestures of cheer surviving in the cold. I pull my hood tighter and start toward the station. The air feels too still, the kind of stillness that belongs to churches or graveyards—like the world is holding its breath before a spell breaks.

Somewhere behind me, a door slams. I turn, but the narrow street is empty except for a single trail of footprints pressed deep into the snow. They're larger than mine, fresh, and they stop abruptly at the curb—as if whoever made them simply vanished. I stare for a moment longer than I should, waiting for movement that never comes. Then I shake it off and keep walking, but the hum beneath my skin answers like a struck tuning fork, vibrating through bone and thought until I can almost taste metal.

The train platform smells of cold metal and sea salt. The harbor wind cuts through the crowd of commuters, tugging at scarves and coffee cups, scattering the faint chatter that never quite fills the space. The tracks sing faintly—a vibration just below hearing that settles somewhere behind my teeth. I close my eyes and count my breaths, pretending I can't feel the city breathing back. When the train arrives, the doors open with a hiss that sounds too alive, too deliberate, like a sigh caught between sleep and waking.

Inside, the car is half-empty. I slide into my usual seat by the window—the same one every morning, familiar enough to feel like a ritual. The glass reflects the row behind me, pale and endless under the fluorescent light. Then, as the train lurches forward, something flickers at the edge of the frame: a figure at the far end of the car, head tilted, watching. I turn sharply. Nothing. Just the sway of the carriage, the hum of the tracks, the echo of something that shouldn't have been there.

Boston creeps closer with every stop—stations flashing past in bursts of light and shadow, faces half-seen, forgotten before the doors close. I check my phone to anchor myself, but the screen stutters once, a white static ripple tearing through the display before clearing to reveal the time. 7:13. The same as the dream. My pulse kicks once, hard, but I tell myself it's coincidence. Everything strange feels easier to name that way.

By the time the train slides into North Station, my hands have stopped shaking, but the hum hasn't left. It's softer now, deeper, curled somewhere low in my chest like a second heartbeat that doesn't quite belong to me. Outside, the city looms—gray towers veiled in exhaust, glass catching what little light the morning offers. Christmas decorations hang from lampposts, glitter dulled by slush and traffic fumes. For a moment, Boston almost feels ordinary again. Almost.

The courthouse waits like it always does, marble and glass swallowing the cold light. As I step through the main doors, the motion sensor flickers, and for one fractured heartbeat the lobby glows red before snapping back to white. No one else seems to notice. The clerks keep talking. The guard waves another visitor through. The world carries on, unaware. I tighten my grip on my bag and move toward the elevators, telling myself it's just the wiring, the storm, the old building's bones settling.

But as the doors slide shut, the hum deepens. It threads through the air vents, the cables, the floor beneath my feet—alive and rhythmic, as if the entire courthouse has a pulse of its own. My reflection stares back from the elevator's mirrored wall, eyes too bright, breath fogging faintly in the cold light. For a moment, I could swear I see movement behind me—a shadow, faint and waiting. Then the doors open, spilling me into another day that doesn't quite feel like mine.

By the time I reach the second floor, the fluorescent lights hum just a little too loudly. They've always been harsh in here—flat, sterile—but today the sound feels alive, like static whispering through my bones. I swipe my badge and push through the glass doors of the stenographers' office. Everything looks normal: the low whir of printers, the steady clack of keys, the shuffle of paper stacks waiting to be filed. But the air feels heavier, denser somehow, as if the building itself has drawn a breath and forgotten to let it go.

Abigail Lockley waves from her desk, her usual morning smile too bright for the hour. "Rough commute?"

"Something like that." I force a smile back and hang my coat, trying to shake the cold from my sleeves.

My desk sits by the window overlooking the street below, the glass streaked with condensation that turns the city into watercolor—smears of gray and amber beneath the constant drift of snow. People hurry in and out of the courthouse, bundled shapes moving through the white, but one figure stands still among them. Black coat. Stillness like intent. Head tilted up, watching the window—watching me.

I blink, and they're gone.

The clock on my computer reads 8:12 a.m. I could've sworn it was 7:45 a minute ago. I tell myself I misread it, but unease slips in anyway, cold as the wind still clinging to my clothes. I shake it off, open my docket, and start logging the morning schedule. Two property disputes, a fraud hearing, an appeal on a malpractice suit—ordinary names, ordinary crimes, nothing worth losing time over.

Still, the hum in my chest persists. Every few minutes a phrase or number on the screen blurs, letters smearing together before snapping back into focus. Once, I blink and the text rearranges itself entirely—curving into symbols that don't belong to any language I know. By the time I lean closer, they're gone, replaced by plain English again.

The bailiff passes behind me, drops off a file, and for a split second the shadow he casts stretches wrong—longer than it should, reaching across the desk like it's trying to touch me. My pulse stutters. I close the file and stand. The walls feel too close.

The restroom mirror offers no comfort. The fluorescent light above it flickers, catching on the edge of my reflection. When I move, the image doesn't follow right away—it lags by a heartbeat, a second version of me trapped in glass, catching up too slow. My stomach twists.

"Get it together," I whisper, gripping the counter until my knuckles ache.

When I return to my desk, a paper cup waits by the keyboard. Chai, extra spice. Steam curls in the air, forming something that looks almost like a symbol before dissolving. There's no note. No one hovering nearby. The scent of cinnamon and clove is warm, grounding—and wrong. It feels like memory, like something that's already happened. My hand trembles as I reach for it.

The first sip burns. The second steadies me. For a moment, the world clicks back into place. My breath slows, the hum quiets, everything sharpens. Then I catch the reflection in my monitor—just behind my shoulder, in the window. The city is inverted, snow rising instead of falling.

"Ms. Duvall."

The voice cuts clean through the static, pulling me upright before my brain catches up. I turn, already knowing who it is. Elias Shaw stands in the doorway, his presence cutting through the dull light like he doesn't belong in this world of paper and screens. His coat's still damp from snow, his eyes sharper than the rest of him, and there's a tension in his shoulders that wasn't there the last time we spoke.

"Detective." My voice comes out steadier than I expect. "You're far from your precinct."

He steps inside, gaze flicking briefly to the untouched cup on my desk. "He bring you another one of those?"

I don't answer. I don't have to. The air between us hums again, faint and electric, like the moment before lightning strikes.

Elias lowers his voice. "Have you noticed anything strange lately?"

The question lands heavy. "Strange how?"

"Anything out of place," he says. "Missing time. Unusual noises. Dreams that feel—too real."

My throat tightens. "You sound like you're building a ghost story, Detective."

"Maybe I am." His tone doesn't waver. "Or maybe I'm trying to keep you from ending up in one."

Something in my chest twists. "You think I'm in danger?"

"I think," he says quietly, "you're standing too close to someone who makes danger look civilized."

He doesn't have to say Silas's name—it's already in the room, heavy as incense. The hum returns, faint but insistent, threading through the air like a low electric current. For a moment, I can't tell if it's coming from the lights or from me.

Before I can answer, my phone rings—sharp, sudden, slicing through the tension. I don't have to look to know who it is. The name flashes across the screen: **Silas Kade.**

Elias's eyes flick down to the phone, and the change in him is instant—subtle, but there. His jaw tightens, his posture sharpens, the muscle near his temple flexing once before he speaks. "You going to answer that?"

I hesitate, pulse jumping. Then I swipe to accept.

"Silas?"

His voice slides through the receiver—smooth, deliberate, the kind of calm that sounds practiced. "Good morning, Celeste. I didn't wake you, did I?"

"No. I'm at work."

"Of course you are." There's a smile in his tone. "Listen, I wanted to let you know—I'll be in court this afternoon, consulting on a civil suit. Maybe we could grab a late lunch? I have something for you."

Something in the way he says it makes the back of my neck prickle. "You don't have to keep bringing me things."

"I know," he says lightly. "But I want to."

Elias doesn't look away. Not once. The longer I'm on the phone, the colder the air between us becomes. When I finally hang up, the silence that follows feels brittle, sharp enough to cut.

He exhales through his nose, a quiet sound that almost passes for a laugh. "You really don't see it, do you?"

"See what?"

"The way he circles you," Elias says, voice low. "The way you let him."

I straighten in my chair, the heat rising up my throat before I can stop it. "You think you know me, Detective. You don't."

He takes a step closer, close enough that I can smell the faint trace of his cologne—coffee, cedar, cold air. "Then help me understand," he says. It's not a challenge this time; it's a plea disguised as authority. "Because from where I'm standing, he's already halfway through whatever game he's playing, and you're the one holding the match."

The lights hum louder, the air thickening between us. "You think this is about him?" I ask quietly. "Maybe the problem isn't what's strange, Elias. Maybe it's what's waking up."

Something flickers in his expression—jealousy, yes, but also something older, rawer. Possession wrapped in concern. He looks at me like he's trying to decide whether to warn me or confess something he shouldn't. Then he sighs, breaking the spell. "If you notice anything else—anything at all—you call me. Don't call him."

His tone is calm, but it's not a request. It's a line drawn.

He turns to leave, shoulders tense under his coat. His reflection passes through the glass, fractured by light, until it disappears down the hall.

I stare after him long after he's gone, the phone still warm in my hand. The chai on my desk has gone cold, but the air around me still hums—alive, electric, waiting. The taste of his name lingers on my tongue longer than I mean it to.

The rest of the day unfolds in fragments.

I try to work, but my focus fractures the moment the elevator doors close behind Elias. His words linger like static in the air—*you don't see it, do you?*—and every hum of the lights feels louder for it. The courthouse fades into the gray rhythm of routine: papers stamped, names called, verdicts read. But beneath it all, I can feel that other rhythm pulsing steady and low, like something waiting under the floorboards.

By the time noon comes, my phone buzzes again.

Silas Kade.

For a moment, I consider ignoring it. Then I think of Elias—his warning, his jealousy—and something stubborn inside me pushes *accept.*

"Still joining me for lunch?" Silas asks, voice smooth and certain, as if the question's already been answered.

I should say no. I don't.

The wind cuts sharp off the harbor when I leave the courthouse. Snow drifts sideways, glinting under the pale sun. My reflection follows me in every window—faint, blurred, almost belonging to someone else. The city hums like a living thing. Each step toward the restaurant feels less like choice and more like inevitability.

The restaurant is all quiet wealth and soft shadow—the kind of place where the light itself feels expensive. Gold fixtures, white linen, muted conversations that sound like secrets. The scent of truffle oil hangs beneath the low murmur of music, threaded with something faintly metallic—money, power, old history.

A hostess greets me by name before I can even give it. "Mr. Kade is expecting you."

Her tone is smooth, practiced. She doesn't ask if I'd like to wait. She doesn't ask anything at all. She simply gestures for me to follow, leading me past the main dining room and down a narrow hallway paneled in dark wood. Each step softens beneath the carpeted floor, the sound of laughter and clinking glass fading until all that remains is the hush of isolation.

She stops at a closed door near the end. "He's inside."

I thank her, though my voice sounds distant in my own ears.

The private dining room feels separate from the world—lit by a single chandelier and a scattering of candles. The walls are lined with old books behind glass, spines etched in gold script. No music, no chatter. Just silence that hums like expectation.

Silas stands as I enter, his movements precise, deliberate. "Celeste."

The way he says my name feels rehearsed, but reverent—like a prayer he's practiced until it became second nature. His dark suit fits him like a confession. The firelight from the corner catches silver in his hair.

"You didn't have to go to all this trouble," I say, slipping into the seat across from him. "I was planning to be on time."

He smiles faintly, settling back into his chair. "I didn't want to be interrupted. There are things best said without an audience."

He gestures toward the table—two crystal glasses of sparkling water, a dish of lemon slices, and a single white envelope resting beside my plate. The wax seal is pressed deep red, a sigil I don't recognize glinting faintly in the light.

My pulse stutters. "What's this?"

"A formal invitation," he says lightly, though there's gravity beneath it. "The Inkbound Society is hosting their winter gathering tomorrow night. They'd like you to attend—as my guest."

I glance down at the envelope again, at the sigil that looks almost alive beneath the candlelight. "I've never heard of it."

"You wouldn't have." He leans forward, elbows resting lightly on the table. "It's an old order. Scholars, historians, archivists. Those who believe words don't just tell the truth—they *become* it. They shape the living record."

"And you think I belong with them?"

"I don't think." His smile deepens, quiet but sure. "I know. You give memory form, Celeste. You witness what others bury. You were made for their circle long before you ever picked up a pen."

The words slide under my skin before I can stop them. I trace the edge of the envelope with one finger. "And if I say no?"

His eyes catch the light, green-gray and knowing. "You won't."

There's no threat in it. No arrogance either. Just faith—like he's certain of something I haven't yet accepted. Devotion, shaped into command.

A server slips in without a sound, setting down two plates—duck glazed in dark wine, roasted fennel, blackberries glistening like drops of ink. Silas doesn't order. He doesn't need to. The table already knows what it's supposed to offer.

He raises his glass, the red wine catching in the flicker of candlelight. "To revelations."

I hesitate, then lift mine. "To clarity."

We drink. The wine is sweeter than I expect, heavier. It burns on the way down, slow and lingering.

When I set my glass back down, Silas is watching me with that same unnerving calm. "You were never meant for the noise of this world," he says softly. "You hear what others ignore. You carry echoes of things long forgotten."

I try to look away, but his voice draws me back.

"The Inkbound have been searching for someone like you," he continues. "No—*for you*. They've known your name longer than you've worn it."

My pulse quickens. "That sounds more like prophecy than invitation."

"Maybe it's both." His tone lowers, reverent. "The solstice is coming. The longest night. When the veil between what was and what is grows thin. That's when you'll remember what you are."

The air shifts—thicker, charged, vibrating just below the level of hearing. I feel it behind my ribs, that low hum that never really left.

Silas studies me, his voice dropping to a whisper. "You can feel it, can't you? The pull."

I don't answer. I don't have to.

He leans back slightly, eyes glinting like light on ink. "When the night reaches its longest hour, Celeste, you'll understand. You'll wake. And when you do—nothing in this world or the next will be able to stop what's already begun."

The words fall between us, quiet as prayer.
A blessing and a warning, spoken like a promise.

"Your detective friend called me earlier," Silas says casually, slicing through his duck with surgical precision. His tone is mild, but the blade in his hand glints under the candlelight. "He had questions about my past cases. I assume you know about that?"

My fork pauses midair. "He didn't tell me."

"No?" His expression softens into something dangerously close to sympathy. "He's worried about you."

The words land between us like a dropped glass—quiet, but sharp enough to cut.

Silas continues before I can answer, his voice smooth again, almost amused. "He thinks I'm dangerous." His smile curves, deliberate. "And maybe he's right. But danger isn't always the enemy of truth."

I set my fork down carefully, keeping my hands steady even as my pulse betrays me. "You make everything sound like a test."

He tilts his head, studying me through the thin veil of candlelight. "Maybe it is." The reflection in his eyes shifts—green, then silver, then something I can't name. "Maybe you've already been passing it without realizing."

The air between us hums, soft but relentless. The sound of the restaurant fades—the quiet murmur of other diners, the clink of crystal, even the faint rhythm of the city beyond the window. It all recedes until it's just the two of us and that low, insistent vibration that matches the beat of my heart.

Silas's voice lowers to a whisper. "Tell me, Celeste. When you write, do you ever feel like the words are already waiting for you? Like they existed long before your hand found the page?"

The question knocks the breath from my lungs. "How do you know that?"

His smile deepens, slow and deliberate, like the answer has always been there. "Because I've read what you haven't written yet."

The room tilts for a moment—just slightly—as if the floor itself exhales. Candlelight bleeds gold across the white tablecloth. I blink, and the world steadies again, but something in it has changed. The air feels denser now, alive, thrumming against my skin.

Silas reaches across the table, his fingertips grazing the back of my hand—barely a touch, but enough to make my breath catch. "Say you'll come tomorrow," he murmurs.

I glance down at the envelope, at the wax seal gleaming dark and red like fresh blood. "And if I don't?"

He withdraws his hand slowly, his voice calm, almost tender. "Then the invitation will find you anyway."

The hum beneath my skin answers before I do. It's low, steady, a pulse that feels both mine and not.

Silas watches me, eyes gleaming like wet ink in the candlelight. "You already know your answer," he says softly.

My mouth is dry. "And if I go?"

"Then you'll understand what's been calling you," he murmurs. "What's been trying to wake."

The words curl through the air, smoke and gravity at once. I should leave. I should stand, walk out, call Elias—anything to break whatever this is. But the thought dies the moment his hand finds mine across the table, fingers tracing the pulse at my wrist like he's measuring the beat for tempo.

"I'll go," I hear myself say. The words feel foreign, pulled from somewhere beneath reason.

His smile is slow, knowing. "Good."

Silas stands first, smooth and unhurried. When I rise, he's already closer than he should be—close enough that his breath ghosts across my cheek, that I can smell the wine on his lips.

"Tomorrow, then," he says, voice low, reverent. "Wear something that remembers who you are."

Before I can ask what that means, his hand lifts to my throat. Not rough—*reverent*. His thumb strokes the line of my pulse, slow and deliberate, like he's imprinting it into memory.

The contact steals the air from my lungs. The candlelight blurs, flickering gold against his collar. My heartbeat stumbles beneath his touch.

Then he kisses me.

It isn't hard or hurried. It's patient. Measured. The kind of kiss that feels like a question and an answer all at once. His hand stays at my throat, thumb still moving in that slow, claiming rhythm—as if he's reminding me who's already found me.

When he finally pulls back, the air feels thinner, the room quieter. The space between us hums, alive.

"Until tomorrow," he whispers.

I don't watch him leave. I can't. My knees feel unsteady, my breath unspooled. The candlelight gutters once, then steadies again, throwing shadows that ripple across the books behind the glass.

I touch my fingers to my throat, to the heat he left there, and find my pulse still racing beneath them.

Outside, snow begins to fall again—soft, deliberate, endless.

And somewhere beneath it, something in me stirs.

Chapter 31
Celeste

The invitation sits on my vanity beneath the soft glow of the lamp, the wax seal catching light like a drop of blood. I've traced its edges a dozen times, half-expecting it to vanish when I blink. But it doesn't. It feels solid. Heavy. Real.

And yet, I can't shake the thought that it's been here before—that I've opened this same envelope in another life, read these same words under the same breath of anticipation.

The Inkbound Society requests your presence.

The script curves elegantly across the page, the ink slightly raised as if freshly pressed. Beneath it, a single line written in Silas's hand:

Wear red. The night remembers its own.

A knock at the door pulls me from the page. I open it to find no one there—only a black garment bag resting neatly against the frame, the faintest trace of sandalwood and smoke clinging to it. My pulse skips.

Inside, folded with impossible precision, waits the dress.

Blood-red silk, trimmed in black lace so fine it looks like shadow spun into thread. The corset dips low, daringly so, its boning lined in velvet, its laces the color of midnight. Beneath it, sheer sleeves whisper down to my wrists, and the skirt flows in a slow, heavy cascade that gleams like spilled wine.

It's beautiful. Terrifyingly so.

I lift it from the bag, the fabric sliding over my hands with a sound like breath. It shouldn't fit, but somehow I know it will—like it was made for me before I ever measured a single inch of myself.

I stand before the mirror, the room hushed except for the faint tick of the clock. The red catches the lamplight, deepening to garnet where the fabric folds. I feel strange in it—powerful, unfamiliar. Like I'm wearing someone else's memory.

When I lace the corset, each pull feels ritualistic, each knot deliberate. My heartbeat slows. My hands don't shake.

By the time I fasten the last hook, the woman staring back at me looks like a secret. Her hair—my hair—catches the light in copper and fire. The dark line of the dress frames my collarbones, my throat, the steady pulse beneath it.

For a long moment, I can't look away.

This isn't vanity. It's recognition.

I add the final touches without thinking—black earrings, a silver bracelet I don't remember owning, the faintest hint of perfume that smells faintly of smoke and winter. When I reach for my coat, I see the envelope again, half-hidden beneath the lamplight.

The words shimmer faintly as if wet.

The night remembers its own.

Outside, the city waits beneath a sheet of frost, its windows glowing faintly in the dark. I slip the invitation into my clutch and step into the cold.

Each breath hangs silver in the air. The snow is beginning again, soft and slow. And for the first time in a long while, I don't feel like I'm walking to a dinner. I feel like I'm walking toward a reckoning.

The night greets me with silence. Snow drifts lazily beneath the streetlights, flakes catching on my lashes and melting against my skin. The world feels muffled—like the city is holding its breath.

At the curb, a sleek black car waits, the kind that doesn't belong in my neighborhood. Its windows are tinted, its chrome glinting faintly beneath the yellow glow of the lamp overhead. The driver steps out as I approach, dressed in a dark overcoat, hat pulled low.

"Miss Duvall?" His voice is polite, almost rehearsed.

"Yes."

He opens the back door with a quiet nod. "Mr. Kade sent me. He said to tell you he's looking forward to the evening."

Of course he did.

I hesitate for just a second, watching the faint mist curl from the car's exhaust, then slide inside. The leather is soft and warm, the air faintly scented with clove and something deeper—amber, maybe. It smells like him.

The city slips past the window, quiet and gleaming. Christmas lights blur into streaks of red and gold as we cross the bridge toward Boston, the water below ink-dark and still.

For a while, I just watch the reflection of the passing skyline. My face looks strange in the glass—half shadow, half flame. The dress glows even in the low light, the corset pressing my breath shallow. It feels less like clothing and more like armor.

The driver says nothing, only glances at me once in the rearview mirror before returning his focus to the road.

I trace the faint outline of the wax seal in my clutch with my thumb, the words echoing in my mind.

The night remembers its own.

The car turns off the main road, winding through a part of the city I don't recognize—streets lined with stately brownstones and iron gates slick with frost. Finally, we pull up before a mansion that looks older than the rest of the street combined.

Light spills from its tall windows, warm and golden, but it's the kind of warmth that feels staged—inviting, but not safe.

The driver steps out, opening my door before I can reach for the handle. "We've arrived, Miss Duvall."

I step out carefully, heels crunching against the thin crust of snow. The building towers above me, its stone façade carved with faint reliefs I can't quite make out in the dim light. The air hums faintly—something electric beneath the quiet.

At the top of the steps, Silas waits.

He's dressed in black, the fabric of his coat catching just enough light to look like it's drinking it in. His hair is slicked back, a few strands escaping to frame his temple. When he sees me, his expression shifts—something softer, almost reverent.

"Perfect timing," he says, offering his hand. "You look…" He pauses, smile deepening. "Like the story the night's been waiting to tell."

I take his hand before I can think better of it. His skin is warm against the cold, steady where mine trembles.

For a moment, neither of us moves. The city feels far away—muted, watching. Snow gathers in my hair, melting on my lashes. He studies me like he's memorizing something he's already read a hundred times before.

"You came," he says softly, the words carrying more weight than they should.

"I said I would."

His smile turns slow, deliberate. "There are promises made in daylight that dissolve in the dark. But not yours."

He steps closer, the distance between us shrinking until I can feel the heat radiating from him, the hum beneath my skin syncing to the rhythm of his breath. His gloved hand rises—hesitant, then sure—fingers tracing the line of my jaw before resting lightly against my throat. His thumb presses into the hollow there, a quiet claim disguised as a touch.

"You feel it too," he murmurs. "The current beneath everything. The call."

I should pull away. I don't.

His thumb moves in slow circles, the contact steady, grounding, almost tender. "Don't be afraid of it," he says. "It's been waiting for you."

Then he kisses me.

It's soft, almost reverent, but there's command in it too—like a vow being spoken without words. The cold disappears, swallowed whole by the heat of his mouth, the slow pressure of his hand at my throat. I feel the hum surge through me, answering something I can't name.

When he pulls back, the air feels thinner, the night sharper. His gaze lingers on mine for a beat longer than it should.

"Come," he says, his voice low, threaded with quiet certainty. "They're waiting for you."

He doesn't have to say who *they* are. The mansion looms above us, its tall doors carved with faint golden veins that pulse like breath beneath the surface.

I follow him up the steps.

And the hum becomes a heartbeat.

The doors open before we reach them. The moment we cross the threshold, the air changes.

Warmth folds over me, heavy and deliberate, carrying a scent I can't quite name—smoke, ink, rain on old parchment. The sound of conversation hums low beneath the vaulted ceilings, a current of voices that somehow feels like one voice speaking in harmony.

The entryway opens into a grand hall lined with dark oak and flickering sconces. The walls are filled with portraits so old their subjects might as well be myths—faces rendered in chiaroscuro, eyes painted with unsettling precision. I swear one of them blinks.

Silas's hand rests lightly at the small of my back, guiding me forward. "Welcome to the Inkbound Society," he murmurs. "Where history is written by those who remember it."

The hall opens into the dining chamber, and I have to stop to take it in.

A single, impossibly long table stretches down the room, draped in black linen embroidered with threads of gold that form an intricate geometric pattern—circles within circles, lines intersecting like constellations. Candles burn in candelabras fashioned from wrought iron and bone-white marble, their flames steady despite the faint draft whispering through the air.

At least two dozen people are seated already, their attire a spectrum of elegance—velvet, silk, brocade, colors that look plucked from twilight. Masks rest on many of their faces—some simple, others carved into shapes that echo animals or mythic beasts. Yet despite the extravagance, each of them turns to look as I enter.

Not out of curiosity. Recognition.

I spot a few familiar faces among them—figures from the Thanksgiving dinner. The woman who'd spoken of "heritage" as if it were a private joke. The elderly man with the silver-tipped cane who had known my name before I'd given it. Their smiles are polite. Knowing.

At the head of the table sits an empty chair carved from black walnut, the crest of a quill and flame etched into its back. A single book lies open before it, pages blank, a fountain pen resting across the spine.

The room hums softly, a vibration I feel in my chest more than I hear.

"Every gathering begins with the Reading," Silas says, his voice pitched low near my ear. "It's an old tradition. Words carry power, Celeste. What we speak tonight will shape what's written tomorrow."

He guides me toward two open seats halfway down the table. The guests watch as we sit, then lower their gazes in unison. The motion feels rehearsed, almost devotional.

From the shadows near the head of the table, a figure steps forward—a woman with silver hair twisted into a crown braid, her gown the color of obsidian ink. When she speaks, her voice carries effortlessly, each word deliberate, weighted.

"Tonight we break bread in remembrance of the written word—the first binding, the first truth."

A server appears from nowhere, setting before each guest a small leather-bound book, no larger than a palm. Mine feels warm to the touch.

"Tonight," the woman continues, "we honor the Keepers of Memory. The chroniclers. The witnesses." Her eyes find me across the table, sharp and knowing. "Those who transcribe the world into being."

The hum rises, subtle at first—like the low thrum of a heartbeat beneath the table. The candles flare, their flames stretching tall and thin, bending toward the center of the room as if drawn by breath.

Silas doesn't move, but I can feel his attention like heat beside me. When the woman's gaze leaves mine, I exhale, unaware I'd been holding my breath.

The first course arrives—bowls of dark soup flecked with gold leaf, served on black porcelain. The scent is rich and unfamiliar. As spoons touch the surface, the liquid ripples faintly, reflecting not our faces, but shapes that shift and blur—crowns, gates, wings of flame.

"Drink," Silas whispers.

My hand trembles around the spoon, but I do. The taste is metallic and sweet, like wine left too long in the dark. Heat blooms down my throat. The hum in the room grows louder.

When I look down again, the small book beside my plate is no longer blank.

My name glows faintly across the first page—written in ink the color of blood.

Celeste Duvall — Witness.

I lift my eyes to Silas. His smile is quiet. Certain. "Welcome home," he says.

The room exhales as one. Candles flicker. Pages whisper.

And I realize the dinner hasn't begun.

It's already happening—around us, through us, written as we breathe.

The hum in the air deepens until it feels almost alive—like the whole room is breathing in unison. The walls seem closer now, the candlelight bending around us in soft ripples that make the edges of everything shimmer.

I try to focus on the clink of silverware, the murmur of voices, the scent of rosemary and wine. Normal things. Real things. But beneath it all, something pulses—a rhythm just under my skin that isn't my heartbeat.

A man across the table raises his glass. "To the record," he says. His voice carries easily, smooth as old ink. "May what is written never fade."

The others repeat the phrase in one voice, the sound too even, too rehearsed. My throat tightens before I can stop it. Silas lifts his glass and turns to me, that unreadable half-smile curving his lips.

"To the record," he says softly, and the way he looks at me makes my pulse trip.

I force the words out, my voice quieter than I intend. "To the record."

The taste of wine burns down my throat, warm and sharp.

As the next course arrives—seared duck glazed with something dark and sweet—the conversation shifts. The woman with the silver braid speaks of *preservation*, of *balance*, of *truth made flesh*. Her words twist together like verses, phrases repeating, building, until it feels less like dinner talk and more like liturgy.

"The written word is the oldest form of magic," someone near the end of the table says. "Every spell begins with a story."

A soft murmur of agreement circles the room. I glance at Silas, searching for irony in his expression, but there's none.

He's watching me.

"You don't believe that," I whisper, half a question, half a plea for something normal.

"I believe in patterns," he says simply. "And in those who are born to remember them."

My stomach twists—not from fear, but recognition. Something about the phrasing—it feels familiar, like a dream I almost woke from once.

When the main course is cleared, servers bring out slender glass cups filled with a translucent golden liquid. It glows faintly in the light.

"Ink of oath," the silver-haired woman says, her tone reverent. "To see, to bind, to remember."

I glance at Silas, whispering, "What is this?"

His gaze flicks to mine. "Don't be afraid."

That should've been my warning.

The liquid tastes like honey and smoke. For a heartbeat, it's pleasant—warm, alive. Then heat blooms behind my eyes, and the edges of the room blur. The gold-threaded tablecloth pulses faintly, the patterns moving like a heartbeat.

The guests speak in low, melodic tones, reciting something I can't quite understand. The hum in my chest responds, rising in pitch.

And then—something shifts.

The air thickens. My fingers tremble. The candle flames stretch and twist, their light bending toward me like metal to a magnet. A murmur ripples through the room. Someone exhales sharply, as if recognizing something sacred.

Silas doesn't move, but his eyes darken, the gray-green gone silver in the flicker of light. "You feel it, don't you?"

My voice is barely a whisper. "What... what's happening to me?"

"You're remembering," he says. "You always do."

The woman at the head of the table rises. "The Witness has returned."

The words strike something deep inside me. My breath catches. The hum inside me becomes a song—low, resonant, endless.

The walls of the room fade into darkness, the faces blur, and for an instant, I'm standing somewhere else entirely—beneath a sky split by fire and shadow, a thousand voices crying my name in languages I shouldn't understand.

When I blink, I'm back at the table. My glass is empty. The candle flames are steady again. The hum is gone.

Silas reaches for my hand, steadying me. "It's alright," he says quietly, too calm. "It's only the beginning."

I glance at the open book at the head of the table. The pages aren't blank anymore. Lines of fresh ink have appeared, shimmering faintly as they dry.

And at the bottom—written in crimson—my name.

Celeste Duvall — Witness Awakened.

Chapter 32
Elias

The snow's falling again by the time I park across from her building in Salem. The street's quiet—most people already tucked away behind warm lights and locked doors. My car engine ticks softly as it cools, the sound oddly loud in the stillness.

I tell myself I'm just checking in. A follow-up. Nothing more. But I've been sitting here for forty minutes, and we both know better.

At 7:42 p.m, the door opens.

Celeste steps out into the lamplight. Even through the thin veil of snow, she looks sharper, more defined against the cold night—her coat cinched tight, her hair catching the faint red gleam from the sign above the café across the street. She pauses, looking both ways, then down at something in her hand.

A sleek black town car glides to the curb, too polished for a small Salem street. The driver—gloved, anonymous—gets out and opens the back door. Celeste hesitates for a heartbeat, glancing over her shoulder like she feels the weight of being watched. Then she slides inside.

I'm already moving.

My engine growls to life, headlights dimmed as I ease into the street. The car ahead signals south, heading toward Boston. The road's slick, but they move like they've done this a hundred times—every turn deliberate, no hesitation.

The drive should take less than an hour, but tonight the weather stretches it thin. Snow dusts the highway, blurring the lanes into a single white ribbon. My wipers fight to keep up, rhythmic and relentless. Through the streaked glass, the town car's taillights flicker—two small red beacons leading me deeper into something I can't name.

I should turn back. I know it.
But I don't.

The miles slide by—Peabody, Lynn, Revere. The glow of the city begins to rise ahead, muted through the snowfall. Boston always looks holy from a distance, domes and spires shining like they belong to something purer than it is.

By morning, the snow has stopped, but the city feels muted—streets washed to gray, sky low and heavy with that dull light that never becomes day. I've been at my desk since six, chasing ghosts across a digital map.

The department's surveillance feed cycles through four monitors, each one flickering with grainy footage from the highway cameras. I scrub through the timeline again, watching my own car glide through the tunnel just before midnight. The timestamp ticks forward. Nothing ahead of me. Nothing behind.

The town car is gone.

I replay it twice, three times, jaw tightening each time the frame rolls over and the screen shows only the empty road. Every other vehicle registers—headlights, license plates, the blur of motion—but not hers. Not the one that carried Celeste.

A muscle between my shoulders tightens, a steady, ghosting ache that feels older than fatigue. I roll it out, but it lingers—a pressure like the memory of a hand that's not there anymore.

Something's missing. Not just from the footage—from me. Like I'm circling an answer I already know but can't pull into focus.

I take another sip of cold coffee, click through the nearby traffic intersections. Same story. The car appears outside Salem, three separate angles confirming it. It passes the toll station on 1A. Then... nothing. No record of it entering Boston, no plates flagged, no trace on any municipal feed.

It just stops existing.

I lean back, eyes burning from the screen. The air in the precinct smells like burnt coffee and paper dust. My partner's desk is empty; the world feels too quiet for a weekday morning.

A faint hum builds in the back of my head—the kind that comes before a headache, or before remembering something you shouldn't.

What if I didn't lose the car? What if it slipped somewhere I can't follow?

The ache between my shoulder blades pulses again, sharp enough to draw breath. I reach back instinctively, half expecting to find something there—heat, weight, a mark. But my fingers meet only fabric.

I close my eyes, press the heels of my hands against them. The afterimage of headlights still burns behind the lids—two red points fading into white.

Maybe the footage is corrupted. Maybe there's a gap in the feed. Maybe I'm just exhausted.

But the hollow in my gut says otherwise.

I reopen the file, frame by frame, eyes locked on the place where the car should be. For half a second, between one flicker and the next, there's something—a distortion, a shimmer that bends the light like heat on glass.

Then it's gone again.

And for the first time since I started this case, I'm not sure I'm chasing something human.

I scrub the playback again, this time slowing the frame rate to half-speed. The timestamp blinks in the corner—11:58 p.m. A line of cars passes through the tunnel, each one crisp, identifiable, traceable.

Then the space where Celeste's town car should be wavers. Not empty, not full—something in between.

The light bends, almost imperceptibly, like heat rising off asphalt. A shimmer that lasts less than a heartbeat. When I freeze the frame, the distortion collapses into static, the edges of the tunnel blurring into gray noise.

I lean forward until my forehead nearly touches the monitor. "Jesus," I mutter under my breath.

It's not a camera glitch. I've seen those a hundred times. This looks different—organic somehow, as if the air itself refused to be recorded.

I flag the file and call down to forensics.

"Hey, Rina? Shaw. I've got footage that needs enhancement—Section

B-42, timestamp 11:58:03 through :06. Can you run a detail sharpen and color analysis?"

"On it," she says, bored. "Expecting a plate number?"

"Something like that."

The line clicks off. I sit there, listening to the low hum of the monitors, the faint pop of old wiring behind the wall. The ache between my shoulders sharpens again—like a warning this time, or a pull.

Fifteen minutes later, the email pings in.

Subject: Re: Tunnel Footage

"Nothing there, Detective. I ran every filter twice. No license plate, no vehicle, no thermal trace. You sure your timestamp's right?"

I stare at the attached still frame. Just a stretch of empty highway.

But I know what I saw.

I replay it again. Frame by frame, second by second, chasing that shimmer like it might prove I'm not losing my mind. But the harder I look, the less certain I am that it was ever there at all.

The ache crawls higher up my neck, settling at the base of my skull. My hand drifts unconsciously toward the spot, fingers pressing against skin that feels too warm.

Maybe I'm exhausted. Maybe it's nothing.

But when I close my eyes, I can still see the distortion pulsing behind my lids—like light caught in water, or a doorway trying to open.

And in the static between frames, I swear I hear something whisper:

You're too close.

By the time the shimmer fades from my mind, the clock on the wall reads 3:17 p.m. I've wasted half the day watching nothing happen. The room feels smaller now, the hum of the lights louder, sharper. My coffee's gone cold again.

I shut the monitor off and grab my coat. Logic can't explain what the footage doesn't show, but instinct says there's something beneath it—something older than evidence and cleaner than coincidence.

Danvers isn't far, maybe forty minutes if traffic's kind. I take the back roads, windows cracked just enough to let the cold air in. The ache between my shoulder blades hasn't eased; if anything, it's worse. Feels like someone's tracing a fingertip along bone, slow and deliberate.

By the time I pull into downtown Danvers, the sky's the color of pewter, and the first flurries of snow drift lazy through the air. The sign hanging over the narrow storefront is hand-painted, the letters flaking but still legible:

The Witching Hour – Books, Relics, Tours.

Inside, it smells like sandalwood, dust, and old wood polish. Shelves bow under the weight of books whose spines are etched with half-legible titles—*Daemonologia Brittanica, The Key of Solomon, On the Properties of Salt and Blood.* Dried herbs hang from the rafters, and a black cat sprawls on the counter beside a stack of flyers advertising *Ghost Walks of Old Salem.*

"Elias Shaw," a voice drawls from the back. "Now there's a ghost I didn't expect to see walk in."

I turn toward the doorway. Jude Morelli emerges, sleeves rolled to his elbows, a smudge of ash on his cheek. He looks exactly the same as he did five years ago—sharp grin, too many rings, a cigarette tucked behind one ear.

"Been a while," I say.

"Not long enough, probably." He smirks, then gestures at the shelves. "You finally ready to admit your job doesn't have all the answers?"

"Something like that." I step closer, pull the folded printout of the still frame from my pocket, slide it across the counter. "Tell me what you see."

Jude picks it up, squinting. "Nothing."

"Look closer."

He tilts the page under the lamplight, the shimmer of the photo catching faintly on its gloss. His brow furrows. "That's not digital interference. It's displacement."

"Meaning?"

"Meaning something's there that your camera wasn't built to see." He glances up, studying me. "Where'd you get this?"

"Tunnel footage," I say. "Midnight. A car disappeared."

Jude whistles low. "You chasing ghosts now, Shaw?"

"I don't believe in ghosts."

He grins. "That's cute."

The cat stretches, knocking over a flyer that flutters to the floor. I bend to pick it up—it's advertising a special *Winter Solstice Night Tour: Crossing the Veil.*

Jude leans against the counter, arms crossed. "You ever wonder what really happens when the veil thins?"

I straighten, meet his gaze. "Not until now."

Jude studies me for a beat longer, then nods toward a back shelf. "There's a book you should see. Old. Came from a church archive in Salem before it burned. Mentions something called *The Inkbound Society.* Sound familiar?"

The ache between my shoulder blades tightens again, sharp enough to make me wince.

"No," I lie.

Jude smiles faintly, like he knows better. "Then maybe it's time you start believing in something, Detective. Because whatever's hiding in that footage? It's not done with you yet."

Chapter 33
Elias

Jude tilts his head, still watching me. "You always did wear your tension like armor," he says lightly, but his tone shifts—less teasing now, more studying. "Except this isn't just stress, is it?"

I straighten instinctively. "What are you talking about?"

He steps out from behind the counter, moving slow, deliberate. The air changes with him—he's always had that presence, the kind that makes rooms feel smaller. "You've got a murky look about you, Shaw. Clouded around the edges. The kind of thing that happens when someone's brushed up against something they weren't supposed to."

"Save the mystic crap, Jude."

He ignores the warning in my voice and circles me once, the smell of clove smoke trailing faintly behind him. "You don't feel it?" he murmurs.

"Right here." His hand hovers near my shoulder blades—not touching, just close enough for the hair on my neck to rise. "Like something's alive under your skin. Trying to push its way out."

A sharp pulse fires down my spine, hot and electric. I jerk away. "Don't."

Jude holds his hands up, palms open. "Relax. I'm not doing anything. That's all you."

I roll my shoulders, trying to shake it off, but the ache deepens into something stranger—a vibration low in the bones, steady as a second heartbeat.

"What the hell is that supposed to mean?"

"It means," Jude says softly, "something bound you. Maybe a curse, maybe a ward, maybe something older. Hard to tell. But it's leaking now."

"Bound me? By what?"

He studies me a long moment, eyes narrowing. "You wouldn't believe me if I told you. But if you've been anywhere near the Inkbound... it would explain the hum."

"The what?"

"The pulse under your shoulder blades. It's not pain, Shaw—it's memory." Jude steps back behind the counter, pulling open a drawer. "Here." He slides out a small glass vial filled with ash-gray powder. "Burn this tonight. Cedar and salt. Won't fix it, but it might quiet it down enough for you to sleep."

I take the vial, feeling the faint vibration through the glass. "You think I'm cursed."

"I think," Jude says, "you've seen something that doesn't want to stay seen."

The ache flares once more, sharp and bright, and for a split second, I swear I hear a whisper—my name, drawn out in a voice I can't place.

I close my fist around the vial. "If I start believing all this, what happens next?"

Jude's grin fades. "Then you stop chasing killers, Shaw. And start realizing you're part of the story."

Jude flips deeper into the tome, the paper whispering like dry leaves. "See this?" he says, pointing to a page where the ink has bled almost to oblivion. "Most of these names are lost. Faded beyond recovery. But two remain."

The drawings on the page are faint but still visible — two books, rendered in old ink and careful hand. Beneath the first, *Ledger of the Damned* curls in precise lettering. The second is harder to read, the words nearly swallowed by time: *Gospel of the Damned.*

"Everything else?" Jude gestures to the rest of the page, where ghost letters drift like ash. "Gone. The rest of the titles burned themselves out, or someone made sure of it."

He leans on the counter, lowering his voice. "The *Ledger* you already know. The Inkbound's masterpiece. A record of judgment written in blood and bound in oath. But the *Gospel*—that one's older. It didn't belong to mortals. They say it sang itself into existence. The Sirens were its keepers."

"Sirens," I echo. "Like the kind that drown sailors?"

"Like the kind that sang kingdoms into ruin." Jude closes the book halfway, eyes never leaving mine. "They used song the way the Inkbound used ink. Both forms of creation. Both bound by rule and price."

I exhale slowly. "And the Bookbinders?"

His mouth twitches—almost a smile, though it doesn't reach his eyes. "Descendants of the original thirteen bloodlines. The first to bridge words and will. Every one of them carried a trace of that old power—voice, ink, fire, shadow. Over time, they forgot what it meant. The families scattered. Some went into law, some into politics, some into ink and parchment." He taps the closed cover. "But blood doesn't forget. It just waits."

My gaze drops to the book again. The drawings seem to shift in the dim shop light, the lines bending like something alive beneath the page.

Jude continues softly, "If the Inkbound have the *Ledger*, it means one of the bloodlines still holds the right to write in it. And if the *Gospel* has started to stir…" He trails off, looking toward the window where the snow drifts pale against the glass. "Then it's calling its keeper home."

The ache between my shoulder blades pulses again, deep and rhythmic. For a heartbeat, I think I hear a faint hum—something like a chord half-remembered, vibrating in the space between us.

I step back from the counter. "You think this is all connected to the murders."

"I think," Jude says, "someone's been writing again—and one of the old bloodlines has started to remember."

I close the book carefully, but the sound of it shutting feels too loud, too final. It's as if the air itself exhales.

Jude's voice drops to a whisper. "You can't stop what's already written, Shaw. But maybe—if you're lucky—you can learn which page you're on."

"I'm not buying this, Jude."

My voice comes out sharper than I mean it to, but I don't care. "Ink that binds souls? Sirens? Bloodlines? You're talking like a man who reads too much late-night Reddit."

Jude doesn't flinch. "You came here because you already know something's wrong."

I laugh, but it sounds hollow even to me. "I came here for leads. Evidence. Facts. I'm a detective, not some occult hobbyist with a crystal collection. There's no such thing as curses, or angels, or demons. Just people. People doing awful things and calling it fate."

"Then tell me this," Jude says quietly. "How does a car vanish off every traffic camera in Boston? You watched it disappear, didn't you?"

The words hit like a gut punch. I freeze before I can stop myself.

"You've felt it too," he continues. "That hum under your skin. The ache between your shoulders that won't go away. The way lights flicker when you walk by." His tone drops to something calm and certain, like he's explaining the weather. "You've been fighting it your whole life. You just don't have the language for it yet."

"I'm not part of anything," I snap. "I'm not cursed. I'm just—" I stop. I don't even know how to finish that sentence. "I'm tired," I mutter.

Jude watches me for a beat, then turns to a cabinet behind the counter. The hinges groan as he opens it, pulling out a smaller book—dark blue leather, worn thin at the corners, clasped with silver that gleams like an eye.

He sets it in front of me. "If you want proof," he says, "start here."

I glance down at the thing. "What is it?"

"A compendium," Jude answers. "Fragments from before the binding wars. It lists what the bloodlines could do—sight, fire, shadow, ink, voice, memory, blood. Abilities humanity buried when the world fractured."

I shake my head. "You're telling me we just... misplaced magic?"

He smiles faintly. "We buried it. Fear is a great shovel."

I huff out a breath and rub the back of my neck. The ache there flares again, sharp enough to make me wince.

Jude notices. "That pain between your shoulders," he says softly. "It's not just tension. It's a seal. Something locked your power away a long time ago."

I glare at him. "Power. Jesus, Jude."

"I can break it," he says simply. "If that's what you want. But once it's undone, there's no going back. Whatever was written into you—once it wakes up, it stays awake."

My pulse kicks hard. The air in the shop feels too thick, heavy with incense and something metallic. "And if I say no?"

"Then you keep pretending it isn't happening," Jude says. "Until something else wakes it up for you."

For a long moment, I just stare at him. The silver clasp on the book catches the light, like it's watching me back.

"You think I'm part of this," I say.

"I *know* you are," he replies. "You just haven't remembered yet."

Something twists in my gut, a quiet warning—or maybe recognition. I push away from the counter, trying to steady my breathing.

He doesn't stop me. "Take the book," he says. "Read. Then decide whether you still want to pretend."

I grab the damn thing because arguing feels worse. The leather is warm under my hand, like it's been waiting.

Outside, the wind howls down the street. The ache between my shoulders throbs again, steady as a heartbeat.

For the first time, I'm not sure it's mine.

Chapter 34
Celeste

The ride back to Salem is quiet.

Too quiet.

The driver doesn't speak. He doesn't even look at me. The hum of the engine fills the silence, a low, steady pulse that settles somewhere behind my ribs. Headlights carve through the dark in thin, liquid lines, scattering across the snow-slick streets before vanishing into shadow again.

Outside, Boston fades—its skyline dissolving into a blur of light and smoke until there's nothing left but my reflection in the glass. Pale skin. Eyes too bright. Lips still tinged with the taste of wine.

My skin still hums.

Not from the drink. Not from Silas's hand guiding me through that candlelit hall. But from something deeper. Something that doesn't belong to the night we just left behind.

The dinner hadn't felt like a social event. It had felt like ceremony. A communion cloaked in silk and gold, where every glance carried meaning and every word sounded like part of an oath I hadn't meant to take. The scent of spice and smoke still clings to my hair, the echo of that single phrase still lodged behind my ribs:

Welcome home, Celeste.

Home.

The word felt foreign in his mouth—and even stranger in mine. I've lived my entire life in this world and never felt less at home than I did surrounded by those people, their perfect manners and knowing smiles. Like they were all in on a secret written in a language I was just beginning to remember.

When the car turns onto my street, the lights of Salem look dimmer than usual—muted, almost brittle. The driver eases to a stop in front of my building, the tires crunching against old ice.

I wait, expecting something—his voice, a message, a shadow slipping from the corner of my vision. But there's nothing.

The driver steps out, opens my door without a word. His face is unreadable beneath the brim of his hat.

"Good evening, Miss Duvall," he says at last. His tone is polite. Empty.

Before I can ask who sent him—or if I'm meant to thank him—he's already gone, the car gliding away into the dark as if it never existed.

The street is silent except for the faint hum still alive beneath my skin, steady as breath, waiting.

Inside, my apartment feels smaller than usual. Too bright. Too human. I set my clutch on the table and catch sight of myself in the mirror—red lace, tousled hair, pupils blown wide. I look like someone I don't know.

I should shower. Sleep. Pretend this was just another lavish dinner with too many secrets and too much wine.

But the moment I unfasten the corset, the air feels electric, my pulse matching the same rhythm that had thrummed through the hall during the toast. A hum I'd thought was in my imagination until now.

I move to the window. Snow has begun to fall—slow, deliberate, like it's thinking about each flake before it lands. The city is quiet. The kind of quiet that listens back.

When I close my eyes, flashes come unbidden:

Gold-rimmed chalices.

Ink pooling in a bowl shaped like a heart.

A voice reciting names I can't quite hear.

My own hand—bleeding, signing something.

I gasp and step back. The vision fades. The glass is clear again. My reflection looks pale, frightened, but the hum under my skin hasn't stopped.

I reach for my journal on the coffee table and open it to a blank page. The pen feels heavier tonight, my hand trembling as I start to write.

Something happened tonight.

I don't remember all of it, but I think they do.

And Silas—he looked at me like he knew what I'd forgotten.

The words pour out faster than I can form the thoughts. My hand aches, but it won't stop.

> *The candles bent toward me.*
> *The air sang my name.*

The room knew me before I spoke.

Ink drags in uneven strokes. The pen scratches across the paper, faster, sloppier—sentences bleeding into one another until they lose shape.

He said welcome home.
He said the ink remembers.
He said I was never lost, only sleeping.

My hand jerks once, hard enough to splatter ink across the margin. The words keep coming anyway.

The book opened.
The light moved.
The hum had teeth.
The witness woke.

The last phrase repeats itself—over and over—until the letters dissolve into a blur of black. My chest tightens. I blink down, breath uneven, and realize I don't recognize what I've written.

The handwriting isn't mine.

It's neater. Precise. Each letter formed with care, almost ornamental, like calligraphy carved into skin. The ink looks darker too—red-black, like it hasn't quite decided which it wants to be.

I flip back a few pages, heart hammering. The earlier entries are mine—messy loops, rushed scrawl—but scattered between them, faintly pressed into the paper, are fragments in that same unfamiliar hand.

> *The ledger must be balanced.*
> *The ink is the blood between worlds.*
> *The sea remembers its own.*

I trace one line with my fingertip, and the ink ripples—subtle, like breath. The hum beneath my skin swells in answer, low and alive.

The radiator clicks once. Somewhere behind me, something shifts—too soft to be real, too close to ignore.

I turn. Nothing. Just my reflection in the dark window, pale and still, watching me.

When I glance back at the page, there's one more line I swear wasn't there before.

You are not writing this alone.

The words shimmer faintly, then fade to black.

My hand shakes as I close the journal, pressing the cover shut as if I could trap whatever wrote with me inside. The room is silent again—almost.

Because beneath the quiet, I can still hear it.

That low hum.

Waiting.

It's darker, sharper—almost carved into the paper.

A symbol sits where my signature should be, one I've never seen before but somehow know by heart: a circle of flame split by ink.

The hum inside me crescendos—pain, pleasure, power—all tangled together until it feels like something breaking open.

I drop the pen.

The light flickers once, twice. Then everything goes dark except for the faint glow bleeding from the pages of the journal, the ink shimmering faintly gold in the dark.

I don't remember falling asleep.

One moment, I'm staring at the glowing pages; the next, I'm somewhere else entirely—weightless, submerged. The world hums like it's breathing with me.

The air—or maybe the water—moves against my skin in slow, deliberate waves. Every breath tastes like salt and honey, thick with something electric. The darkness isn't empty. It's alive. It hums. It knows me.

When I move, the world moves with me. My body feels different—fluid, stronger, too aware. My skin shimmers faintly beneath the surface, light rippling over it like fire refracted through water.

A voice hums just below hearing. It's not words at first—just vibration sliding along my spine until it blooms behind my ribs. When it finally shapes itself, it sounds like mine, layered over something deeper.

You remember now, don't you?

Shapes swirl in the dark—a silhouette made of mist and flame, its edges dissolving with every breath. It steps closer, and I realize it's me. Or what I was before this life pretended to tame me. Eyes like molten amber. Hair floating in the water like threads of blood and gold. Lips parted, whispering the truth I've been running from.

"You're not dreaming," she says. "You're remembering."

The world tilts. I see flashes—faces, lovers, prey. Men and women both, drawn by the same magnetic pull, their desires unspooled in my hands like threads of light. I see the power of it—how easily hunger becomes devotion, how love becomes ruin.

The voice—my other self—circles me, close enough that I can feel her breath against my ear.

> *You were born to be worshiped.*
> *Born to feed.*
> *Born to unmake.*

Her words slide through me, leaving a shiver that's not entirely fear. My pulse quickens, echoing the rhythm of waves. Images flash behind my eyes: a song rising from my throat, glass shattering, men sinking beneath black water with my name on their lips.

"I'm not that," I whisper, but it sounds small, unconvincing.

The reflection laughs softly. "Not yet."

I reach out, desperate to touch her—to understand. My fingers meet her skin, and the contact burns. Not pain. *Awakening.* A surge of heat, pleasure, and memory all at once.

I see another world: spires of glass and obsidian, seas made of flame, voices chanting my name as the sky split apart. I see a ledger bound in skin and ink—and a hand, my hand, signing it.

Then everything goes white.

I wake with a gasp, tangled in sheets, the taste of salt still on my lips. The air in the room is cold, but sweat beads along my skin. My hair clings to my neck as though I've just surfaced from the ocean.

On the nightstand, my journal lies open again. A single line glows faintly across the page, written in that same golden ink:

The song is returning.

The hum inside me answers like a heartbeat.

And it hasn't left since.

It lingers low beneath my heartbeat—too steady to be imagination.

I tell myself it's just adrenaline or lack of sleep. But the mirror doesn't

lie—not completely.

There's a light under my skin this morning, a faint shimmer that moves

when I breathe.

I shower too long, hoping the water will wash it away, but the heat only

makes it worse.

When I close my eyes, I can almost feel the waves from the dream lapping

against me again—the phantom touch of hands that were my own, the pull

of the tide that isn't.

By the time I step outside, the world feels sharper.

Colors too bright.

Air too thin.

Salem in December looks postcard-perfect—snow dusting the eaves,

wreaths on every door, the smell of cinnamon and wood smoke curling

through the streets—but everything vibrates slightly, like reality's half a

note out of tune.

At The Witch's Brew, I order my usual dirty chai, and June gives me

a look I can't quite read. It isn't judgment—something softer, almost

reverent.

When she passes me the cup, her fingers brush mine, and for a heartbeat

her breath catches.

"You look different today," she says quietly.

I laugh it off, but the sound feels wrong in my throat. "Guess the caffeine's working early."

"Mm." Her gaze lingers, unfocused, like she's listening to something I can't hear.

"Whatever it is... it suits you."

I leave a bigger tip than usual and step out before she can say anything else.

The cold hits me, but it doesn't bite the way it should.

I walk toward the station, my reflection moving beside me in the frosted shop windows. Every time I glance, there's something off—my eyes catch the light like gold flecks in dark water, my hair burns deeper into crimson under the sun.

On the train, people keep staring. Not openly, but in those quiet, darting glances that feel like static crawling over the skin. The man across the aisle fumbles his coffee when our eyes meet. The woman beside him smiles without meaning to, then blushes and looks away.

I tuck my scarf higher and focus on the blurred landscape outside. But the glass shows my reflection again—lips redder than they should be, pupils too wide, a faint shimmer along my throat where the pulse beats steady.

I close my eyes and whisper, "It's nothing. Just exhaustion. Just stress."

The hum answers anyway—a low purr beneath the words.

By the time I reach Boston, my nerves are raw. The courthouse rises like a monument to order—cold, solemn, predictable. It should steady me, but instead it feels like walking into a current I can't fight.

The metal detector shrieks when I pass through, sharp and accusing. The guard checks my bag, then waves me on, muttering about false alarms.

Inside, everything is too bright. Every sound—heels, phones, paper shuffling—lands harder than it should. I take my seat, pretending not to notice the shift in the air.

People are looking.

Not in the usual passing way.

Their gazes stick.

A clerk I've spoken to a hundred times pauses mid-sentence, eyes lingering too long before he clears his throat and looks away.

A woman by the copier smiles as I pass—uncertain, like she isn't sure why she did it.

The attention crawls under my skin. I can feel it—the heat of it, the pull. My pulse kicks up in response, a rhythm I can't control.

I tell myself they're imagining things. Or maybe I am.

This is what I was raised to avoid.

Be still. Be quiet. Be good. Don't draw eyes unless they're looking for salvation.

My foster mother's voice whispers it like a hymn. *Vanity is a sin. Desire invites ruin.*

I fold my hands in my lap, trying to still the tremor that's started there.

But it's not fear. Not really.

It's something darker.

Older.

Like part of me is stretching awake after too long asleep.

I sip my chai to hide the shaking. It burns my tongue, but the pain feels grounding. Necessary.

Something's changing.
And I don't know whether I should fight it—
or finally stop pretending I want to.

Chapter 35
Elias

The city feels half-asleep under a thin layer of frost when I pull into the precinct lot. The air bites, sharp and clean, but it doesn't clear the fog in my head. I haven't slept much—just drifted between case files and bad coffee, trying to find a thread that makes sense.

Freddy's latest report sits on my desk, neat handwriting, clipped tone: **Sedative present—traces of ketamine analog.** It's clinical, but the meaning is simple. The victims weren't fighting. They were made to *watch*.

I drop into my chair, rubbing the tension between my shoulders. It's been there since Jude's little reading—his talk of magic, bloodlines, curses. I don't believe in that crap. Still, something in me hasn't felt right since that night. The world feels... heavier. Like gravity learned my name.

I flip through the file again. Photos. Reports. The same pattern—the precision of the cuts, the strange stillness in every scene. Whoever's doing this isn't improvising. They're performing.

And somewhere in the middle of all of it sits Celeste Duvall.

I shouldn't think about her, but I do. The way she looked at me in the diner—steady, searching, like she already knew the questions I hadn't asked yet. Like she was waiting for me to catch up.

Her name's on several transcripts connected to the victims—Wexler, Corbett. She's not listed as a witness or consultant, but she's always there, sitting close to the truth without ever being called to speak it.

I scroll through her background check again. Perfect record. No priors. No inconsistencies. No life, really—just routine. Work, coffee, the train. Nothing out of place. Which makes it worse. People that clean are either saints or hiding something sharp.

The file says she aged out of the foster system in Washington—no parents listed, no birth certificate on record until she was twelve. Her first verifiable address was a group home in Tacoma, then a foster placement outside Seattle. From there: community college, a certification in court reporting, and a transfer east at twenty. Salem by way of nowhere.

No criminal record, no traffic violations, not even a parking ticket. She doesn't exist anywhere before that. No social media, no emergency contacts, no long-term leases. No one's ever listed as next of kin.

It's the kind of paper trail that looks honest until you read between the lines. She's not just private—she's erased.

I lean back in my chair, staring at the faint reflection in my monitor. A woman like that doesn't just disappear from the system without help. Or without reason.

No partners. No old coworkers listed for references. No past addresses except the one she's in now. Foster care, foster care, then nothing.

There's a photograph attached—her ID from the courthouse. Clean lines, steady gaze. Most people fidget in pictures; she looks like she's bracing for judgment. Like she's been doing it her whole life.

She moved across the country at twenty, alone, with no family and no ties. People don't just start over like that unless they're running from something... or toward it.

I can't tell which one she is yet.

But if I've learned anything—it's that ghosts always leave fingerprints somewhere.

The door creaks open behind me. Captain Rivera leans against the frame, arms crossed. Her expression's the same one she wore when I botched the Jensen case—a mix of concern and warning.

"You look like hell," she says.

"I feel worse."

"Take a day off, Shaw."

"Can't. Not when it's this close."

She sighs. "You've been saying that for six months."

I don't answer.

"Just... don't lose the line between instinct and obsession again."

"Funny," I say, "that's exactly what my old captain used to tell me right before I turned out to be right."

She studies me for a long moment, the kind that feels like she's weighing whether to argue or write the paperwork now.

"Shaw," she says finally, "go home."

"I'm fine."

"You're not. You've been living on caffeine and bad instincts for weeks."

"It's working."

Her voice hardens. "You've been circling the same case for months. The department's starting to notice. I'm not asking—you're taking tomorrow off."

I look up, half-ready to push back, but the expression on her face makes it clear this isn't up for debate.

"Captain—"

"No," she cuts in. "Go home. Eat something that didn't come out of a vending machine. Sleep. Whatever this thing is you're chasing—it'll still be here when you come back."

She stands, the conversation already over in her mind. "You burn out again, I can't protect you. Not this time."

I sit there in silence as she leaves. The door clicks softly behind her, a small sound that feels heavier than it should.

I stare out the window, watching the snow drift past. The city looks too clean under the white—like it's pretending it hasn't bled.

The phone on my desk buzzes. Unknown number.

I answer.

For a few seconds, there's silence. Then a voice—low, calm, distorted like it's passing through water.

"Stop looking where the light is brightest, Detective. Shadows tell a truer story."

The line goes dead.

I sit there, frozen, the hum of the lights pressing in. No trace. No caller ID. Just that single line echoing in my head.

Shadows tell a truer story.

I grab my coat, the ache in my shoulders flaring. I don't know what the hell is happening—but I know one thing.

Whatever this is, it's not over.

And it's getting closer.

The city feels half-asleep when I leave the precinct. Snow has thinned to a restless drizzle, just cold enough to sting when it hits my face. I drive without the radio, headlights cutting through the fog that's starting to roll off the harbor. Boston at night always feels like it's holding its breath.

By the time I reach my apartment, the world's gone quiet—no cars, no neighbors, just the low hum of the streetlight outside my window. There's something waiting on my doorstep. A small package, wrapped in plain brown paper, edges damp from the melting snow. No return address, just my name written in black ink.

I crouch, pick it up. The handwriting is familiar—careful, deliberate. Jude.

Inside, beneath a layer of waxed paper, lies a small glass vial stoppered with dark wax. The liquid inside glows faintly gold in the dim light, swirling slow like honey caught in sunlight.

Tied around its neck is a note written in Jude's script:

When you're ready for the truth, break it. But be certain, Elias. Once unbound, there's no going back.

Beneath the vial are books—old ones, heavy and worn. Their spines read like half-forgotten warnings: *The Choirs and the Fallen: A Study of*

Angelic Descent. The Siren Lineage and the Voice of Flesh. The Shifting Veil: Creatures Between. Bloodlines of the First Thirteen.

I thumb through one at random. The pages smell like dust and candle smoke. Handwritten notes fill the margins in faded ink—Jude's or maybe someone older.

One passage catches my eye, underlined twice:

When the body forgets what the soul remembers, the binding cracks from within. The pain between the shoulders is not affliction but awakening.

I rub the spot instinctively, the dull ache still there, sharp now under my touch.

The vial catches the light again. For a moment, I swear it hums—low and steady, like a heartbeat too close to hear.

I tell myself I'll throw it away in the morning.

I don't believe it.

Instead, I leave it on the table beside the stack of books, turn off the lamp, and stand in the dark for a long time. The room feels smaller somehow, the air charged, the silence full of breath.

Somewhere outside, a train horn sounds—distant and low, cutting through the night like a warning I don't yet understand.

Sleep doesn't come easily.

When it does, it doesn't feel like rest—it feels like falling through someone else's memory.

The first thing I see is light. Not the clean kind that breaks through clouds, but something older—raw, molten, alive. It bleeds through the cracks of a broken sky, washing the world below in gold and crimson.

Then comes the sound.

Wings. Thousands of them.

Feathers like shards of glass, the air humming with the rhythm of something vast and terrible. Seraphs—six-winged, crowned in fire. Their faces are veiled, their eyes burning through the cloth like stars through smoke. They move in unison, forming a circle over what looks like a city half drowned in light.

Below them, the water churns—and from it, voices rise.

Sirens. The sound is beautiful and unbearable all at once, a harmony that bends the air until it feels too heavy to breathe. Their song isn't meant for ears; it's meant for the soul. Each note drags something inside me to the surface, memories that don't belong to this life.

And between them—something darker.

A shadow walking on two feet.

No wings, no song, only eyes that catch the light and reflect it like polished obsidian.

Silas.

I don't know how I know, but I do. The shape of him. The quiet authority in the way he stands among gods and monsters like he's always belonged there.

And then—Celeste.

She stands at the edge of the water, her hair tangled with gold and red, her reflection shifting in ways the light can't explain. She opens her mouth as if to speak, and what comes out isn't words—it's a call. A melody made of want and warning.

The Seraphs stop.

The Sirens bow their heads.

Even the shadow moves closer.

The water rises around her ankles, glowing faintly as it climbs higher, covering her hands, her throat, until only her eyes remain above the sur-face—bright and endless, like the sky before it burns.

She looks at me.

Not through me—*at* me.

And I feel the air split open.

The light collapses inward.

The song breaks apart.

And I'm falling—through sound, through heat, through the echo of my own pulse pounding like wings behind my ribs.

I wake with a gasp, the sheets twisted around me, skin slick with sweat. The room smells faintly of ozone and stone dust, sharp and ancient.

For a moment, I can still hear it—that song.

Not a dream. Not entirely.

The ache between my shoulders burns, sharp enough to bring tears to my eyes. I reach back, fingers brushing skin that feels too warm, too alive. Beneath it, something stirs—something that's been sleeping far too long.

On the table, the vial glows faintly gold in the dark, as if it's heard the same song I did.

I sit up slowly, head spinning, breath coming fast like I've just run a mile. The room is too quiet. The air too heavy. My heart doesn't know whether to slow down or keep running.

The dream—or whatever it was—still clings to me. The wings, the song, the light that didn't belong to this world. It felt ancient, like memory in-stead of imagination. My skin hums with it, the ache between my shoulders pulsing in time with my heartbeat.

I drag a hand down my face. "Get a grip, Shaw."

But the words sound thin, even to me.

The books Jude sent are still on the table, their covers catching faint morning light. *The Choirs and the Fallen. The Siren Lineage. Bloodlines of the First Thirteen.* The pages seem to breathe when I look at them too long. I shove them aside and stand, pacing the apartment, trying to shake the feeling that something followed me out of that dream.

I stop at the window. The city is pale and blurred, still waking. Somewhere a siren wails, a sound too human to comfort me.

The ache in my shoulders sharpens again, spreading down my spine. I grip the edge of the counter until the pain fades, until I can breathe without shaking. None of it makes sense. Seraphs, sirens, wings—Christ. I don't even believe in angels.

And yet—

I can still *feel* the feathers against my skin.

I cross to the medicine cabinet, fingers fumbling for the orange bottle buried behind an unopened box of bandages. Zolpidem tartrate. I haven't touched them in months. I don't like the fog they leave behind. But the thought of closing my eyes and seeing that light again makes my stomach twist.

On the counter sits the small glass vial Jude gave me, the ash-gray powder glinting faintly in the dim kitchen light. *Burn this tonight.* His voice echoes in my head—half warning, half challenge.

I almost laugh. It's absurd, all of it—magic, curses, bindings. Yet I find myself reaching for a dish anyway. I tap the powder in, strike a match, and watch the flame catch. It burns slow, smoke curling upward in thin gray ribbons that smell of cedar and salt, like the ocean pressed into ash.

The air shifts—cooler, heavier. My skin prickles.

I shake two pills into my palm. Then, after a moment, one more.

"Just sleep," I mutter. "That's all this is. Stress. Nerves."

I swallow them dry. The bitterness clings to the back of my throat. Behind it, the faint trace of cedar smoke still lingers—soft, almost sweet—curling through the apartment like a memory that refuses to fade.

When I finally lie down, the apartment feels foreign—like someone else's life left on pause. I stare at the ceiling until my vision blurs, until the pull of exhaustion starts to drag me under again.

Just before I slip under, the faint hum returns—soft, rhythmic, almost like wings.

I tell myself it's the sound of the radiator.

But deep down, I know better.

Chapter 36
Celeste

The night hums differently.

It isn't the wine or the candlelight or the murmur of conversation—it's what hides beneath it. The air itself feels charged, as if the walls are listening.

The Inkbound Society has gathered again, but this dinner isn't like the others. No polite laughter. No clinking of glass or talk of grants and legacies. The house has gone still. Reverent. Even the servants move like wraiths, careful not to disturb whatever waits in the silence between heartbeats.

Silas stands at the far end of the long mahogany table, firelight washing his black suit in liquid gold. His composure is flawless, but when his eyes find mine, something shifts—gravity, focus, the pull of a tide that knows where it's going.

I take my seat, every motion deliberate. A dozen guests tonight, maybe fewer. Faces I've seen before—judges, scholars, benefactors with immaculate reputations and rot behind their smiles. The sigil carved into the back of each chair glows faintly in the candlelight: a circle of flame split by ink. It throbs, almost breathing.

A single bell chimes. The sound threads through the air like a command. The room stills.

Silas raises his glass, the reflection of the fire catching in the red. "Tonight, we honor tradition," he says, voice low and resonant. "And we welcome what has long been waiting."

The words settle into the bones of the room.

The silver-haired woman steps forward from the shadows—the one they call the Keeper. Her gown drips black silk, her eyes bright as cut glass. "The Witness approaches her threshold," she intones. "The night before rebirth, when the veil between ink and flame thins."

A tremor ripples through the air. Candles gutter, their flames stretching thin, bending toward the center of the table.

Silas's hand hovers above the glass before him, palm open as if feeling the current. His voice is softer now, meant for me alone. "Every story requires a catalyst, Celeste. A moment when the ink finally remembers the hand that guides it."

My pulse stumbles. "And if I don't want to remember?"

"You already are," he says simply.

The Keeper gestures. Two attendants carry in a basin wrought from black stone and place it at the center of the table. Inside: water so dark it reflects nothing at all. Steam coils upward, tinted faintly gold.

"The first rite," the Keeper says, "is of reflection."

The guests stand as one. The movement is soundless, practiced. Silas circles the table and stops beside me, his hand brushing the back of my chair—a whisper of contact that still sends heat crawling up my spine.

"Look," he murmurs. "See what's been waiting beneath your skin."

The air thickens as I stand. The surface of the water trembles when I lean over it, catching not my reflection but flickers of something else—flame, wings, waves breaking in slow motion.

My breath fogs the surface. The images sharpen. I see myself there, but older, endless. Eyes like molten gold, mouth curved in something both tender and terrible.

The hum builds. I can feel it beneath my ribs, inside my teeth, threading through the soles of my feet.

Silas's voice drifts beside me. "The solstice is the pivot. Tomorrow, the sun stands still, and so do you—between what you were and what you are. After tonight, there's no going back."

He reaches out, fingertips brushing my throat, his thumb tracing the steady pulse there. The gesture is reverent, possessive, grounding and un-mooring all at once.

"Say the word," he says. "And it begins."

I open my mouth, but the air moves first. The candlelight bends in-ward, drawn into the basin. Gold light bursts from the water, rising in slow spirals until it touches the ceiling. The guests whisper something in unison—words older than language.

Heat floods my chest, bright and unbearable. The hum inside me answers in full.

Silas's hand steadies me as the light surges higher, wrapping us both in the glow. I can't tell where his touch ends and mine begins.

Then the room exhales—candles flaring once before going still again. The water in the basin is calm, black, ordinary.

But the mark at my wrist burns faintly through the skin. The circle of flame, split by ink.

I glance down at my hands—steady, but my pulse betrays me. Something is coming. I can feel it at the base of my spine, a quiet thrum building under my skin, gathering with every breath.

When dinner begins, it feels almost ceremonial. Each course arrives in silence, silver utensils glinting beneath the dim light. The food is decadent—roasted lamb, honeyed figs, spiced wine—but every bite tastes faintly metallic, like memory or blood. I eat because everyone else does. Because not doing so would mean admitting I already know this isn't dinner. It's initiation.

At the end of the meal, Silas rises. "Celeste," he says softly, and the sound of my name in his mouth feels like a summons.

The others don't look up. It's as if they've been waiting for this moment all night.

I follow him down a narrow corridor lined with portraits so old the paint itself seems to be decaying. Faces fade into the shadows as we pass, but the eyes remain—watchful, knowing. The air grows cooler. Quieter.

At the end of the hall, a door stands slightly ajar, candlelight spilling through the crack. When Silas pushes it open, my breath catches.

The chamber beyond is circular and made entirely of stone. The air tastes of iron, paper, and something older—like burnt sugar and rain on dust. In the center lies an intricate sigil carved into the floor, spirals of ink, ash, and gold leaf that shimmer faintly, alive beneath the surface. The patterns pulse in time with my heartbeat.

Silas steps inside, his voice low and steady. "This is where it begins."

I hesitate at the threshold. "What begins?"

He turns toward me, and for a moment he looks less like a man and more like a reflection caught in candlelight—too bright around the edges, too still. "The remembering."

He lifts a small leather-bound book from the altar at the center. Its cover is blackened at the corners, the title burned into the surface in letters that glint like cooled gold.

The Ledger of the Damned.

My chest tightens. "Silas—"

"You've felt it," he says, cutting gently across the distance between us. "The pull. The hunger. The blurring between dream and waking."
He takes another step closer, his eyes catching the firelight. "It isn't madness, Celeste. It's memory."

The candles bend toward me, flames lengthening, whispering. The sigil hums faintly, threads of light crawling outward until they brush the toes of my shoes.

"Tonight," he says, "we remember who you are."

My mouth goes dry. The air thickens with the scent of ink, smoke, and spice.

And somewhere deep inside me—something answers. Slow. Inevitable.

A recognition older than language.

The room exhales. Every candle flares at once, a low vibration spilling from the walls, through the floor, through me.

Movement stirs at the edges of the light. One by one, figures step forward from the shadows—members of the Society, cloaked and masked. Porcelain and obsidian faces gleam in the dark, each marked with shifting sigils that seem to breathe. Their robes are stitched in crimson thread that glows faintly as they form a circle around us.

Silas opens the ledger. "Ink remembers flame," he says, his tone ritualistic. "And flame remembers name."

The others echo him, voices overlapping in perfect unison. The sound threads through my bones like heat.

When he looks up again, his gaze pins me where I stand. "Speak it," he whispers. "So the world can find you again."

The air thickens. My vision swims. I try to speak, but the name that forms isn't *mine*.

It's older. Heavier.

A name the room already knows.

Someone closes the door.

The sound is final.

Silas stands at the center of the sigil. His jacket is gone, sleeves rolled, dark silk clinging to the shape of his frame. His hands are steady, but his eyes—gray-green, sharp as stormlight—are fixed entirely on me.

"Come here," he says, and the words leave no room for refusal.

I step forward. My heels click against carved stone until I reach the circle's edge. The air inside is heavier, charged, each breath carrying the faint taste of salt and copper.

I glance down at myself—the gown they left for me earlier. It's nothing like the one from the first dinner. This one is meant for ceremony. Blood-red silk that drapes low across my shoulders, cinched at the waist with black lace. The fabric moves like liquid when I breathe. Beneath it, my skin prickles with awareness, heat curling low in my belly.

Silas raises his hand. The circle's outer rim glows faintly, lines of ink shifting into runes I can't read. Around us, the masked figures begin to chant—low, rhythmic, a language more sung than spoken. The sound vibrates through the stone, through my bones. My pulse stumbles to match its rhythm.

My gaze meets Silas's again, and the world narrows to the space between us.

"What is this?" I whisper, though I'm not sure I want the answer.

"The truth," he says. "The call that's been waiting for you."

He takes a slow step closer. My breath catches. The hum in my veins grows louder, echoing the chant's cadence. I can feel it—something deep beneath my skin responding to him, drawn like the tide to the moon.

When he reaches me, he doesn't touch. Not yet. He lifts a hand, hovering just shy of my throat. The air between us crackles. My heart stumbles against my ribs.

"Do you hear it?" he murmurs.

At first, I think he means the chanting.

But then—something else.

A faint melody threads through the sound. Not quite music, not words either, but calling. It's soft, ancient, and impossible to resist.

My body sways toward it before I can stop myself. The others' voices rise, twining like currents around us. The air shimmers, thick with heat and salt and something bright that tastes like lightning.

The moment his fingers brush my skin, the world breaks open.

Light bursts behind my eyes—gold and deep ocean blue. The sound becomes a song, vast and endless, echoing through every part of me. I can feel the water moving in the air, the pull of it in my blood. The hum I've lived with for months blooms into something bigger—beautiful and terrifying.

The chant stops. The room falls silent, except for the faint rush of waves I swear I can hear somewhere far away.

Silas lowers his hand, voice reverent. "Welcome back, Celeste."

I try to speak, but my throat is full of sound that isn't human. My reflection in his eyes ripples like water—like a mirror disturbed by its own truth.

And beneath it all—

I feel the world shift.

The first note of an old song rising again.

The light fades too fast.

One heartbeat I'm floating, radiant, every nerve alive with that impossible melody—

and the next, it turns sharp, discordant, pressing against the inside of my skull.

My knees buckle.

Silas catches me before I hit the floor. "Easy," he murmurs, voice steady, grounding. His hands are warm where they hold me, but the world trembles at the edges.

The circle beneath us shifts, sigils pulsing in time with my heartbeat. The air thickens—ink and iron. My vision fractures: flashes of red, of faces I can't place, of hands slick with blood that looks too real to be memory.

"I—" My voice breaks. "Silas... what's happening?"

"You're remembering," he says softly, almost tenderly—as if the word shouldn't terrify me.

The chanting fades, replaced by whispers I can't locate. They slide beneath my skin, old and familiar. *Ledger. Balance. Blood.*

I try to pull back, but the floor feels alive beneath me, the carved runes burning faintly through the silk. My pulse pounds in my ears, matching another rhythm—one I've felt all along.

The hum.

It swells again, not just in me, but around me—pages fluttering in an invisible wind, the scent of parchment and smoke rising thick as breath. The light bends toward the altar where the book lies open, ink shimmering red-black like a wound that refuses to close.

For a heartbeat, I see it writing itself.

A name.

My name.

"No—"

The word tears from my throat, raw and small. But the images don't stop. They rush in: Corbett's lifeless eyes. Harren's slack jaw. Blood glinting on old blueprints. My hands tremble, and for an instant—they're not clean.

I stagger back. "That's not me," I whisper. "That's not—"

Silas is there, steady, but his eyes are unreadable. "Not yet," he says.

The Ledger hums once more, low and resonant, sinking into my bones. I can feel it pulling—calling to something buried deep inside me. A hunger I've tried to name as guilt, as grief, as anything but what it really is.

The masks around us remain still. Watching. Waiting.

"I can't—" My voice fractures.

Silas steps closer, close enough that his breath grazes my ear. "The Ledger calls to its Keeper. You've heard it before, haven't you?"

I shake my head, though part of me knows it's a lie. I've heard that hum for months—low, persistent, the rhythm behind my heartbeat. I thought it was anxiety. I thought it was madness.

Now I know it's neither.

The pull sharpens—magnetic, insistent. My gaze drifts to the open book again. I can almost feel the parchment under my fingers, almost see ink waiting to obey.

Silas's voice threads through the chaos. "You can fight it, or you can understand it. But you cannot ignore it."

The world tilts. The air tastes of iron. My pulse stutters, the room collapsing into fragments of color and sound—pages turning, whispers rising, water rushing somewhere unseen.

And then—darkness.

The last thing I hear is Silas's voice, soft and certain:

"Happy birthday, Celeste."

Chapter 37
Celeste

The first thing I notice is the silk.

Cool sheets, smooth as water, tangled around my legs. The bed is too large, too soft, the kind of decadent comfort that feels earned by someone else's life.

The second thing is the scent—chai and smoke and something faintly metallic.

When I sit up, the room spins slow and golden. Sunlight filters through gauzy curtains, striking gold veins across dark wood. Everything gleams—polished furniture, a fireplace flickering low, the edge of a mirror carved with sigils I don't remember seeing before.

For a moment, I can't move. My body feels wrong—no, not wrong. *Different.* Every sound brushes against my skin. Every beam of light feels alive, warm and sharp at once.

Then the memory hits—the circle, the chanting, the way the world split open when Silas touched me.

"Good morning."

His voice pulls me back like gravity.

Silas stands in the doorway, sleeves rolled, a tray balanced in one hand. The scent of chai fills the room again, richer now, dusted with cinnamon. He looks the same—composed, effortless—but there's something new in his eyes when he looks at me. Recognition. Reverence.

I pull the blanket tighter around myself, though I'm still in the red dress from the night before. The corset unlaced, the silk clinging to my skin like second breath.

"Where am I?"

"In my townhouse," he says simply, setting the tray on the bedside table. "You fainted after the ritual. I brought you somewhere safe."

Safe. The word hums oddly against the edge of my thoughts.

He pours the tea into a porcelain cup and hands it to me. "Drink. It'll help with the dizziness."

The first sip burns sweet and steady down my throat. My pulse evens, though the air between us grows heavier with every breath.

"What happened?" I ask quietly. "Last night—"

Silas studies me for a long moment before answering. "The first awakening is... intense. The Siren blood always calls loudest. It stirs everything else beneath it." His gaze lingers on my throat, my wrists, the faint shimmer beneath my skin. "But it isn't finished."

Something deep in me tightens. "Finished?"

"There's one more ritual," he says. "To complete what's been waiting in you all this time."

I shake my head, though I don't mean it. "I don't understand."

"You will." He moves closer, the air shifting with him. "The Siren is only half of what you are, Celeste. The other side of your blood is older. Stronger. And it won't stay sleeping much longer."

A flicker of warmth unfurls low in my stomach, spreading like liquid fire. I set the cup down before it slips from my hands. My heart beats too fast, the rhythm strange—*hungry.*

Silas's voice softens. "You've felt it already, haven't you? The pull. The way people look at you now."

I want to deny it, but I can't. I see flashes in my mind—the way strangers' eyes linger, how their smiles tilt, the heat that curls in my chest even when I don't want it.

He reaches out, fingertips brushing the back of my hand. My breath catches.

"This isn't corruption," he murmurs. "It's truth. The body remembers what the soul forgets."

I can't tell if he's warning me or tempting me. Maybe both.

"Rest for now," he says finally, straightening. "Tonight, we finish what the world started."

He leaves before I can answer.

The door clicks softly shut. The taste of chai and smoke lingers in the air, and under it all—the hum returns.

Low. Steady. Alive.

The sound of something ancient waking in my blood.

The door closes, and the silence settles like silk over my skin.

The chai cools on the table. I lean back against the pillows, but the room keeps pulsing — slow, steady, like a heartbeat not my own. The exhaustion hits all at once, heavy and irresistible.

Just a few minutes, I tell myself. Just to rest.

The world folds in on itself.

And then I'm standing somewhere else entirely.

The air here glows like the inside of a candle flame — gold bleeding into scarlet, the light alive and breathing. Water runs in thin ribbons along the marble floor, but it doesn't make a sound when I step through it. Every movement leaves a ripple of color behind me, faint as smoke.

Something hums in the distance. Not music — not yet — but the promise of it.

I know this place. I shouldn't, but I do.

The walls are carved with symbols I've seen before — in the Ledger, in my dreams. Hands reach up from the stone like they're trying to escape. I pass them, drawn forward, every nerve whispering that I'm not alone.

Then I see *him*.

At first, I think it's Silas. But this version of him isn't bound by flesh or shadow. His eyes burn too bright, the lines of his body shaped from darkness and light at once. He watches me with something older than recognition.

"You came back," he says, his voice layered — echoing, endless.

"I'm dreaming," I whisper, though the air tastes too real, heavy with salt and spice and heat.

He steps closer. The water rises around us, warm as breath, curling around my legs. His hand hovers near my face — not touching, but near enough that I can *feel* it.

"Not dreaming," he murmurs. "Remembering."

Images flood in — flashes of other lifetimes, other faces. Lovers and gods, war and fire, a circle of light where blood once spilled freely. Each one burns through me, fragments of stories I never lived and yet *did*.

I stumble back. "No. This isn't me."

His hand closes around my wrist — gentle, but unbreakable. "It's always been you."

Something cracks open inside me. The air thickens, sweet and electric. I can feel my heartbeat echo in his, the rhythm identical. The hum builds until it's almost unbearable, until the entire room seems to pulse with it.

"Who are you?" I ask, though I already know the answer isn't meant to comfort me.

His smile is all light and ruin. "The one who woke you first."

He leans in, and when his lips brush mine, the dream explodes.

Every nerve ignites. The hum becomes a song, low and dark and infinite. Power floods through me — heat and hunger, fire and ache — until I can't tell where I end and he begins.

Then, through the blinding haze, I see flashes again — Corbett, Harren, Vennett — and the ink bleeding from the Ledger like blood. The song twists, sharp and discordant, and I choke on the taste of metal.

I pull away, gasping.

He catches my chin, his voice a whisper that shakes the air. "You cannot unmake what you are, Celeste. You can only *become* it."

The world tilts. The floor splits open like a mouth.

And I fall—

—back into my body, back into silk sheets and fading sunlight.

I jolt upright, breath ragged, skin slick with sweat. The chai cup lies shattered on the floor beside the bed. The air still hums, faintly, like the echo of a song not yet finished.

For the first time, I'm afraid to close my eyes.

The air still hums when I swing my legs out of bed. The floorboards are warm beneath my feet, though the fire in the next room has long since died. Every breath feels like standing too close to a storm — static prickling just under my skin, the taste of iron and rain lingering on my tongue.

The red dress clings when I move, the silk cold and heavy against my skin. It feels wrong now—too decadent, too alive, like it's still breathing from the night before. I unlace the corset with shaking fingers, each pull a soft gasp in the quiet room. When the final ribbon slips free, I let the fabric fall in a crimson heap at my feet.

The air against my skin is cool, startling. Goosebumps rise along my arms. I cross to the armchair and reach for Silas's shirt draped over the back—a dark button-down, faintly wrinkled, smelling of smoke, spice, and something that feels like him.

The cotton is soft when I pull it on, the hem brushing my thighs, sleeves hanging too long. It's warm from his body heat, grounding in a way I can't explain. I roll the cuffs up, inhale once, and let the scent steady me.

My body aches, but not from sleep. It's a deeper ache—like something beneath my skin is shifting, stretching, remembering how to exist.

The house is silent when I step into the hall. Shadows stretch long across the walls, the sconces burning low, casting the place in molten amber. I pass portraits whose eyes seem to follow me — men and women bound in time, their gazes soft but knowing.

The hum leads me downward, to the library.

It's darker here, the kind of dark that feels alive. The air tastes of old parchment and something faintly metallic. My fingers trail the spines as I move — leather, vellum, silk, their titles embossed in gold and silver. Some in languages I recognize. Others in scripts that twist when I look too long.

A book shifts beneath my touch.

Not slides — *moves.*

I pull my hand back. The spine gleams faintly, the letters reshaping themselves. My breath catches when I realize it's the same title I found before:

The Ballad of Ash and the Thirteen Gates — only this time, the words glow red, as if written in light.

I reach for it, and the hum deepens, echoing through my bones. The air vibrates. The scent of smoke and salt blooms around me, thick and sweet.

When I open the cover, the ink shimmers — alive, shifting between black and gold. But the pages aren't the same as before. The poetry is gone. In its place, names.

Hundreds of names.

Each one written in the same elegant hand. Each one crossed out.

My vision blurs. The letters twist, bleeding together until I can make out a single phrase beneath the last name:

Balance must be kept.

The same words from the dream.

My fingers tremble as I turn the page. The next one is blank. But when I touch it, ink blooms across the paper in a slow, deliberate curl — my name, written as if by an invisible hand.

"Celeste."

The sound of my name pulls me up short.

I turn toward the doorway. Silas stands there, shadow cutting across his face, his expression unreadable.

"What are you doing?"

"I don't—" My voice breaks. "It moved."

He steps closer, his gaze flicking to the book, then back to me. For a moment, something like concern passes over his features — and then it's gone.

"The Ledger answers to its Keeper," he says softly. "Even when she doesn't understand what she's asking for."

"I wasn't asking for anything."

"Weren't you?"

He closes the book gently, his hand lingering on the cover. The hum fades, but not completely. It's still there, faint beneath my ribs, whispering.

Silas looks at me, eyes gray-green in the low light. "You should rest. The next ritual will demand more of you than this."

"What ritual?" I whisper.

He doesn't answer.

Instead, he brushes his thumb across my jaw — light, reverent — and turns away.

I stand there long after he's gone, the echo of his touch burning through the dark. The book still thrums beneath my palm.

The page beneath the cover feels warm — alive — as though my name hasn't stopped writing itself.

Chapter 38
Elias

I wake like I've been dropped back into my body from a great height. The air feels wrong—too still, too charged. My skin hums, the faint echo of something I can't name pulsing beneath it. The sheets are twisted, damp with sweat, and the taste of smoke clings to the back of my throat.

I sit up slowly, heart thudding in that offbeat way that comes after adrenaline. My apartment is dim, the gray light of dawn pressing against the blinds, but everything feels *brighter* somehow—edges too sharp, shadows too defined. Like the world's been tuned to a frequency I wasn't supposed to hear.

The air hums around me, faint but constant, as if some invisible circuit has finally come alive. I run a hand through my hair, fingers trembling slightly. My body feels... different. Lighter, but heavier too, every breath dragging against something unseen.

It's not just exhaustion. I've known that kind of tired before. This is something else.

I swing my legs out of bed and brace my elbows on my knees, staring at the floor until the blur steadies. There's a residue in the air—a feeling, almost, like the echo of a door left open somewhere.

I don't remember dreaming. I don't remember anything, really. Just flashes—light like fire through water, wings made of shadow and flame, voices singing in a language I almost understood. The kind of dream that leaves more behind than it takes.

I stand, but the moment I do, my knees nearly buckle. There's a rush of vertigo, heat curling low in my spine, then a flicker—an image not from my mind but through it. A place that isn't here. A memory that doesn't belong to me.

I steady myself against the wall, dragging in a breath that doesn't seem to fill my lungs.

Whatever Jude's "binding" was—it's breaking. I can feel it.

And whatever it's holding back... is waking up.

I press my palms to my face and exhale, trying to steady the rush in my chest. Whatever happened last night—whatever *this* is—I'm not ready to face it. Not now. Not with so much on the line.

If the pattern holds, the next kill will hit within the week. The last two were timed to holidays—ritual dressed up as coincidence. Which means Christmas might carry a murderous ring to it if I don't stop this first.

The thought lands heavy, cold. I can almost feel the clock ticking somewhere in the back of my skull, each second pulling me closer to something I don't understand and can't afford to believe in.

I move through the apartment on autopilot, bare feet against cold tile, the floor creaking under my weight. The coffee pot sits where it always does—ancient, dented, reliable in a way I'm not sure anything else in my life is.

I brew it strong enough to strip paint. The smell hits first—bitter, dark, grounding. The kind of brew that could wake the dead or at least keep me from joining them. When I take the first sip, it burns all the way down, settling like grit in my stomach.

It tastes like my probie days back in New York—stale donuts, sleepless nights, and the kind of optimism I used to think counted as armor. Back then, the worst monsters I chased were human. Now, I'm not so sure.

Mug in hand, I cross to the wall where the case board waits—its surface a patchwork of headlines, photos, string, and half-formed theories. I stare at it until the faces blur into one. Wexler. Corbett. Harren. Vennett.

Each one part of the same equation I can't solve.

Each one connected to Silas Kade.

And now, somehow, to Celeste Duvall.

The coffee turns cold in my hand as I trace the lines between them, the red thread running like veins through the chaos.

There's a rhythm to it, I realize—dates, symbols, placements. Like a song I can almost hear but can't translate.

And whatever's coming next...

it's already started.

The apartment hums in that too-quiet way that only happens after too many nights alone. My phone buzzes across the table, screen lighting up with an unknown number. The Boston PD prefix. I grab it before it can ring twice.

"Shaw."

"Detective, it's Vega. You got a minute?"

Her voice carries that dry efficiency I've come to depend on—sharp, precise, already halfway ahead of the conversation.

"Always," I say.

"I've been combing through the Corbett files again. Something didn't sit right with the donation trail. I finally cracked the dummy accounts. Turns out a good chunk of her money was funneled into something called *The Second Light Foundation*."

I frown. "Never heard of it."

"You wouldn't have. It's a ghost org—front for something bigger. It popped up in an old human trafficking investigation two years ago. Holiday abductions. Mostly women in their twenties. Vanished between Thanksgiving and Christmas. The case never went to trial—was dismissed during pre-hearing review."

"Who represented them?"

There's a pause, the faint rustle of paper. "Kade & Rhoan LLP. The law firm."

Not Silas by name. But close enough that it hits like a gut punch.

"Any record of him on the filings?" I ask, voice low.

"Not directly. His signature's nowhere on it. But Rhoan was still under his mentorship then. My guess? He's the one who set the strategy."

The ache between my shoulder blades sharpens, that same strange pressure crawling up my spine like static. "Send me everything. Financials, transcripts, any surviving witness statements."

"You got it," Vega says. "One more thing—you might want to keep this off the books. Someone upstairs tried to lock the file an hour after I accessed it."

"Who?"

"I didn't stick around to ask."

The line clicks dead.

I stare at the wall of names, faces, strings—a web of patterns that's no longer abstract. The red thread cuts through all of them: Corbett. Lexington. Harren. Vennett. *Second Light.*

And now, Silas Kade's shadow running through it all.

The taste of old coffee coats my tongue, bitter and grounding. Outside, the wind sharpens against the window, carrying the first hint of snow.

Whatever this is, it isn't done.
And the closer I get, the more I feel it pressing back.

I stare at the board until the words blur together. *Second Light Foundation.*

The name looks too clean for what it's tied to.

Official channels won't get me anywhere. Not if Vega's right about someone already locking the file. Which means it's time to make a call I promised myself I wouldn't.

I scroll through the contacts on my phone until I hit the one saved under a name that doesn't exist—*Kellan R.*

He picks up on the second ring. "You sound like you haven't slept in three days."

"Try four."

"That's not an improvement." The click of a lighter filters through the line. "What do you need this time, Shaw? I told you, if it's about Jensen—"

"It's not." I rub the back of my neck, feeling the pulse there. "You ever heard of *The Second Light Foundation*?"

There's a pause long enough to make me think the line dropped. Then, "Yeah. And you should be careful saying it out loud."

"That bad?"

"That buried," he says. "Last I heard, it was supposed to be a charity out of Boston. Fronted as a humanitarian org—rehousing displaced women, victims of violence, that kind of thing. But there were whispers it was a feeder network. Moving people, not saving them."

My stomach turns. "And the donors?"

"You wouldn't like the list."

"I don't like any of this."

He exhales, slow. "You want me to dig?"

"I need everything you can find—financials, donors, operating heads, old staff lists, the works. Especially if there's anything connecting them to Kade & Rhoan LLP."

"That's a big ask, Shaw. You know what happens when I poke too deep into sealed data."

"I'll owe you one."

"You already do." Another pause. "All right. I'll pull what I can. You'll have it by morning. But if it smells rotten, I'm not calling you first—I'm burning it."

"Fair enough."

The call ends, leaving me with the hum of the city bleeding through the thin apartment walls.

I lean against the counter, thumb pressed to the edge of my mug until the heat bites. My reflection stares back at me from the dark window—eyes hollow, jaw tight, the faint shadow of a man who can't tell if he's chasing a killer or the ghost of something older.

The ache between my shoulders flares again, sharp and insistent, like something underneath my skin is trying to wake up.

I close my eyes, exhale through my teeth.

"Not yet," I whisper.

Outside, a siren cuts through the night—high, distant, lonely.

A warning, or a promise.

The coffee's gone cold again before I realize I haven't moved.

The city hums beneath the silence, that same low frequency that's been following me since dawn. It sits under everything—the fridge motor, the pipes, even my pulse—like a sound too low for hearing but too deep to ignore.

I try to shake it. I run water over the mug, pull on my jacket, tell myself movement is logic, that motion keeps the ghosts from catching up. But when I step outside, the air doesn't help. Boston feels... off. Too bright, too brittle. Like the light itself is holding its breath.

The streets glisten with half-melted snow. Steam curls from sewer grates, and Christmas lights blink against the gray like someone trying to remember hope. Every sound feels magnified—the rush of passing cars, a door slamming blocks away, my own boots against wet concrete.

I don't realize I'm driving until I'm already halfway across the bridge to

Salem.

Habit, I tell myself. That's all it is.

But it's a lie.

There's a pull in my chest—small, steady, magnetic. The same one that hums under my skin. It leads me here, to the quiet streets I've come to associate with her.

Celeste Duvall.

Even her name feels strange now, weighted. Like saying it out loud might wake something I don't understand.

Her building sits at the end of a narrow street near the harbor, the kind of place that should feel safe. Familiar. But as I park across from it, I get the same feeling I used to get standing over a crime scene before anyone pulled the tape—a shift in the air, a wrongness that doesn't need evidence to be real.

The lobby lights flicker when I step inside. The woman at the front desk gives me a polite nod, eyes darting from my badge to my face and back again. "She's not in," she says before I can even ask.

I blink. "Excuse me?"

"Ms. Duvall," she clarifies. "Left early this morning. Black car picked her up right out front. The driver had her name on a placard."

My stomach tightens. "Did she say where she was going?"

She shakes her head. "Didn't have to. He said it was *for the event.*"

I frown. "What event?"

Her lips press together, uncertain. "I assumed it was one of those... society things she's been attending. She looked beautiful, though. Like she was walking into a photograph."

I thank her, but my voice sounds far away. I step back outside, into the cold. The wind cuts off the harbor, sharp with salt. The air tastes metallic.

Her windows are dark. No lights, no movement. But something still hums inside the building—faint, rhythmic, like distant machinery or the echo of a heartbeat.

I tell myself it's nothing. That she's fine. That Silas Kade probably whisked her off to another one of those immaculate dinners he uses as excuses for control. But my hand still tightens around the steering wheel until my knuckles ache.

He's dangerous. I've known it since the first time I looked into his eyes and saw how empty they were.
The kind of empty that isn't absence—it's hunger.

I stay parked for too long, watching the front of her building through the windshield until frost begins to creep along the glass. My instincts—the same ones that got me through twenty years of casework—won't shut up.

Something's wrong.
Not provable. Not visible. But wrong.

I can feel it in the pulse behind my ribs, the same rhythm that's been haunting me all morning.

I start the engine, force myself to drive away.

At the next red light, I catch my reflection in the rearview mirror. My eyes look different in this light—paler, sharper, almost luminous around the edges. For a moment, I don't recognize the man staring back.

I turn the mirror up. I don't want to see.

The radio crackles to life on its own, static breaking into the faint hum of a song. It's barely there, almost lost under the engine's growl—a woman's voice, soft and distant, humming a melody I shouldn't know but do.

It's the same tune that's been threading through my dreams.

I shut the radio off.

The silence afterward is worse.

By the time I reach the edge of the city, snow has started to fall again—thin and quiet. The world feels like it's waiting for something.

I don't go home. Not yet.

Instead, I park beneath the bridge, the one that overlooks the harbor, and stare out across the water until the horizon blurs. The waves below glint faintly gold in the dark, catching a light I can't see the source of.

For the first time in my life, I don't know if I'm chasing a killer—or if I'm watching one rise.

Chapter 39
Celeste

The drive shouldn't take long.

It never does. But tonight, every turn feels slower, stretched thin between heartbeats. The city glides past in a wash of amber light and wet cobblestone, Beacon Hill rising around us like a memory too old to belong to this century.

We don't leave Boston—just slip beneath it somehow. The streets grow quieter, narrower, the glow of the skyline fading behind the veil of falling snow. Gas lamps flicker along the brick façades, their light bending strange through the mist, as if the air itself remembers what it once was.

When we stop, I already know.

The same house. The same threshold that breathes when you cross it.

But the air is different tonight—denser, charged.

The Siren in me recognizes it instantly. She stirs beneath my skin, restless, alert, humming low like the tide turning toward a deeper current.

Silas cuts the engine and sits for a moment, his hands resting loosely on the wheel. The silence between us is heavy, the kind that carries too many truths waiting to be spoken.

Finally, he turns to me. "There's something you need to understand before we go inside."

I nod, though a shiver works its way through me. "What is it?"

His eyes find mine, gray-green and unflinching. "Your binding."

I blink, the word catching somewhere between curiosity and fear. "My binding?"

He exhales, as though the act of saying it out loud carries its own weight. "When you were born, your power wasn't dormant—it was sealed. Suppressed before it could fully take root. Whoever did it knew exactly what they were doing. They bound your magic to your thirtieth year, to the solstice alignment of your birth. Soon that seal will break on its own."

I stare at him. "And if we don't—?"

"Finish the ritual?" His mouth tightens. "Then it breaks *without guidance*. Without balance. The Siren you've already awakened will pull against the seal. The Succubus will tear through it. You'll burn from the inside out."

The words hit harder than they should. "You mean die."

Silas's voice is quiet, almost reverent. "Not in the way mortals understand it. But yes. Your body wouldn't survive the release."

I look past him toward the house—the windows still dark, the forest pressing close on all sides. "Why bind me at all?"

"That's the question," he says softly. "Maybe to protect you. Maybe to protect everyone else."

His hand hovers near mine, not quite touching. "The ledger recognized you before I did. It started calling to you weeks ago—that pull you feel, the lost time, the dreams. That's the seal beginning to crack. Tonight, we finish what your blood started."

My pulse thrums. "And if I say no?"

Silas looks at me like he already knows the answer. "You won't."

The truth is, I can't. The ache in my chest, the electric hum under my skin—it's too strong now, too hungry.

"What happens tonight?" I ask finally.

His gaze flicks to the house, then back to me. "The second awakening. The one that breaks the binding. It's the most dangerous part, and the most intimate. You'll need to trust me completely. Once we begin, there's no stopping it."

The words hang there between us, heavy as prophecy.

Outside, the wind stirs through the trees, carrying the faintest scent of cedar and myrrh—the same as the oils he used to cleanse me.

"Come," Silas says softly, opening his door. "It's time."

I follow him into the night, the Siren inside me thrumming in time with my heartbeat. The air seems to part for us as we walk, as if the world itself knows what's waiting inside.

And beneath the fear, beneath the anticipation, one thought pulses steady and certain:

Whatever I was before, I won't be after tonight.

Silas opens the door, his movements deliberate, reverent. "You've crossed one threshold," he says softly. "Now comes the second."

The chamber glows with candlelight—hundreds of them, arranged in spiraling patterns across the floor. But the center of the room has changed.

Where the sigil once burned alone, a bed now stands. A four-poster altar carved from blackened oak, etched with symbols that shimmer faintly in molten gold. The sheets are dark red—silk that seems to move of its own accord, catching the light like living flame.

It feels... alive.

It feels like it's waiting for me.

"This isn't the same ritual," I murmur, unable to tear my gaze away.

"No." Silas steps closer, his voice low enough to feel rather than hear. "The Siren is already awake. She's your song, your lure, your voice. But the other half—the Succubus—she's the vessel. She's how your power takes form."

A tremor ripples through me. "And this ritual—"

"—will call her to the surface," he finishes. "You've felt her already, haven't you? In your dreams. In your skin."

I can't deny it. The hunger. The heat that never fades. The way touch—any touch—feels like it might undo me.

"She's the part of you that remembers," Silas continues, stepping into my space. "The one who knows what it means to take and give in the same breath. To feed. To create."

The words crawl under my skin, settling deep. The candles flicker in rhythm with my pulse, their flames bowing toward me.

"I don't know if I'm ready for this," I whisper.

"You are," he says, and for a moment, the authority in his tone feels older than him—like something speaking through him. "You've been ready since the first moment you started remembering what you are."

The hum in my veins swells into a low vibration, spreading through my chest, my throat, my core. My body moves before my mind can follow, drawn toward the center of the circle. The bed's carved sigils glimmer faintly beneath the silk, gold lines pulsing in time with my heartbeat.

As I reach the edge, I can feel the air tighten—the invisible tether between us stretching, snapping back, pulling. Silas watches me, eyes bright, unblinking, his control fraying at the edges.

"This is how she wakes," he says, voice roughened now. "Through want. Through truth."

The Siren in me sings at the sound of it. The Succubus answers.

The world narrows to breath and pulse, to flame and shadow, to the soft rasp of silk under my fingers as the ritual begins.

The light in the room seems to shift with every breath I take. Candles gutter low, their flames bowing toward the copper tub I hadn't noticed before.

It's massive—deep and wide enough for two, its sides engraved with sigils that glow faintly when I look at them too long. Steam rises from the surface in soft ribbons, carrying the scent of jasmine, sandalwood, and something darker—like smoke caught in silk. White rose petals float on top, glimmering faintly against the water's golden sheen.

Beside it, folded with reverence, rests a black silk robe. It gleams like spilled ink, waiting.

"This portion of the ritual is sacred," Silas says quietly, stepping closer.

"Your Siren side has already awakened. But the Succubus... she must be called through the body. Through trust. Through touch. Through desire"

My breath catches. "Touch? Desire?"

His gaze holds mine—steady, solemn. "Intimacy is her language. To awaken her, the vessel must be honored. Cleansed. Made ready."

He gestures toward the tub, the heat shimmering between us. "Undress, Celeste. Let the mortal weight fall away."

The air thickens. My fingers move before thought can intervene. The dress slides from my shoulders and pools at my feet, silk against stone. The air kisses my skin, cool and electric.

Silas doesn't leer. He doesn't even smile. He looks at me like he's looking at an altar—something ancient, sacred, inevitable.

"Step in," he says softly.

The first touch of water makes me gasp. It's hot—so hot it borders on pain—but the ache in my body melts beneath it, replaced by something deeper. The petals cling to my arms, my thighs, the hollow of my collarbone, as if the water itself recognizes me.

Silas kneels beside the tub, sleeves rolled to his elbows. He opens a small brass basin filled with soap and oils that shimmer like molten gold. "These were made for this," he murmurs. "Blends of amber, cedar, and moonflower. Each meant to draw out a part of you."

He dips a cloth into the water, wrings it out, and presses it gently to my shoulder. The touch is slow, reverent. Steam rises between us as he traces the cloth down my arm, over my hand, across the curve of my back. The sensation is unbearable in its tenderness.

"This isn't submission," he says quietly, as if reading my thoughts. "It's devotion. The conduit serves, so the vessel may awaken."

I turn toward him, water glinting down my shoulders. "Conduit?" The word feels heavy in my mouth, like it carries a truth I don't want to name.

Silas's eyes lift to mine, and the candlelight catches the faint traces of runes beneath his skin—ink that seems to move with his pulse. "Every awakening requires balance," he murmurs. "A vessel cannot rise alone. Power that strong, that ancient, would consume her from the inside out. The conduit absorbs the excess—anchors it in flesh, in blood, in will."

My heart stumbles. "You mean pain."

He nods slowly. "Pain. Pleasure. Memory. Whatever she needs to remember herself." His gaze doesn't waver. "To bring a Succubus into her power is to bind desire to the physical world. To feel everything she feels. To take what she cannot yet bear and hold it until she learns how to live with it."

My breath hitches. "So you—"

"I take it," he says simply. "Every ache. Every surge. Every ounce of what you are becoming. It will move through you, and into me. That is the sacrifice. I bear the breaking so you don't have to."

The room hums faintly around us, the copper tub glowing in rhythm with his words. The candle flames bend toward him like they're listening.

I shake my head, voice low. "That doesn't sound like devotion. That sounds like dying."

Silas smiles faintly—sad, knowing. "It is. In its way. But that's what the conduit is for. To die a little, so something divine can be born."

He reaches into the water again, his touch deliberate, reverent. "This ritual doesn't just cleanse you, Celeste—it rewrites what your body remembers. Every scar, every wound, every moment you denied what you were. The Succubus carries the ache of every incarnation. She is hunger and mercy in the same breath. And she must be met by someone willing to bear both."

He leans closer until his voice is almost a whisper, low enough to vibrate through the steam. "That's what I am. What I was born to be. A book-binder, a conduit, a keeper of thresholds. My purpose is to hold open the gate between what you are and what you will become. Until you no longer need me to stand in between."

The words burn through me, more potent than any touch. The water ripples, the sigils in the copper flare bright gold, then fade to ember.

He looks at me one last time, eyes steady, unflinching. "When your power comes through, it will seek me first. It will hurt. It will want. It will burn. And I'll take it, all of it. Because this is what it means to wake a god from mortal skin."

I close my eyes. The heat seeps through me, deeper than flesh. I feel the Siren's hum shift, a low vibration settling into my bones. But underneath it—something else begins to stir. Heavier. Hungrier.

Silas works methodically, pouring water over my hair until it clings to my skin in dark ribbons. His fingers massage the perfumed oil into my scalp, the scent dizzying—spice, salt, and something sweet enough to ache.

"Let go," he whispers near my ear. "Stop holding her back."

The sound of his voice vibrates through the air, through the water, through me. My pulse stutters. The surface of the bath ripples faintly with each exhale, golden light blooming outward from where his hands touch me.

When he finally stills, he exhales—steady, quiet, controlled. "It's done," he says.

I open my eyes. The water glows faintly beneath the petals, the sigils on the copper pulsing in time with my heartbeat.

Silas rises and reaches for the black silk robe. "Now, rise. Leave the water behind. The mortal part of you has been washed away. What remains is what was always meant to be."

I stand, trembling, the water cascading down my skin like liquid light. The air feels alive—thick with warmth, incense, and something older than both of us.

Silas rises wordlessly and takes a waiting towel from a nearby chair. It's black linen, embroidered with faint runes along the hem. He unfolds it slowly, stepping close enough that I can feel the heat still clinging to his skin.

"May I?"

My voice catches in my throat, but I nod.

He begins at my shoulders, pressing the towel against my skin with steady, deliberate hands. Each motion is careful, methodical, as though drying me is part of some vow he can't speak aloud. He moves down my arms, over the curve of my back, tracing the drops of water that cling stubbornly to my collarbone. Every touch hums faintly with restrained magic, the kind that feels like prayer and promise at once.

When he kneels, gathering the towel to dry my legs, I can barely breathe. His hands are firm, reverent—never possessive, never careless. Only when every last trace of water has vanished from my skin does he set the towel aside and reach for a small glass vial resting on the table beside the tub.

"This is the final part of the cleansing," he murmurs. "To seal the purification. The oils are sacred—myrrh, amber, blood orange, and dragon's blood. They awaken the senses, call what's hidden to the surface."

He pours a few drops into his palms. The scent blooms instantly—rich and dark, threaded with smoke and warmth. When his hands touch my skin again, it's not just warmth I feel—it's current, like energy seeking somewhere to go.

He starts at my throat, fingers brushing lightly along the pulse beneath my jaw, then down to my chest, my shoulders, the hollow of my back. The oil gleams faintly where it touches, a sheen of gold against bare flesh. The runes carved into the copper tub seem to respond, glowing softly, flickering in time with my heartbeat.

"This isn't meant to tempt," he says softly, though the tremor in his voice betrays him. "It's meant to bind. Energy to energy. Flesh to memory. You to yourself."

His fingers slow as they reach my wrists, pausing over the faintest shimmer beneath my skin—veins pulsing with new rhythm. "You're changing," he murmurs. "Your body knows it before you do."

When he finally steps back, he takes a long breath as if steadying himself. He retrieves the silk robe, now warmed by the firelight, and wraps it around me. The fabric slides easily over my oiled skin, clinging like shadow and smoke. He fastens the clasp at my throat with care, his knuckles brushing my skin.

The spark between us flares—soft but undeniable.

His eyes meet mine, the gray-green gone dark. "Every act of awakening requires devotion," he says quietly. "But devotion comes with cost. The conduit must bear the echo of what he awakens. When your power comes, it will find me first."

The air thickens between us until it feels alive, pulsing with something more than heat. I feel the hum beneath my ribs—the pull of power that isn't just his or mine, but both, bound by something neither of us can name.

When he finally steps back, his voice is low. "Rest now. The next ritual begins soon."

But I know rest won't come. Not when my skin still glows faintly under the silk. Not when the scent of myrrh and smoke still clings to the air like a promise that hasn't yet been fulfilled.

He leans close enough that I can feel his breath against my ear. "One more ritual," he murmurs. "And you'll remember everything you were. Everything you are."

The world seems to narrow—steam, silk, breath, heartbeat. The Siren hums. The Succubus stirs. And deep within the copper tub behind us, the water darkens to red.

Chapter 40
Celeste

The chamber hums differently tonight.

Not louder—deeper. The walls listen. Candlelight spills across the carved floor, catching on the copper and gold sigils that seem to breathe in time with my pulse.

Silas moves around me with quiet precision, each motion deliberate, ritualistic. When his eyes meet mine, there's no hunger—only recognition.

"This part will hurt," he says softly. "Not because it's meant to, but because the body always resists what it already knows."

He steps closer. The air thickens, heat building between us until it hums in my bones.

When his fingers brush my wrist, the sigils flare. Light races up my arm, searing bright through my chest. I gasp—every nerve igniting, awake.

"The first seal," he murmurs, his hand rising to my throat. "The one of silence. It taught you to forget your voice."

His palm rests there—warm, steady, possessive without cruelty. The pressure isn't suffocating. It's grounding. The touch sends a rush through me so sudden it steals my breath, heat unfurling low in my belly, a wave that spreads until even the air tastes electric.

He leans in, his lips barely grazing mine—a whisper of contact, the spark that turns want into memory. The circle responds, light flaring gold and violent beneath our feet.

The hum inside me deepens, vibrating against his hand, against my pulse, until it feels like the world is waiting for me to speak.

"Say it," he whispers. "Claim what was taken from you."

The words rise before I can think—old, instinctive, alive. They taste like salt and smoke on my tongue.

"I am the storm that remembers its own name."

The sound fractures the air. The sigils ignite, the flames bending inward, gold bleeding into white. The chamber breathes once—then exhales light.

The light explodes, then folds back into my skin, settling as warmth that lingers long after the sound fades.

Silas steps back, his expression caught between reverence and relief. "Good," he says softly. "That was the first."

He leads me to the bed, the sigils glowing faintly as if waiting for us. The air hums with something alive—anticipation, maybe, or the pull of power gathering beneath the surface.

He looks at me, searching. "Are you ready for the next step?" His voice is low, steady, reverent. "To lean into your desire. To feed your Succubus."

My heart stutters. The word *desire* hums through me like a forbidden prayer. Every lesson from my childhood—every warning about restraint, control, purity—rises up, begging me to turn back. But the power in the air feels older than shame. Older than sin.

I nod once. "Yes."

The glow deepens, copper brightening to gold. I can feel it now—the hunger that isn't hunger, the need to connect, to draw and give in the same breath. It isn't lust exactly; it's resonance. A song the body sings when the soul finally listens.

Silas reaches up, fingers brushing my jaw. The contact sends a spark down my spine. "Then stop fighting it," he whispers. "Let it move through you. Let it teach you what you were meant to feel."

The world narrows to warmth and light and breath. He lays me onto the bed, a gentle press of his hand at my back guiding me down. The sigils pulse in rhythm with my heartbeat, each flare loosening something bound deep within me. Feather-light kisses trace a path along my jaw and down to the hollow of my neck, sending shivers through me. The pull between us builds until it's no longer physical—it's elemental, magnetic, an exchange of energy that burns and heals all at once.

One hand tangles in my hair, pulling my head back slightly, exposing the vulnerable curve of my throat. His other hand, warm and calloused, slides beneath the silk robe, finding the peak of my breast. A shiver, not entirely of fear, traces its way down my spine as his thumb begins to massage, circling the sensitive nub, sending a jolt of awareness through me. My breath hitches in my throat, a silent gasp caught between my lips.

His kiss swallows the gasp, deeper, nipping at my bottom lip. I arch into him, wanting to bring him closer, to meld our bodies and souls into one. The pull of power and energy rises around and through us, a tangible force that crackles in the air, humming with an ancient, primal song. It's a symphony of desire and burgeoning magic, each note vibrating through my very bones.

His hands, warm and possessive, slide from my waist to cup my face, thumbs tracing the curve of my cheekbones, tilting my head just so. Our eyes lock, a silent conversation passing between us – a recognition of shared destiny, of a bond that transcends the physical. In their depths, I see not just passion, but a fierce devotion, a promise of things yet to come.

My fingers tangle in the silk of his hair, pulling him even nearer, if such a thing were possible. The scent of him – an intoxicating mix of earth, old books, and something uniquely his own – fills my senses, a potent elixir that makes my head swim. Every touch, every breath, every beat of our synchronized hearts echoes with a profound significance. This isn't just a kiss; it's an awakening, a claiming. It's the moment when two disparate halves finally find their whole, igniting a flame that threatens to consume everything in its path. And I, for one, am more than ready to burn.

The hum rises to a crescendo. I gasp, and the light from the sigils rushes up around us, gold dissolving into white. Silas exhales, his expression unreadable but reverent. "That was the second," he murmurs. "Desire without shame. Hunger without fear. You're almost free."

My breath hitches, shallow and ragged, each inhale a desperate gasp for air that does little to cool the fire coiling in my core. Desire, raw and demanding, builds within me, a fervent heat spreading through my veins, begging for release. The world seems to narrow to the thrumming pulse in my ears, the insistent ache that intensifies with every beat of my heart.

"Second?" I manage to whisper, my voice a barely audible tremor. The word feels foreign on my tongue, heavy with an implication I am only just beginning to grasp. "How many are there?" The question is more than just curiosity; it is a desperate plea for understanding, a fragile attempt to anchor myself in a reality that feels increasingly surreal and overwhelming.

Silas rises from the bed slowly, the faint light from the sigils painting his skin in moving gold. My gaze is drawn to the lean planes of his stomach, the subtle definition of his chest and shoulders as he moves. He doesn't speak at first. The sound of fabric shifting fills the space — the slide of buttons, the soft whisper of linen as he pulls his shirt from his shoulders. Piece by piece, the armor of his civility falls away until only the man remains — the conduit, the keeper, the one who's chosen to bear the weight of the ritual.

"There is a third and final seal," he says, his voice steady, low enough to make the air itself listen. "The one that binds your hunger to fear. That makes you mistake longing for sin."

The words settle over me like smoke. I can't look away. There's reverence in the way he stands — unguarded, unashamed — a study in control and surrender all at once.

"This isn't about desire," he continues, stepping closer. "It's about truth. The body remembers what the soul tries to forget."

The distance between us vanishes, replaced by his familiar weight and hands untying my robe. As the silk parts, I'm bared to his gaze, and a powerful, ancient current flows between us. His touch is a language I'm only just learning to understand—reverent, unhurried, utterly devoted. He starts at my shoulders, tracing the line of my collarbone, a faint hum rising from his touch that makes my skin prickle with awareness. His fingers follow the curve of my neck, then linger at the pulsing hollow of my throat, as if listening to the song that lives there.

He kneels before me, the candlelight casting long, dancing shadows around us. His gaze, dark and intense, moves over every inch of my form, from the faint shimmer of my skin to the gentle swell of my breasts. He cups them, his thumbs circling my nipples until they tighten into hard buds. A soft moan escapes my lips, and his eyes darken further, acknowledging the sound, accepting it as an offering.

His lips follow the path his hands have traced—a whisper-soft kiss at my throat, a slow, deliberate suction at the peak of my breast, drawing a gasp from deep within me. The sensation is exquisite, a perfect balance of tenderness and raw hunger. My hands tangle in his hair, pulling him closer, arching into his touch, needing more.

He moves lower, a trail of fire in his wake. His tongue paints patterns on my belly, teasing the sensitive skin, eliciting shivers that rake my body. The air grows thick with the scent of aroused skin, of desire uncoiling, of ancient magic stirring. When his breath ghosts over the delicate skin of my inner thigh, my legs tremble, parting instinctively, inviting him closer.

He takes his time, worshipping each curve and hollow, each pulse point and tremor. He licks and sucks, bites and nips, exploring every secret place, every forbidden curve, until I am a symphony of sensation, a living, breathing testament to his devotion. My hips begin to buck, a primal rhythm taking hold, my body crying out for a release that feels both imminent and impossible.

His head dips lower still, his hot breath stirring the delicate curls at my core. My eyes flutter shut, anticipation a sweet agony as he begins to explore with his tongue. He licks the swollen lips, a soft, teasing swipe that makes me whimper. Then he zeroes in on my clit, a firm, sucking draw that pulls a gasp from deep in my chest.

At the same moment, a single, smooth finger slides into me, stretching and filling, a delicious invasion that makes my core clench around him. Then a second, then a third, each one steadily increasing the pressure and fullness, a delicious invasion that makes my core clench around him. He works me with a rhythm that quickly becomes intoxicating, his tongue a masterful dance of pressure and release, sending streaks of white-hot pleasure through me, amplified by the slow, deliberate thrust of his fingers.

A low moan escapes my lips, lost in the hum of desire that fills my ears. I dig my fingers into his hair, pulling him closer, lost in the delicious torment he's inflicting. My hips begin to buck of their own accord, a silent plea for more, for everything. The world outside this moment fades into a hazy blur, replaced by the exquisite sensations coursing through my body. Each movement, each touch, is a direct hit to the very core of my being, unraveling me piece by glorious piece.

His intense emerald and gold gaze never leaves mine, even as he expertly pushes me to the edge of my control, a thrilling point where pleasure is about to turn into total surrender. In his eyes, I see not just raw, wild desire, but a deep, ancient connection, an understanding that goes beyond words, echoing a language only our souls get. He's not just taking; he's receiving, absorbing, becoming completely intertwined with every part of me, every trembling nerve, and every beat of my heart. His worship, a mix of touch and taste, is more than just physical intimacy; it's an act of creation, building a new me from the ashes of my past, bringing dormant desires to life, and uncovering the woman I was always meant to be.

With a gentleness that contradicts how intense he was earlier, he trails light, teasing kisses back up the soft skin of my inner thigh, past my hips, and across my stomach, until his lips finally find my mouth again. A soft, involuntary whimper escapes my throat when he pulls away, suddenly stopping the exquisite rhythm of his tongue and lips that had been devouring me. A low, throaty chuckle rumbles from his chest, a sound that vibrates through me, sending shivers of anticipation down my spine. His eyes, still locked with mine, sparkle with a mischievous delight as he murmurs, his voice a husky whisper that promises both ecstasy and release, "Ready to break the seal, my love?"

"Yes," I breathe out, the word barely a whisper against his lips. My hand moves instinctively, tracing the line of his back, the curve of his shoulder, the warmth of living heat beneath my fingers. His breath hitches—a sound caught somewhere between restraint and surrender.

The sigils carved into the bedposts flicker in response, their light pulsing to the rhythm of our hearts. The air feels alive, thick with something ancient, something watching. Each heartbeat draws us deeper into the current that hums between us, a tether of energy that feels older than either of us could ever be.

Silas presses his forehead to mine, his voice unsteady. "This isn't just desire, Celeste. This is the moment the final seal breaks. Once it does, the power won't ask for permission—it will claim you."

"I know," I whisper, though my voice trembles. "And I'm not afraid."

He answers with a searing kiss, a hungry possession that deepens as his lips claim mine. His hands, firm and knowing, slide to my hips, lifting and tilting me, positioning the throbbing head of his cock at my slick, eager entrance. A guttural moan escapes my throat, a sound of both anticipation and surrender, as the blunt tip presses against my core, a silent promise of the exquisite invasion to come.

He shifts, a low growl rumbling in his chest, a sound that vibrates through my very core as his hardened length presses intimately against me. My breath catches, caught in my throat, and a soft, involuntary moan escapes my lips. A primal awareness, ancient and undeniable, thrums between us, a silent language spoken by our bodies. His eyes, dark with a hunger that mirrors my own, bore into mine. "Ready, love?" he rasps, his voice a gravelly whisper, thick with unbridled desire, a promise of what's to come. I can only nod, my eyes wide, a captivating mixture of eager anticipation and complete surrender. The world narrows to just us, to this moment.

The air crackles with unspoken desire, a silent battle between restraint and a hunger that demands release. He leans in, his lips brushing my ear, his voice a low thrum that sends shivers down my spine. "Tell me you want this, love. Tell me you crave me."

My breath hitches, a silent plea escaping my lips, as his hips subtly rock against mine, a tantalizing preview of the pleasure to come. He enters me slowly, deliberately, a masterful dance of control and exquisite sensation. Each deliberate thrust is a brushstroke, painting a masterpiece of growing heat within me. He pulls back, almost out, then plunges deep again, a rhythmic tease that has my senses reeling. A sigh, deep and profound, escapes both our lips, a symphony of pure pleasure as our bodies finally, perfectly align, completing a circle that feels as ancient as time itself. He keeps me teetering on the precipice, each movement a promise of release, each slow, agonizing withdrawal a testament to his masterful restraint, until I'm breathless, desperate, begging for more.

When he finally pushes me over the edge, it is with a long, deep kiss, his tongue tangling with mine, tasting my surrender, claiming my ecstasy. The world explodes in a rush of white-gold light, the hum of the ritual cresting into a silent, shattering climax that vibrates through every cell, leaving me breathless, reborn, and utterly, irrevocably his.

For a heartbeat, I see everything—the echo of wings, the memory of fire, the hunger of the sea—and then it folds back into me.

The air stills. The light fades. I'm trembling, but not from fear. I feel *whole.* Silas's hand still rests over my heart, his thumb brushing a slow, reverent circle against my skin. "It's done," he says softly. "You've crossed the threshold."

I draw in a shaky breath, feeling the afterglow of something more than touch—something elemental, cosmic. The hunger inside me has changed; it's no longer absence, but power made flesh.

"I feel it," I whisper. "Everything. The world, the pull, the hum beneath it all."

He meets my gaze, gray-green eyes lit with equal parts awe and warning. "Then the Ledger has awakened its Keeper."

Chapter 41
Elias

I wake drenched in sweat, heart hammering hard enough to shake the room. The kind of waking that leaves you unsure whether you dreamed or remembered something you weren't supposed to.

Gray light leaks through the blinds like it's been scraped from metal. My shoulders ache again—deep, hot, wrong. The pain isn't muscle; it's buried somewhere older.

The coffee brews thick and black, bitter enough to wake the dead. I drink it standing, staring at the board across the room. Five faces. Five crimes the world still calls "unrelated."

Corbett. Harren. Lexington. Vennett.

And now I can see it—one red line winding through all of them.

The phone vibrates against the counter. Rivera.

"Shaw."

"Got your data pull on Second Light," she says, voice too careful. "You sure you want this on your plate?"

"Spit it out."

"Okay." A breath. "The firm's charity arm—Second Light Initiative—filed zoning paperwork for a chain of 'rehabilitation centers' under another shell: The Haven Initiative. On paper, it's real estate and victim outreach. In practice? Money runs through three dummies, then lands offshore under phantom names."

My jaw tightens. "Trafficking."

"Yeah," she says quietly. "Moving people, not property. Runaways, foster kids, mostly women. The first known survivor disappeared after a deposition—case dismissed before trial. Guess who handled the defense?"

"Second Light."

"Bingo. And here's the kicker—Vennett's last development permit was for waterfront housing in Gloucester. Funded by Corbett's trust. That trust is now transferring to a new signatory—Dahlia Merrow."

The name lands cold. "Merrow," I mutter. "Environmental exec. Christmas gala host."

"Right. Her foundation's next public fundraiser is December twentieth. Pattern lines up to the day."

I scroll through the file—donation ledgers, press clippings, guest lists. The same faces. The same smiles. A gallery of benefactors funding rot behind glass.

"Good work, Rivera. Send it all. Unfiltered."

When the call ends, the apartment goes too still. The radiator hisses like it's trying to warn me.

Corbett laundered the money.

Vennett built the shells.

Harcourt covered the clinics.

Harren handled the disappearances.

Every one of them touched the pipeline.

And every one of them is dead.

I stare at the board. Red thread twists tighter, circling one last name.

Dahlia Merrow.

Outside, Boston crouches beneath a low gray sky, the air heavy with snow and silence. The whole city feels like it's holding its breath.

If I'm right, she's next.

If I'm wrong, I'm running out of time to be right again.

The ache beneath my shoulders flares, sharp enough to double me over. For a second, I swear something moves under my skin—a pulse, a whisper.

The Ledger must be fed.

I shake it off, pour another cup, and grab my coat.

If someone's cleansing the past, they're almost finished.

And the only thing worse than catching the killer...

is realizing what they're cleansing the world of.

The case board stares back at me—threads tight, faces blurring. Every instinct I've ever trusted tells me the next move is hers. Or his. Or both.

I grab my phone before I can talk myself out of it and scroll to her name.

Celeste Duvall. The contact photo is blank, just a gray silhouette and the memory of her voice. I hesitate, thumb hovering over call, then hit it.

It rings longer than it should.

Once.

Twice.

Three times.

"Celeste," I mutter when the voicemail clicks on. "It's Shaw. Call me when you get this."

I pause, listening to the silence between the static. "Something's shifting in the case. I just need to know you're okay. Or that you're not with him." Another breath.

"I'll swing by your place if I don't hear from you."

The message ends, but the unease doesn't. It crawls up the back of my neck and settles there, heavy and certain. I grab my keys.

The drive to Salem is short—too short. The sky's gone the color of steel, snow slanting sideways in the wind. Streets blur past in shades of gray and salt until I turn onto hers. The lights in her building are out except for the flicker of one hallway bulb that can't decide if it wants to live or die.

Her door looks the same as always. Too neat. Too quiet.

I knock once, knuckles against wood.

No answer.

"Celeste," I call, voice low but sharp. "It's Elias. You home?"

Still nothing.

I try the handle. Locked. I knock again, harder this time, the sound echoing down the narrow hall. Somewhere below, a radiator groans and hisses, the only reply.

When I crouch to peer through the gap at the threshold, I catch the faint smell of chai and dust. The kind of still scent that comes from a place untouched too long.

Her mail's piled on the floor—three days' worth, maybe more. One envelope stamped *Final Notice*. Another from the courthouse, unopened. I pick it up, then set it back down.

Through the frosted window by the stairs, I can just make out the edge of her reflection—the same window I saw her silhouette in weeks ago. But this time, there's nothing behind it.

I press my palm to the door, half-expecting warmth. It's cold.

Something twists low in my gut, sharp and certain. She's not here. And wherever she is, it isn't safe.

The hallway light flickers once, twice. The hum that's been shadowing me all week stirs again, faint but familiar.
For a second, I swear I hear her voice on the other side of the wood.
Not words. Just breath.
Then nothing.

I step back, jaw tight, the cold bleeding through my coat. "Hang on, Celeste," I murmur. "I'll find you."

The snow starts again as I leave, steady and silent, covering my footprints before I reach the car.

The drive back to Beacon Hill feels longer than it should.
Snow drifts down in soft, soundless sheets, muting the city until even the tires on pavement sound distant. The closer I get, the worse the feeling gets—that gut-deep pull that isn't logic or fear, just something older whispering, *Go.*

Silas's townhouse sits dark at the end of the street, its windows glowing faintly amber through frost-laced glass. Warm light, but no movement. No shadow crossing behind the curtains. Just stillness.

I kill the engine and step out, breath fogging in the cold. The air smells faintly of woodsmoke and iron. On the front steps, a thin dusting of snow—perfect except for a single set of footprints leading up to the door. Light tread. Heels. Hers.

The lock turns easily beneath my hand. Unlatched.

Inside, the house is warm but wrong. Too still. The kind of quiet that feels placed there. The faint scent of clove and cardamom lingers in the air—hers, caught between perfume and memory.

The fire in the hearth has burned to pale embers. On the low table before it sit two wine glasses—one upright, half-full; the other tilted on its side, a dark stain bleeding into the rug. Both glasses smell faintly sweet. A bottle sits open beside them, the cork resting neatly beside the label. Nothing messy. Nothing frantic.

A single folded napkin rests beside the upright glass. Lipstick stains trace the rim—a deep rose shade I've seen her wear before.

My pulse stumbles. "Celeste," I murmur under my breath.

No answer.

I scan the room—everything perfectly arranged, but too deliberate. No sign of struggle. No forced entry. Just absence, as if the life here stepped quietly out and shut the door behind it.

Upstairs, the faintest glow spills from a doorway. The study.

Her bag sits just inside the threshold—open, but not rifled through. Phone missing. Notebook still inside, pen tucked neatly in the spiral. Her coat hangs over the back of the chair, the silk scarf she wore last week draped across it. Still faintly warm when I touch it.

The desk lamp burns low. Papers are scattered across the surface—maps, ledgers, notes scrawled in multiple hands. But one page lies separate, centered as if placed there on purpose.

The handwriting isn't hers.

Dark ink glimmers faintly red in the light.

THE WITNESS HAS AWOKEN.

The words look carved, not written—pressed deep enough to indent the paper beneath.

My throat goes dry. The hum I've been carrying in my chest for weeks stirs again, low and insistent, matching my pulse beat for beat.

I look around once more—the two glasses, the lipstick, the bag, the open door—and every instinct tells me I'm too late, but not by much.

She was here.

She didn't leave alone.

And whatever has woken... hasn't finished yet.

The house exhales a soft creak as the heat kicks on, and for a heartbeat I swear I hear something faint beneath it—a sound like a page turning, or a whisper.

Then it's gone.

I back out slowly, leaving everything as I found it. The snow outside has already covered her footprints. Something's moving now, quiet and certain, like a storm gathering offshore. And I'm standing dead center of it.

I step back from the desk, leaving the page exactly where I found it.

THE WITNESS HAS AWOKEN.

The words burn behind my eyes, heavy as prophecy. Whatever this is, it isn't just a message—it's a warning.

I pull my gloves tighter, make one last sweep of the study, then head for the door. I don't touch anything else. The air feels thick in there, like it remembers what happened. Outside, the cold hits hard—brutal, clean, grounding.

The snow's coming down steady now, dusting Beacon Hill in white. I keep walking until I hit the corner café still open past midnight. Inside, the barista barely looks up. I order black coffee, no sugar, just something to keep my hands from shaking.

Back in the car, the heat's slow to kick in. The cup burns against my palm as I make the call.

"Vega."

She answers on the first ring, dry as ever. "Please tell me you're calling with good news."

"Not even close. I need a trace on two phones—Celeste Duvall and Silas Kade. Off the record. Fast."

There's a pause long enough for me to hear her pulling up the system. "Give me five."

I sip the coffee, staring out at the quiet street. Everything feels wrong—the silence, the timing, the warmth leaking from that townhouse like nothing ever happened. Five minutes stretch into eight before she's back.

"Okay," Vega says, voice tighter than before. "Got both. Last confirmed ping for Duvall and Kade was from the same address—his place in Beacon Hill. That was about two hours ago. Then both signals move together, headed west across Charles. Route ends in Back Bay."

"Destination?"

"The tower puts them right near Gloucester and Commonwealth. Guess what's there?"

I already know, but I ask anyway. "What?"

"Dahlia Merrow's foundation. The same one tied to the Second Light accounts. And before you say it—yeah, the Christmas gala's tonight. Started at nine. She's got half the city's power players in one ballroom."

I grip the steering wheel until the leather creaks. "Tell me the phones are still active."

"They're not." Vega's voice flattens. "Both went dark about thirty minutes after arriving. No outgoing calls, no data packets. Clean shutoff."

"Meaning someone wanted them quiet."

"Exactly."

The coffee cools in my hand, but I don't feel it. I stare through the windshield at the snow-slick street, the faint reflection of the townhouse in the rearview mirror.

Celeste's phone. Silas's. Both moving toward Merrow. Both disappearing in the middle of a black-tie event.

"What's your play?" Vega asks.

"Merrow," I say. "If the others were part of the pattern, she's either next on the list... or she's hosting the end of it."

"Shaw—don't do anything stupid. The whole damn PD's on security detail for that gala. You show up, you'll light up every radar in the city."

I hang up before she can finish.

The streets of Back Bay aren't far. I start the engine, toss what's left of the coffee out into the snow, and pull away from the curb.

The hum in my chest starts up again—low, steady, alive. The kind that doesn't belong to nerves.

If Vega's right, they're already there.

If I'm right, something's about to happen inside that ballroom.

And if I'm too late—

the next name in red ink won't be Merrow's.

It'll be hers.

Chapter 42
Celeste

The world is too still when I wake.

For a moment, I can't tell if the silence is real or just the echo of the chant still winding through my head. The air smells of smoke and salt and something sweet burning low—like the room itself remembers what we did here.

Light leaks through the curtains, pale and fractured. My body feels heavy, but not tired. *Fed.*

Silas's arm lies draped across my waist, the weight of it anchoring me to the sheets. His breath moves slow against the back of my neck—steady, human—but what stirs beneath my skin isn't. The memory of last night hums there, low and steady: the circle of flame, the rise of heat through the sigils, the sound that wasn't quite a song but still carried my name.

I close my eyes and it floods back—power moving through me in molten waves, pleasure and fear tangled until I couldn't tell them apart. The moment his hand closed around my throat, the seal broke. I felt the world bend, fill, ignite. I remember his voice at my ear, coaxing, commanding.

And then came the hunger.

It started like thirst—sharp, unbearable—and then it was everywhere. In the air, in the sound of his heartbeat, in the taste of his breath when he kissed me. I fed on it without meaning to, every pulse of his desire answering the ache in mine. He didn't resist. He offered it.

Now, in the morning light, the memory glows under my skin like fever. My mouth still tastes faintly of smoke and skin. His fingers twitch once against my stomach, as if he can feel the current still alive inside me.

I slip from beneath his arm carefully. He murmurs something—maybe my name—but doesn't wake. I stand by the window, naked in the half-light, the sheet dragging across my legs like fog. The city outside is quiet, frost clinging to every edge, the sky the color of old glass.

My reflection startles me. My eyes catch the light, gold threaded through green, too bright to be ordinary. A shimmer dances along my throat where his hand had rested—a mark that feels more like claiming than bruise.

The hunger stirs again, lower now. Not painful. Familiar.

I press my palm to the cold glass, watching the breath bloom beneath it. "It's still in me," I whisper. The words fog, then vanish.

Behind me, Silas stirs. "It always will be," he says softly, voice rough from sleep but certain. "You just stopped pretending it wasn't."

I turn, meeting his gaze. There's no remorse there, no apology—only understanding.

For a heartbeat, I think of Elias—his warning, his suspicion, the way he looked at me like I was still something worth saving. The thought twists, but what blooms beneath it is sharper. Need. Awareness. A hunger that's finally found its name.

Outside, a clock tolls nine. The sound rolls through the room like a reminder.

Silas sits up, the sheet falling low on his hips. "Tonight's Merrow's gala," he says, calm and deliberate. "You'll be there."

I don't argue. The ritual may have ended, but its rhythm hasn't. The world feels tuned to it now—each breath another note in a song that isn't finished.

I dress slowly, his eyes following every movement. The hunger doesn't fade. It never will.

When I glance back once more before leaving, he's still watching, that faint, knowing smile playing at his mouth.

"Remember," he says, almost tender, "you're not the prey anymore."

The words follow me out into the cold,
and the hum beneath my skin answers like agreement.

His words echo long after the door closes behind me.

You're not the prey anymore.

Something breaks open inside me. Not loud, not violent—just a shift, quiet as glass cracking beneath frost.

The air moves differently now. Each breath carries a charge, sharp enough to taste. The hum that's been under my skin for weeks surges higher, cresting like a tide that finally found its shore.

And then—

the memories come.

Not all at once, but in flashes, disjointed and merciless.

A basement washed in blue light.

The smell of rain and rust.

A man—Vennett—his voice high, panicked, cut short by the sound of something wet and final. My own breath steady, detached. The song rising from somewhere deeper than my throat.

Then another—Corbett. The marble of her foyer slick under my hands. The mirror catching my face in its reflection—not shocked, not remorseful. Exalted.

Each image hits like lightning, searing itself behind my eyes. The weight of bodies, the silence after. The way the world went still every time, the way the hunger ebbed only once it was done.

I stumble into the street, boots slipping on the thin crust of ice. The city hums around me, alive and indifferent. A siren wails somewhere far off, then fades.

You're not the prey anymore.

He didn't mean it as comfort. It was a reminder. A truth I'd spent years pretending wasn't mine.

I see it now—the pattern Elias kept circling, the red line through all the names. They weren't random. They were offerings. Each death a verse in the same song that woke me. Each one necessary to break another seal.

The Ledger didn't choose me to witness.

It chose me to balance.

To feed.

I press a hand to my mouth, but it doesn't stop the sound that slips out—half sob, half laugh. My pulse races until it feels like the world is moving through me instead of around me.

People on the sidewalk glance up, then glance away. They can *feel* it—the shift, the weight of what I've become—even if they don't understand it.

I move faster, heading toward the harbor without knowing why. The water calls, low and steady, the same pitch as the hum in my bones. The same rhythm as the song from the ritual.

The memories keep bleeding through, clearer with every step. Harren's terrified whisper. Lexington's last look. The way their eyes glazed not in fear—but recognition. Like they *knew* me. Like they'd been waiting for it.

By the time I reach the edge of the pier, the sky's turned the color of ash. My reflection stares back from the dark water—eyes gold as flame, lips parted like I'm about to sing.

The truth settles over me like a second skin.

I wasn't being hunted.

I was completing the hunt.

And now, with every heartbeat, I can feel it calling for more.

I close my eyes, the wind biting my face, and for the first time since I can remember, I don't fight it.

The hum resolves into music.

The water answers.

And somewhere deep below, the Ledger turns its next page.

The title settles on me like a crown I didn't earn but can't refuse. Keeper. The word hums in my bones, both vow and sentence.

My pulse slows. The hunger steadies. The fear recedes, leaving only clarity.

I understand now. The ritual wasn't an end. It was a beginning. The killings weren't the purpose—they were the prelude.

There's still one life left to claim before the song completes itself.

The final seal.

The last offering.

And somewhere deep inside, beneath all that heat and knowing, something darkly beautiful unfurls.

I turn from the water, the wind at my back carrying the faint scent of salt and smoke.

The night feels thinner now—porous, waiting.

The gala's lights glitter in the distance, warm and inviting against the winter haze.

The Keeper is almost born.

All she needs now is the final verse.

By the time I reach Silas's townhouse, dawn has burned itself pale. The city looks washed clean, streets slick with thawing frost. Every sound feels too sharp—the hiss of a car's tires, the groan of the gate as I push it open, the faint hum that's still alive beneath my skin.

The front door isn't locked. It never is. The house greets me in silence, warm and dim, the air thick with cedar and smoke. The faint scent of ink and clove trails down the hallway like a memory trying to find its shape.

He's waiting in the parlor. No surprise flickers in his expression when he sees me—only recognition, the quiet certainty of a man who's known I'd come.

"You left before sunrise," he says, voice soft, like he's afraid to startle what I've become.

"I needed air." My throat feels dry, every word catching on the hum beneath it. "I needed to remember."

He studies me for a long moment, eyes tracing the faint shimmer still moving under my skin. "And did you?"

"I think so." The confession tastes like confession and victory all at once. "But it won't stop."

"It's not meant to."

Silas rises, closing the distance between us. He doesn't touch me yet, but I can already feel the pull—his desire like a current tugging against mine, inevitable as gravity. "You're burning," he murmurs, almost reverent.

I nod once, barely breathing. "I can't quiet it."

"You're not supposed to."

When his hand slides to the back of my neck, the hum spikes, sharp and electric. My breath catches. The world narrows to the warmth of his skin, the way his pulse flutters beneath it—steady, offering, unafraid.

"This," he says, voice low, roughened, "is how your kind feeds. You take what's freely given. You turn hunger into balance."

His mouth finds mine before I can answer. The kiss is deep, deliberate—heat and surrender tangled until I can't tell where his breath ends and mine begins. The taste of him floods my senses, sharp and alive, like the first inhale after drowning.

The energy between us shifts—no longer hunger, but exchange. The air thickens, pulsing with every beat of our hearts until it's indistinguishable from the rhythm of the house itself.

He breaks the kiss only long enough to whisper against my lips, "Take what you need."

I do.

The world tilts—heat, pulse, sound, everything folding inward. I draw on him, on the edge of his want, until the ache in me settles into something steadier, quieter. The hunger hums low now, purring like a satisfied thing.

When it's done, I rest my forehead against his, breathless but calm. He brushes his thumb along my jaw, then down to the hollow of my throat—where my pulse beats steady again.

"Better?" he asks.

"Yes," I whisper. "For now."

He smiles faintly, the kind of smile that holds both pride and warning. "You'll need control tonight. The gala isn't just spectacle—it's a stage. Every eye will be drawn to you."

"Because of what I am."

"Because of who you are." His thumb lingers at my throat. "The Keeper doesn't hide in the dark. She walks in it."

I step back, steadying myself. The energy still hums under my skin, but softer now—obedient, waiting. The morning light catches the window, scattering gold across the floor. It looks almost like the circle from the ritual, fractured and glowing.

"I'll be ready," I say.

He studies me a moment longer, then nods. "Then let's prepare. The night won't wait."

As he turns toward the stairs, I catch my reflection in the dark glass of the window—eyes like liquid fire, lips still red from his kiss.

The hunger has been sated, but the power hasn't faded.

It's only waiting to be used.

By the time evening falls, the city has remade itself in lights. Snow drifts lazy and slow past the streetlamps, haloing the air in gold. The hum inside me is quiet now—contained, but alive, coiled beneath the surface like something waiting for its cue.

Silas waits by the door, coat dark against the faint gleam of the townhouse. The black car idles at the curb, headlights cutting through the mist.

He offers his hand, the gesture smooth, almost old-world in its grace. "Ready?"

I glance at my reflection in the glass—hair swept up, the faint shimmer of gold dusting my collarbones, a gown the color of deep wine that clings like a secret. I barely recognize the woman staring back. "I think so."

He studies me for a moment longer, something reverent flickering in his eyes. "Then tonight, the world will remember you."

The ride to the Merrow estate is short, though it feels longer. Boston glides by in streaks of frost and light, all sharp edges softened beneath falling snow. Neither of us speaks. There's nothing left to say.

When the car turns onto the long drive, the estate rises from the dark like a cathedral of glass and stone. Lanterns line the walk, flames bending in the wind. Strings of white lights spiral the trees, reflections trembling in the frozen pond beyond the gate. The sound of distant music seeps through the cold—a low hum of strings and laughter and crystal.

The driver stops at the awning, the tires crunching over ice. Silas steps out first, then turns to me. His hand finds mine, grounding and possessive all at once.

As I step onto the carpet, the night exhales around us. Cameras flash. The light catches on my skin like heat through smoke. Heads turn. Conversations falter. For a moment, the world stills as if it recognizes what it's seeing but can't name it.

"Smile," Silas murmurs, low against my ear. "You were made for this stage."

I do. And the crowd parts.

Inside, the air is warm, thick with perfume and expensive fear. Crystal chandeliers drip light across the marble. The music swells, the room turning in slow, glittering motion. Dahlia Merrow stands near the grand staircase, silver and white sequins catching the light, her laughter bright and brittle as glass.

Silas's fingers graze the small of my back. "There she is," he murmurs. "The final seal."

The hum in my chest stirs again—soft, predatory, certain. I can feel the pulse of it under my skin, the Siren and the Succubus moving in unison.

Across the room, Dahlia's gaze meets mine. She stills. A flicker of recognition—fear or awe—crosses her face before she masks it with a smile.

Silas leans close, his breath a whisper against my neck. "One more step, Keeper. And then it's done."

I lift my chin, the smile never leaving my lips. "Then let's finish the story."

The orchestra swells. The crowd shifts. And together, we move through it—two shadows wrapped in light, walking toward the inevitable.

Chapter 43
Elias

The valet barely glances at the borrowed suit when I step from the car. Good—means I blend. The tux fits tighter across the shoulders than it should, the collar brushing the raw skin where the ache beneath my shoulder blades hasn't stopped since the solstice. The pain hums, low and steady, like static threaded through my spine.

The Merrow estate glitters ahead—stone and glass spilling light into the night. Music drifts out through the open doors, low and refined, but beneath it there's something else—a vibration just at the edge of hearing. It's the same sound I woke to two nights ago. The same frequency that hasn't left me since.

I flash a badge at the front security detail—generic enough to pass for private protection—and step inside before they can ask questions.

The ballroom hits me like a wave of heat and perfume. Crystal, silk, money. Champagne laughter floating over a symphony that doesn't belong in this century. The kind of room where power wears a smile and secrets clink in glasses.

And then I see her.

Celeste.

For a heartbeat, I don't recognize her.

She's standing in the center of the dance floor, moving with a kind of grace that doesn't belong to the woman I've watched fall asleep over transcripts and coffee-stained pages. The red gown shimmers with every turn, catching the chandelier's light like it's spun from blood and gold. Her hair gleams dark against her bare shoulders.

And Silas Kade's hand rests at the small of her back.

They move together like they've done it for centuries—her body following his in quiet rhythm, each step practiced, perfect. His mouth dips close to her ear, and she laughs—a low, soft sound that wraps around the room like smoke.

Jealousy hits first, sharp and visceral. Then awe, because I can't look away. She's magnetic, untouchable, the whole room bending toward her like metal to flame. The air around her hums faintly, a resonance I can feel even from across the crowd.

Every instinct I have screams *get her out of here.*

I move closer, weaving through clusters of donors and dignitaries, their conversations blurring into static. I keep my eyes on her, the red of that gown flashing like a beacon between shoulders and champagne glasses.

Silas spins her once, hand trailing up her spine. The touch looks casual, but I see the control in it. Possession disguised as elegance.

She looks up—right at me.

The music slows. For a moment, no one else exists. Her lips part slightly, surprise flickering through the poise, and I swear the air shifts. The chandelier light bends—just a fraction, just enough.

Silas follows her gaze. His smile never wavers. If anything, it deepens.

He leans close to her ear, murmuring something I can't hear over the music. Her shoulders stiffen, then ease. She turns back to him, her expression smoothing back into calm perfection. The spell reasserts itself.

The song ends. Applause rises like a tide.

I find myself at the edge of the floor, jaw tight, pulse thundering in my throat. When Silas guides her from the dance, I catch the faint shimmer along her throat—a golden sheen that wasn't there before.

The orchestra slides into something slower—strings like smoke curling through the air.

Silas turns her effortlessly, hand at the small of her back, the movement too perfect to be casual. Celeste glows beneath the chandeliers—red silk, pale skin, eyes like fire under glass. Every step she takes looks deliberate, divine.

And before I can stop myself, I'm moving toward her.

"Mind if I cut in?"

Silas's smile doesn't reach his eyes. "Detective Shaw," he says, smooth as ever. "You look out of place."

"Guess I like changing the scenery." My gaze finds hers. "One dance?"

Her breath catches—barely—and then she nods. "It's fine, Silas."

He hesitates, studying her for a long beat. Then, with a quiet smile that feels like a warning, he steps aside. "Don't keep her long."

"I'll try not to."

Her hand fits into mine—warm, alive, charged. The orchestra rises, and we move.

For a moment, the world shrinks to the sound of violins and the scent of her perfume. Cardamom and smoke. The kind of smell that lingers. The kind that ruins.

"You shouldn't be here," she murmurs.

"Neither should you."

"That's not an answer."

"Neither was yours."

Her mouth curves faintly, though her eyes don't soften. "You think this is a game, don't you?"

"No," I say, my voice low, steady. "I think you're in danger."

"From who?"

"From him."

Her breath hitches just enough for me to feel it. "You don't know what you're saying."

"Then tell me what I am saying, Celeste."

Her gaze flicks to Silas across the floor, still watching, still smiling. "You don't see it," she says. "You never could."

"I see enough to know he's using you."

"You think this is something he made me?" Her voice is quieter now, the kind that trembles not from fear, but from truth too heavy to say out loud. "You have no idea what I am, Elias."

I lean closer. "Then show me."

The words slip out before I can stop them, but I mean them. Every one.

The orchestra swells. She looks up at me—eyes burning gold under the light, pulse thrumming against my palm. For a moment, she stops fighting the current between us.

"I'm trying to protect you," I say, breath unsteady.

Her voice is a whisper against my mouth. "Maybe you shouldn't."

The last note holds—violins trembling, the world balanced on its edge. And then she closes the distance.

Her hand slides up my chest, fingers curling at my collar. The kiss is slow at first, testing, then deepens—hungry, inevitable. The crowd disappears. The music blurs. For one impossible second, there's nothing but heat, breath, and the taste of her.

When the orchestra falls silent, she's the one who pulls away. Her lips are parted, eyes dark, pulse wild beneath her skin.

"Thank you," she whispers, voice trembling with something I can't name. "For the dance."

Before I can say a word, Silas is there. Calm. Composed. Too calm.

"Celeste," he says softly, like her name belongs to him.

She glances at me once—guilt, warning, longing all tangled in one look—then takes his hand.

They vanish into the crowd as the next song begins, red silk trailing behind her like smoke.

I stand there long after they're gone, breath uneven, heart still beating to a rhythm that doesn't belong to me anymore.

The applause swells around me, polite and distant, but it sounds wrong—too thin, too far away.

My hands still burn. My mouth does too.

Her taste lingers like smoke and something sweeter, the kind of sweetness that cuts if you hold it too long.

I can still feel the imprint of her hand against my chest, the way her pulse raced beneath my thumb. It wasn't just heat—it was something alive, moving between us, like static finding its circuit. I've been kissed before, but never like that.

Never like being recognized.

The lights blur. Conversations hum at the edge of hearing. I can't focus. Every nerve in my body feels rewired.

When I glance toward the crowd, I catch sight of red silk disappearing through the arch that leads to the terrace. Silas follows, hand at the small of her back like he's claiming what's his.

My gut twists. Not jealousy—instinct. The kind that screams when something's about to go wrong.

The hum that's haunted me for weeks grows louder, crawling beneath my ribs. I tell myself it's adrenaline. It doesn't feel like adrenaline.

I move.

The terrace doors are half open, curtains shifting in the cold breeze. The night air hits like a shock—crisp, salt-laced, and full of static. Boston glows in the distance, a thousand fractured lights scattered across the harbor.

The crowd swallows them before I can reach the terrace doors.

One moment, she's there—red silk trailing like a flame through smoke—and the next, she's gone.

I push through the sea of guests, shoulder brushing velvet and perfume and too many practiced smiles. The hum under my skin doesn't fade; it sharpens. Every instinct I've ever trusted is screaming that I'm already too late.

By the time I reach the terrace, they're there—Silas and Celeste—standing at the far end near the balustrade, the city lights glinting off the harbor below. She's turned slightly toward him, head tilted in that way that makes it look like she's listening, but her posture's all wrong. Tense. Wound tight.

I take a step forward just as she laughs. The sound hits me like static—too controlled, too brittle—and then Silas touches her arm and leads her back inside through another set of doors I hadn't noticed before.

Not the ballroom doors.

A private entry.

I follow, but I wait long enough that I won't draw attention. Guests pass me—laughter, champagne, the hollow thrum of polite decadence—but all I can see is the ghost of that red dress vanishing into shadow.

The corridor beyond the terrace feels different. Quieter. Older. No music here, no chatter. Just the faint echo of heels and the hum of old radiators somewhere behind the walls. The floors are marble, the kind that remembers every footstep.

Their trail cuts left, deeper into the residence. I follow the way the air still stirs—warm perfume, candle smoke, something faintly electric.

Then I hear it.

A door closing. Soft. Measured.

When I round the corner, the hall is empty except for the faintest shimmer of movement at the far end. A figure—tall, poised, wrapped in silver and white—her blonde hair catching the light as she reaches for a door handle.

Dahlia Merrow.

Even from this distance, I recognize her from the photos—polished, powerful, untouchable. She hesitates for just a heartbeat, glancing down the hall as if she senses she isn't alone.

Our eyes don't quite meet.

Then she slips inside the room and shuts the door behind her.

The click echoes too loud in the stillness.

I move closer, every nerve on alert. The hum inside me has changed—lower now, heavier, like it's syncing with something just beyond the door. The hair on my arms rises.

Something's wrong here.

Not just with Celeste. Not just with Silas.

The whole house feels like it's holding its breath.

I move closer, heart hammering against the hum under my skin. The air grows thicker with every step—like the walls themselves are leaning in to listen.

By the time I reach the door, the noise inside me has become a pulse. Low. Relentless. Alive.

I don't think. I just reach for the handle.

Chapter 44
Celeste

The world hums differently now.

It's not chaos anymore—it's harmony. Purpose. Every sound, every breath, every pulse in the room moves with me, not against.

The candles burn steady, their flames long and pale, bending toward the sigil carved into the floor. The air is thick with heat and iron, but I'm no longer trembling from it. The hum that once rattled my bones now answers to my heartbeat.

Silas stands near the door, his posture precise, his expression unreadable—but I feel the pride behind it. The quiet reverence.

"You understand now," he says, voice low, certain. "You always were meant to."

I smooth a hand down the silk of my gown. The color looks deeper tonight—darker, almost black where the shadows catch it. "I don't just understand," I murmur. "I remember."

He steps closer, the faintest smile touching his mouth. "Then you know what comes next."

I nod. "The Keeper completes the circle."

He inclines his head slightly, as if confirming a vow already made. "And this time, you will not run from what you are."

"I'm done running," I say, and it's true. Every fragment, every piece of what I was—siren, succubus, witness—has settled into one current. One rhythm. I can feel the Ledger in my veins now, its song woven through my pulse like fire threaded through silk.

The latch clicks.

The door opens.

Dahlia Merrow steps inside, and the air changes.

She looks exactly as she did on the gala floor—silver gown like liquid starlight, hair twisted in an immaculate chignon, every inch of her composed, expensive, practiced. But her eyes betray her. They're wide, darting, searching for Silas first.

"Silas," she breathes, relief and unease tangled in her tone. "They said you needed to speak with me—privately."

Her gaze finds me next. The relief dies.

Recognition takes its place.

"Miss Duvall," she says, uncertain. "You—"

"Celeste," I correct softly. "You can call me Celeste."

She blinks, faltering. "Of course. I—what is this place?"

The door shuts behind her with a quiet click. Silas doesn't move from his post beside it. He's the silent witness now—watching, guiding, letting me lead.

I take a slow step forward. "You've been here before," I say.

"I haven't," she insists, too fast.

"You have," I counter, voice barely above a whisper. "Not in this life, maybe. But you've stood in circles like this. Signed ledgers like the one waiting on that altar."

Her pulse stutters visibly at her throat. "I don't know what you're talking about."

"Yes, you do."

Something flickers behind her eyes—like a film catching light, showing a frame of something she shouldn't remember. Her lips part, but no sound comes.

"You donated to Second Light," I continue, each word deliberate. "You funded the houses. The transport. The cover stories. The disappearances."

"I was told it was—"

"Charity." I step closer, and she backs into the circle without realizing it. "You thought good intentions would erase what you paid for. But memory doesn't forgive so easily. It just waits."

Her breath catches. "What do you want from me?"

"Balance," I say simply. "Truth has to keep its own accounting."

The runes carved into the floor begin to glow faintly—soft gold light tracing the circle around her feet. The air hums low, answering me, hungry and patient.

Silas's voice slides through the heat. "She's ready."

Dahlia looks between us, panic rising. "Silas, please. Whatever this is—"

He doesn't answer her. His attention is on me. "You know what must be done."

I nod. The Keeper completes the circle.

When I lift my hand, the heat gathers instantly. It coils around my wrist, alive and waiting. I can feel the Ledger's pulse—the same rhythm that carried through every ritual, every awakening, every death.

"This is mercy," I whisper.

"No," she breathes, tears slipping free. "This is judgment."

"They're the same thing."

Light flares beneath her. The sigils bloom in gold and red, spiraling outward in waves. Dahlia's body arches once, a cry caught somewhere between pain and revelation.

Her memories pour out like smoke—images and fragments that strike through me: a ledger stamped with blood, a child's bracelet, a scream that never reached daylight.

For a heartbeat, it feels like drowning. Then the energy breaks, and the room stills.

The circle fades. The light dims. Dahlia stands motionless, eyes open, breath shallow but steady. Not gone—transformed. Her soul added to the record.

I exhale slowly, lowering my hand. The air tastes like rain after lightning. Clean. Complete.

Behind me, Silas moves from the door, his steps soundless on stone. "You've done it," he murmurs, reverent. "The Keeper has remembered."

I turn toward him. The power still hums beneath my skin, softer now but no less certain. "There's one more step," I say quietly. "And then it's finished."

His gaze flicks to the door, expression darkening. "He's here."

I can feel Elias before Silas says it—the steady heartbeat, the mortal rhythm pounding behind that thin layer of oak.

"I know." My lips curve faintly, neither smile nor threat. "Let him see what the world has awakened."

The hum shifts before the door moves.

It's how I know he's there.

Elias.

That mortal heartbeat—steady, stubborn, still searching for logic in a room built on the undoing of it.

I turn slightly, the hem of my gown whispering over the stone. Dahlia sways where she stands, eyes glassy, body trembling with the aftershocks of what's just been drawn from her. She's not broken—just emptied. Waiting.

"Sit," I murmur.

Her body responds before her mind can argue. I step behind her, guiding her gently toward the high-backed chair by the altar. She obeys, folding into it with a shuddering breath, fingers twitching against her lap as if she's still trying to remember what to hold onto.

Her pulse steadies. The circle quiets. The balance holds.

That's when the door opens.

The sound is small—barely a whisper of wood on stone—but it hits like thunder.

Elias stands in the threshold, every line of him taut with disbelief. The sight of him catches in my chest—his suit sharp, his expression sharper. He looks like he belongs here and doesn't, all at once.

Our eyes meet. The hum answers.

"Celeste," he breathes, not a question, not a warning—just my name, stripped bare.

Silas doesn't move from the shadows. His gaze finds me instead. "Use your voice," he says softly, the words neither command nor permission. "Show him what you are."

I turn toward Elias, the air tightening between us. My voice rises, quiet at first, then clear and deliberate, threaded with the melody that has lived under my tongue since the first seal broke.

"Elias," I whisper, and the sound shivers through the room.

He takes a step forward, then stops. His hand tightens on the doorframe like he's bracing himself against a storm he can't see.

"Don't," he manages, his voice rough. "Don't do this."

I smile—small, rueful. "You think I haven't already?"

He shakes his head, but I can feel it—the way the sound coils around him, winding through his breath, his pulse, the spaces between each heartbeat. My siren hum merges with the succubus pull, seamless now—pleasure and command balanced on the edge of a single note.

"Look at me," I say, and he does.
Of course he does.

The air between us crackles—heat, memory, the ache of all the words we never said. His pupils dilate, his lips part, breath catching in sync with mine. I step closer, slow, deliberate, the light bending around us as though the room itself holds its breath.

"Stand and watch," I whisper. The syllables curl through the space like smoke, silk, sin. "Do not look away."

His body answers before his mind can fight. His jaw tightens, eyes locked on mine, every instinct screaming to move—and yet he stays.

The song lingers between us, low and haunting, tasting of salt and iron and longing. Power and ruin braided together.

I turn back to the circle, to Dahlia, to the work that still needs finishing.

Behind me, Elias breathes my name again—this time not as a plea, but as a confession.

And I know he'll stand there until I decide to let him go.

I step around the chair until I stand close enough to see the pulse at her throat—too slow, too human. The room narrows to nothing but her face, pale and perfect in the candlelight, and the ledger waiting like a judge on its altar.

"Dahlia Merrow," I say, my voice soft but every syllable a blade. "You signed papers that sent children into trains they never boarded. You capped calls from mothers and smiled as foundations bought silence. You watched homes empty and called it progress. Tell me their names."

Her hands curl in her lap, nails digging into the silk as if she might claw memory back into place. She opens her mouth, closes it. Sounds come out like a sob first, then a string of denials—defensive, practiced.

"You can speak," I tell her. "You can say the names of the girls who vanished. You can stand in the light and own what you paid for."

She shakes her head, a tiny, pathetic motion. "It was money—donations—mistakes—" Her voice cracks. "We thought we were helping. I never—"

"You bought silence," I interrupt, and my words are not accusation but catalog. I say the names as if reading from a list: the charities, the shell corporations, the safe houses that weren't safe. Each name lands like a verdict. The sigils under our feet gleam; the air tightens, waiting.

Silas stands at my shoulder, steady as a stone. "Make it right," he murmurs.

I don't raise my voice. I do not need to. I place my palm against the hollow at her throat, feeling the fragile beat there—human, urgent. I let her feel me there: the calm, the certainty. "Say their names," I tell her. "Speak for the ones you let go."

Her eyes fill. She tries—clumsy, broken, a whisper of a name that catches on guilt and dies. For a second she reaches forward, as if to touch redemption, then pulls back. The choice trembles across her features. I give her time. She cannot meet it.

That's when I take the blade.

It is small and warm where I hide it against my palm, ceremonial and ordinary both. I don't brandish it. I don't raise it for theater. I lay the edge at the soft skin beneath her jaw and draw it once, clean and certain.

Her first sound is a surprised little sound—half prayer, half apology. The movement is quick, the motion more intimate than violent: a single, precise cut. She inhales, fragile and sharp; the next breath is gone. Her hands fall limp into her lap. Her eyes find mine for a fraction of a second—no terror, only the stunned recognition of someone finally forced to look—and then they cloud.

The room exhales.

There is no flourish. No image to gape at. Only the slow, undeniable silence of consequence. The sigils along the floor dim, then steady, like a scale settling. Somewhere across the house a clock resumes its tick as if it had only been paused.

Silas's hand closes once at my back—firm, approving, almost parental. "Balance," he says simply, and there is gratitude in it that tastes strange and old.

I release the knife and let it rest on my palm, then close my fingers around it. The metallic tang at the edge of the air is there, but I do not watch what I have done. I have been a witness my whole life; tonight I am the ledger.

Elias is at the door. He has watched the whole thing, or at least he has watched enough—his face a map of betrayal and disbelief. He looks as if the world has rearranged itself around a truth he was never taught to hold. His hands clench at his sides. He breathes my name like a question that cannot be answered.

I step back toward the altar, toward the book that remembers. My fingers hover over the page, ink already darkening where the pen will move. There is room in the ledger for what we decide; there is no room for excuses.

The circle brightens. Gold light ripples through the runes, spilling across the stone until it pools beneath the altar where the Ledger waits open, its pages trembling like something alive. The air thickens, humming with power that vibrates up through the floor and into my bones.

Ink blooms across the parchment, dark and shimmering. The pen doesn't move—no hand touches it—but the words appear all the same, letter by deliberate letter.

Dahlia Merrow — Account Rendered.

The handwriting is ancient, looping, unmistakably not mine. It glows faintly before settling into the page, final and absolute. The Ledger closes itself with a soft whisper, as if exhaling her name one last time.

The hum subsides. The light fades.

Silas steps from the shadows, his gaze steady, reverent. "The Keeper has spoken," he says quietly. "And the record remembers."

I exhale, the power still burning low in my veins. It doesn't frighten me anymore. It feels like truth—like balance returning to a world that forgot how to weigh itself.

Behind me, I feel Elias's presence in the doorway. He hasn't moved. His breathing is uneven, ragged, caught somewhere between awe and horror. He's seen everything—the circle, the light, the way the world bent to my will.

I turn toward him slowly, the candlelight catching on the silk of my gown, the faint shimmer still alive beneath my skin. His eyes meet mine, and I know what he sees isn't the woman he thought he could save.

He sees the truth.

The Witness.

The Siren.

The Keeper.

I meet his gaze and say, softly, "Now you understand."

And the Ledger hums again—satisfied, alive, waiting.

Chapter 45
Elias

The sound doesn't leave me.

Even after the room goes still, after the light fades and the air stops trembling — I can still hear it.

That low hum. The whisper of her voice when she said *speak*. The silence that followed when Dahlia didn't.

I can't unsee it.

The blade.

The light.

The way the ledger wrote her name on its own like it had been waiting all this time.

My body feels locked between two instincts — run or reach for her. Neither feels like survival.

Celeste stands at the center of the circle, skin catching the candlelight like the reflection of something divine or dangerous — I can't tell which. The blood on her hand doesn't look human. It looks ceremonial, necessary. Holy, even.

And somehow that's worse.

Every case, every body, every whisper that's crossed my desk since I met her — they all collapse into one line that leads here.

Not to Silas.

Not to the Society.

To *her.*

My mind wants to call her killer, cultist, criminal.

My heart calls her something else.

Something ancient that doesn't fit in any report I could ever file.

I take a step forward before I can stop myself. The sound of my shoe against the stone feels like sacrilege.

Her eyes find me — slow, deliberate — and everything inside me goes quiet.

No fear.

No anger.

Just recognition.

I should cuff her.

I should draw my weapon.

But the truth is, I'm not sure which of us is the danger anymore.

My voice comes out rough, like it's been dragged through glass. "Tell me it wasn't you."

She doesn't answer. She doesn't have to. The room already has.

The memory plays itself behind my eyes: every file, every pattern, every murder I tried to map. All the signs I ignored. All the times I thought she was running from something — when all along, she was *becoming* it.

The part that breaks me isn't the truth.

It's that I understand it.

I understand why she did it — why the killings followed guilt instead of chance, why every one of them was someone complicit. She wasn't hunting the innocent.

She was balancing a scale the rest of us pretended didn't exist.

And I hate that a part of me agrees with her.

The air still hums faintly. The scent of copper lingers, mixing with jasmine and smoke — her scent.

I take another step.

Silas moves between us, calm as ever. "Careful, Detective," he says quietly. "You're standing at the edge of understanding. There's no way back once you cross."

"I'm already there," I say.

He studies me for a long moment, then inclines his head slightly — not a challenge. A kind of acknowledgment.

A silent *welcome.*

Celeste watches me, expression unreadable. The light has softened around her now, the gold fading into something human again, but the power hasn't left. It's under her skin, alive, patient.

She looks like herself.

And not at all.

"You shouldn't have come," she says softly.

"Too late for that," I manage. My throat feels tight. "Tell me what you are."

Her lips curve — not a smile, not quite. "I'm what happens when the world forgets to listen."

Something in me fractures at that.

Because I know, without question, that she's right.

The room smells of salt again. My shoulders burn — that same ache, the same heat that's been crawling under my skin for weeks. The mark I've been trying to ignore pulses once, hard enough to stagger me.

I catch the wall, but the hum answers — *her* hum.

And for the first time, I wonder if whatever is waking up in me isn't hers after all.

Maybe it's the same thing.

The same ledger.

The same call.

I look at her again, and the truth settles like a blade between us:

I didn't come here to arrest her.

I came here because I couldn't stay away.

She steps closer, slow, measured, her gown whispering across the stone. The distance between us folds like it was never there.

Her eyes soften, just a little. "You can't stop this, Elias."

The air changes.

It's not a shift so much as a surrender. The candles bend toward her like they're caught in the gravity of her name. The temperature drops, and yet the heat in the room rises until the air tastes like lightning and salt.

The glow starts beneath her skin — faint, gold at first, then bleeding into crimson. Her hair loosens, spilling over her shoulders like dark water catching fire. The silk of her gown ripples as if moved by an unseen tide. And her eyes—God, her eyes—turn to molten amber, alive and ancient, as if every star that ever burned learned how to look back.

I should look away. I can't.

Her wings unfurl slow from her shoulder blades, not feathered but translucent, opalescent — the edges dripping with light that curves and shimmers like oil over water. They don't so much emerge as *remember* themselves, as though the world is rearranging to make room for what she's always been.

Her voice, when it comes, is layered — hers, and something beneath it, a harmony that shouldn't exist in a human throat. "The last seal is broken," she says, and the words vibrate through the floor, through the air, through *me.*

The sound isn't destructive; it's creation wearing a sharper edge.

Light pours down the walls, tracing the sigils in gold and red. The ledger on the altar reopens on its own, pages fluttering as if in a storm that only it can feel. The final page glows—ink spreading, writing her name one last time, sealing it in flame.

Celeste Duvall — Keeper Awakened.

The letters burn bright, then settle into something eternal.

She exhales, the sound soft and tidal, like the sea breathing in her place. Light moves under her skin, steady now, tracing the shape of wings that fold close and horns that catch the dim glow like burnished gold. When her eyes find mine, there's nothing hidden left—no mask, no mercy, just truth.

The woman I thought I knew is gone.

And in her place stands something greater—terrible, beautiful, inevitable.

My pulse stutters. "Celeste," I breathe. It's not a name anymore. It's a prayer.

Her lips curve, a ghost of a smile that feels older than language. "You see it now," she says softly. "What we are."

We.

The word hits like thunder behind my ribs. My shoulders burn again—heat flaring so sharp I gasp. The ache that's been building for weeks ignites, carving through muscle and bone until I can feel something unfurling just beneath the skin.

She steps closer. The scent of her—salt, smoke, memory—wraps around me like a tide pulling home. "Don't fight it," she whispers. "You were never meant to."

And for a moment, I almost believe her.

Because looking at her now—wings half-spread, eyes burning like dawn breaking over ruin—I can feel the truth in my bones: whatever she's become, it isn't separate from me. It's the same current, the same hum, the same awakening that's been waiting under my skin all along.

And as the walls of the world begin to hum again, I realize the thing I've been hunting has already found me.

She moves toward me.

Not walking—gliding, the air itself bending to her will. Every breath I take tastes like her—salt and smoke and something older, electric. The glow beneath her skin softens to a living pulse, casting faint gold across her collarbones, the curve of her throat.

I can't move.

Not from fear—something deeper. The kind of paralysis that comes when instinct and hunger become the same thing.

"Elias," she says, my name falling from her mouth like invocation. Each syllable lands low in my chest, thrumming through my veins.

She stops inches away, tilts her head, studying me like she's seeing what's still bound. Then her hand lifts—fingers brushing my jaw, then tracing down to my chin. The heat of her touch burns and soothes all at once. My breath falters.

"You've been carrying chains that aren't yours," she murmurs, her thumb brushing the corner of my mouth. "Tied to guilt. To silence. To mortal law."

Her gaze holds mine, molten and steady. "But you were never meant to serve their truth."

Before I can answer, her lips are on mine.

The kiss is slow—unhurried, deliberate, dangerous. It's not a question. It's a claiming.

The hum that's haunted me since the night we met surges until it becomes sound, until the air around us vibrates with it. My hands find her waist on instinct, and the moment my fingers touch her, the world ignites.

The walls dissolve. The candlelight fractures. My body arches toward hers, caught between pleasure and pain, life and something brighter. Every nerve feels rewritten, remade in her image.

She deepens the kiss, and I taste it—saltwater and blood and memory. The pull of something ancient and infinite, a current that's been waiting for me to stop fighting it.

When she finally breaks the kiss, her breath ghosts against my lips, her eyes gleaming with power that doesn't belong to this world.

"Look at me," she whispers.

I do. I can't not.

Her other hand lifts, palm hovering over my heart. The mark between my shoulders sears in answer, every pulse syncing to hers. Her voice lowers, rich and resonant—each word a command wrapped in tenderness.

"By breath and blood, by name and memory—your bonds dissolve."

The words strike like lightning.

Every muscle locks—then releases.

The heat rips through me like wildfire, starting deep in my chest and spreading outward in violent waves. It sears through sinew and bone, burning away whatever was left of the man I thought I was. I choke on a gasp—half agony, half relief—as something deep beneath my shoulder blades *shifts,* pushing against the skin like it's been waiting centuries for permission to exist.

The ache becomes unbearable. Then—release.

The world explodes in light and shadow all at once. My knees hit the floor. The air trembles around me, thick with smoke and energy, the taste of iron sharp on my tongue. My vision fractures—gold and black, flame and ink—until I can't tell where the pain ends and the power begins.

Celeste kneels before me, calm amid the storm she's unleashed. Her hand slides up the back of my neck to cradle my jaw, grounding me as something vast and ancient unfolds from my spine.

The sound is primal—like thunder tearing through a cathedral.

I look up, breath heaving, and see them.

Wings.

My wings.

Black as obsidian, dripping shadow and light in equal measure. Feathers like smoke, edges fading into inky tendrils that pulse with faint luminescence. They're heavy and weightless all at once, as though gravity itself hasn't decided how to hold me yet.

Celeste's lips curve into a small, knowing smile. "The Seraph blood remembers," she says softly. "Noctevaris runs deep, even in exile."

Her words hit something deep inside me—a truth older than faith, older than fear. I can feel it now, thrumming through my veins, ancient and furious and alive.

She leans close, her voice brushing the edge of my ear, equal parts tenderness and command.

"Reveal yourself, Elias."

The words ignite whatever's left of restraint. The light inside me surges, spilling out in black flame that coils around my wings before fading into the air. The ground itself seems to hum in answer.

When I open my eyes again, she's watching me—reverent, proud, maybe even fond.

"This," she says, her palm pressed briefly to my chest, "is my thank-you. For trying to protect me, even when you didn't understand what you were protecting me from."

"Celeste—" My voice breaks, raw. "Don't."

But she only smiles, that same slow, devastating smile that started all of this. Behind her, the air fractures like glass under pressure, light bleeding through the cracks in shades of gold and crimson. The sigils carved into the floor begin to turn, spiraling toward the opening vortex.

Silas appears in the doorway—composed, unhurried, the edge of his coat catching the wind pouring from the portal. He meets my eyes once, something almost human flickering there, then offers his hand to her.

She takes it without hesitation.

When she looks back at me, her expression softens. "This isn't goodbye," she says. "Only distance."

The air around them ignites—heat, light, sound collapsing into itself until the portal swallows them whole.

Then silence.

The light fades. The room stills. The scent of ozone and smoke lingers in the air.

I'm left alone in the circle, wings spread wide, breath shaking, the echo of her touch still burning against my skin.

And for the first time in my life, I realize what it means to be *unbound*.

The silence stretches.

I stay there longer than I mean to—kneeling in the echo of her absence, wings still half-unfurled, breath ragged against the weight of the air. The portal's light fades to embers, and for a moment the chamber looks almost human again.

Almost.

I stand slowly, the ache behind my shoulders now something deeper—an ache that feels like belonging. My fingers brush the sigils carved into the floor. They're cool now, lifeless, but beneath the stone I can still feel the pulse. The residue of her.

Celeste.

The name hits like an invocation, and for the first time, I don't flinch from what it stirs.

I fold the wings in close. They obey reluctantly, ink dissolving into smoke until the room smells faintly of rain and burnt pages. The faint shimmer lingers under my skin, like the hum never really left—it just changed frequency.

When I push open the heavy door, the cold hits hard and clean.

Outside, snow has started to fall again, soft flakes catching in my hair, on my coat, melting as soon as they touch. Beacon Hill lies quiet beneath it—gaslight reflections and long shadows, the city pretending it doesn't know what's just woken beneath its streets.

I walk until the night air burns in my lungs.

The world feels different. Thinner. Like I can see the seams of it now—the lines between what's written and what's real. Every heartbeat carries a whisper I can't unhear, every streetlight flicker feels like a message coded in flame.

Above me, clouds roll in slow and heavy, black threaded with gold. The storm she called is coming.

I can feel it.

I stop at the edge of the hill, the wind tugging at my coat. Somewhere in the city below, a bell tolls midnight—the sound low, resonant, like the turning of a page.

I close my eyes.

And in the hush that follows, I hear her voice. Soft. Certain. Eternal.

"Remember."

The word slips through me like light through glass—gentle, unyielding, alive.

I open my eyes to a world that's still falling apart and just beginning again.

Wings gone. Breath steady. The snow glows faintly gold where it lands.

And for the first time, I understand what the others never could—

the Ledger doesn't just feed on blood.

It feeds on truth.

And mine has only just begun.

To everyone who has followed me into the dark corners of this story — thank you.

Writing *Ledgers of the Damned* has been a journey through shadows, obsession, and the weight of consequence. It's a story that demanded everything from me, and it wouldn't exist without the people who reminded me why I started in the first place.

To my husband, Ricky — thank you for your endless patience, for supporting me through late-night writing marathons, and for standing by me through every degree, deadline, and wild creative idea. You are the calm to my chaos and the constant in every chapter.

To B. Wills and Letta, my partners at Golden Light Publishing House — thank you for every call, brainstorm, and "what if we just..." moment that somehow turns into something beautiful. This journey would mean far less without the friendship, chaos, and shared vision we've built together.

To my readers, reviewers, and the incredible ARC and street team — you are the reason the words keep coming. Every post, message, and reaction fuels the fire behind the pages.

And finally, to those who read between the lines — who see the nuance, the ache, and the intent buried beneath the surface — this one's for you.

Thank you for finding the beauty in the damned.

— Yvonne Hamilton

About the Author

Yvonne Hamilton is a fantasy author, world-builder, and co-founder of Golden Light Publishing House, where myth, madness, and meticulous storytelling collide. Based in West Virginia, she writes the kinds of stories that blur the line between beauty and ruin—realms forged in fire, characters stitched together with secrets, and worlds that refuse to stay quiet.

With a background in business management and data analytics, Yvonne brings the same precision she uses in spreadsheets to crafting sprawling universes filled with celestial bloodlines, shadowed magic, and rebellions that burn brighter than the stars. Her work—spanning dark fantasy, romantic thrillers, and multi-realm sagas—often explores redemption, betrayal, and the cost of truth in worlds built on lies.

When she's not writing, Yvonne can usually be found buried in coffee, orchestrating publishing schedules, or chasing down the next story that won't let her sleep. She believes good fiction should set something on fire—preferably expectations.

Also by Yvonne Hamilton

The Breakfast Murder Club Series

Blades Over Breakfast

A Hexed Valentine Romance

Hexes and Heartbreakers

Flickers of Betrayal: The Unauthorized Rewrite

Upcoming Connected Parallels

No Vacancy for the Damned